Moira's
Way

Moira's Way

A NOVEL BY
Susan Sullivan Saiter

DONALD I. FINE, INC.

New York

Library of Congress Catalogue Card Number: 93-70902

ISBN: 1-55611-372-2

Manufactured in the United States of America

10   9   8   7   6   5   4   3   2   1

Designed by Irving Perkins Associates

To David and Amaryllis,
wherever they are.
And to Laura for believing in Moira
all the way through.

Part I

One

THEY SAY SHARKS need to keep swimming to keep from sinking to the bottom and dying of suffocation from the weight of their internal organs. The McPhersons had a similar survival system—Daddy had to drink and Mother had to make sarcastic jokes. Otherwise, they seemed to think they'd sink to the bottom and die from the weight of their unhappy marriage.

Maybe the marriage would have been better off if they hadn't drank and fought. Or maybe the marriage would even have broken up.

But it didn't. And they swam on.

And fought on. There were times when you'd almost think Daddy needed a drink in order to defend himself against Mother, otherwise he couldn't stand up to her.

Even when Daddy was drunk and he did stand up to Mother, he was no match. He'd furiously hurl his anger here and there, but totally out of control, while Mother's mind was working fast, working on the next insult. Mother's words had a quick bite.

Drunk, Daddy would attack, but clumsily, because even then he was a little afraid of her.

Daddy wasn't afraid of his daughter, Moira, however. So when Daddy got mad at Mother, Daddy convinced himself that it was Moira he was mad at, because she was easy. And by the time Moira was twelve, thirteen, Daddy often forgot that Moira and Mother were different people, especially when he was drunk.

The odd thing was, Mother sometimes did too.

Moira made a convenient scapegoat for their drinking and fighting problems, which were really a coverup for their sexual problems.

* * *

Daddy had something of a system: beer during TV shows, whiskey during commercials. The whiskey bottle never left the kitchen, while a beer bottle traveled right along with Daddy anywhere he went.

Evenings, the beer bottle would be on the table next to him. If it was his first, it would be sort of hidden, behind the lamp or a standing-up TV Guide or Reader's Digest in the back corner of the end table, or if no magazine was around, perhaps the beer bottle would be peeking out from behind a pack of beer nuts or some other snack.

If it was a second or third or so, the bottle would begin to lose its inhibitions and step toward the front of the table, standing boldly next to the ashtray, shining under the harsh light of the lamp.

The first beer might pretend that it was being drunk slowly, sitting there shyly, modestly, totally in control, its level lowering in respectable stages. But the fifth beer or the sixth or the tenth or the fifteenth wouldn't care who saw how fast it went.

Before Moira had all this figured out about Mother and Daddy—that she was the scapegoat for their problems, particularly their sexual problems—she tried to please them, but always fell short, the opposite of her sister, Taryn. Taryn was perfect, innocent, and even had sort of an angelic face because she'd been born premature and never quite lost those big-eyed, rosebud-mouthed preemie features. Taryn lived only to please. Moira felt as if Taryn was like the beer—moderate, acceptable, Daddy's allowable companion, while she, Moira, was the whiskey—the family secret, the closet case, inherently evil and lurking there just to entrap some potential sinner.

If you came out to the kitchen in the early stages of Daddy's day's drinking, say, at noon on a weekend, or right after work on a weeknight, he'd try to hide the whiskey bottle from you, even though you knew he had it, even though you knew he kept it in the top cupboard with the potato chips and crackers and cookies, the family fun foods of which he disapproved because they lacked nutritional and moral fiber. When Daddy was around, everyone pretended to maintain their own health and refused to open those cupboards where the whiskey lived, so as not to embarrass him by shining the light of day on the pint of Canadian Club and thereby acknowledging its existence (and it was always a pint, not a fifth, because, Moira imagined, a pint implied restraint, even if it was regularly, religiously replaced).

If anyone accidentally wandered into the kitchen a little later, say two hours into his drinking, he'd be breathing heavily and his face would be purply blood-red and sagging, as if the alcohol had sunk to the bottom of it and was sloshing back and forth. He'd be jumpy, his arms crooked and the muscles tight at the top, and he'd give the intruder a look like what the hell are you doing in the kitchen, my kitchen, because unlike in most homes, the McPherson kitchen was the realm of the man of the house.

Mother and the girls knew that if you walked in on him accidentally, you held your breath and stared straight ahead and just made a tense walk to the sink, got a glass, and took a drink of water. You put the glass down in the dish drainer without making a sound, you didn't make a false move or gesture, and you got the hell out with the same kind of walk-don't-run gait you would use if you had just stumbled on a bear in the woods.

If you went into the kitchen any later than, say, ten o'clock, you deserved no pity because you were asking for it, the same way you would be asking for it by heading into the woods or a dangerous city neighborhood at that hour.

Of course, sometimes drinking would put him in a good mood, at least for an hour or so. You knew when he'd had a few because he'd pop the beer nuts a little higher into the air before catching them with his tongue, and he'd sort of lunge out at you in a jokey way when you passed his easy chair or came upon him in the hallway. But then the inevitable would arrive, and he'd have had a few too many and he'd get to the point where everything, *everything,* pissed him off. Then it was time to retreat to your bedroom.

Daddy drank, he said, because Mother was always nagging and bitching. Mother said she was always nagging and bitching because of his drinking.

Mother blamed him because the family never seemed to fit in. It was all his fault. And he didn't disagree, either; he accepted the blame, accepted being crucified dead and buried, because it was his fault that the McPherson family did not fit in.

Fitting in had always been a problem. Here in Sioux Falls, Mother complained that they weren't nicey-phony-perfect like their wholesome, middle-class neighbors. But when they'd lived out in the country, up in Codington County, surrounded by corn and oat fields and prairie instead of green lawns and concrete, they hadn't fitted in either. The McPhersons had been better educated than most everyone else, and more ambitious. Except for the few rich farmers and a doctor or two, people in their neighborhood out there always had a bunch of rusting cars out front and mud all over their yards. Some were rough and scary, like Mr. Hinkley, who chased Moira with a pitchfork the day he caught her riding one of his mules around in the pasture (which she'd been doing for years—it was the closest she could get to living her fantasies after reading *Black Beauty* and *The Black Stallion* and seeing *National Velvet),* and like Mrs. Porst, who punished her daughter Cecily by scratching her all over with dirty ragged fingernails. Cecily would show you her back sometimes, seeming almost proud of the evidence of how much her mother cared, and there'd be a recent tirade's deep, long red scars crisscrossing the whitened old ones. Of course, there were people in that town who were nice, but they were going nowhere—even their twangy accents made them sound hesitant and unsure of themselves.

Mother was from a small town halfway between Watertown and Aberdeen, South Dakota. Daddy grew up in International Falls, Minnesota. Daddy had gotten a hockey scholarship and went to the University of Minnesota. He met Mother when the bus the team was taking to a game in North Dakota got sidetracked during a blizzard and they had to wait out the storm in Watertown.

They were married three months later. Daddy dropped out of college. Mother didn't even finish her last year of high school until she took an evening class years later, after Moira and Taryn were born. She loved drama class, just as she loved drama class at the school she attended before meeting Daddy. Nowadays she sat around reading her old eleventh-grade drama book; she had all those Shakespeare plays and *Our Town* and a couple of others just about memorized.

After he dropped out of college and they had Moira, Daddy worked as assistant manager in a feed store near Aberdeen. When Taryn was born three years later, he tried selling snow shovels door-to-door for extra income, and found that he had a knack for sales.

Daddy got his big break in 1956, when he was hired to be a regional rep for Heartland Sporting Goods, Inc. Those were optimistic times for everyone, from the guy down the street who clubbed the cattle over at the stockyards, to the guy down in the White House who made all the optimistic speeches. It was downright unpatriotic not to be optimistic then.

Daddy got to go to Chicago for a sales training program. He called long distance and raved about the plane ride—how it had dim lights and little curtains you could open and close, and how they got free gum in tiny packages that he was saving for the girls and a little pack of cigarettes he'd keep as a souvenir. The hotel was as fancy as a palace, he said, and in it was a Polynesian restaurant with totem poles and hula music and nets all over.

When the class was done four weeks later, Mother and the girls drove to Watertown to meet him at the airport.

Daddy came walking down the steps from the plane with his hair slicked back and wearing a brand-new yellow tie with great big black ovals on it that looked like great big optimistic eyes. "They were impressed with me, Eleanor. We're moving to Sioux Falls," he said.

Moira and Taryn jumped up and down happily. Mother's mouth twitched up on one side into something resembling a smile. When they got home, Daddy opened up the three sample trunks. All excited, they dug through the contents. The trunks were crammed with brand-new, leathery smelling items of masculinity, the masculinity that was going to lead them to a better life. Daddy took things out and handed them around—baseball mitts, ping-pong paddles, hockey pucks, hunting jackets.

Inside the last trunk they opened was a gun. The girls stood back as Daddy took it out and held it up with both hands.

"I'll demonstrate a little of what I learned in Chi-town about sales technique," Daddy said with a confident smile. "Here's your initial call on a prospect, say some jasper that owns a small gun store or a hardware store." Daddy reached out to shake Mother's hand. " 'H'lo there. Aloysius McPherson here. Friends call me Wish.' "

But Mother wasn't one to stay optimistic and patriotic for long, and lapsed into her wise-guy-in-a-fairly-good-mood role. "What friends?" she said.

Daddy ignored her. " 'Nice weather we've been having,' or: 'Crappy weather we've been having'—whichever is appropriate, of course."

As Daddy went on playing straight man to Mother's still-jovial wisecracker, Moira leafed through an instruction manual. It showed different positions you could use when shooting the gun: standing, kneeling, sitting, prone. The illustrations, of husky, bland-looking men, reminded her of the drawings demonstrating positions for sexual relations in a book she'd come across at the Watertown public library.

Daddy put the gun down and went to the kitchen to get a beer. When he returned, he broke into his "drinking" mode of speech, mixing pronoun-verb agreements so that it sounded like he was telling a story about himself as another person.

"Then you shoots the shit with the prospect for a while, and then when he's not looking you launches into your pitch. 'Say, uh, before the snow flies, might not be a bad idea to stock some of these hockey skates.' Or," he said, and picked up the gun again. " 'Now that duck season is approaching, can I interest you in the new High Standard Duck Rib Twelve? Same specs as the Duck twelve-magnum, except for the vent rib.' "

The three females stared at the gun, impressed with the big words. Daddy must be very intelligent, Moira thought, to be able to learn all that so quickly.

"Even women should be familiar with guns in order to protect themselves," he said, leaving his sales pitch mode. "Basic parts of a shotgun. Any gun for that matter. Barrel, stock, action, sights."

"This is the heel." He patted the end of the rifle, the wooden part. "And of course, you've got your muzzle." He ran his hands over the end of the gun and cupped it and for a moment Moira winced at the thought of a bullet coming out and hurting his hand.

By the time Daddy had had another beer he was into his explaining-things-more-than-anyone-wanted-them-explained mode, the same mode he got into when he helped the girls with their homework.

Taryn had her eyes wide and was now dancing around asking all kinds of questions about the gun, but Moira knew she was just humoring him. Taryn's major survival skill was in humoring Daddy (and Mother, but that was a whole different thing). The sad thing was, he was far more interested in the two women he often didn't get along with—Mother and Moira—and there were times when he seemed hardly to know that Taryn existed.

"What's that, Daddy?" Taryn said in a cutesy-poo voice, pointing to something on the gun. "And that, and that, and that."

"Front sight, magazine, magazine loading port, trigger, trigger guard, safety, stock, comb."

Moira wished he would put the gun away, but he went on to tell how the caliber was measured by the gauge. Or something like that. It had something to do with the weight of the lead shot. There were single-barrel guns, double barrels, and single barrels with automatic magazines that held several cartridges. He said repeating shotguns were more popular in America than in other countries. Some of these guns were for hunting birds, some for deer. The reason you used a cartridge full of buckshot was that it was more efficient than a bullet, because you had a better chance of hitting your target. Moira winced at how a bird must feel when that buckshot hit and only tore its wing apart instead of killing it.

It was still all pretty jovial until much later that evening, after Daddy had had several beers and a couple of trips to the whiskey cupboard, when he roused himself from watching "Highway Patrol" and asked if anyone wanted to hold the gun. Everyone shook their head no.

"Oh hell, what's wrong with you women. Come over here, uh . . . uh . . ." Sometimes he forgot Taryn's name when he was drunk. Sometimes when he was drunk he called Moira by her mother's name.

"Come over here, uh, Taryn," he said. Taryn got that smug look on her face like she did whenever Daddy chose her over Moira. He handed her the gun.

"Pretend there's a nice fat mallard over there," he said, raising his beer bottle and gesturing toward the big picture window. "Let's see you get him."

Taryn raised the gun and squinted her eye. "Bang! Dead!" she shouted timidly, as only Taryn could do.

Daddy walked the walk he did when he'd had at least a half dozen drinks, kind of lurchy and swaggering and angry and joking all at the same time, and roughly fixed her fingers on the trigger. "Okay now, pull the trigger and put that bird where it belongs—on your dinner table."

Taryn squealed happily and pulled the trigger. It made an empty, impotent click.

Daddy took the gun and went over to Mother, who was on the couch. "Who's next? Eleanor?" he said.

"No one," Mother said, pushing the barrel of the gun. "Put your toys away now, Aloysius." She looked at the beer. "And your baby bottle."

Daddy put his beer on the hutch next to the baby pictures of Taryn and Moira and held the gun up and pretended to shoot something outside the window. Then he lifted it and pretended he was going to shoot the lamp out. He patted the gun. "Eleanor, you're looking at the latest in a full-choke, twelve-gauge gun that will kill anything wearing feathers up to sixty, seventy yards away."

Then he pointed the gun at Mother and said, "Where's that hat of yours with the feathers on it? That one Bill Krenshaw thought looked so swell that day in town. Go put the hat on. I'll use it for shooting practice."

Mother screamed and ducked as he let the trigger snap. He laughed. Daddy didn't laugh often, so Moira remembered that laugh. The laugh of someone who doesn't expect to be loved, who expects to be feared and pitied and hated.

Moira got a sick feeling in her stomach because Mother didn't laugh or even make a sarcastic quip, but instead yelled, "Get that disgusting gun out of here before I pack up and leave."

Now Moira was really sick. She understood what they were doing, her parents. They were now playing the game where Daddy tried to impress Mother and Mother refused—for good reason, usually—to be impressed. So then he tried to bully her if he couldn't impress her, and when he couldn't bully Mother, he bullied Moira. And now a happy time—Daddy coming home, everyone thrilled about the new job and the new move and the new life—was going to get ugly.

To save face, Daddy pretended to shoot some Indians, then some Commies, then some Democratic politicians, then a rock-and-roll singer.

"Why don't you come here and learn how to use it, Eleanor?" he said.

"Don't tempt me," she said, and picked up her book and walked off into the bedroom.

Daddy pointed it at her as she walked out of the room, then looked at Moira. "Moira, get over here. You're going to learn how to use the goddamned gun." Taryn ran for her bedroom. "Get over here, Moira."

He put his arms around Moira and she felt the heat from his anger and the booze. His skin got hot and soft when he was drunk and angry, and his breath came faster. "Hold this." She wanted to cry as he put her finger in the trigger. She hated guns. Never wanted to have anything to do with a gun. She felt his chest against her neck, the buckle of his belt lightly touch her spine, then she felt him quickly back off. "Now aim. Aim at something. Pretend you're shooting some punk bastard at school that you never liked."

Moira was crying now. He went to the kitchen for a shot of whiskey, then came back and pulled Moira outside, and in the backyard in the twilight he loaded the gun. He grabbed her arms and put the gun in them. It was heavier than you'd think, and the cold steel felt like she imagined a cold coffin would on her bare arms. The gun smelled, too, of steel and gunpowder.

"See that crow up there? Shoot it."

"I can't," she said in a watery voice. He knew Moira loved animals. She wasn't allowed to have a pet, but had all kinds of rabbits and birds she fed, and pretended the mule over at Hinkley's farm was hers, named it National Velvet in fact and rode it around and jumped ditches on it, pretending it was a show horse when Farmer Hinkley was gone.

"Shoot the goddamn bird," he said, and held her and pulled the gun up so that he was squinting through it, then he put her fingers in the trigger and made her squeeze. With a boom and a kick that felt as if it were blowing the side of her head off, the rifle knocked her back into Daddy's arms and the crow flapped safely away just as a piece of wood from the garage blew off into the air.

Moira felt something pressing against her back, Daddy's pants, or maybe just his belt, she didn't know, but she yelled, "Let me alone."

"Oh, goddammit all to hell," he said, pushing her away. "I can't teach you anything."

She ran to her room. If he came in after her, she'd have a heart attack and die.

Moira lay in the black night of her room, wondering. Did other people's parents do the things that Mother and Daddy did? Maybe she and Mother were too critical. Daddy probably only thought he was impressing them with the gun. And no matter his motives, Mother did that sort of thing—she'd dive into anyone trying to be nice to her, to impress her, to get her to like them, and she'd torture them with it. Like she'd take that shotgun he was trying to impress her with and turn it around on him and mentally shoot him dead with it.

The next day she went out past the woods, past the river, past the farms, to the plains and the secret hiding place to meet her friend, Paul Whitefeather.

She had to tell him they were moving away. But she also wanted to talk to him about what had happened with Daddy. To find out if his dad did things like that. Got drunk and made him shoot guns. Was there a connection somehow? Drinking, men, shooting off guns?

Paul would know about drinking because his father was an alcoholic, too. But Paul's father's drinking was so bad he couldn't hold a job—not that there were a lot of jobs for an Indian man, anyway. His mother had a night job mopping floors at the meat packing plant. They could never play at his house—his father was drunk in the evenings and his mother wanted quiet during the day so she could sleep. They didn't play at Moira's either; Moira had never really asked her parents, but it would have been too shocking for them and the neighbors if she brought an Indian into the house.

Moira always felt she knew the true meaning of the word peace from those days of running, wrestling, and talking out on the flat, endless, forever prairie with her friend. Peace, Paul said, was realizing that you were made up of the dirt of the earth and wind of the sky. Whenever she was scared of something, like death, she'd remember that feeling of kinship with the earth and sky, because that was where those molecules of yourself seemed to want to return. She and Paul both felt part of all those little molecules of prairie land and wind out there.

Moira wanted to tell him about how Daddy had made her shoot off that gun.

"My parents had a big fight again. Dad got so drunk he brought out his rifle."

Paul made a sound of understanding.

She stopped, though, when she got to the part about bumping into Daddy. She couldn't say it. But she knew she'd never forget it, either. And neither, probably, would Daddy.

All she could say to Paul was, "He made me feel like there's something wrong with being a girl."

Paul looked at her and said, "Girl?" as if he'd never thought of her as one before. But she'd certainly thought of him as a boy before. She'd always been aware of his greater freedom.

"Remember what I told you," Paul said. "When your old man gets drunk, you go hide. Anywhere. They're stupid when they're drunk. They get mixed up about who they're mad at."

Moira thought how true that was. Daddy was always yelling at her when he was mad at Mother. Even when he wasn't drunk.

They sat quietly, listening to the advice of the wind. The wind told you to shut out the bad things in life, to listen to your inner self, to do things your own way. It said you knew deep down what was right and wrong. The wind said everything was going to be okay.

And then she broke her news. "Anyway, that's not what I came to tell you. We're moving away."

As he turned to look at her, the pale light went across Paul's broad cheekbones like a half-mask. Paul's eyes were very intelligent and also rather wary, except when he looked at her and they glowed and seemed to grow bigger. "Moving?"

"To Sioux Falls."

They just sat and stared at the calm sky and thought about not seeing each other any more.

She didn't look at Paul. She knew he'd have that serious, calm, quiet look on his face, but when his gaze fell on her, his squinty eyes would narrow even more to a wary trust that made her feel like she had some sort of extra burden of responsibility because he and the wind had shown her happiness they didn't show to everyone.

"You going to remember me?" he finally said.

"Of course."

He reached over, without looking at her, and touched her hand. "We're moving, too, someday. My old man wants to move to the reservation."

That was a little better, if it was a mutual abandonment. Maybe white girls and Indian boys weren't supposed to be together, anyway.

"I'd like living on the reservation," Moira said. "Out under the stars, away from all the problems of the world."

Paul laughed hard at that one. "You can't live on the reservation, you're a white girl." Then he squinted at her again, and said, "On second thought, maybe you're not white. You don't act like it. And as a matter of fact, you don't act like a girl, either. Maybe you're not a girl. Maybe you're something else."

He seemed to mean that as a compliment, and Moira wasn't sure it couldn't be seen as one. And there was some truth to it. She'd never liked playing with dolls. She'd always preferred plastic animals and Tinker Toys and board games and reading. And she didn't have a clue as to how girls made friends with each other, and how they got any pleasure out of running around in giggling groups, when a person could just as easily be sprawled on the grass keeping charts on anthill activity, or up in a tree with a science book trying to figure out the tree's age from the rings on a sawed-off branch.

Paul was the same way. He had no boy friends. Moira was the only person she knew of who loved instead of looked down on or pitied Paul because of his poor family and because he was an Indian.

Moira pitied him only when kids at school let their gazes pause on his whisker-straight black hair, or when they ran their eyes too long on the dark shimmer of his skin when turning to see him as a teacher announced results of a test he'd just scored tops in. Paul was just about the smartest kid in fifth grade. They were pretty much tied on this, and always ended up the last kids standing in the spelling bees and the arithmetic bees, as well as the lines for gym teams.

Snow began to flirt its way through the air. The wind had gotten cold and now there was a real bite to it. "It feels awfully good, doesn't it?" Moira said.

"Yup," Paul agreed. "Cold wind lets you know by God you're alive."

They thought about that while the wind whistled through their souls.

"Let's walk around and just be," Paul said.

When they were just being, they pretended they were animals or trees or something that wasn't burdened with a human brain.

Watching the horizon, where a skimpy sun was setting, they listened to the whirr of the wind and waited for something to happen. It usually did. Moira usually got something like a religious feeling when that something happened.

Paul said he had had visions out on this spot. Moira wasn't sure she hadn't had visions herself. In those visions, she felt that she had to do something wonderful in life, had to be really good, had to make the world better even if it was only a little bit, as long as she left it better than the way she found it. And she would hear, she swore she heard, someone whispering in her ear that even if things were awful at home with her family, *Everything is going to be all right.*

She picked the milkweed tufts apart and sent them fluffing off into the air. Someday she would come back and see if a whole bunch of milkweeds were growing here from the seeds. And she'd picture herself and Paul, their faces glowing in the soon-to-be setting sun, the landscape brown and quiet, their bodies keeping each other warm.

Moira looked again at the horizon, waiting for that vision to appear, but all she felt this time was a surge of hope and peace. That was enough to remind her that life was just wonderful, even though when you went home likely as not there'd be a musty gloom hanging in the air, a tired gloom waiting to descend and slowly sink its fangs into the members of the McPherson family.

Moira prayed to this wonderful wind to whisper its secrets to her family the way it did to her. To keep calling them to this spot the way it did to her, to whisper love and goodness and peace and happiness to them the way it did to her. To make her mother and father and sister happy, as happy as she was.

"Your old man," Paul said. "He made you shoot that gun because he knows you're not a girl. Not an ordinary girl. Maybe he wishes you were a boy."

"Yes. He thinks girls are bad. So does Mother," Moira said.

Paul said, "Maybe he's afraid of a girl like you. Because you're different. Anyway, you stay away from that man."

Paul wanted to protect her. But how could he protect her? They were moving away. She would have to protect herself. She was all she had in life, and she would have to protect herself.

And she could. And optimism took her over again. Playfully, she took Paul's arm and twisted it behind his back. "You better not ever change."

They arm-wrestled around, then he got her down on the ground and they wrestled some more. When they were both panting, they stopped and lay on the ground holding each other for a brief second, then sat up and looked around.

"Don't you ever become a white girl," he said.

"I won't."

"If you do, if you become one of *them,* you won't be happy."

"I know."

"We'll meet back here someday."

And now she knew it. Paul loved her, and she loved him. And she would love him forever. She would look for his face in other people. And for his soul.

They looked back at each other and understood that each had heard the voice that whispered *Shhhhhh . . . everything is going to be all right.*

* * *

The McPhersons moved into Sioux Falls that summer. Here, they were going to become successful. It looked like a place to be successful in. Unlike back in the old town, their spiffy new subdivision had no weeds poking up through the snow in winter, no patches of mud in summer. Instead, there were stretches of low houses with melancholy low-horizon views of those perfect lawns couched quietly under the bright Dakota sun, minty green new lawns against minty blue skies.

Daddy poured his heart and soul into that lawn. And his pocketbook. The family could go without things—the "in" clothes and dancing lessons for Taryn, a chemistry set for Moira or the new-style swoopy framed glasses to replace the scratched, old square frames she had. And the house could go without things—a mirror to replace the broken one over Moira's dresser, or a dining room table to replace the one ruined last Thanksgiving after Daddy got drunk and sent everyone to their room and forgot about the candles still burning.

But the lawn got the VIP treatment. Daddy had control of the new, perfect lawn in their new, perfect neighborhood, and yet Daddy would stand staring at the lawn, constantly nervous that he didn't have the right fertilizers or grass seed or little rocks around the shrubs.

Daddy sometimes said the more out of control the world and all the people in it got, the more he needed to control the lawn. And the more he needed to control the family's work on it in what Mother called the chain-gang approach to yard work. When the impulse to teach the Protestant ethic via the chain-gang approach struck Daddy, usually after a couple of beers, he'd start yelling at everyone to go outside and do some yard work.

Standing out there in the morning daylight with a hangover, his eyes could look cruel, the pupils shrinking to pinpoints within the blue eyes that allowed no sympathy as he barked out his orders.

"Eleanor, roll out that lawn mower."

"Roll it out yourself," Mother would say from the kitchen as she sipped her black, Scandinavian-style "hard boiled" coffee.

Daddy would turn to Moira. "Goddammit, roll out the lawn

mower." Then, as an afterthought, "And Taryn, you pull weeds, then you can both trim the evergreens."

If you asked him how many weeds you had to pull, or how much to trim the bushes, he'd glower at you and tell you to quit smarting off; he'd let you know when you were done.

Then he'd go inside and watch "Meet the Press" or something while you did your weed-pulling, and when the whim struck him—that could be in fifteen minutes or it could be in two hours, depending on his mood—he'd come out and stand on the door stoop and let you know that it was time to stop. Later, during the baseball game and after a few more beers, he'd tell you that he was just trying to teach you discipline and that you'd thank him for it later in life. From the ironing board in the kitchen, Mother would sarcastically say she'd think of some way to express her gratitude and he'd get pissed off and tell her she had no sense of pride in the appearance of the house and then yell at Moira and tell her she'd better not be such a smartass.

But of course there was a payoff: obviously, good citizens lived here. The McPherson lawn was a brighter, more lustrous green than anyone else's on the block. Not that they had anything to do with anyone in this new neighborhood—Daddy felt uncomfortable with the neighbors, as he did with everyone. He liked being alone, with his big moat of perfection surrounding his castle.

And not that the neighbors were anything to be physically scared of. Here there were no tough guys or screeching tires or whining hillbilly or rock-and-roll music. Here, families with haircuts as neat as their lawns went out together in four-door sedans. Here, they kept their car radios low, but you could bet when they drove off it was someone like Mitch Miller they were listening to and not someone like Hank Williams or Elvis Presley.

Worry over the lawn and the rigors of his white-collar job and Mother's nagging, though, weren't the only reasons Daddy drank. He was starting to act more and more weird toward Moira, not just bullying her, and he seemed almost to need a drink to keep from bothering Moira too much.

He wouldn't even look her in the eye anymore, and averted his eyes when she came into the room.

Moira didn't know what to think. Maybe all this had something to do with the jiggle under her sweater.

In fact she came to believe that she and her jiggle were the cause of Daddy's standing around drinking late at night in the kitchen and being pissed off and lunging out at her in the hallways and pounding on the bathroom doors when she was in there, and of its all getting worse. And as it got worse, life for them was getting scarier; in fact Moira thought it was odd that they'd moved here because they wanted a nice, clean, safe part of town to live in, and yet there were lots of dangerous neighborhoods around the Mc-Pherson household.

Two

Moira was definitely going to have to do something about that jiggle under her blouse.

Lately, a group of boys who hung out by the staircase whistled and made their heads bounce along with her breasts as she hurried to class. And then just last week, when she was wearing that Banlon sweater that made them look so pointy, she'd been stopped in the hall by Mr. Smealz, her English and geography teacher.

Mr. Smealz had eyes as blue as those maps he was always pointing at with his yardstick, cold as the Antarctic Sea. Eyes that reminded her of Daddy's, except Daddy's had those thick black lashes that gave them a sort of hurt look, and Mr. Smealz's eyes had light lashes that gave them a naked look.

Mr. Smealz had that yardstick in his hand, the one he always carried around with him and used to whip boys in front of the class when they acted up. He'd stopped her by holding the yardstick out. It had grazed her stomach, then her breasts, and she swore to God he stared at her breasts for a moment before pulling the yardstick back and holding it with both hands like a sword and saying in his whispery voice that was much scarier than a yell, "No running in the hall."

Speaking of running, the jiggle was a real handicap in gym class, not only in running games on the gym floor, but also in the locker room. She was embarrassed to have people know that she didn't have a bra, that she still did her jiggling beneath an undershirt.

She supposed she should do something about it. Moira did a lot of things for herself that her parents didn't do—signed notes from school, got herself into AP classes, figured out the school bus routes and did other school-related parent tasks. But in a hundred million years Moira would never get up the nerve to go into a store and buy a bra for herself. She wasn't even sure if it was legal for a thirteen-year-old girl to buy one. She imagined being arrested for trying to buy a bra and having a big headline in the local section of the newspaper: THIRTEEN-YEAR-OLD GIRL ARRESTED FOR ATTEMPTED BRA-BUYING.

The problem was, sex didn't exist in the McPherson household. As with Red China at the U.N., sex was not officially recognized at 47293 N. Boxelder Court East, Sioux Falls, South Dakota. And yet somehow, as you vaguely knew that Chinese people lived on the other side of the world, and there were armies of them—millions or maybe billions—you also vaguely knew that sex lived on the other side of the silences in the McPherson household, and that if it ever decided to march in and invade there'd be no stopping it.

She'd hinted to Mother a hundred times that she needed a bra. Each time, Mother had smoothed her hair and said, "Moira, do you know what happens to girls who become preoccupied with things they shouldn't think about at too young an age?"

Moira shook her head.

"Good. Keep on not knowing." Then she turned and looked in the dining room mirror. "Besides, do I look old enough to have a daughter who wears a bra?"

Moira shook her head again.

But it got too embarrassing at school. Moira practiced getting her nerve up to approach Mother, and decided to ask for a training bra, which might be more acceptable.

In the same matter-of-fact voice and with the same matter-of-fact face that she would use to say she needed a new protractor for math, Moira said to Mother that she needed the training bra. "For gym class."

Mother looked up from *Adventures in Drama,* her old high school book she dragged around with her all the time, rereading *Macbeth* and *Romeo and Juliet* and *Our Town* and all those other plays from it. She fingered the words *Oh You Kid* written by some boyfriend long ago in ink on the edge of the pages, and stared at Moira as if she'd truly been hoping all this time that Moira would never, ever need anything so disgusting as a brassiere.

"Everyone else has a training bra, or even a real one," Moira said quietly.

Mother looked at Moira's chest, then down at her own. She looked up and gave Moira her "ain't life shitty" smile.

Mother wasn't the only one who gave the "ain't life shitty" smile. It was sort of the McPherson signature, a tentative little smile that more or less communicated the basic message of their existence.

Right now the ain't-life-shitty smile meant Mother had been gypped. Gypped out of a decent set of the things they weren't allowed to talk about. Mother was always complaining about how Marilyn Monroe and Jane Russell and Elizabeth Taylor had brought hourglass figures into style, and how Mother could never keep up because she had the figure of a lady and not that of a flashy-looking tramp.

"I don't know what the rush is, Moira. I didn't need a brassiere and girdle until I was seventeen." Then she switched moods and laughed. "I still didn't need one, but I was afraid of getting in a car accident, and then what?" She ran her hands over her chest. "And I still don't need one." She looked at Moira's chest again where the unbrassiered breasts stuck out all wrong in jelly-pyramids instead of nice, firm conical bumps.

Moira was ready to give up on the whole idea when, of all things, Mother brought it up a few nights later, while the family was watching President Eisenhower make a speech.

Moira was sprawled on the floor doing her science homework, when she suddenly understood a section she'd read on how nerve impulses pass through synapses, and she felt the elation she got when things made sense.

Mother said, "Moira, I've been thinking . . . hon."

She looked up and smiled. "What, Mother?"

Mother chewed her gum in a smartass way she had of chewing it when she was in one of her moods.

"Come over here, hon."

Moira got up and went over to the couch where Mother was sitting. Mother had called her *hon*, but Mother's face wasn't saying *hon*. It was saying something else. And it was also suspicious and saying no one was going to put one over on her. Moira wondered what she was trying to pull on Mother. Mother sometimes made Moira feel guilty about things she didn't know she had done or was doing.

"Yes?" Moira said.

Mother said. "Are you wearing falsies?"

Moira could feel embarrassment rays emanating between her and Daddy over in his easy chair. In this household, bosoms didn't officially exist—Daddy didn't mention them, and you didn't mention them around him—and yet here was Mother all of a sudden talking about them. But of course that was Mother, always doing things out of the blue and switching moods like lightning and doing bizarre out-of-context things. And this was as out of context as if President Eisenhower had just mentioned that it had come to his attention that Moira McPherson of Sioux Falls, South Dakota, might need a training bra, and he was going to appoint a congressional panel to look into the matter.

"No, I don't have falsies on," Moira said quietly. She saw Taryn out of the corner of her eye. She was staring so hard at the TV she could have set fire to the President's speech script.

"Come here closer."

Moira moved toward Mother. Mother had that smartass look on her face as she chewed and snapped her gum. Moira was frightened of that look, just as she was frightened of mean kids at school. In fact, Mother often reminded her of kids at school because Mother seemed more like a kid, or at least a teenager, than she did a mother. Moira sometimes thought that if their family were a classroom, Daddy would be the teacher, Moira the egghead no one liked, Taryn the perfect girl with a bow in her hair, and Mother would be the smartass kid in the back slumped down in her chair, throwing paper wads and making wisecracks.

Mother reached out and pinched her nipple. She didn't let go, kept pinching, pinching. Moira cried, "Ouch."

Mother let go and smiled out of a corner of her mouth. Mother said to Daddy, "Moira needs a bra. A training bra, or so she says." There was a silence, then Mother repeated, "Moira says she needs a training bra."

Daddy stared at the television set and cleared a frog out of his throat and said in a forced tone of voice, "Is that right?"

Something passed through that message, from Daddy to Moira, and Moira got a creepy feeling.

"Training bra," Mother said, staring at Moira's breasts as if they were fungal growths she had to come up with a home remedy for. She reached up and pinched again and wriggled the nipple as she talked. "I wonder what they're supposed to put you in training for."

If only the earth would open up and swallow her, Moira prayed.

"Huh? What do they put you in training for?"

Daddy cleared his throat again. "You got me."

Moira pulled away from Mother, who was still holding on. Mother raised her half-moon eyebrows in Daddy's direction. "If you ask me, training bras are a gimmick to get money out of people. That's all they're for."

"I guess," Daddy said, trying to sound like he wasn't embarrassed.

"Well, finances are tight for us right now since you didn't get that raise you thought you were going to get and the only expense we aren't cutting back on is booze. I don't know, do you think we can spring for a brassiere for Moira?" Mother made a tiny laugh.

Daddy grunted something, and Moira ran to her room and cried.

That night when she went to bed, Moira's nipple throbbed. As it throbbed, it seemed to grow bigger and more sensitive. She hated herself, wished she didn't have these things, but she couldn't help it, could she?

Moira didn't ever ever want the subject to come up again.

The next evening, Mother told Moira she was going to take her out shopping for a brassiere.

It had snowed the night before, and a good two feet of blue-glazed snow covered the lawns. Snowplows had cleared the roads and left cindery stacks along the roads. The tire chains jingled off and on as Mother backed out of the driveway in her jerky way and then at her slow, scared speed. The tire chains marking the slow beat, they headed for Sears Roebuck.

They went straight to the lingerie department and Mother loudly asked a salesclerk where the bras were. While Moira stood wishing she were dead and that no one she knew would come in, Mother searched through the racks of bras, picked out a few, and took Moira to the dressing room.

Moira turned around and took off her undershirt. Mother

handed her the first one, a soft nylon bra with a bow between the cups. Size 30AA.

It made her bosoms look like enormous lumps of bread dough stuffed into cupcake pans.

"A little snug," Mother said and handed her another bra. "Here, try this one.

It was smaller than the first one, if possible. She couldn't even snap it in back.

Mother handed her another. Size 32A.

"Let me see, turn around." Mother said. Moira turned around and gave Mother an apologetic look.

Mother studied her breasts smashed into the bra as if Moira's chest were an abstract painting she was trying to make herself like. Afraid Mother would decided she liked it, Moira turned back around and quickly took the bra off. She held up her undershirt to hide the offending breasts.

"This is ridiculous," Mother said, grabbing the bra and storming out to the sales floor. Moira held her shirt over her breasts, wishing they would shrink back down to where they used to be. Mother returned with three more, a 32A, 32B, and 34A.

Still too small.

Moira took the last bra off and held her blouse in front of her breasts and Mother disappeared through the curtain again. Moira let the blouse drop and looked at her breasts. They looked sad, unloved.

Mother appeared again. No more frilly, delicate nylon bras this time. This was a heavily stitched cotton job that looked like it belonged in a hospital. Moira turned around so that Mother couldn't see and put it on. So far so good. She turned to look in the mirror.

They looked like new breasts. Brand-new, pumped-up, fresh new breasts. Moira couldn't believe what a relief it was to have a nice comfortable bra. It felt like suddenly being rich.

Moira turned and smiled at Mother. Mother seemed mad.

"I wouldn't go showing those things off," she said. "Now take *that* thing off and I'll go pay for it."

Mother took the bra out and paid for it while Moira got dressed.

She pictured herself walking into school the next day, the boys not making fun of her, Mr. Smealz not staring.

Mother was in a completely different mood by the time Moira came out of the dressing room. She held the little brown package out in her index finger and thumb and other fingers arched up as if it contained smelly garbage.

"Look, the old man is out of town, and Taryn is over at whatsername's house for the night. Let's go to a movie."

Moira nodded, even though she would like to have gone home and put on her new bra and worn it while she did the math problems she hadn't finished before they went out shopping. But Mother was in her odd mood where she acted like she and Moira were teenagers, best friends together.

They drove through town, past the Jewel Theater, which was showing a boring John Wayne film, and past the Granada, which was showing *Francis, the Talking Mule.*

"Let's just go home," Moira said.

Mother agreed and pulled the car into a driveway to turn around. But then her face lit up and she said, "Wait, how about a drive-in?"

Moira said she had homework but Mother told her she was turning into a grind, so Moira reluctantly agreed to go. They drove through the deserted city with its walls of piled-up snow and headed out into the country, the car chains clinking on the iced-up road. It was a black-and-white scene of moonless sky and empty cornfields with a crust of spun-sugar snow. They got to the Star Lite, where the McPhersons had spent many a summer Friday night with hundreds of other Sioux Falls families and dating teenagers. But this was a winter weeknight, and the lot was a sorry-looking mess of ice and snow and only a few dozen cars.

The marquee said the drive-in was showing *Let's Make Love.*

They drove in and Mother asked the woman in the ticket booth who was in the movie.

"Marilyn Monroe and Yves Montand," she said. She pronounced the French name *Wy-vees.*

"Did we miss much?"

"Only about fifteen minutes," she said. "You didn't miss nothin' important. You'll still understand the movie."

They bounced in over the partly plowed, icy ground, chains clinking more noisily now. To make matters worse, the car was a new one with a stick shift, and Mother kept popping the clutch and gunning the engine, all the while driving at a snail's pace. Someone yelled for Mother to turn out her lights.

Mother paid no attention and kept driving with her lights on. Someone honked and yelled, "Turn out the goddamn lights."

"Please, Mother, turn them out."

"How on earth can I see without the lights? Now let's find a good spot."

They roared through the drive-in with the lights on and the chains jingling and more people yelling and honking for Mother to turn off the lights. Mother stalled the car, then rammed into a speaker. She finally pulled into one spot but there was a car full of kids fighting on one side and a couple making out on the other, so Mother started up the engine and ground the gears and people started honking again. Moira slid down as far as she could in her seat and took off her glasses so she couldn't see the people staring. Was this going to be the story of her life? No friends, just a weird Mother to hang around with?

They found another spot but the speaker wouldn't turn on loud enough so they had to move. Mother backed out, right into a pile of dirty snow. *Whirrr, clink clink, whirrr, clink clink,* the tires went in the snow. More cars honked. Mother rocked the car, racing the engine and popping the clutch. *Harrruuun. Harrrrruun.* Moira tried a yoga breath like the beatniks did on some TV show she'd seen in order to tune this whole awful scene out, and watched the movie screen as Marilyn Monroe wiggled around in a silver-sequined dress while a skinny middle-aged man ogled her goofily.

A couple of teenage boys got out of their cars and came over to theirs. Moira put her hands over her face. "You stuck?" they asked Mother.

"I guess so," Mother said.

Moira could hear Marilyn Monroe singing breathily on the other car speakers as the guys rocked the car while Mother spun the tires and pretty soon no one in the lot could hear the singing. Moira's face was so hot with embarrassment it felt as if it would be permanently colored red.

With a mighty heave from their helpers, the car finally lurched out of the snow, and Mother found a spot in the front row near the playground. Thank God there were no other cars because they were too close and the picture sort of hurt your eyes. But up here all anyone could see would be the back of Moira's head, thank God.

They were so close that Marilyn Monroe's breasts were like dirigibles in those sequinny dresses.

"Look at those things," Mother said.

Moira worried that hers were going to get that big. It was hard to tell if that was good or bad. If you were at school, it was bad, and if you were in the McPherson household, it was bad, but if you were in movies, it was good.

And the clothes were designed to show off Marilyn Monroe's dirigibles. Moira couldn't understand why bosoms were okay on Marilyn Monroe but not on Moira. Maybe because Marilyn Monroe was beautiful and Moira was—to quote Mother—only on the homely side of average.

"Those bosoms are obscene," Mother said, but then she laughed so you didn't really know if they were obscene or not. "She'd better not turn around too fast or she could punch that French guy to death with them."

Moira watched and worried about her math homework. Maybe she could finish next day in homeroom. She always hated homeroom because other kids talked to each other and laughed and horsed around and she sat with her hands on her desk staring a hole in the clock and waiting for classes to start. "Let's get popcorn," Mother said.

Moira didn't want to go out into that parking lot full of staring eyes, but Mother insisted. They smushed across the gravel, Mother talking loudly about the old days when you had Maureen O'Sullivan and Katharine Hepburn and other actresses who were appreciated for their beautiful bone structure.

Moira put her hand to her cheek as they entered the refreshment stand. Her face was long and thin, and if there were beautiful bones in there, they were hiding.

There was something comforting about the sleaziness of the refreshment stand, the popcorn and grease and salt smell, the coffee, the hotdogs of suspect freshness, the fat guy behind the counter with sweat all over his round face.

The fat guy said, "What do you two lovely ladies want to-night?"

Mother raised her eyebrows and made a big deal of not respond-ing to his flirting.

They got their candy and walked back to the door over the flat-tened popcorn boxes and blackened pieces of gum and Mother burst into a wild giggling. "How'd you like that man in there trying to pick us up?"

"I don't think he was actually trying to pick us up."

"You don't?" Mother said, sounding sort of disappointed. She pointed out the poster on the cement-brick outside of the refresh-ment stand that showed Jayne Mansfield in a gold low-cut dress. "Maybe that'll be you someday, Moira," she said with something that was either a laugh or a sarcastic noise or both.

Moira's stomach did a turn because she couldn't figure out Mother or the world on the subject of breasts. She felt sick when she opened her box of Jujubes, and thought she was going to puke in the parking lot just to put the final touch on their disruptiveness at the drive-in.

But then as they got back to the car, someone whistled at them and Mother took Moira's arm as if they were a couple of teenage friends. "Hey, Mama, come on over here," someone said, and now Mother was laughing and making wisecracks.

And then Mother jabbed Moira with an elbow the way she some-times did when she wanted to be buddies instead of mother and daughter, and started teasing Moira about the size of her breasts. "I can see why you're embarrassed. You've certainly got an embarrass-ment of riches there."

Mother tried to make Moira feel bad about her breasts, and yet Moira detected a bit of ambivalence in Mother's attitude. Moira herself certainly felt ambivalent. And as they drove home past the empty winter wheat fields whose smooth snow glittered like dia-monds on one of Marilyn Monroe's white dresses, Moira felt that maybe the only thing to do with breasts was to accept them as

something glamorous, accept yourself as glamorous if you ended up
getting big ones, and give up on ever being one of those nice sweet
innocent girls who walked around school with modest little nice-
girl bumps in their Orlon sweaters.

A few days later, Moira found something on the bathroom floor
that looked like a sponge. She picked it up to put it on the bathtub,
but then hesitated. It wasn't a sponge at all. It was a falsie, complete with a fake nipple. She found another one behind the clothes
hamper.

Mother came out of the bedroom in her nightgown. "Oh, those
are mine," she said, grabbing them from Moira. "I decided that my
clothes would hang better if I wore these. The styles now, you
know, are made for curvy figures." Briefly, Moira noted, her eyes
ran over Moira's body.

Moira noticed later that Mother did look different with her falsies. Better, maybe. She stood up taller.

What Daddy thought of them Moira didn't know; he made no
comment in front of Moira, anyway.

Mother bought more falsies. Bigger ones. And true to Mother's
lackadaisical style, the falsies ended up all over the house. On top
of the stereo, on the radiator, on the kitchen table, in the basement
on top of a pile of tools, in the garage. Mother must have had a
dozen pairs of them of varying sizes, some with nipples, some without. Over the winter, as they got washed and worn a lot, they
changed shapes. Some got hard and misshapen, some got starched
accidentally, some came out miraculously puffy and soft, if yel-
lowed, by the washing and chlorine bleaching. Some looked like
stuffed animals or old bread rolls left around the house, while others were very obviously imitations of the real thing. Moira found
the whole thing rather sad, but Taryn found it quite embarrassing
because she had to check the house for errant falsies before bringing
friends in.

Meanwhile, Mother refused to buy Moira another bra. Moira
had to hand wash it, because the laundry was Mother's to do (since
Daddy's underwear might be in it).

As the year went on and Mother's falsie collection grew, Moira's bra developed underarm stains from all her nervous perspiring under her navy blue sweater, and soon her big new bra had permanent dark semicircles underneath the armpits.

Not exactly the kind of bra Marilyn Monroe would wear.

Three

THE MCPHERSONS rarely made it to church, and they weren't particularly religious. But they sent the girls to Sunday school every now and then.

One afternoon when her parents were out shopping and Moira was looking around the house for the Bible so she could do her Sunday school homework, she discovered something shocking about Mother.

She looked through the drawers in the living room, then went to her parents' bedroom. She felt a book way in the back of the nightstand on Mother's side of the bed, and though it wasn't a Bible, it certainly was interesting: a ragged copy of *Peyton Place*.

Moira had heard all about books like *Lady Chatterley's Lover* and *Peyton Place*. That Mother would read something like this—and on top of that, hide it—was too much to believe at first. But on the other hand, Daddy reading it was not only unbelievable, it was unthinkable; Daddy was the most moralistic person in the world—increasingly these days, in fact, because the more he drank, the more moral he became.

Somewhere around the house there was a spare Bible or two left over from the classes they had to attend to get the girls baptized. As a little girl, Moira had often leafed through these Bibles.

She'd stop to immerse herself in those pictures of Jesus in his white robe with his arms out as if to reach for you, pictures washed with perfect aqua skies and soft rays of light emanating down on him from heaven. It was really strange, but in some of those pictures, Jesus reminded her of Paul Whitefeather. Maybe because both Jesus and Paul Whitefeather were dark-skinned and long-haired and sort of wild-eyed and hurt-looking, and because it often seemed that they were the only people who accepted Moira McPherson.

* * *

Yes, *Peyton Place* had to be Mother's book, even though Mother pretended to be such a Puritan. Mother was always catching you off-guard; the minute you thought you understood her, she'd turn around and do something completely out of character. Actually, when it came down to it, maybe there was no character for Mother —she was like an amoeba, constantly changing shape.

It seemed to Moira that Mother was hiding the book from Daddy, and maybe in a way she was hiding it from herself too. But she couldn't really succeed, because, it occurred to Moira, this whole family was walking around with *Peyton Place* hidden inside their heads.

Every time Mother and Daddy went out, Moira sneaked into the bedroom to read the dirty parts in *Peyton Place*.

And then one lazy Sunday afternoon as she was lying on Mother and Daddy's bed reading, picturing the *Peyton Place* characters' bathing suits sliding off, imagining their groping hands in the dark, she heard Daddy and Mother come in the front door. She jerked open the nightstand drawer and stuffed the book in. She wasn't sure she'd closed the drawer all the way, but they would catch her if she didn't get out of the room fast. Slipping and sliding in her socks on the bare wooden floor, she raced out of the room. Halfway down the hallway, she thought she heard the book fall to the floor and she skidded to a halt, but it was too late to go put it back because Daddy was rounding the bend that led into the hallway.

She hid in her room and listened. It wasn't long before Daddy's voice boomed out: "What on earth—hey, Eleanor, what the hell kind of trash is this?"

"What's that?" Mother called from the living room.

"This book, this garbage," Daddy said, walking into the living room, his voice rising and cracking like a teenage boy's that was changing.

There was a pause, then Mother said crisply, "Oh, that. Ella Randolph down at the end of the cul-de-sac gave it to me." Moira heard Mother walk into the kitchen, her ankles cracking and her mules clacking behind her in the quick sparky way that usually preceded a big fight.

"Ella Randolph always did have a smutty mind," Daddy said. "Sits out in the garage drinking beer with the men and telling those traveling-salesman jokes. I went over there one time and joined them for a beer and I couldn't believe my ears when I heard the kind of language that woman used."

"What does a smutty mind have to do with anything?" Mother said, her voice as pure and clear as spring water.

"This book. It was made for filthy minds and nothing else."

"Why don't you spray some Lysol on it, then?" Daddy was always spraying Lysol around the house. He sprayed chairs before he sat in them. If anyone came to visit, when they left he dusted everything they might have touched with Lysol, saturated every chair they might have sat in.

Maybe his drinking had something to do with all that, too, Moira thought. Every time he got mad, he got a drink, maybe because alcohol killed the germs inside his mind, too. Or the dirty thoughts.

"I have no idea what that book is about," Mother said crisply. "I haven't even looked at it yet."

"You know goddamn well what this book is. Filth." Then Moira heard Daddy go to the refrigerator. She heard the clinking of his rummaging around in the silverware drawer, then the whoosh of a beer bottle being opened. He went on. "I wouldn't be surprised, in fact, if it wasn't someone other than Ella Randolph who gave it to you."

There was a pause, then Mother said in a slightly quivery voice, "What do you mean?"

"I'll bet it was that skirt chaser at the library. That asshole that minces around the library and thinks he's goddamn Andrew Carnegie. Is he the one who gives you all those books you've been reading?"

"You and your ridiculous jealousy."

It was true. Daddy *was* jealous. He'd once bloodied the nose of a parking lot attendant for telling Mother that she was wearing an attractive hat. Mother had bad teeth and ankles that cracked all the time from her childhood calcium deficiency, and she was always going to the dentist for fillings. But they'd switched dentists three times since moving into Sioux Falls. Once because Daddy thought the hygienist was a floozie, another time because the dentist told Daddy that drinking might be the reason his gums were bleeding, and another time because Mother came home laughing and told him the dentist had a habit of laying his instruments on the little bib on her chest while he worked. "And a couple of times when he reached for his little mirror, it took him a lot of searching to find it."

Daddy had gone in the next day and grabbed the dentist by his shirt right in front of a patient and told him he'd drill a hole through his head if he ever bothered Mother again.

"What if the girls see this book?" Daddy continued. "Especially Moira."

Mother's voice came out dry and clear. "Moira? Why is Moira constantly on your mind, Aloysius? Huh? I sometimes think you have improper thoughts about your daughter. I ought to call the authorities."

"I've had it with your gutter mind."

It sounded like Daddy threw *Peyton Place* across the room, and then Moira heard him and Mother scuffling, in the kitchen. She heard some more yelling, then the moaning of the dinette chairs being pushed around, then there was a bang and Mother started screaming, "Don't you ever hit me again."

"You tell that soft-assed sissy if he has any more books for you to read, to call me up. I'll get them for you and shove them down his throat."

"You don't seem to understand. He's the *librarian*. If he recommends books, I consider them."

"Yeah? What other things does he recommend?"

Moira heard a lawn mower turn off and the boys outside who'd been playing and laughing stop, and then there was silence in the neighborhood as if everyone was waiting to hear what else the librarian recommended.

"He recommends you see a psychiatrist for the way you stare at your eldest daughter."

"What the hell are you talking about?"

Mother's ankles cracked into motion and her mules slapped into her bedroom and now there was a tense quiet. Moira's mouth filled with saliva that wouldn't go down.

Soon, the symphony of the usual drinking sounds began—the sawing of cupboard doors opening and closing and the banging of drawers and tinkling of silverware and the squeaking of the refrigerator door and plinking of beer-bottle caps, all against the counterpoint of the rhythmic shuffling of feet on the kitchen tile. Sometimes Moira thought Daddy welcomed a big blowout fight so he'd have an excuse to get drunk. Sometimes she thought Mother welcomed a big blowout fight so she'd have an excuse to get depressed and give up on life and hate everyone—her husband, her kids, herself, the world—and then leave them all and go out alone to a movie.

Moira closed her eyes and took breaths to get more oxygen and hemoglobin into her blood. She had to relax, she had to escape from these fights.

But what was wrong with her? This wasn't right. Fathers didn't think things like that about their daughters. That was the sickest thing Moira had ever heard of.

Yet Mother thought so.

And yet Daddy seemed so innocent in his own way—always worried about doing the right thing, even watching television to find out what was right and wrong because his parents had never taught him.

But Mothers always know best. Maybe if a person loved you too much, that was bad. Maybe you had to be mean to them so they wouldn't love you too much. Maybe she shouldn't love Daddy anymore.

Oh, but she did. After all, he patted her head when she got A's on her report card.

Daddy used to take her skating. Pulled her around on the sled on the ice. Then, while she made snowmen, he played hockey with some of the teenage boys, waving to her, wanting her to be proud of his hockey playing.

Told her she was smart. Told her she was a good girl. And a couple of times he'd told her she was pretty.

But that was back in the old days. Back when they lived in the country, before they became civilized and moved to the suburbs and were going to have money and the girls were going to go to Dakota

State Normal College to become teachers and respectable people, and before Moira became a walking menace around the house. Moira, the ghost of sex future, ghost of sex present, and somehow, she felt, the ghost of their sexual past.

She got up and closed her bedroom door. Now there was silence. She got out her homework. She stared at the blank white sheet in front of her until her mind was blank and white, too. Then she began, slowly at first: y plus z minus x . . .

Moira was awakened in the middle of the night by banging, then a noise in the kitchen of ripping paper. She wondered if she had put her homework away, reached for her pile of books on her nightstand, and felt for the reassuring sheaf of papers as if she were patting a baby in a cradle.

Next there was the squeak of the cupboard door, then the hubbubabubbub as the door gently bounced shut. She heard Daddy pour a shot, heard his footsteps do a little shuffle the way he did when he was enjoying the shot, then she heard him pour another, then another. She heard him mutter, "Sons of bitches at work. Cutthroat sons of bitches. And now this garbage. How the hell much can you take? Whole goddamn world is screwed up." He yelled out into the silence of the house, "All right, Eleanor, this is the end of the matter."

Soon she heard the back door slam. She knelt on her bed and cautiously pulled her curtains apart. Moonlight streamed down on Daddy as he went to his tool shed and emerged with a spade. Moira's throat closed up and her face froze numb; while everyone was asleep, he'd killed Mother and was going to bury the body.

He began to dig a hole, his heel kicking down on the shovel with all the anger of the ages, coming up with earth, throwing it in a pile, thrusting the spade back into the ground.

But he stopped after just a few minutes. Then he came back inside the house, and went back out. He was carrying something in his index finger and thumb as if it were contaminated.

Moira saw that it was a book. He opened it and ripped the pages, muttered something, and threw the book into the hole. It wasn't a grave for Mother, then—just a grave for sex.

But thank God, Mother was still alive, maybe watching from her own bedroom window. He stared for a moment, then took the spade to the tool shed and reemerged with the gallon can of gasoline for the lawn mower. He sprinkled gasoline into the hole and lit a match. There was an explosion louder than with the barbecue, and for a moment Moira thought he was going to go up in a puff of smoke. But as the flames leaped up he frowned, his face blazing yellow and red and black. When the fire went out he replaced the soil, burying sex in the backyard. And Moira never once again looked at that spot without thinking of it.

In the middle of the night she awakened again, and Daddy was standing in her doorway staring at her. She closed her eyes and prayed for him to go away. When she opened them, he was gone.

The next morning she felt guilty, as if she had betrayed Mother, even though she hadn't done so on purpose. She had just been careless about the book.

At breakfast, she thought Mother gave her a look that said she knew Moira was the one who'd brought it out of the hiding place, but since *Peyton Place* was sex, Moira couldn't very well be blamed for bringing out in the open something that didn't exist.

Everyone froze as Daddy came in to the kitchen, an unwashed smell about him, his eyes swollen so tight that they looked like black slits, his curly hair popping out all over his head.

Noisily, he slammed around looking for a frying pan to make one of his famous big hangover breakfasts.

He examined the pan for cleanliness next to the window, and put it on the stove. As he stood in front of the refrigerator looking for eggs, he said without turning around, "Moira, I want to look at every book you bring into this house."

But it was Mother's book. *It was Mother's.*

"And another thing, Eleanor. Moira is not going out with punks in cars. I read in the newspaper yesterday that three teenagers were killed in a car crash over in Duluth. Moira is not going out with boys. Not while she lives in this house."

And he slammed the refrigerator door shut.

Four

COULDN'T GO OUT *with boys. Not while she lived in this house.*

Moira came home from school. She'd gotten two A's on tests today and a warning note for her poor attitude in gym class because she had gone into the bathroom to cry after she was chosen last for the gym team (as usual—you'd think she'd be used to it by now). The teacher had written on the note: *Unsportsmanlike conduct.*

But she was in the sanctity of her home at last. Daddy was nowhere in sight, so Moira turned on "American Bandstand" (an illegal show when Daddy was policing the house). Moira adored "American Bandstand," and felt reassured that there was happiness out there to be had when she saw all those teenagers dancing.

The song "Mack the Knife" came on, and the Bandstand kids stopped chewing their gum with that glazed look in their eyes and looked around for partners. They giggled and tried to figure out whether this was a slow or fast dance. Myrna Horowitz, the one with the polio brace on her leg, pulled her partner out onto the dance floor and began to jitterbug. The camera showed her for a minute, to underscore her courageousness for dancing with the leg brace, and soon everyone else was out jitterbugging with Myrna.

That song over, "Mr. Blue" began, and the teenagers reached for each other to slow-dance as if there were magnets inside their chests. Moira's own chest ached as she watched.

She went to the kitchen. Taryn was giggling on the phone. Taryn must have just washed her hair because a halo of light shone around the top. Moira automatically smoothed her own thick, curly hair which, like Daddy's, seemed to grow up and out instead of down. As a toddler, Taryn used to say it was easy to draw Moira— "You just make messy scribbling all around her face."

Moira mussed the smooth bangs of her sister's halo and pretended to push down the receiver button on the phone. Taryn reached out with her foot and tried to kick Moira. Moira grabbed her ankle and playfully shook it, then got a glass of milk and went back to the living room and spread her books out in front of her. Frani and Justine, the two prettiest girls on the show, were laughing with Dick Clark as they rated a new song. As Moira opened her algebra book, the Bandstand couples erupted into a fast-dance while Dick Clark played "Sea Cruise."

Fabian came on the show and all the girls screamed as he sang "I'm a Tiger." Dick Clark interviewed him, then they played "The Stroll," a new slow-dance, and Moira's algebra was done. Time to start English. It felt as if her period had started. She went to the bathroom and checked. It had. She washed out her pants in the sink and hung them in the bathroom.

There was one Kotex in the box.

She went to her mother's bedroom. Mother was in the spot she went to when she was depressed, in a swirl of sheets on the bed, staring at the wall.

Mother turned, her face as lifeless as the white wall.

"We're out of Kotex," Moira said.

Mother stared at the wall for a moment and then slowly rolled over and sat upright on the side of the bed. She was wearing her stretched-out panty girdle and a bra that had little circles of stitching that went round and round and came to a point that crumpled because her breasts didn't reach. She searched around through the bedclothes, then looked under the bed and found a falsie, then another, and fished them around under her bra until the crumples were gone and the bra was bursting.

"I'll go to the store for you. You don't want people knowing you've started all that business at such an early age." She went to the bathroom to get ready.

Moira settled back down in front of the TV. Mother came rushing out of the bathroom with Moira's washed-out pants. "What if your father saw these?"

Feeling like a criminal who should hide the evidence, Moira took them to her room and hung them on her bedpost to dry.

Mother fumbled with the old Brownie camera that she'd gotten out from the bottom of the same drawer in which she'd kept *Peyton*

Place. Her hair was in pin curls with a pink hairnet over them and her yellow-pale face shone with cold cream. She went around like this all day, and then, if Daddy was on the road, wiped off the cold cream and brushed out her hair and went shopping or to a movie, usually by herself at night.

"Stand still so I can get your picture. Move back a little. I want it full-length."

Moira, flattered, took off her glasses and moved back and smoothed her hair down and sucked her cheeks in to make a smile like Gina Lollabrigida's.

Mother held up the camera, her face serious, puckered, as if this were as important as Matthew Brady photographing the Civil War. "Hold still."

"Velveeta," Moira said, laughing and making a silly exaggerated model's pose with her hips forward and her head back like she'd seen Tuesday Weld do in a movie magazine.

"Now turn to the side."

Moira turned to the side. "What is this, a mug shot?" she said, laughing self-consciously and now trying to look star-struck and cuddly like Sandra Dee.

"It's not your mug I'm interested in."

The radio that they turned on when Daddy wasn't around played "Bobby Sox to Stockings." Frankie Avalon's nasal voice sang about when a girl was old enough for giving away her heart.

Mother sang along for a while, then suddenly she seemed to re-member that she was a mother and not a teenager and was sup-posed to disapprove. Mother stood up erect and said, "Old enough to give *what* away?" She stood back a little further, and snapped again. "Got your period. I don't know what this world is coming to when children get that sort of thing. Periods, for God's sake."

"Mother, almost everyone at school does." She knew because in gym class you got to take a sponge bath during that time.

"I went around telling everyone I had my period, too, even though I didn't get it until I was fifteen. No, there's something very precocious about you, Moira, and I don't just mean with the straight A business. You'd better watch it, young lady, or you're going to be in trouble some day."

"What sort of trouble?"

"None of your business, Miss Precocious."

Moira hung her head. Maybe Mother was right and no one else really had their period yet. Maybe she was a freak. A sex maniac.

But she didn't want Mother to see that she felt bad. Sometimes she got the idea that Mother liked it when she felt bad. Then Moira was easier to control. But she wanted to rise above all that, so she made a cheery face and said in a cheery voice, "Hey, Mother, what is it with the picture taking? I didn't know I was all that beautiful."

"You're not. You're on the homely side of average-looking, like the rest of us. Your father is the only one with any looks. Those curly black eyelashes and blue eyes, wasted on a man. And don't look so offended. I would do you a disservice if I didn't tell you."

"Oh," Moira said, feeling the smile abandon her face even though she wanted to keep it so Mother wouldn't know how much she'd been hurt again, and also to show Mother she wasn't one of those vain girls who wanted to be pretty, that she was trying to accept her lot in life as an untouchable in the beauty caste system.

"Your hair's too dull and curly, your face is too long, your eyes are too low in your face, your nose is too flat, your lips are too thin and wide." She paused for a breath, then moved on to new territory. "Your shoulders are too high, your fingers are too fat, your feet are too long, you're slightly duck-toed. I don't think I drank enough milk when I was pregnant with you."

Now Moira felt like crying. Taryn walked into the room with a smug expression. Mother raised her plucked and penciled eyebrows and said, "Taryn, you needn't feel so superior. Your face is flat as a pancake, you're short as a dwarf, and you'll never lose that dazed look. Oh, it's all my fault. If I hadn't had that weird craving to inhale gasoline from the spare can all the time when I was pregnant you probably wouldn't have been premature."

But lest anyone might think Mother was being unloving, she added in a somewhat apologetic tone, "At least you girls aren't some stuck-up little show-off snots who think they're better than anyone else."

Mother put her eye to the camera, and snapped again. "Oh, don't look so offended, Moira. I never said you were ugly. I just said you weren't beautiful." Mother always did this, said something mean, then repented and made her voice soft and retracted a little of what she'd said. "Do you want to be beautiful like that made-up floozie that ran off with my father? What good is she to anyone, except the cosmetic companies?"

Moira wasn't sure that the beautiful woman who stole Grandpapa from Grandmama was so bad off for being beautiful. Look at all the attention she got from Mother. But Moira had to deal with her own relationship with beautiful, or rather her own non-relationship with it, so she asked Mother, "Why are you taking so many pictures of me, then?"

"If you really want to know," Mother said, putting the camera back into the case. "They're to show people that you weren't pregnant, in case some day they ever accused you of anything like that."

"Like what?"

"Having been pregnant and deserting a baby when you were young. There was a girl in my school they accused of that. She went away for six months to visit a sick aunt in Watertown. She never shook that reputation."

Moira looked at Mother to see if this was a joke. It wasn't. Moira wondered what was wrong with her, that Mother had to do this. No one had ever accused her of being pregnant. And then she remembered what a sensitive issue the whole thing was, as when she asked the other night if she could go and see the new Sandra Dee movie, *A Summer Place*.

Mother hadn't even answered but clacked off in her mules to the kitchen and said something to Daddy. Daddy had jerked the kitchen faucet off so hard it made the pipes in the basement groan. He came into the living room breathing loudly and glowering and obviously past the three-beer stage of the day and therefore not to be reckoned with lightly. He yelled at Moira that it was past her bedtime.

Mother took some snapshots out of the drawer and said, "See, the date is printed on these. And there's a picture of you with all your belly showing. Now, if anyone ever accuses you of anything when you were young, here's the proof. And we'll take these pictures every few months."

She tossed the snapshots onto the table, ammunition against the world's army of dirty minds.

Moira walked stiffly, with as much dignity as she could summon up, to her room. She put her hands in her face and cried at what a dirty, filthy, disgusting girl she must be for her parents to have to take such extraordinary precautions.

Was she going to be crazy some day? Was she going to be a slut? And what were the choices? Was she going to be like Mother— depressed and married to an alcoholic? It was getting more and more difficult to hang on to her dream of going away and making something of herself, because she was sometimes beginning to wonder if she wasn't doomed, fated to be a failure. Moira wanted to be her real self and grow up to be important so that she could help people who were less fortunate, and at the same time she wanted to please Mother and Daddy by being normal. Was it possible to be both?

Five

MOTHER MADE FUN of people for sport—the neighbors, Taryn and Moira's teachers and friends, casual acquaintances, everyone.

While she made fun of real people for sport, she took television people *very* seriously. Maybe because some teacher had once told her she had acting ability, and her parents had told her that if she ever set foot on stage they'd throw her out of the house so that she could be done with it and just go ahead and be a streetwalker, which as far as they were concerned was a cut above an actress.

In watching TV, Mother's anger came through more harshly than she probably intended sometimes, especially when an actress was a notable show-off. With some of them, Mother would watch an entire show, and then at the end, when the commercial came on, come out with, "What ever gave her the idea that we would want to sit here and watch her for half an hour?" With others, like the soap-opera actresses, she'd try ridicule: "Did you hear that? Martha wants to know what she can do about George. Well, I'll tell her what she can do—she can get the hell off TV and go out and get herself an honest job like anybody else." Or sometimes the silent treatment seemed the only thing, as when an actress was being so outrageously show-offy that it didn't need comment, the whole family could see it for themselves. Other times, if the family wasn't catching it, Mother would get the vaguest hint of a sarcastic smile, and turn and sort of spread the smile around the room to make sure everyone was tuned in to the fact that the person (usually but not always a woman) was showing off in a particularly outrageous fashion. Sometimes when an actress she couldn't stand appeared on the TV, Mother would give her the ultimate insult of simply refusing to look at her, letting her eyes travel across the room to something else, just to teach the actress a lesson for having the nerve to show off on Eleanor McPherson's TV set.

But to be perfectly honest, sometimes it felt good to come home to Mother, Moira's best friend. The only person who accepted her. Sometimes.

One reason Mother could accept her was because Mother had a strange attitude about clothes where the girls were concerned. While Mother bought herself a new outfit every payday, she said kids didn't need a lot of expensive clothes.

Mother said it was vain for little girls to have "excessive concern about clothes," and it was bad for their developing characters. "Clothes are like coffee and cigarettes and makeup, one of the rewards for being an adult. God knows there has to be some compensation for getting old."

So Moira had just three outfits to wear. Mother had bought them at the dime store. Taryn was luckier. The Ettingers had a girl just two sizes bigger than Taryn, and they gave her nice, expensive hand-me-downs. Plus Taryn had girlfriends who wore nice, expensive clothes, and they lent her things now and then. Moira, Miss Science with Coke-bottle specs, didn't have those kinds of girlfriends.

Whenever she was rejected at school by other girls because her cheap clothes were often torn or dirty—because Moira was very nearsighted and couldn't always see the dirt and besides, she was always in a trancelike state over her homework—she would think about Paul Whitefeather saying she wasn't really a girl and she wasn't really white. That helped. If she wasn't really a girl and wasn't really white, then she didn't have to be accepted by the white girls. She could be her own person. She was going to be her own person all her life. She was going to leave South Dakota and become someone important. But that didn't mean she would waste being important on just getting things for herself. She would dedicate her life to humanity.

One eerie thing was that Moira and Mother and Taryn had once been watching an old Shirley Temple movie on TV, *Bright Eyes,* and Moira noticed that the girl who played Shirley Temple's foil, the "homely brat," as Mother referred to her, wore a hat and coat just like the one in which Mother had dressed Moira for a picture that she kept up on the hutch. And Mother had combed Moira's bangs down over her face like the girl's in the movie, too, even though Moira's bangs liked to roll back and stick up in the air, and Mother having to practically blind Moira with hairspray in getting them to stay down.

It was probably just a coincidence, but Moira sometimes wondered if Mother thought of herself as Shirley Temple stuck with a couple of homely brats.

Moira wondered what it would be like to have a mother who thought you were attractive, that you were worthy of boys' love, and who bought you clothes, fixed your hair in perfect pigtails with painstakingly straight parts the way Sharon Thompkin's mother did. Who fussed over you the way Christine Larkster's mother did her, fashioning long corkscrew curls that danced on the lace collars she wore with her pastel sweater sets.

Mother hated kids on TV almost as much as she hated women on TV. Actually, Mother hated show-offy kids anywhere, and when they encountered a show-offy kid—at the grocery store, on the playground, at school, in the neighborhood—trying to get attention by doing something, Mother's advice was simply to ignore him or the spoiled brat would end up thinking he was something special.

Mother's criticism of her daughters was for their ultimate good, Mother stressed, because she wanted nothing more than for her daughters to be normal and normal meant average. That, she made it clear, was why she was the way she was. Lax mothers produced lax children.

Six

"MISS AMERICA" would be on in ten minutes. Eleanor was making fudge for them to eat while they watched the program—her way of showing the Miss America show-offs that the McPhersons weren't buying into their beauty game. If that's what you wanted to call it. A lot of the contestants stretched the meaning of the word beauty to its limits, as far as Eleanor was concerned. Minutes to go. She beat the fudge furiously. In truth, she loved watching this show, as she loved watching other shows with supposedly beautiful women so that they could play "Who's the Ugliest?" "Miss America" was a once-a-year bonanza for that game. Fifty of the world's biggest show-off, ripe-for-the-kill contestants.

She took a tiny spoonful of fudge and dropped it into cold water. Almost soft-ball stage. Hurry, the Miss America music was coming on. She turned the heat off under the coffee and poured herself a cup. She liked her coffee strong, Scandinavian-style. Aloysius, being of British Isles extract—a little English, a little Scottish, a lot of Irish —teased her about her Norwegian ways, even her big-boned size (which he nevertheless claimed to admire).

He had, in fact, teased her out of some Scandinavian habits— those jelly-filled bismarcks in the morning, the strict Lutheran church that she'd been brought up in, the spareness of her taste in furniture. She'd agreed to some furniture more to Wish's taste, like the bright red sectional modern sofa and the blond wood cabinet with the combination radio, TV and hifi. But she wouldn't be teased out of her two-quart pan of strong boiled and bitter coffee, her lifeblood. She made it in the morning and drank it all day long. Kept the pan on the stove all day for reheating. By late afternoon, it would have a grease rainbow. Twelve cups or so later the pot was gone and it was bedtime. It never kept her awake. Eleanor didn't react to things the way other people did—alcohol kept her awake, coffee put her to sleep. Funny.

The fudge was done just as Bert Parks began to introduce them. "Hurry, Mother," Taryn said.

Eleanor poured the fudge onto a plate and grabbed a knife for it and ran to the living room just in time to see Miss Alabama's homely phony smile. She scooped a bit of fudge, not quite hardened, onto the knife and stuck it in her mouth and passed the plate to Taryn, saying, "Ugly as sin" as Miss Alabama strutted across the stage.

"Miss Alaska," Bert Parks said.

"She's pretty," Moira said.

"Are you *kidding?*" Eleanor said, but then calmed down as she reminded herself that Moira always had to be the spoilsport in this game.

"Fat legs," Taryn said.

"Are those legs?" Wish said. "I thought they were tree trunks."

Even Wish, over there in the corner with his Reader's Digest, was going to join in. That sounded like about a four-and-a-half, five-beer joke. But only a rough estimate. He went through various stages in his drinking, from the slightly jovial two-beer, to the cocky four-beer stage, to the "everyone's a wonderful person" six-beer stage, to the pissed-off stage, and so on. Actually it varied, depending on the phases of the moon, Eleanor guessed. But one thing was sure: Wish didn't make jokes until he'd had at least two beers, and the quality of the jokes deteriorated the more he drank until he turned the corner and suddenly, without warning, it was no joke at all. She took a quick glance. He was holding a beer but you didn't really know if it was number three or number thirty-three. He didn't keep them all on the table. Made a small collection, then put the bottles away before starting a new collection so you couldn't keep track.

When a commercial came on, Eleanor ran to the kitchen for milk. Actually, she was now in a good mood and reminded herself that she kind of felt okay when she had companions—her family—to hate the world with. Otherwise, it was a very lonely life.

In fact there was always a depression right behind her head, always tapping hesitantly on her shoulder, reminding her that it was still there, waiting, saying *Come with me.*

Usually Eleanor would reach back and wave it away as if it were

a pesky mosquito. But it would come right back and buzz lightly
near her ear, waiting patiently. It was very patient. And persistent.
You could chase it away a hundred times, a thousand times, and
still it would be there, circling nearer, farther, back again.

As the show came on again, she tore into one of the contestants.
"Look at that hair. Rope. It looks like rope. Why do some women
let their hair grow into a long rat's nest and think that looks attractive? Much better if she had it cut and arranged into a real style."

"Yeah," Taryn said. "She's ugly."

"She has pretty eyes, though," Moira said, blinking behind those
thick glasses. Eleanor poked Taryn in the ribs, and Taryn turned
and gave Eleanor a little smile and nodded toward Moira. It really
pissed them off when Moira didn't hate the world along with them.
Moira had always been a traitor to this family. She had these
phony-baloney highfalutin' notions about honor and generosity and
all that nicey-nicey crap that along with a dime would buy you a
cup of coffee. Eleanor suddenly stopped herself from thinking that
way. Oh my God, she thought, I sound like a catty high-school girl.

Well, those goody-goody emotions were the kind of emotions
other people could afford, but not the McPhersons. And look where
it got Moira. She was the freak of the school anyway.

"How can you say she has pretty eyes when she might not say the
same thing about you?" Taryn said to Moira.

Moira shrugged.

And the parade went on. Miss California wasn't bad but her eyes
were too narrow. Miss Delaware was a dog and made you wonder
what *wasn't* pretty these days. Miss District of Columbia had a
horse face, Miss Georgia had that southern belle stupid look, Miss
Iowa had a nose that wouldn't quit and her hair was too long, Miss
Indiana looked like the next thing to a prostitute with that puffy
hair and all that eye makeup and the way she wiggled, Miss Illinois
had a phony smile, Miss New York was pretty if you liked the dark-
skinned type—foreign or something, and they certainly weren't going to go that far, would they? Making a foreigner Miss America?

Miss Louisiana looked like a redneck queen with all that infuriat-
ing long black hair, Miss Michigan was pretty but her ankles were a
little thick and her teeth were too small (Eleanor liked a good-sized
set of teeth), Miss Minnesota had too much makeup and you just

knew she was some little whore back home despite what they pretended, Miss Ohio was so tall and gawky she looked like Ichabod Crane, Miss Pennsylvania—now she was a good-looking gal, she might get it. In fact, she looked a little like Eleanor would look if she were the type of woman to spend all day in front of the mirror primping to draw attention to herself, which, thank God, she had more important things to do than, yes, this girl had nice small features, smooth short brown hair, a good-sized but straight nose, nothing too cute and boopsy boop like these men liked, and a modest smile. Miss Pennsylvania should win.

They all checked out Miss South Dakota carefully. She was a huge disappointment.

"Bleached blonde," Eleanor said.

"Bump in her nose," Taryn said.

"Fat cheeks," Moira said, trying now to get into the spirit of things.

When a commercial for Toni home permanents came on, they critiqued the models. "Her cheeks are too low," "Her hair is too kinky with that permanent," "She looks uglier after than before the permanent." "Big teeth," Eleanor pronounced. She might like a good-sized set of teeth, but there were limits.

Eleanor let it flash through her mind again that she could have fixed herself up with enough makeup to look like one of these girls. All you needed was a can of face paint and some hair dye and a phony smile. But Eleanor remembered the rules she had read—that the Miss America contestants could never have had a child. And much as Eleanor wanted to forget about that baby boy she'd had and had to give up, back when she was fourteen, she couldn't forget.

She'd hidden it from Wish. Why wouldn't she have been able to hide it from the Miss America judges?

But she wasn't going to dwell on that. She glanced at Moira, Taryn. Too bad her own daughters were so homely they could never be Miss America. But wait. She had always been homely too. That was why she had homely daughters. Because she was ugly. Not worthy of love. That was why her father had run off with that beautiful woman. Beauty was everything.

Were her daughters ugly? People sometimes said Moira was

pretty. But they didn't have the high standards that Eleanor had.
They didn't notice how long Moira's face was, how thick her waist
was. And they must pretend not to see those glasses. Those thick
glasses that gave Moira's eyes the look of bug-eyed confusion all
the time. Eleanor made Moira wear the glasses all the time. Moira
took the glasses off sometimes when she left the house, Eleanor
knew that. But what could you do? Send a policeman to school
with her to make sure she wore her Coke-bottle glasses?

And Taryn was no beauty. She still had that preemie look. People
said Taryn was cute, but only because she was little. But didn't they
notice those buggy eyes, that sallow skin?

Let's face it, none of them was beauty-contest material, and the
world unfortunately was filled with people who thought that was
all that mattered.

But you had to keep these hostile thoughts to yourself. People
were always getting mad at her for criticizing things they held sacred. For laughing at things they took seriously. But then, she had
to survive, didn't she? She had to have some release. Instead of
drinking she made fun of things, laughed at them. When life got
tough, Wish took a drink, Eleanor took a joke. Joking, her drug of
choice.

This thing that Moira had about right and wrong, good and bad
—Eleanor wondered what was missing in her. Why didn't she just
know things like other people did? What the hell was wrong with
her?

Eleanor, on the other hand, was constantly having to judge a
situation by thinking what would seem right to other people, what
would make them think that Eleanor and her family were decent
people. She went overboard, trying to give the appearance of old-
fashioned decency, in order to try to fit in. Why? Because her parents hadn't offered anything to believe in, or *not* believe in? That's
probably what Miss Smartass would say.

On "Miss America" there was just a bunch of dumb singing and
dancing right now. She looked out at the black of the picture window of their house. All you could see through the rain-speckled
window was the Ettingers' half-drawn drapes with a lamp on in the
living room. They had a rec room in the basement. That's how Phil
Ettinger spent his free time, sawing knotty pine and doing things

like going out for just the right drill bit. She'd heard him asking around at all the other neighbors' houses to borrow a drill bit in a size he didn't have, a number something or other. But she noticed he didn't stop here at the McPhersons', most likely because he knew that Wish McPherson's hobby wasn't drilling holes in knotty pine but more like sawing logs when he was passed out on the sofa.

She smiled at her joke.

Jokes, and *Adventures in Drama,* which brought back the old days when she had been the star of Miss Barton's class. Memorizing those poems, everyone's amazement at how fast she memorized them, reading from the plays, especially Shakespeare. And what good had her poetry and plays and short stories done her? They'd provided an escape, that's what, from the life she had to keep as a nasty little secret from the world.

Talent competition. Eleanor had been so talented way back when. Those dramatic readings in high school. The high school play she got the part in, then had to drop out of because her belly was growing and her mother found out and then she had to go and stay at her aunt's.

Everyone in town had heard about it. But Aloysius was from another town. He didn't have a clue. In fact, when he got her in a fix again he thought he was the Devil who had just impregnated the Holy Virgin Mary. She'd made him think she was a virgin. Ha-ha, Aloysius, have I got news for you.

It was really starting to rain now. She liked a good rain, it could substitute for a good cry. Eleanor Bergstren McPherson didn't cry. She refused to cry because that would somehow diminish her problems, reduce them to something that could be cried about, real problems evoking real tears. *Her* problems were invisible, evasive, nasty problems that hung in the air above you and came down to ankle level and nipped all the time and tripped you every so often.

She looked out the window again. Yes, maybe the Ettingers had their nasty little secrets, too. She felt her smile leave and chewed her fingernail and thought about the Ettingers. Maybe they had a cloud of poison gas in their house, too, but just were better at pretending it wasn't there.

Oh, but she knew the truth, that the Ettingers didn't have a house full of poison gas, that most people didn't.

No cure for weirdness, just learning to live with it. Or deciding not to live with it.

Commercials over, there was Bert Parks with the shit-eating grin, and there were the Miss America contestants. Why was it that everybody else had to walk around in regular clothes, and these broads got to wear bathing suits and high heels and probably hose, that's why their legs looked good, and makeup—and they weren't at the pool?

Eleanor knew why they did this; they did this just to make the women watching feel inferior and jealous. Well, she wasn't falling for that. She'd stage her own little protest right here in the living room.

"Pass the fudge. Look at the busts on that one," Mother said of Miss Mississippi as the ten finalists lined up. "And on the one from Tennessee." She looked over at Wish.

Wish took a look at the busts, too. He emptied another beer bottle and as the five finalists were about to be announced he got tired of the Miss America pageant and got up and changed the channel.

It was as if he'd jumped up and shouted at the top of his lungs, *Fuck you,* to all of them.

Except *fuck* was the one swear word he never used.

She felt like telling him he was out of style. If he wanted to be up to date on his swearing, he should cut out the *bastards* and *sons of bitches* and update his vocabulary.

Eleanor looked at her daughters out of the corner of her eye. She could feel the disappointment almost crackle out of them. She could see them slump in their chairs. She was enraged herself, but what could she do? Start a fight? Leave? By the time they went to a motel, Miss America would have been crowned. Anger felt like a jolt of hot water being forced through her veins. She could almost bawl. Or better, she could go over there and slap him. Knock the beer out of his hand. Club him over the head with a Louisville Slugger out of his samples trunk. Take the girls to a motel and never see him again. Take herself alone to a motel and never see the lot of them again.

Oh, but to hell with it. Just to hell with it. To hell with it all. She kept repeating that to herself, and soon she felt an odd pleasure at the anger, at the audacity of Wish's doing something like this.

And getting away with it.

Yes, the anger almost felt good. It almost felt like sex. It was a good substitute for sex. Anger as masturbation, she thought, and half-smiled.

Slowly, the two girls got up and slumped quietly off to bed. Eleanor looked out the window through the rain at the Ettingers' half-opened drapes, and then drifted off to bed herself. The game of "Who's the Ugliest?" was over for the night. Aloysius had won.

Seven

MOTHER INSISTED on short hair for the girls. She had almost a fetish about hair. The girls went to the beauty parlor once a year, the day before their birthday, for a shaping, and Mother cut their hair the rest of the time, usually during a depressed mood, coming after them with the scissors swishing, complaining about what a rat's nest they had grown, cutting hair in quick, deliberate snips of the scissors, long, cold dangerous blades that swished and snapped loudly close to ears, eyes, noses. After Mother was done, she'd look at Moira or Taryn with her mouth puckered, eyes narrow and appraising, and her face always concluded that the haircut was her best effort but of course there was nothing she could do about the face. She'd blow on their faces to make the little cut hairs scatter, and it would tickle and everyone would be in a good mood again.

Moira hated the way she looked in those pictures that Mother took. Part of the reason she was ugly, she decided, was because her face was long and thin and the short frizzy hair emphasized it. Moira had wanted to let her hair grow long so she could wear it in a ponytail and keep it from sticking up and out, but Mother said only cheap tramps wore long hair.

The most recent picture of Moira made her look odd—thick glasses, thin, serious face, then a curvaceous body with clothes that were too small and childish. It showed her from the knees up, standing in front of the blank wall in the hallway. It reminded Moira of the pictures in her health ed book where they showed people with harelips or elephantiasis or another deformity, large, three-quarter-page pictures, and you always wondered why they ever let someone take their picture in the first place and then put it in a book. And now she knew why—because maybe you hated yourself for having this deformity and wanted to punish yourself for it by getting in a book for millions of school kids to go *ugh* at and then laugh about you.

Moira's deformity was her breasts. Like the diseased leg of that poor elephantiasis man in the science book, her breasts were getting too big to ignore. Maybe she had elephantiasis of the breasts.

Moira went to her room and took her clothes off and stood on her bed and leaned so she could see her body in the mirror. From the neck up, she was respectable. Her head was respectable on the outside with her short hair and on the inside where she was top math and science student at North Prairie Junior High. From the neck down, she was a slut. Ask Mother.

Mother hated anything fancy. Ruffles, long or curly hair, heels higher than two inches, hair dye, and most jewelry were the stuff of tramps as far as she was concerned. She prided herself on always dressing like a lady, always tailored, always severe, no makeup except for the arches she penciled on her eyebrows to show disapproval, and on dressup occasions a little coral lipstick to show she wasn't a frump or a beatnik.

Mother made it clear that if a boy was interested in Moira, he couldn't possibly like her the way he liked girls who were really pretty, and it was for terrible reasons that he showed an interest in someone like Moira. Like when Jimmy Hawkmeier sat behind Moira in math one day and told her he liked her.

"You're real pretty, Moira, when you take the specs off," he said.

But Moira thought of Mother's instructions and literally ran away from Jimmy.

Over Cokes and "American Bandstand" with Mother after school, Moira told Mother that Jimmy Hawkmeier said she was pretty. Mother jumped up, spilling her Coke, and grabbed Moira by the hair and pulled her around the kitchen. "Pretty, huh? Is that what he thinks? I'll tell you what *that* translates as. He's thinking filthy thoughts, that's what."

"You mean he doesn't think I'm pretty? Am I pretty, Mother?"

"Take a look in the mirror, dear."

Later that evening, during a raging snowstorm, she heard Mother tell Daddy that the Hawkmeier boy over on Pierson Street wanted to do unspeakable things to Moira, and the next thing she knew, Daddy was stomping around looking for his parka and gloves and was going out into the blizzard to beat the shit out of Jimmy

Hawkmeier. As he was heading for the door in his jingling galoshes, Mother went clacking after him in her mules, accusing Daddy of liking Moira too much.

"You're obsessed." Mother said. "Obsessed with that girl. Just because she's smart, Daddy's little girl that gets all A's."

Daddy threw his gloves into the utility room and grabbed a beer out of the refrigerator. The drinking began and the females of the house all went to their rooms. And they got through another night.

Yes, if boys at school were interested in her, it was not because she was pretty, but only because there was something wrong with them or because they wanted to do dirty things to her.

Hey though. Maybe if she were pretty, Mother would love her. The way other mothers loved their daughters.

But Moira couldn't be pretty? She thought about it some more. Moira may have been the smartest girl in science and math in the whole ninth grade at North Prairie High School—that was easy—but she couldn't figure out this "pretty" business. Strange—getting all A's came naturally to her. The hard part of being a girl was making yourself pretty.

Well, if she wasn't pretty and no one could love her the nice way they loved girls, well then, maybe they were going to have to love her the wrong way. Eventually she'd find some way to be loved. Maybe sometimes she could disguise herself as a pretty girl with the right makeup and clothes. If she was loved only for her disguise, it was better than nothing, wasn't it?

Eight

IT WASN'T TOO FAR from the spot where *Peyton Place* was buried that Daddy caught Moira and Dennis Wildersen kissing.

Dennis wasn't in any of Moira's classes—she was on the college prep track, and he was in general studies. But then one day she got after-school detention, and there he was, climbing onto the bus in front of her, wearing his big black leather jacket.

She'd gotten detention this time because she had refused to undress in gym class. Other girls were developing figures, but Moira still felt as if she were exploding one. And she couldn't stand the staring, the whispering.

He took a seat up in front. Moira went to the back of the bus.

She sat down and stared at the bus floor, which bore the happy, well-adjusted remnants of the happy, well-adjusted normal kids who had already been driven home because they didn't have detention. The floor was gaily decorated with M&M packages, Popsicle sticks, notices of PTA meetings for parents, a stray homework paper or test with a nice, happy, passing grade on the top of it. By the time this group got off, the bus would be littered with cigarette butts and gum and graffiti, and test papers with *F* or *Poor* or *Incomplete* written at the top.

Except for Moira's papers, of course.

Her being an A student wasn't the only thing that set her apart from the rest of the detention-bus students. She was usually the only girl in detention.

Lately, she got detention a lot. She was always in trouble, and she wasn't even sure why. Oh, she knew *why*—because she was shy in gym class, because she ate lunch hiding in a stall in the girls' bathroom rather than sit friendless and alone in the cafeteria, because she didn't do the homework in easy classes so she could concentrate on the harder classes and still got A's in everything and it pissed off her teachers.

It was so lonely at school that Moira began to feel almost like a different species to explain herself to herself. And yet it had to be admitted that Moira survived—thrived, even—on little pockets of happiness. One pocket of happiness came from being smart, just about the smartest kid in the school.

But Moira was lonely, so lonely that sometimes she'd walk down the hall alone, or carry her tray through the cafeteria with a pretend smile and wave to an imaginary friend off in the distance.

In detention hall, Mr. Smealz walked around the front of the room smacking the yardstick on the side of his thigh as a warning to people not to talk or horse around. The one good thing about detention was that since Mr. Smealz made it so utterly quiet in there, Moira was often able to get all of her homework done, and then when she got home she could concentrate on extra-credit work or projects.

Mr. Smealz kept her after school a lot. Then it seemed like he was always staring at her when she looked up. She never knew for sure what she was doing wrong, but it seemed he was always staring at her with those sucked-in cheeks of his, scowling and thinking of what a troublemaker Moira McPherson was. A bad, bad egg.

As the last of the delinquent students got on the bus, Moira was ready to sink into isolation. All those boys were leering, or at least it felt like it. She hunched over so her breasts wouldn't show and pulled some of her short bangs as far as she could over her face.

Dennis Wildersen didn't seem to mind being on the detention bus. He wore the same expression he always wore, like he had just asked a question and was waiting for the answer.

Dennis took the seat behind the driver—a jovial, tough, middle-aged woman—and offered her a cigarette. The driver took one and lit it, then pulled the door shut and turned the transistor radio up loud. The bus went sailing off and the radio started playing the calypso rhythms of "Oh Carol," by Neil Sedaka. Moira closed her eyes and thought about what it must be like to be this Carol and have someone write a song about you. When she opened her eyes, Dennis was leaning over the back of his seat with his pointed chin resting on the sleeves of his big leather jacket, staring at her. His eyes were big brown disks under shaggy eyebrows. Her stomach felt like it did when the bus hit a dip in the road.

The calypso rhythm of Neil Sedaka was crazy now and the bus seemed to be rocking its hips to the beat. Dennis got up and jerkily came to the back of the bus, holding onto the seats. He took the big black leather jacket off and sat down right in front of Moira and turned around. Staring at her, he crossed his white, unathletic arms on the back seat. They had little boomerang-shaped black hairs all over them. He pulled out the pack of cigarettes and, still staring at her, stuck one in his mouth and lit it.

Moira was withered with self-consciousness, and yet she was actually enjoying this, too. Nobody had ever shown so much interest in her in her entire life. She had makeup on and felt almost attractive. Maybe this disguise as a pretty girl was working.

He looked down at the books in her lap. Her latest science test was sticking out of her notebook with a *100%—A* dashed off in red. She put her hand over the grade.

He held his cigarette between his thumb and middle finger and offered her a smoke. She shook her head.

"Nice girl, don't smoke, huh? What else don't you do?"

The bus lurched around a curve, then coasted over the easy bumps of the tar road, swaying its rear and doing the calypso along with Neil Sedaka. She turned away, her face pounding. If she wasn't mistaken, somebody was actually flirting with her. What next?

The song ended and Dennis sang out along with Neil Sedaka, "Cha-cha-cha."

But so what if someone was flirting? Daddy wouldn't let her go out with Dennis or anyone else.

Moira acted like she didn't want to talk to Dennis, and so he got up and walked up to the front of the bus, gripping the backs of seats as the bus lurched back and forth in its sexy dancing rhythm. When the bus came to his stop, Dennis sent a smile to Moira and skipped down the steps. She burst into a blush and looked down at the books in her arms.

"Dinner's ready," Daddy called out. The smell of corned beef hash sizzled from the kitchen. Daddy often cooked dinner when Mother was in one of her depressions.

Taryn got off her fifth phone call of the afternoon. Moira reread a paragraph in her history book, squeezed her eyes shut, and made a copy in her brain and then went to the table. Daddy called out, "Eleanor, time to rise and shine."

Mother came shuffling in from the bedroom, but dinner wasn't ready. Daddy was still only cutting little potatoes into the pan. He liked an audience, but the audience had to remain quiet and attentive. One false move and you could end up in the Siberia of your room without even bread and water.

They sat in tense silence, waiting for him to cook the potatoes and corned beef hash and then to fry the eggs, all this punctuated with trips to the high cupboard for a quick sip from the bottle of Canadian Club, which they were all supposed to pretend not to see.

He stood over the three seated women, his tension gripping each of them by the shoulders with invisible hands. But the cooking food smelled delicious. His meals were always nice and filling and starchy. Lately, Mother was very often too depressed to make dinner, so they got to eat a lot of these kinds of dinners, man-dinners, trucker-three-A.M.-type dinners.

When the potatoes were charred, he took a drink of his beer, then turned, his face slightly redder than a minute ago, and told Taryn to set the table.

When she sat down, he began tapping his toe. She looked up. "Is something wrong?"

"What do you think?"

They all surveyed the table. Milk carton, mayonnaise, ketchup, mustard, salt and pepper in the center of the table with the bowl of waxed fruit.

Taryn said, "It looks okay to me."

They sat stiff-shouldered, waiting for an outburst, for him to kick the legs from under a chair and send everyone to their room. But instead, he went to the bread drawer, jerked it open, and took out a bag of cookies.

"You forgot a plate for dessert." He had a wide grin.

They all laughed out some nervous energy as Taryn got a plate for the cookies. For a moment, Moira's childhood love for her father came out from somewhere and took a deep breath.

But then Moira picked up the bag and saw that the cookies were coconut, which they all hated and he knew it. She opened her mouth to say something, but Taryn read her mind and violently shook her head and mouthed the word *no*. Moira decided to keep the peace tonight. He brought over the pan of corned beef, the grease sizzling under each face as his shaking hand dished out food onto their plates, exactly the amount of each food he wanted them to eat—corned beef and potatoes, egg, canned lima beans with his own special garnish of bacon and pimentos, a salad with exactly one tomato slice and one Italian hot pepper placed in the center, and a slice of white bread he had already slathered with margarine.

With a touch of the fork, the eggs broke into thick, golden pools atop the corned beef hash, which with Daddy's own special touch of potatoes was so good.

Daddy asked, "Well, how did everyone's day go?"

Mother and Taryn shrugged and said in their best let's-humor-Daddy voices that their day had been okay.

Moira felt reckless, brave. After all, didn't the teacher in health ed class say that if you have a problem, you should bring it up to your family rather than just letting it fester inside you? "I have to eat lunch all alone at school. It's embarrassing."

"What's so embarrassing about that, Eleanor?" he said loudly. "I mean, Moira. You're there to get nutrition, not to join the yakkety-yak Ladies' Aid Society."

Taryn said, "I'd be embarrassed, too, if I had to eat alone."

"Embarrassed," Daddy scoffed. "How'd you like to arrive home for lunch and find there's nothing but a raw potato in the house? Huh, how'd you like that, Eleanor?" he said, looking at Moira. "Now that's what I call embarrassing. You gets home after stealing a few pieces of coal from a neighbor's bin so your family won't freeze, and you're so hungry you can eat a horse, and you sees not a goddamn thing in the ice box. So you goes to the neighbor and asks for a piece of bread. Now *that's* embarrassing. You want to hear what else is embarrassing?" His voice was growing louder and angrier. "You're a scholarship student at the University of Minnesota and you walks to class with newspapers and notebooks stuffed under your shirt because you can't afford a coat."

Mother gave Taryn a look with her eyebrows up. Taryn returned the look.

"I went all through college with no coat. No goddamned winter coat. Try *that* for embarrassing."

"Yes, try that one on for size," Mother said, and both girls giggled.

"Don't be such a smartass," Daddy said, looking at Moira.

Mother said, "Aloysius, there are—were places to get free clothes. You could have gone to the Saint Vincent de Paul Society if it was all that bad."

Daddy stabbed a potato as if it were trying to get away. He stuck it into his mouth with the prongs of the fork facing down the way he did when he was tense and drunk. "Aloysius Wesley McPherson never took a handout in his life. Never will. And neither will you kids."

"Well, then, how can we feel sorry for you?" Mother said.

Daddy turned and glared at Moira.

Mother went on. "If you didn't get a coat, then it sounds like you chose to freeze. Maybe you wanted everyone to feel sorry for you. Did you ever think of that? Poor me, poor Aloysius McPherson, poor little me." If Daddy were in a really bad mood, a smart remark like that could have been Mother's death sentence. But he wasn't in a particularly violent mood—you could tell by the shade of his face and the half-pleasant expression in his eyes, which were crinkly and blue as a clear northern winter sky.

"There's a girl I know from last year who was my partner on a science experiment, but she has a different lunch hour. Maybe I should have gotten it changed at the beginning of the school year. Maybe I could still get it changed," Moira said.

Daddy said, "Bullshit, you're not getting it changed. You learns to stick with things, you goes the distance, takes whatever the hell is handed to you and makes the best of it."

"I agree, you mustn't think you're better than anyone else," Mother said, her plucked halfmoon eyebrows unpenciled and looking like a connect-the-dots-and-dashes picture. Moira wondered what would be in that picture if you ever connected all of Mother's dots and dashes—some message of what was inside of Mother's brain.

Moira tried to tune them out and think about her science project, a papier-mâché Neanderthal village diorama.

"Can't you make friends with someone in the lunch hour you've got?" Taryn asked, her eyes wide. "I eat lunch with the same group every day."

Moira looked at Taryn, and for a split-second she hated her enough to tear her apart.

And she wondered how on earth Taryn did it, found kids to laugh and joke with and dress like and think like.

Dennis was standing behind Moira in the lunchroom line.

Moira had worn a dark brown shirtwaist dress that someone had handed down to Taryn that was way too big for Taryn and which Moira had begged her for. The deep clear color made Moira's eyes sparkle, and Moira felt as close to pretty as a girl who was on the homely side of average could ever get. She had pulled the belt in two holes tighter than was comfortable. She could hardly breathe, but she felt like Marilyn Monroe.

"Hey there," she heard him say. "Got detention tonight?"

She shook her head no. He tapped her back. A tickle went up her neck. She turned, and saw that he had a black eye.

"It must be a day for miracles," he said. "I don't got detention either. I guess the teachers felt sorry for me because I'm an invalid today."

"What happened to your eye?" Moira asked quietly.

"Big helluva brawl at my cousin's wedding." He smiled broadly.

Moira would have laid down her life for one single cousin that the family saw regularly. But she had no cousins that she knew of, no relatives that they were on speaking terms with.

"It was just like on TV, right there in the VFW hall. Best wedding I ever been to, best fight, too."

Moira made a little noise to acknowledge what he was saying, then turned away the way Mother told them to. Mother taught them to act like they didn't like the other person. The logic behind that was they probably didn't like you, so you had the advantage if you were first to show it.

"What'sa matter? Oh, I bet you go to weddings where everyone's just nicey perfect, huh?"

"No, I've never been to any wedding."

Dennis looked at her as if that made her an unbelievable innocent, virginal in a way. "You'll go to at least one some day—your own."

She blushed. Weddings were not a fit subject for conversation around her house. Moira assumed it was because of the filthy things people did on wedding nights.

"Know what that same cousin that gave me this black eye did? He almost blew my hands off with a cherry bomb last Fourth of July. The guy's funnier than hell. Dangerous, but funnier'n hell."

His eyes jumped into a little smile to wait and see if that was interesting.

Moira just said, "Oh," and they took cartons of milk and moved down the row to where women in hairnets and green nylon uniforms were ladling wet-dog-smelling gravy over mashed potatoes and porcupine balls and green beans that had cooked so long they lay open with the bloated seeds spilled out.

Then she thought of something that was normal. "On the Fourth of July we get fireworks. My Dad sticks sparklers into the ground and lights them. We stand and watch."

"Sparklers stuck in the lawn?" he said, his voice cracking. "Hey, you're supposed to hold sparklers, not put them in the lawn."

Moira wished she hadn't said anything. Here Daddy had that gun in the house, and the shells for it in the utility room, always replaced every year in case he needed them, in case someone tried to break into the house—a dangerous weapon like that in the house—and yet Daddy wouldn't let them hold the Fourth of July sparklers because he thought they were unsafe. It was all too weird. Her family was too weird. Daddy worried about them getting hurt as much as he worried about germs. He couldn't stand the sight of blood, the sight of any—human or animal—blood. He'd fainted once, in fact, when he got a nasty gash in his toe from the lawn mower and Mother had had to send for the ambulance.

"My father said that he read someone was blinded that way, though."

Dennis looked perplexed. Uh-oh, here it comes, Moira thought. Weird, my family is too weird. Moira regretted mentioning the sparklers and started feeling like one, sputtering and twinkling over on the weedy part of the lawn, while big fireworks were going off somewhere else; and Moira wasn't even sputtering and twinkling in someone's hand but in the midst of the weeds, a safe forty feet away from the others.

But, surprisingly, there was a glimmer of respect in his eyes, and she saw that it was because he wanted to hear more about her sparkler-in-the-grass life, which maybe to him was okay after all, because no matter how strange her family was, Dennis thought she was okay.

They turned to face the clattering cafeteria full of friendships. They sat down, and Moira gasped as the tight belt dug into her ribs, and wondered how she was going to swallow her porcupine balls.

That evening, as she leafed through her movie magazines, Moira decided that the best bosom pictures weren't even the ones that showed everything but these, where actresses leaned across tables in low-cut gowns, a long line running down the middle of their chest, the longer the line, the bigger and softer and droopier their bosoms.

Her breasts had gotten so sensitive. Inside her bra they called out to her, glowing, aching, and feeling good at the same time. Water on them in the shower sometimes felt so good she was ashamed. She stood up on her bed and undid the four hooks on her stiff new bra and looked in the mirror.

They were pooching out and she was scared they'd always be high and pointy with light pink nipples instead of long and droopy with brown nipples the way they were supposed to be. And the nipples seemed too far apart and not perfectly round, and she worried that they might end up shaped like panda eyes. She so wanted grownup lady bosoms, soft, mature, thirty-five-year-old ones, with tops that would pour out like cake batter when she bent over in a bathing suit.

She woke up that night at four A.M. and wanted to go outside to find out what the world felt like at that hour. She stood on the back porch and let her nightgown fall off. The breeze stirred and her nipples hardened. She imagined that Joe from "American Bandstand" was blowing on them. She practically doubled over from a feeling that ran all over her abdomen. She pretended that Joe was saying he loved her.

Then she thought about Dennis, and hid her face in her hands. Her right nipple, the one Mother had pinched, ached.

The breeze blew again and she got to breathing so hard she was afraid someone in the house would hear. She lay down and let herself feel the night air and Dennis's kisses on her mouth and throat and nipples.

Then she reached back and gripped the porch step behind her and when she pulled she felt a good feeling in her abdomen. She pulled some more and then pulled herself up and felt air rushing into her. She pulled and pulled and wondered if this was fucking, if this was what they meant by fucking, fucking the air and having it feel so good you didn't care how bad you were.

One afternoon while they were watching "American Bandstand," the phone rang and, unbelievably, it wasn't for Taryn.

With a loaded voice, Mother said, "Just a moment" into the receiver, then in the same loaded voice said, "Moira, it's for you."

It was Dennis and he wanted to know if she wanted to play miniature golf.

A date. She was being asked for a real date. Yes, maybe she really was a girl.

But of course she couldn't go. "No thanks. I'm busy," she said.

"What is it?" Mother wanted to know. "Who is it?"

Moira put her hand over the mouthpiece. "Dennis Wildersen. He wants me to play miniature golf."

Mother said, "Tell him to wait a minute." She wanted Moira to tell her all about him. Moira said she didn't know much, that he always seemed to be on the detention bus with her. Mother thought the whole detention bus thing was funny. Maybe because it took away from Moira's image as a science freak. Or maybe just because Mother would laugh at anything, even nuclear war, Moira sometimes thought.

"Why don't you go?" she said. Mother's personality of the moment was grownup, concerned, kindly, understanding. Motherly.

But Moira felt guilty because Daddy thought she shouldn't go out with boys. He'd always say he didn't want Moira to go out because he was worried about her getting into a car accident, even though the boys her age couldn't drive yet. He never came out and said it was sex he was worried about, since sex didn't exist for Daddy. Sex was so bad, worse than death, because you not only couldn't talk about it or do it, you couldn't even worry about it.

"You need some experience at dating. Just remember, your father will be home by six."

Moira's heart pumped so hard, she could barely talk or hear over the phone.

As they played miniature golf, Moira thought maybe she had more power than she knew. And when Dennis cradled his arm around her to help her get a shot through the windmill, she remembered Daddy doing this with Mother. Taryn, too, come to think of it. He didn't do it with her. He seemed afraid of her.

After miniature golf, Dennis walked her home. It was a hot Indian summer day, and she was in a purple-and-white houndstooth shorts outfit. She had just a smudge of purple eye shadow over her eyes, which seemed to change color from brown to gold. She felt pretty and dared anyone, even Mother, to tell her she wasn't.

It was only four o'clock, so she suggested they take a little walk through the field behind her house. They drifted back toward Moira's house, and when they got to the edge of the green lawn at the bottom of the little hill, they sat down. He let his cheek touch hers. She thought about going to a sock hop at school, maybe, and dancing and being a couple gazing at each other in the damp dark of the gym with crepe-paper streamers licking the top of their hair.

"Hey, I like you. You're different."

"Different from what?" Moira dared to ask.

"Different from everyone." He pulled out a Lucky Strike and offered her one. She decided to try it, holding the cigarette with a shaking hand while he lit it with a shaking hand. "You're a nice clean girl." He told her about his brother who got involved with a wild girl and had to get a penicillin shot in the ass that lasted for five minutes, and then the doctor's nurse went and told everyone in town about it. Moira felt lightheaded and relaxed from the cigarette, and smiled now with all the happiness in the world. Dennis said they should meet at Rollerama on Friday.

She had a boyfriend now. She was a real girl with a real boyfriend. She felt as if she were a puzzle and someone had just put her together. He leaned down and kissed her softly and said, "Me, I'm gonna get a nice girl, like you."

And then it happened. Daddy appeared at the top of the hill, looking about ten feet tall. He had the hedge clippers, holding just one handle so they dangled open in a big X.

He charged down the hill and stood in front of them. He was going to kill them with the hedge clippers.

With his teeth clenched, he said to Dennis, "You ever touch my daughter again, I'll kick your head in."

Dennis looked like he was trying to figure out which direction was the safest to get up in.

Daddy moved a little closer. In Moira's line of vision were the creases in the crotch of his gray chinos. Dennis got up, slapping the grass off his pants. "Yeah, Daddy-O, don't blow a gasket."

He didn't look back at Moira, but to his credit, he didn't run. He walked, and none too fast, putting on his jacket slowly, then disappearing into it.

Daddy watched him go, then turned to Moira, still crouched on the ground. "Get up to the house, you little . . ." He was either groping for a word or trying to keep from saying one. As she started to get up, he aimed a slap at her. She covered her face with her hands, and though maybe he aimed for her face or her arm, his hand smacked loudly on her left breast.

She stared at the rain gutters on the Mankowskis' house next door, trying not to think about how her breast had wriggled dumbly like a bad puppy under the impact of the slap, like a poor dog being struck.

She lay down and thought about school but then her mind kept returning to the slap.

A few hours later, Mother walked in, less ashen, for some reason, than usual. Moira noticed that her eyebrows had been drawn in with that Maybelline sable brown eyepencil she kept in the medicine cabinet. She sat down on the edge of the bed. "I hear you were kissing that boy out in back."

Moira didn't say anything.

"Your father came home early from work. He decided to do

some yard work. The next thing I know, Taryn comes in and says you're out in back kissing that hoodlum boy. I asked Taryn how you were kissing him, on the lips, or where."

"It was just once."

"Once, twice, and pretty soon, you're . . . well, you're too young to discuss this subject, but you should be warned."

Mother stared at her for a few minutes and her mouth twitched, then she said, "To be honest, Moira, when I said you should go on a date, I had no idea you would do such a thing. And I told your father that. That you were acting like a floozie. The next minute, your father was storming toward the back yard with the hedge clippers."

They let silence circle the room, then Mother said, "He wanted me to come and talk to you. He thinks you've become much too . . . provocative."

Now it felt like Mother was slapping her inside on her heart, just below where Daddy's slap had landed.

"If you don't watch it, the only thing boys will want from you is you-know-what."

Tears began to roll down Moira's cheeks. Mother stared at her for a moment, superior, older, bigger, wiser, cleaner, and more decent than her daughter, then got up and, careful not to look in the mirror, went out of the room, closing the door softly.

Nine

MOIRA SAT in homeroom the first day of the school year staring straight ahead and saying a prayer to God that the teacher wouldn't call on her to go to the board.

It had always been bad enough wearing those three outfits from the dime store to school, but now Moira's fashion statement had hit rock bottom. Mother had started making her clothes.

There were a couple of other girls whose mothers made their clothes, but they tried to imitate department store clothes so their daughters could keep up with the rich girls at school.

Mother's purpose was different. She wanted to show the girls that sewing had its merits. That was to fit with the plan she and Daddy had to send the girls to Dakota State Normal College to become home economics teachers. Home economics teachers, Daddy always said, had the best of both worlds—they could be mistresses of housewifely skills, and earn a full-time salary in the bargain. And if they were to become home-ec teachers, they were going to have to know how to sew. And what better way to develop their interest in sewing than to have a mother who made their clothes?

"I'm going to set an example," Mother said one July day as she came in with an armload of rustling packages from Meyers Fabrics. "Be a role model, as they say."

The problem was, Mother was a horrible seamstress. Moira's first-day-of-school dress was one of the new "sacque" dresses. The style was supposed to be roomy, but for some reason Mother had bought a size-thirteen pattern when all Moira wore was a seven. The dress hung to an inch above her ankles, and it was made out of a rough wool plaid and had no lining because Mother didn't know how to do linings. It itched like crazy, plus she was sweating constantly because it was September and still officially summer and eighty-seven degrees out. Mother couldn't sew a straight seam to save her life, and she didn't bother to match the thread, so there were wild orange seams going all through her red and blue plaid on one side, and then when she'd ran out of orange thread she'd grabbed for the first spool in her new sewing basket and it had been green, so there was a visible seam of bright green up on one shoulder. The zipper looked like a cross-eyed person had put it in. And since Mother lost interest in any project long before it was done, she hadn't bothered to finish off the sleeves right and Moira couldn't lift her arms up very high without cutting off her circulation and she couldn't walk too fast or she'd tear out the hem she'd hastily sewed in herself this morning while waiting for the bus.

Moira had begged Mother to let her babysit for the little Henderson boy down the street that summer to buy some new clothes, but Mother said she didn't like the idea of Moira babysitting. "Especially for a boy," she had added.

"What's different about a boy?" Moira asked. After all, this was babysitting.

"Moira," Mother said in an exasperated voice. "Do I have to answer a dumb question like that? Anyway, this is a subject you shouldn't even be thinking about. Now just get your mind out of the gutter."

Mother had made Moira model her new dress for Daddy the night before. He'd popped a beer nut high, said, "A little roomy, isn't it?" and Mother had flown into a tirade.

"You want her going around in skin-tight clothes the way she did last year? Is that what you want? So she'll be leered at?"

"No," Daddy had said wearily. "I just wondered if that's her size."

"Daddy's right, it's not my size. I wear a seven, Mother," Moira had said. "This is from a size-thirteen pattern."

"Oh, baloney," Mother had said. "How do you know what size you are?"

Would there ever be someone to help her? Or just someone to be on her side for a change? Maybe not. Pulling the itchy dress over her head, she scratched her throat with one of the pins Mother had forgotten and drew blood and that was all she'd needed to flop onto her bed and have a nice, sorry-for-herself cry. She wondered if

it had ever been there, if there'd been any love from anyone anywhere, at school or at home. She sometimes felt that she could just
curl up and die.

And now, sitting here in homeroom with all the other kids lock-
ing eyes with their friends while Moira sat staring a hole in the
blackboard, if God had come along and given her a choice—"Do
you want to go through this, or do you want to be put out of your
misery with a quick but painful death?"—she wasn't sure which she
would choose.

What was wrong with Mother? If Mother insisted on sewing,
why didn't she make imitations of the best fashions, like Suzanne
Weathers' mother did when she got those good fabrics from a trip
to Chicago once a year and then sewed her those lovely sheath
dresses? What was it like to have a mother who wanted to be a
mother instead of your best friend because she didn't have any of
her own because she hated the world?

Moira was ready to throw in the towel again, and then Rosemary
Jenks walked into her life.

It happened just as the teacher looked at Moira and said,
"Moira, you topped the honor roll last year. Would you go to the
board and . . ." and just then the door opened and the principal
came in, followed by a pale girl in a navy-blue knife-pleated skirt
and a plain white blouse and gray cardigan drooping off her arm.
She wore white nylon anklets and oxford lace-up shoes like the
mail-order kind in little newspaper ads, and they made her calves
look stubby and ghostly white.

The girl stared at the floor but you could sort of see her face and
she was kind of pretty even though she didn't fix herself up. The
principal announced that this new girl had just moved in and her
name was Rosemary Jenks.

Moira felt so sorry for the girl that she couldn't stand to look
anymore. But she was grateful to her, too, because maybe she
wouldn't have to go to the board now. She looked down at her
hands and pretended they were together and said, "Thank you,
God," and breathed a sigh of relief as the teacher forgot all about
calling her to go up to the board and had to get the new girl her
desk assignment and write her name on the class roster and then
merciful God made the bell ring.

* * *

Moira's first class was algebra, but she had five minutes until it began. Now was the time to do something about this hideous dress. The geometry teacher knew that Moira was a top math student so she wouldn't complain too much if Moira walked in late.

Moira ran to the girls' room. She went inside a stall and rolled up the sides of her dress and got some safety pins out of her purse and pinned here and there. The dress was kind of tight now, but at least it wasn't billowing around and at least the orange thread didn't show. The hem had started to come out so she rolled it up again and pinned some more. When the bell rang and all the other girls had left, she came out and looked in the mirror. Her face looked tanned and freckly from the summer, and that gave her brown eyes a nice sort of luster, she thought. Sometimes she thought she wasn't as bad-looking as Mother said. With difficulty, because Mother had made the buttonhole too small, she unfastened the top button and spread out the collar. She got out her makeup and redid her face, using a little less than she used to because her face seemed to be getting more and more acceptable. She came out of the girls' room hurriedly and as she hurried she realized she'd made the dress too tight. Howie Snyder whistled and she decided that was better than having them laugh or feel sorry for her.

The new girl, Rosemary, was in her first class.

A couple of the popular girls gave her contemptuous looks when she walked into algebra. Moira sat down next to Rosemary. She half-turned and aimed a smile in Rosemary's general direction. Rosemary said "Hi" and smiled back with her mouth shaking. She had slightly buck teeth, which Moira thought gave her an awkward but appealing appearance.

She saw Rosemary later at the bus stop, standing so still she looked like a statue. Marie joined her and Rosemary didn't move away. Thanks, God. At least now she had someone to stand with. It felt so comfortable, so right, to have a companion instead of standing alone. The next day, Rosemary invited Moira to come over after school. A week later, Moira could honestly say that she now had a friend; in fact, since she didn't have any other friends, she had a best friend.

The day Moira brought Rosemary home, Mother at first acted like Rosemary was her own friend and Moira had intruded.

They sat down to do their algebra homework, and Mother came in and stood next to Rosemary.

"Look at the way Moira's eyes bug when she's doing her homework," Mother had said to Rosemary, giggling. "She's so-o-o-o *intelligent.*"

Rosemary looked surprised, then smiled a little smile. Moira took off her glasses, and Mother said, "Moira, you know the optometrist said you have to wear them all the time."

Moira put them back on.

Then Mother went and turned on the radio, and when the song "Money" came on, Mother started singing along and dancing and wiggling around the living room.

"Come on," she said, waving to Rosemary.

"My parents don't allow me to dance," Rosemary said.

Mother's hips stopped wriggling. "What? Why not?"

"Because they consider it sinful."

Mother looked at Moira and rolled her eyes. Moira looked down at her homework. Mother left the radio on and disappeared into the bedroom.

Moira asked Rosemary, "Do your parents allow you to listen to the radio?"

"No, we don't believe in any kind of . . . frivolity."

Moira got up and turned off the radio. She wondered what religion wouldn't allow you to listen to the radio, but she didn't want to embarrass Rosemary by asking about it, just as she wouldn't want any probing questions about why her father wouldn't let her date and why her mother took pictures of her to prove to posterity that she was never pregnant as a teenager. Rosemary seemed like she wanted to be Moira's girlfriend, and Moira needed a friend and she didn't care if the friend believed she was reincarnated from a goldfish or if she slaughtered lambs on altars or cast virgins into volcanoes—Moira was going to have a girlfriend to giggle and whisper with.

"Want a drink?" Moira said.

"Sure," Rosemary said. "But I'm not allowed to have soft drinks. Anything with carbonation is considered too stimulating."

They went to the kitchen to get a drink. "Is orange juice okay?" Moira asked.

Rosemary looked a bit doubtful. "My parents believe that orange juice should be drunk only at breakfast, and then that it is to be appreciated for its nutritional value and not for its exciting taste. They prefer me to drink milk or water after school." She looked around the kitchen, at the red-and-white-checked wallpaper that Moira feared was too exciting, at the moderately nice appliances that Moira feared were too exciting, then back at Moira. "But it's okay this one time."

Moira poured glasses of orange juice and then looked in the cupboard for something to eat with orange juice. There was a can of peanuts—Daddy's, but Moira was going to open them anyway, if Rosemary didn't find peanuts too exciting. Peanuts were okay for her new best friend. Moira got a dish out of the cupboard and opened a drawer to find the can opener, and one of Mother's old stiffened falsies was in it. Moira slammed the drawer shut.

Either Rosemary hadn't recognized the falsie for what it was, or she didn't find falsies too exciting or too sinful or anything. Still best friends, they finished their homework and promised to meet at the bus stop next day.

After Rosemary went home, Mother came out of the bedroom making her upper lip ride up over her gums like Rosemary's and said in a buck-toothed way, "Gee, Moira, I hope your father doesn't drink Coke. I'd just about die if my father drank Coke or . . . oh my God. That would be terrible."

Moira laughed a little laugh to keep Mother company, then went to the bedroom to do her extra-credit problems.

Rosemary's parents were Christian missionaries, and they had just come from living in Africa.

Greeting you as you came into their entranceway was a small blond wood cross, a simple Protestant cross without a Jesus on it. Under it was a small bookshelf with a few dozen books. Moira had leafed through those books and got the same feeling she got when watching performers on TV variety shows and hearing semi-classical music or looking at the paintings in the dime store—a feeling

that the messages in those books were an off-the-mark version of
the real thing.

The cross and the books were there to remind Moira that this
was not your ordinary household but one with a slant. You weren't
going to get off that easily, having a textbook friend. Nope, if you
were Moira McPherson, you were going to have to have a friend
who came from a household that took a sharp turn from the normal mainstream household.

Of course, Moira had nothing against God or the Jesus that you
were supposed to remember from that cross up there on the wall,
but she still found the cross, as well as all those religious books on
the shelf under it, as depressing as a voice on the telephone that was
incredibly friendly and oh-so-glad to hear it was you and then
turned out to be someone trying to sell magazine subscriptions.

Moira knew why Rosemary was her friend—because Rosemary
was just as weird as Moira. They had stopped off at the drugstore
to buy candy bars, and people had given a little wry smile at the
pair of them—Moira slinking around in the tight dress she altered
as soon as she got out of the house and too much lipstick and
Mother's eyebrow pencil shading her eyes top and bottom, and
Rosemary hesitantly stepping along in her anklets and sensible
shoes and the same gray cardigan every day, her limp blond hair
severely fastened back with barrettes like a little girl's. Yes, Moira
knew why Rosemary accepted her, but her family was another matter—sometimes she had the uncomfortable feeling that Rosemary's
family put up with her because they were missionaries; they had
lived in the African jungle so long they didn't know what normal
teenagers were supposed to be like, so neither she nor her parents
knew that Moira wasn't the normal kind of girl you wanted to
hang out with. Moira, anyway, admired Rosemary's calm, her neat
appearance, and her features that even Mother couldn't find much
fault with.

Rosemary's was as ordinary a house as you could get in Sioux Falls
—a two-bedroom ranch with a chain-link fence and a carport for
just one car. The kind of house that was a good setting for the bare
cross and the handful of religious books on the neat, blond wood
shelves.

But just as you walked in and were ready to get all weirded-out over the severe, spare religious overtones, you went around the hall corner and saw two African masks on the wall above the piano, one of ebony, with an expression that seemed to be trying to figure the people out in this household that it was overlooking, the other of light wood and painted red and green and yellow, looking down-right scared of all it saw from up there on the wall.

As if that wasn't enough, over in the corner was another mask with white rings around the eyes and some sort of animal skin—a baby leopard, it looked like—hanging down from the chin like a beard, and under it a mahogany stool with parrots and monkeys carved all over it. In her parents' bedroom there was a bow and arrow on the wall and a horn made out of ivory that must have been nine feet long. In the tiny rec room in the basement there was the usual knotty pine paneling and a red wall-to-wall carpet and an old sofa, but instead of the usual plug-in picture of a lake over the unused bar there were an African shield and spear and a blow-gun.

Rosemary's parents were older than anyone else's. Her quiet, plump father now did some sort of administrative work at the Baptist church, and her salt-and-pepper-haired smiling mother ran the Sunday school.

The family had odd conversations, odd mannerisms, odd facial expressions—and Moira felt confirmed in her suspicions that they couldn't judge critically like the normal people in town, and that was why they accepted her. And yet despite their strangeness, Moira genuinely liked and admired the Jenks family; they were truly kind people, and their sincerity was not to be doubted. Best of all, there was no drinking (not even of caffeine or carbonation because caffeine and carbonation caused excitement), no shouting, no anger, no loudness of any sort, and not a breath of cynicism in this household. Moira, in fact, had once tried to bring a little of her family's smart-aleck attitude to all this politeness and had gotten nowhere; one afternoon while Moira was helping Rosemary with some homework, Rosemary's mother came in her quiet way into the dining room and said, "Did you girls want some cookies?" And Moira said, "I *did* but I don't right now," and gave a little laugh.

Rosemary looked at Moira with a condemning, you're-a-sinner
look, her mother looked perplexed, and Moira would have shriv-
eled up and fallen into one of the tight little cracks in the floor if she
hadn't glanced up at two colorful African masks laughing along
with her at her dumb joke.

Rosemary was cautiously friendly with Moira and always waited
for her after school at the main door so they could walk to the bus
stop together and not have to stand alone among the cool kids.
Rosemary would never meet Moira's eye in classes they had together but stared straight ahead, timid, afraid of the teachers but
listening, listening with all her ability, trying to get good grades,
doing the homework but never hitting the top echelons of the class,
which Moira did in a way that Rosemary told her seemed almost
natural, as if it never occurred to Moira not to be at the top of her
classes.

"How do you do it?" Rosemary asked one day after school as
they compared algebra tests—Rosemary's with a respectable ninety-
two on it; Moira's with a flashy one hundred percent.

"I don't know, Rosemary. I study like everyone else does," Moira
said.

"I study too. Just as much as you do." Her mouth quivered as a
boy she liked walked by. Even though she acted the opposite, Rosemary was the most boy-crazy girl Moira knew. Rosemary stared at
the floor until he was gone, then looked accusingly at Moira. "You
must have a high IQ or something."

"Yes, I do," Moira said. She wasn't supposed to know her IQ,
but Mr. Bailey told her it was high, really high, and she hadn't
wanted to know any more about it. Ever since he told her that,
she'd gone around wishing her IQ were lower. That might be what
her problem was, that she was too smart. But then sometimes a
little voice told her that being smart wasn't her problem, it could be
her salvation.

Moira politely never made reference to Rosemary's offbeat household, just as Rosemary never made reference to the fact that Daddy
was always nervous and uncomfortable around company, or that
Mother was often in bed in the middle of the day. But when they

stopped off at Rosemary's for a glass of milk or water, Moira would often sit on the one African seat-cushion and gaze around at the masks howling or staring or smiling from the walls and feel a strange togetherness with them. More togetherness than she felt with Rosemary, she sometimes admitted to herself.

As they were walking from the shopping center, Rosemary in her gray cardigan and a gathered gray skirt that sagged gloomily to a few inches above her anklets, Moira in pants that Mother herself had made too short in the crotch and too tight in the waist and knees so that Moira could hardly straighten her legs to walk, a truck driver slowed down and yelled, "Hey, girls, how about it. Hey, you in the blue pants . . ."

Rosemary turned to Moira with raised eyebrows the way Mother did it and said, "There's no doubt about it. You have a nice figure."

"I guess I do," Moira said. It was hard to tell what kind of figure lurked under Rosemary's loose clothes, but Moira added, "So do you. You're well-proportioned. And I wish I had long straight hair that I could flip, and perfect skin like yours."

"I'm not pretty and my hips are too big. Sometimes I wish I were more developed on top like you. I cried last night for an hour. Then I said my prayers and asked forgiveness, then thanked God that I don't have more of a figure than I do so that I'm not out there all the time asking for temptation."

Moira didn't say anything back to Rosemary and tried to look at Rosemary's remark as she did the cross in the living room that shared some space with the wild and rather frightening African masks.

Moira didn't know which was worse, being pointed out as different because of her figure or because of her intelligence. Whenever Rosemary or one of her parents complimented Moira on her grades and her brightness, she'd smile shyly and look around the room at the African purples and reds and yellows, brilliant and at odds with the quiet beige of the people in the household. It was all so strange. She'd accept their compliment and feel grateful that she had this second family, this missionary family out to save the souls of the minorities—racial and otherwise—of the world.

"Whatever you do in life, don't hide your light under a bushel," Rosemary's mother said.

And as they looked at Moira as if she were special, Moira tried to ignore the African mask behind Mrs. Jenks's face and tried to accept their acceptance.

Ten

ELEANOR CROUCHED DOWN with her bowl of potato chips and pulled the drapes apart to peek out.

Girls in chiffon and crinolines got out of convertibles and clickety-clacked down the street with dates in white dinner jackets on their way to the party across the street. A 'pre-prom party' that the Ettinger boy was having.

When the girls' high heels scraped and scudded particularly loudly on the sidewalk and the little center metal part on the heel hit and made that perfect-pitch scrape, it struck a nerve in Eleanor, right in the most sensitive part between her shoulder blades, and traveled up her spine, resonating in her head.

Eleanor had never had a senior prom. Never had a senior anything. She'd missed all this. And oh, going to the prom would have been so lovely. She'd watched this same view back when she was seventeen, through the curtains, with Moira screaming and crying for attention in the bassinet in the bedroom. She'd closed the door so she could hear the music. The Andrews Sisters.

Eleanor could just cry. If Eleanor were the kind of person who was able to cry. It was getting dark, but she could still see the girls' carefully sprayed French twists, the boys' swept-back hair, the front in a little bump atop their heads that made you think of the bump in the front of their bathing suits.

Filthy mind. I have a filthy mind.

The image of Aloysius burning that stupid book came to her. What a jerk. Flying into a fury like that over a little book. One that wasn't even all that dirty.

Well, Aloysius, the joke's on you, because you don't know the half of it, do you? Don't know who really gave me that book. You'd like to think it was the librarian. That skinny librarian I flirt with every now and then. Little do you know it was one of the many men who find me interesting and attractive. Who don't get so drunk at night that they can't even see that I pin-curled my hair and brushed it out all pretty for them. That I put on some lipstick.

Eleanor munched a potato chip and tried to picture herself in one of those prom dresses. If it hadn't been for Aloysius . . .

God, but she regretted marrying that man. Well, then, why did she stay now?

Well, let's see, Eleanor, how's two kids, for starters? How's about no education and, if you left, getting a job as the flunky in some office? Or maybe she couldn't even do that. Didn't they always pick those young cuties? What the hell good am I? I'm retarded, old, spastic, crazy, and a bitch.

She munched more chips and sighed out loud again as a girl sashayed by in a lime green ruffled strapless dress.

The song "To Know Him Is To Love Him" floated out from one of the car radios. The sparky click of another girl's pointed-toe prom shoes skated across the night, traveling over the street and entering Eleanor's nerves again as if she were a lightning rod of loneliness.

Eleanor lisped along to the song, then caught herself and turned away from the window.

She hated Aloysius now, but there were times when she could remember loving him. Like when she first met him. Handsome freshman hockey player college boy, here she was, sixteen years old. Next thing you knew, she was in trouble and he was Mr. Honorable, besides being Mr. In Love, and the next thing you knew they were married and he had to drop out of the University of Minnesota.

What the hell was Wish wishing for? To be sober? To have Moira all to himself? To be drunk? To be loved? Yes, that was it. To be loved. Wish McPherson with those hurt blue eyes surrounded by thick curly black lashes that gave his eyes that brimming-over, glisteny look, made them look like they'd been crying, crying all his life over his sad lot.

And now it was her sad lot. Oh Jesus God get me out of this situation.

Wish and his sporting goods. Hockey. Though she'd always preferred the artistic type. Eleanor herself could have gone on the stage. Her drama teacher had once told her she had quite an ear. That she had incredible mimicry ability. She knew she had something of a photographic memory, too.

All that talent gone to waste. All that talent gone to hate.

She fixed the drapes and got up and paced around the room and settled into the couch and called out to the girls, who were in the kitchen making chocolate-chip cookies, "How are the cookies coming along?"

"We're out of margarine," Taryn said.

"Use Crisco. Hey, how about some more chips out here?" she called. Now she felt a little better. Now she felt almost like one of the girls. One of the teenagers. Poor Eleanor. Never had a chance to be a teenager. Life can be a son of a bitch the way it works out sometimes.

The satiny voices of The Teddy Bears floated in on pink and powder blue musical notes that danced on silvery staffs into Eleanor's living room.

Maybe that's why she was such a sex maniac now—never got the chance to be a teenager. All she thought about was sex. Afternoons, she lay in bed thinking about sex with whomever she had a crush on at the moment—the milkman, the pharmacist, the dentist, the guy over at the traffic bureau that time she'd had to go in and protest the parking ticket, the grocery store assistant manager, and yes, Aloysius, even the librarian. Ed Moorland down the street and the assistant principal. Even, she laughed out loud, even that new garbage man, the young one who always looked at her and reminded her of John Garfield in that movie where he's the low-class guy in love with the upper-class woman, who was it, Lana Turner, Barbara Stanwyck?

Eleanor couldn't help it, she liked the attention these men gave her. Besides, Aloysius couldn't even get it up these days. If she'd wanted him to, which she didn't, thank you very much. The thought of it revolted her.

And with some men she didn't only just think about it. How do you like them apples, huh, Aloyisus?

Maybe she should even go out tonight. To the library. Wish was out of town again. Handy being married to a traveling salesman. That librarian seemed to think she was a pretty swell kid. Thought she was talented and intelligent and funny and attractive. Eleanor hadn't gone to bed with him yet. And she didn't go to bed with everyone, she'd have them know. She had some discretion. She mostly just flirted. And it was funny the way Aloysius got so jealous.

Moira came into the room with the bag of potato chips for her. "Wait, Moira, here's one for you," Eleanor said, opening *Adventures in Drama*. "If music be the food of love, play on." Which play?"

Moira shrugged.

"Guess."

"I can't."

"Twelfth Night."

"Oh."

"I thought you were so damned smart."

Moira turned and looked at her mother through her new swoopy glasses that had set them back $19.95 because Moira—probably on purpose—broke those old-lady glasses.

"Shakespeare's not my thing," Moira said, and Eleanor's heart in spite of itself went out to this mess of a daughter using the cool talk, trying to be just like anyone else, a child trying so goddamned hard in this goddamned world to be cool. Tears burned at the rims of Eleanor's eyes and she had to let out a little noise to make them stop.

All that aside, Moira thought she was better than everyone. So see how much pity she'd get from Eleanor.

Some boy had invited Moira to the prom. He was a sophomore, and Moira was too young. Eleanor knew exactly what that boy wanted. What any older boy wanted from a younger girl.

The more she thought about it, the more angry she got. A sophomore wanting to take a younger girl to the prom. Whoever heard of such a thing? It had never happened to Eleanor when she was in high school.

Briefly, very briefly, she flirted with fantasy of what it would be like to go to the dance herself with that sophomore. If the truth were to be known, sometimes Eleanor couldn't tell herself apart from Moira. Sometimes she looked at Moira studying over there in the corner, and she felt as if it were she, Eleanor, who was the straight-A student, Eleanor who had that body with the big bosoms, Eleanor who was thirteen going on thirty.

Because that's all she was, thirty years old in a few days. Three-O. Eleanor's life was supposed to be rocking chairs and knitting and Moira's was supposed to be fun and proms and pointed-toe shoes . . . well, Eleanor would be damned if she was going to play washed-up old bag in this household. Let someone else take that part. Eleanor wanted to be the debutante.

Ha. Yes, sometimes she couldn't tell mother and daughter apart. Sometimes, she also suspected, Aloysius couldn't tell either.

With Taryn it was different. Taryn was the baby. Always would be. In fact, Taryn saw herself that way. She was so tiny, underdeveloped.

Back at the window again, Eleanor pictured herself in peach satin. With enormous breasts and pointy shoes to look down at. Laughing stardust into the warm May air with a sophomore—her own sophomore with slicked-up hair and a carnation in his lapel—telling her she was irresistible.

But he had invited Moira. Well, as far as Eleanor was concerned, the boy was obviously a sex maniac. But Eleanor wasn't going to play the heavy in all this. That wasn't her role either. She had decided to tell Wish about it and let him make the decision.

"Some hotshot sophomore invited Moira to the prom," she had said to Aloysius. "That Ettinger boy is having a party beforehand. I know they'll be drinking. And I know what sophomore boys want from younger girls."

You should have seen Aloysius's face. Eighty-seven shades of red and purple before he slammed the cupboard door shut and called Moira to the kitchen and bawled her out for getting mixed up with an older boy who drank.

"You tell that punk if he shows up on our step he'll wish he'd never been born." Then Wish took a quick shot. The whiskey breath sent a poisonous perfume through the air. "Tell the little sissy bastard he ought to be out playing football instead of going to dances, anyway."

No mention of the sex part, but then Wish didn't like to talk about that.

That librarian was a little effeminate, but maybe that was why

Eleanor liked him. He was so gentle. Even his eyes, as they traveled over the bare part of her shoulders left by the new halter dress Eleanor had treated herself to, even his eyes were gentle. Oh yes, Eleanor thought about sex a lot. If Aloysius ever found her stash of pornography that she kept in a safe-deposit box. Ha. Took it to the park in summer and read about spanking and bondage and doing it with older men, younger men, and oh my God, why was she admitting this to herself?

The car radios sang out in unison, "Will You Love Me Tomorrow?" Eleanor danced around the room, then stopped.

That's what it's all about. A brief time in your life. Four, maybe five years. Five years when you feel that spark that tells you to go out there and fall in love with the next pair of long limbs with a blond bump on the top of his head and a bump in his jockey shorts, who will whisper to you how beautiful you are, who will put goose pimples on your arms and back and shoulders.

Eleanor watched a girl in blue taffeta laugh up into the starlight as her blond date pulled her toward him.

The car radios belted out, "This Is Dedicated To the One I Love." The music was as strong as Aloysius's whiskey.

Moira peeked out of the kitchen to say the cookies were almost ready to go into the oven. The girls giggled and the electric mixer growled on and off and on again. Poor girls, learning how to be girls. And by God, they were going to be the right kind of girls. Home economics teachers. Decent, respectable, well-educated girls who could fit in.

Oh God, but Moira was becoming so sexy. Well, just great. Moira could get pregnant. She could just see Fran Ettinger breaking her neck to get the word out on that around the neighborhood.

Taryn made those tap-dancing shoes out of bottle caps and her hand-me-down Mary Janes. She wanted so much to take tap classes. But Taryn was so sweet and meek now, if she started all that dancing business she might get big-headed. And what if she actually liked that ballet crap? Wasted her life on it?

When Eleanor made it clear to Wish that Moira had dirty thoughts about boys, that that was how teenage girls were, Wish said he wouldn't let his daughters go out on dates. They'd raise them the respectable old-fashioned way.

Here was a double-dating couple. Getting out of a convertible. A white convertible. Wish would know what make. Wish who was out of town tonight. Thank God. No drinking, no tension overtaking the house as if it were perched on the peak of a mountain and the slightest wrong move would make it topple.

Moira came through the room. She was wearing old slacks and had her frizzy hair half in curlers, half sticking up, a smudge of flour from the cookies she and Taryn had been making on her glasses.

Eleanor hated getting old. A useless, homely, old, unwanted, unbeautiful, unlovely, unyoung woman. Eleanor reached inside her blouse to her bra and adjusted a falsie. Sometimes when she was in bed with a man—and she didn't do it that often, really, not often at all—she would pretend she was Moira with those big tits instead of falsies she had to hide in her purse.

Oh God, she was bored. I don't fit in, she said to the teenagers still pouring into the party. Light flashed out of the front door every time a couple went in and loud music—Elvis, wasn't it?—from the hi-fi blared out as if hurling taunts and insults across the street and then closing the door to whisper about Eleanor. I don't fit in anywhere. I want to go to your prom, I want to be part of your prom party. Can't you give me one more chance?

She remembered the carnation corsage Wish presented her with the day of their shotgun wedding. How she'd come home and put it in the refrigerator to keep, to pretend she had a happy memory of the prom. How it had wilted and smelled like lettuce the next day.

She'd tried so many things to be happy. Tried those jobs. She'd never forget the frustration of trying to concentrate on her typing. "I can't help it. My mind is going a mile a minute," she said at lunch one day to Arlene Fitzsimmons, one of the gals she worked with she had thought was a friend and someone she could confide in. "Bells and whistles go off—I think of songs I've heard, poems I've memorized. I think up new poems."

Arlene had taken a puff of her cigarette and stubbed it out in the ashtray and stood up. "Eleanor McPherson, I think you need professional help," she had said, and picked up her purse, opened her compact, powdered her nose, and walked out of the cafeteria.

Eleanor had seriously thought of going home and hanging herself.

A car radio was now playing "Come Softly to Me." Eleanor put her face down in her arms and tried to cry. She couldn't cry. She could just feel like this. She saw a couple kissing in the back seat of a Thunderbird.

She wondered if people who had been happy as teenagers lived the rest of their lives in a kind of limbo.

There was happiness out there, across the street at the Ettingers, out there in the world, and Eleanor was not getting a piece of it.

Taryn came into the living room and plopped down on the couch next to Eleanor. "I wish they wouldn't be so noisy across the street," Taryn said.

Eleanor again looked out the window at the party. The warm purply evening breeze that blew in the smell of May was making this all the more unbearable.

A car radio began to play "Stagger Lee." Eleanor took Taryn's arm and began to laugh. The only thing she could do when she felt like crying was laugh.

"Hey, Taryn, do you hear your father's song?" To Taryn's quizzical look, she explained, "That's him when he's had a snootful— Stagger Lee."

She and Taryn had a good laughing fit over that one. Eleanor felt a little better. Let a smile be your umbrella, let a sarcastic quip at someone else's expense be your raincoat. That was the way to handle things, just laugh 'em off.

Eleanor thought of making a bumper sticker for her own car: LAUGHING IT OFF.

Taryn turned on the TV. Eleanor got up and closed the window and pulled the drapes. Moira looked at the closed drapes, looked at the floor like she was thinking about something, and went to her bedroom to do some homework.

Maybe, Eleanor thought, she would go out to a movie tomorrow night. Maybe she'd let that librarian know that she was going to the movies.

Eleven

ONE LATE FEBRUARY AFTERNOON when it was so cold the air seemed ready to shatter, Daddy came home unexpectedly from an out-of-town trip.

As he pushed open the front door, the cutting air whooshed in on Taryn, lying on the couch watching "The Fugitive," and Moira, sitting in the big lounge chair reading her history book and watching the TV.

Daddy's curly black hair blew in the wind as he held the door open with his foot and lugged in his big sample trunk and his two-suiter.

Slowly, so that he wouldn't notice, Moira moved the ottoman in front of her legs. She was wearing nylons and had shaved them the night before, even though Daddy wouldn't allow it. It was Mother who had suggested it, and instead of lending her her own razor, handed her Daddy's. (Daddy took his electric razor when he traveled).

Out of the sides of her eyes, Moira took a quick glance at Daddy. She estimated his face to be about a two-whiskey shade of red. On the other hand, she thought hopefully, maybe it was just the cold.

He put down his two-suiter and his sample case and stood staring at the TV. But it wasn't the show he was looking at. It was the flowers that had come for Mother, a small bouquet of tea roses surrounded by several sprigs of baby's breath.

"Where'd you get the flowers?" Daddy said.

"Mother ordered those," Moira said.

Daddy went into the bedroom, then came out again loosening his tie. He saw Moira's legs, but didn't look mad.

Maybe he wouldn't get mad. Maybe he didn't care.

"What have you got on your legs, Moira?"

Moira swallowed and took a deep breath. When Mother suggested Moira shave her legs, she had said, "Don't let your father see or he'll tear the house apart." She braced herself. "Nylons. I bought them with my allowance, instead of a candy bar and Cokes this week."

"Aren't you a little young?" he said, staring doubtfully at the hose.

"All the girls wear nylons now."

Daddy made a noise that expressed a lack of interest more than a lack of approval. What relief. "Where's your mother, girls?"

"Out at a movie," Taryn said.

Daddy stopped in the middle of loosening his tie and looked out the window. A cold mean wind howled in the eaves. He went to the kitchen for a beer.

By dinner time, Mother still wasn't home, so Daddy fried some eggs and potatoes for everyone. He put the flowers as a centerpiece on the kitchen table and stared at them all through dinner.

By the time Mother got home, Daddy had found a cowboy show to drink to. Taryn was on the kitchen phone with a girlfriend and Moira was at the kitchen table working on her algebra.

"What are you doing home tonight?" Mother said, not even trying to hide her disappointment. Moira could see her take off her coat and hat and gloves slowly and thoughtfully and put them in the hall closet.

"The head office wants me to go to Fargo tomorrow instead of Moline. So I came home. It's on the way."

"Oh."

"Sorry to disappoint you."

"Well, if I'd known you'd be home, I'd have . . . ."

"You'd have what?"

"Baked a cake." Mother headed down the hall toward the bedroom, her high heels making smart, confident clicks.

"I thought you ordered those flowers for the occasion. Or wasn't it *you* who ordered them?"

"Who do you think sent them? Cary Grant?"

"That's what I was wondering. Who?"

"Can't I order flowers for once in my life, to brighten up my drab little life?"

"You certainly are all dressed up," Daddy said as she went toward the bedroom.

Mother came back into the living room. "If you call not wearing the clothes I wear to scrub the kitchen floor 'dressed up,' then I guess I'm dressed up."

Daddy sat down in his chair. He tossed a beer nut high into the air and caught it on his tongue. "Movie good?"

Mother didn't say anything.

Daddy asked again, "How was the show?"

"Mediocre."

"That's too bad. Uh, what'd you see?"

Mother went to the bedroom.

"I said, 'What movie did you see?' "

But Mother kept walking. Daddy came into the kitchen, where Moira and Taryn sat tensely. He replaced his empty beer bottle with a full one.

Daddy went into the bedroom and the girls heard some arguing. Mother came stomping out in her bedroom mules, her ankles cracking, and went to the refrigerator and opened it and looked in.

The phone rang. Mother's mules scuffled to the living room. She answered it, then spoke in a more polite voice than Moira had ever heard her use.

"Uh-uh," Mother said. "Uh-uh, uh-uh. Yes, uh-uh, well, you know. Uh-uh, that's right. Okay . . ." Her voice trailed off in the most polite and sweet tone Moira had ever heard *anybody* use.

When she hung up, Daddy didn't look at Mother. He just made a barely audible little smacky sound and said, "I suppose that was a wrong number."

"Oh, leave me alone. You've been drinking."

Daddy got up to go to the bathroom. He came out holding his razor in the air. "Who the hell was using my razor?"

There was a stunning silence. And Moira thought she'd breezed through the shaved-legs controversy.

"Eleanor, were you using my goddamn razor on your legs again? Ruining the blade so that I'd cut myself in the morning?"

Mother and Taryn stared at Moira. Moira stared at the wall in front of her, fully expecting Daddy to come and slit her throat.

"Take a look at Moira's legs," Mother said.

"Moira?" Daddy said, and went over to her and grabbed one of her legs. His motion pulled the nylon out of one of its garters.

"Shaving her legs?"

Mother sat over in the corner, like a kid who's on base and can't be tagged. She was staring at Moira. So was Taryn, from second base over on the couch.

"Moira, what are you? A tramp? Eleanor, doesn't she have any more socks, what the hell is going on? The next thing she'll be smoking cigarettes. Drinking. What the hell is going on around here?"

"Moira," Mother said. "Take off the nylons."

"Throw them in the garbage," Daddy said.

Moira tore off the nylons and took them to the garbage can and threw them in.

"There," Daddy yelled, his face purple. "Are you happy, Eleanor?"

Mother said, "Why don't you just leave, go away. Go back to Fargo or wherever the hell you were."

There was a brief silence, then the yell came like a sonic boom trailing the rage that was jetting ahead who knew where. "Can't stand me, can you?"

"You got that right."

Daddy went over to the TV and slammed it off. He picked up the flowers and threw them at the wall. Then he grabbed the rabbit ears off the TV and hurled them at the wall just over the couch where they were sitting. The rabbit ears missed them all, but the cord that snapped off with it whipped Moira on her right cheek, missing her eye and knocking off her glasses. Moira yelped in pain. Daddy came over and grabbed Moira's shoulder and shook her. "What the hell is wrong with you? No more phone calls for you." Then he suddenly seemed to remember that it was Mother who got the call, not Moira, and he turned and yelled, "No more phone calls for anyone."

"Okay. When your boss calls, I'll tell him you're not allowed to get any phone calls," Mother said.

Daddy yelled at the top of his lungs, *"Everybody get the hell out of my sight. Everybody get to bed,"* and they all scattered in differ-

ent directions like insects when you turn the lights on in the basement.

The familiar sounds of Daddy's drinking started in the kitchen.
The phone rang again and Mother's footsteps in her clacky mules
headed down the hallway. But Daddy's heavy footsteps were already on the way.

"Hello," he yelled.

"Hello, hello, hello. Speak up, you son of a bitch, whoever you
are."

He slammed the phone down and he yelled out, "Moira, Taryn,
get the hell out here."

He yelled again and they all appeared from their bedrooms.

Ignoring Taryn, he said, "Moira, tell those greaseballs you can't
take any phone calls."

Moira made little gasps to keep from crying, to keep from going
crazy. Nobody ever called her, he knew that. Rosemary knew better. Dennis would never call her again even if he saw that the house
was on fire.

And then, something new happened; Moira heard Mother's bare
footsteps in the hallway, timid at first, then quickly stepping into
the living room. "This is the last straw. I'm not going to put up
with your treating us this way anymore. As soon as you've had a
drink, you're like this. I'm not putting up with your drinking any
more."

"I'm not going to be treated like an intruder in my own house
anymore. *Go on, get the hell out of here,*" Daddy yelled at the top
of his voice, and they ran to their rooms again.

There was some slamming, and Mother came into Moira's room.
Moira had her glasses off and she couldn't read Mother's expression; it was just white with dark shadowy suggestions of features in
the spots where eyes, nose, and mouth go, like a skeleton of her real
mother without the sad fleshy parts life had molded onto her face.
"Come on, Moira," she said. "We're going to a motel."

Moira felt a strange new excitement as she grabbed the first pair
of pants and shirt she could find—a sleeveless summer blouse and a
pair of wool slacks she'd outgrown that she couldn't get the zipper
all the way up on—and crammed her bare feet into the first shoes
her toes could find in the closet, her patent-leather dress flats.

Mother searched for the keys and her purse, making a jingling like a gym teacher getting her team ready as she went to Taryn's bedroom and came out leading Taryn, still in her nightgown and slippers and clutching her special pillow with the ballerinas on it. Daddy shifted his stance to block their view of the whiskey bottle from the hallway, and stared out the kitchen window, pretending he didn't see as they headed for the front door. Moira thought it looked like he was crying. She hesitated. She wanted to love Daddy. But she was afraid of him, too. As he turned, she turned away. Something cruel came into her and said *"Let's all hate Daddy together."* The cruel feeling became a feeling of power. Better to hate someone if you're not allowed to love him. The only cure for love was hate.

Moira managed to get her three-ring binder and math and biology books, then realized halfway to the car that she'd forgotten her glasses and the sheet with the biology extra-credit problems Mr. Bailey had given her because he was hoping to get her into advanced placement classes next year. She ran back and grabbed them off the desk just as Daddy was coming out of the kitchen.

And now, oddly enough, she felt sorry for him. Sorrier than she had for anyone ever in her life.

Daddy was mad at Mother for being out at the movie when he got home, but he was afraid of Mother so he yelled at Moira. She heard Mother start up the car engine in her mechanically clumsy way. No, she couldn't leave. When Mother wasn't around, Daddy was nice to her. She loved Daddy.

Then he noticed her cheek. "Oh my God, did I do that? Oh my God, you're hurt. Let's put something on it."

But then Mother was back in the house, her ankles cracking, her keys jingling with her newfound adrenaline-charged power.

"Come on, Moira," she said.

Daddy's weight shifted on his feet. He wanted to do something about this fight, get it over with, but he didn't know how.

As they were getting into the car, Moira heard the phone ring again. And as they backed down the driveway, she saw Daddy open his sample trunk, and it looked as if he had gotten a gun out. Or maybe it was just a hockey stick. It was hard to tell because the sheer drapes were drawn and it was only shadows inside. Then she thought she saw him put whatever it was back in the trunk and close the lid and then they were heading out on the street toward their new life without Daddy.

Once they were on the highway, the tires making smacking sounds on the road, night wrapping a comforting blanket around them, Moira began to feel safe, hopeful, then excited, as if their life was going to work now, be normal, without Daddy. The only way to deal with all this was to hate Daddy. She put spit on her finger and put her finger on her cheek to cool the welt from the rabbit ears and hoped there wouldn't be any scars to carry into her new life.

Mother seemed somewhat excited herself as she drove down the black highway lined with telephone poles and corn fields, driving with the trucks full of cattle and hogs looking out at you with glowing eyes that you could see when the car lights shone on them. They were packed in so tight their hides bulged from between the slats.

Mother talked about how Daddy always ruined everything, about how great life would be without him coming home drunk all the time.

"We'll live a normal life," Mother said.

A normal life with no drinking and fighting. Was something like that really in the cards for Moira? For her little sister? For her mother? Why not—didn't they deserve a normal life? Yes, they did. Now Moira felt so alive and happy she couldn't believe it. A normal life at last. She knew she was destined for one, always had been. Moira sometimes felt happiness so strong from things like a stretch of prairie, a bank of fresh snow, a sky so blue a kite could disappear and carry you forever in it, that she could explode and spread happiness all over the world.

"We'll get a little house, I'll get a full-time job. We'll make friends. I'll find a man. A normal man," Mother went on, her pale face even more pale in the light of the occasional car that passed.

Moira turned to see if Taryn was getting all this. But Taryn was asleep, her still neatly parted hair dark against her special pillow with the ballerinas pirouetting all over it.

Moira saw the world opening up in front of her, a long life, a long, happy life with herself right smack in the center of it. It would be so wonderful—she felt she could split herself open with happiness. Oh, it would have awful parts too, like tonight, but the wonderful would knock those nights away, knock away the evil. Good over evil, she really believed things worked that way.

They drove and drove and drove until the car clock with the elongated numerals said midnight and Mother said she couldn't take any more, and stopped at the Tip Top Teepee Motel. There was a neon sign with a dancing Indian wielding a hatchet, the sign jumping from one image to the next as he chopped a cowboy's head. A bunch of semis slept in the parking lot like a herd of beef cattle with their necks pulled in and their backs to the wind. Mother looked at Moira and Moira looked at Mother, and Mother made a little nervous smile and pulled into the parking lot.

It was just starting to snow as Mother and Moira went into the motel office. Moira's feet were swollen and numb from the patent leather shoes with no socks and her cheek still smarted from the welt and the cold.

The motel office floor was covered with old gray carpet remnants streaked with slush and mud. Mother rang the little bell on the counter and it brought a man who had that burnt-ironing smell of body odor under the armpits.

Mother paid for the room and then she and Moira went back out into the swirling snow. Moira wrapped her arms around Taryn and lifted her limp body in the frilly nightgown. Taryn's bones were like a canary's. She carried Taryn with her head resting on the ballerina pillow through the swirling snow. Moira was so excited about their new life with no fighting that it seemed like she was carrying a bride over the threshold into their new life.

Moira helped Taryn get under the wool blanket and thin, cigarette-burned bedspread. Taryn curled up.

Mother put the suitcase up on the rack and said, "Hungry, Moira? I'll go ask Mr. Hospitality if there's anything to eat. I'll be right back."

Moira looked around the room, all browns and grays, with a picture on the wall of a Sioux Indian on his horse. A picture out of a magazine that someone framed. She thought there was something sweet about that, in a pitiful way, that they would bother to decorate the room for a bunch of truck drivers and people running away from home.

Moira wondered then what Sioux Indians had to do with this

motel, and remembered what her best friend when they lived out in the country, Paul Whitefeather, had said about white people, that they liked to name places after something they'd destroyed.

Mother came back in sipping a steaming cup of coffee the size truckers got. Her hair was dandruffy looking with those tiny hard snowflakes. She handed Moira a Nehi grape pop and tossed a stale-looking Danish roll wrapped in a napkin onto the table along with a Chunky, an Almond Joy, and a maple Bun candy bar. "Party time," she said.

Mother's face went so lonely and worried and little-girl-looking that Moira started thinking that maybe this wasn't going to be the breaking away from Daddy that they needed. Maybe they'd end up back home and things would be just the same.

"I wish we had a TV," Mother said, "then at least we could play Who's the Ugliest . . . I'll bet all those women on TV have nights like this, too," Mother said. "Driving to some fleabag motel because their drunken husbands got violent with them. That'll be the next episode on 'Lassie'; Uncle Petrie gets drunk and slaps whatsiz's name's mother. . . ."

"Timmy," Moira said.

"Timmy, that's it—Jesus, I can't stand that puke of a kid—nice and sweet and perfect on the TV screen, then when the cameras are off the spoiled little bastard probably throws shit tantrums right and left."

Moira laughed in a voice that she hoped sounded natural. She almost wished Daddy were here to be a rock against Mother's sometimes craziness that didn't even need beer or whiskey to set it off.

"Uncle Petrie throws the rabbit ears at Timmy, and Lassie drives them to a fleabag motel." Mother went to the window and pulled the curtains aside. "In the middle of a blizzard."

Moira made another nervous little giggle to keep Mother's mood company.

"Hey, here's a radio," Mother said, her face losing a little tiny bit of the wracking concern on it.

The radio sounded like a very loud growling stomach except in one staticky spot. The station, WNAX, playing a yodeling cowboy song, faded in and out as the wind outside howled. "Doesn't work," Mother said, snapping it off.

Moira unplugged the radio and moved it to another part of the room and plugged it in and fiddled with the knobs until it came in better. They listened to the square-dancing show from Luverne, then "Polka Party," from Yankton. Mother raised her arms and did polka-dancing gestures to the accordion music as the snow danced through the air in the black window behind her head. She got depressed-looking again and stared at the dusty corners of the motel room. Moira got out her math book. When she opened the page to the chapter they were on, it was like looking at your dearest friend's face. She began to work on the math problem and ate the Chunky and the Almond Joy, trying to avoid the cavity she already had on the back upper left, and sipped at her Nehi.

The station went off the air and they were left alone with the static. Just as Moira was about to give up on the math problem, Mother broke the silence.

"What in hell are we going to do?" she said. "What—in—hell—are—*we*—going—to—*do?*"

Just then the wind stopped howling and there was a buzzy kind of silence.

Moira looked down at her math book. It looked like a jumble of impossibly hard problems to her now, like it had when the school year had first started and she'd looked ahead in the book.

"Maybe we could go to Mitchell," Moira finally offered. Sometimes when Mother and Daddy had a fight, Mother drove off to Mitchell and got a banana split at Fipps' Drug Store. Sometimes she took Moira and Taryn. "We could live in Mitchell."

"Mitchell," Mother repeated, then turned angrily on Moira. "Now what on earth would I do in Mitchell?"

Moira tried to ignore Mother, but Mother wouldn't quit staring.

"I don't know," Moira finally said.

"Something bigger," Mother said. "Let's think big. Yes, thinking big, we could go to Minneapolis."

"Or even Chicago," Moira said.

Mother looked up at her. Obviously Moira had thought too big. "Let's be realistic."

"Yeah," Moira said, trying to think of a place that would be realistic.

"I could always go back to Mama's," Mother said. "Back to Aberdeen." Mother thought for a few minutes as she looked off at the black little motel window, and said, "But that was worse than this."

Moira didn't know much about Grandma Bergstren, except that she had a cruel sense of humor. She was cruel in a different way than Daddy's parents had been to him. Daddy's parents had been more traditional, drinking and beating him up, but Grandma Bergstren did slightly crazy things like taking Mother and her sister to funerals of people she hardly knew. She'd walk the girls up to the casket and make them look in, then laugh and tease them on the way home for being scared.

Mother and Moira sat in silence for a while. And then her face went all weird and creepy like something in the funhouse at the carnival. Then she went on, "Don't ever get married, Moira. And don't ever have any kids, because then you're stuck. That's how I got stuck, by having you kids."

Moira just sat feeling her cheeks burn with guilt and self-hatred and trying to control the big empty sick feeling filling her.

"I should run off," Mother went on. "I could run off with a gigolo. Ha, then you'd really be in trouble—life with Aloysius Wesley McPherson." Then mother smiled. "They could turn it into one of those cute little sit-coms on TV, like 'Bachelor Father,' huh? Call it 'Bachelor Gigolo'—no, 'Gigolo Knows Best.' "

Moira laughed nervously.

"I always wondered about that guy on 'Bachelor Father,' all alone with his teenage daughter. 'Uncle Bentley, Uncle Bentley,' " she mimicked in a sugary, bratty tone. "Although let's face it, that moon-faced girl is so homely that you wouldn't really suspect anything was going on, would you?" Mother asked the empty dead air, then turned and looked at Moira again for an answer.

Moira shrugged, then said no, you wouldn't suspect anything and laughed again, and pretty soon both she and Mother were laughing. Then Moira could see Mother drifting off into her little fogland. Mother took off her slacks and sweater and stood there in her slip and too-big bra with the falsies stuffed in crookedly.

She put the toilet lid down and sat on it. "Moira, don't ever have kids," Mother said. "There's no way any of us can have normal kids. They'll either be crazy or they'll be alcoholic."

Moira tasted something acid in her mouth.

"You know what, Moira, I have a secret and I should tell you about it. About a baby."

Moira looked up at her mother. Mother had a smile, a crazy smile on her face. And it came to Moira—her Mother was mad. Stark, raving mad. Trying to pass. Almost passing. Was it true? Was she doomed too?

Moira looked at the floor. "Never mind, Mother."

They sat in silence for a moment, then Mother said, "Hell with it. Let's get to bed."

If Moira went to bed now she'd have nightmares. She needed something to blot up the nervousness that was leaking out of her. Maybe she could do her homework. She got a few sheets of motel stationery and went into the bathroom and closed the door and turned on the light. She spread a towel on the floor of the shower and wrapped her coat around her like a blanket and opened her math book. She concentrated on the extra-credit problem, and when she reached her arm back to write down the figures, her arm bumped the rickety metal of the flimsy shower wall. It sounded like thunder.

Pretty soon the breakthrough came and the scared sadness in her head cleared as much as if she had a cold and had just sniffed some Vicks VapoRub.

She sometimes thought that she wouldn't be as smart as she was if she didn't have such a screwed-up family. She wondered if anyone had ever had that theory and done anything with it, some scientist or psychologist, that extremely high IQs usually come from people in extremely screwed-up families because they have to think harder and develop extra brain cells to survive.

Moira was awakened by the sound of trucks grunting their way out of the parking lot and cars whizzing and flailing around and the authoritative grumble of a snowplow. She wrapped her coat around her and went to the window. The parked cars in the lot were nothing but big white humps. Beyond the parking lot was an endless field of smooth, soft white. How could anyone feel angry and depressed or without hope on a morning like this? It looked like a whole new world out there to start a fresh life in. Their lives could be like the new snow after an overnight blizzard, a life of fresh, untrodden snow. Moira stood looking out, relishing the quiet happiness she felt as Mother and Taryn slept and she thought of life's wonderful possibilities.

It took until ten o'clock for a trucker and Moira to push the car out of the snowed-in parking lot onto the street that the snowplow was scraping. Mother drove to one of the better truck stops, where families went for big late breakfasts of pancakes and bottomless-pot coffee on weekends.

They walked in staring at the floor, Moira with her scarf pulled in front of the welt on her cheek, her coat over the summer blouse and pants that didn't zip up, and her no-socks and snow-caked patent leather shoes from which her bare red feet bulged. Taryn was behind Moira, her nightgown showing under her jacket. Mother brought up the rear, shuffling along and looking confused.

The way they looked they didn't want to sit in the middle of the room, so they slid into a drafty booth next to the window where blinding snow-reflected sunlight blazed in on them.

Mother didn't believe in any more makeup than a dab of coral lipstick and eyebrow pencil on raised eyebrows in order to emphasize your disapproval of people. She hadn't even bothered with those this morning, and across the table under the harsh sunlight, her plucked-out eyebrows with the tiny hairs growing in in some spots looked vague, unfinished.

Mother smiled and said, "You can order anything you want."

Taryn ordered blueberry pancakes and Moira was going to try the Highway Hero special—two fried eggs, pancakes, sausage, home fries, toast and jelly. Mother just wanted a donut and coffee.

Moira watched the trucks bouncing heavily into and out of the lot under the now sparkling sun as she sipped her coffee, black and strong. She felt grownup and almost in control, sipping with Mother. She dared to ask, "Well, are we going to Minneapolis?"

Mother rubbed her eyes with all her fingers. "Oh my God, Moira, I can't think of anything to do, anywhere to go on thirty-seven dollars. I don't know what the hell's the use. We might as well go home as do anything."

Moira felt heavy, defeated. Mother took three dollars of that thirty-seven to pay the bill and they got up to leave the restaurant, people staring at Taryn's slippers and their defeat.

Daddy was asleep on the couch in his chinos and T-shirt. He was on his side, snoring loudly, his stomach pushing in and out with the suggestion of the deep and peaceful sleep of a baby. The sample trunk was closed back up and if he had shot the gun off, he hadn't done any harm that she could see. The rabbit ears were back on top of the TV, the dangling cord hanging down the side with the two little sharp prongs that had hit Moira's face. Moira felt embarrassed about her wound, the same kind of embarrassment she had felt one time when Daddy accidentally walked in on her in the shower and had spun and slammed the door.

She put her hand over the little wound as she walked past him into the kitchen. All the beer bottles had been put neatly back in the case under the wall oven. The whiskey bottle was shattered among some garbage inside a grocery store paper bag.

He began to stir as they returned to the living room, so they hurried to their rooms. Moira could hear him groaning and making pitiful sounds as he got himself up and went into the bathroom. She felt bad hearing him in the kitchen making himself a lonely breakfast. Moira could hear it sizzling and snapping in the kitchen. It would be eggs, sausage, home fries with onions—his usual hangover breakfast.

Moira was looking in the mirror at the welt across her cheek and wondering how she was going to explain it to her friend Rosemary, when she heard Daddy in the living room, moaning and crying out. They all ran to the living room. He was on the floor rolling around, crying.

"I'm having an attack. I feel faint. Can't breathe. I need a drink and I'm out of Canadian Club, Eleanor," he said. "Be a doll and run out and get me a pint."

Mother looked at him with a half-interested expression that had become familiar to Moira, and it came to Moira suddenly that

Mother didn't know any other way to be married than this way, and that she'd never leave Daddy. "Go get it yourself."

"No, I mean it, I'm sick, I'm going to faint, I need a pint."

Moira knew what was wrong. She'd looked up things about alcoholics in the library, and they had low blood sugar all the time and had these dizzy spells.

Daddy sobbed and cried like a little boy. Taryn went to the bedroom and closed her door softly. Moira looked at Mother. She knew Mother felt sorry for him. That was Daddy's ace in the hole, always would be—getting people to feel so sorry for him that they'd forget how mad they were at him until the next time.

As Mother got the keys, Moira heard Mother's calcium-deficient ankles from her neglected childhood cracking with a burst of renewed energy. Moira went to her room and got out her Latin. The door opened and shut, and Moira heard Mother's tentative footsteps breaking through the now-crusted snow and the dainty way she closed the car door and started the car engine.

Moira wondered what Mother would do if she hadn't married an alcoholic. Maybe Mother had to marry someone she hated, because she didn't know how to be married to anyone she liked. And for his part, maybe Daddy didn't know how to be married to anyone who liked him.

Twelve

THE SUN WAS HIGH in the brilliant blue sky as the McPherson station wagon pulled off the highway and headed toward Chippewa Campsites, the Lake Superior camping area in which they were going to pitch their tent for one whole week of sun and fun.

Pine trees rustled under the unbelievably blue sky and shimmered so sparkling bright it looked as if someone had just come through these woods and scrubbed furiously with Spic 'n' Span and then rinsed it all with a million buckets of clear, cold Minnesota lake water. The air scorched your lungs, it was so blue and hot-fresh.

A convertible floated by the McPherson station wagon. A half-dozen teenagers in sunglasses laughed and shouted out. Elvis Presley singing "It's Now Or Never" trailed the car like perfume. Both cars came to a halt at the light. Moira saw out of the corner of her eye a boy and girl in the back seat kiss and laugh out loud afterward. It felt as if they were laughing at her. Loneliness grabbed her by the throat and shook her and said *Why aren't you in that car? Why don't you have a crowd of friends?*

A boy in the back seat with his arm back over the trunk of the convertible ran his eyes absently over the station wagon, then let his glance linger when he saw Moira.

Moira felt thousands of pinpricks of embarrassment to be seen with her family. It wouldn't be so bad if she had a group of friends back home to go to the pool with, but she didn't; she was doomed through eternity to go to the beach with her parents and little sister because her parents wouldn't let her date.

Past tent after tent—mostly green army-type tents but some happy yellow ones and a few fancy striped ones—they rumbled slowly over the dirt roads toward the campsite office. Clotheslines were strung from tent ropes to trees, with faded towels and bathing suits hung from them—big, matronly suits in dark, "slimming" colors, with the foam rubber linings hanging out the wrong way like someone relaxing and letting her stomach out when no one was looking, as well as bright, smaller size suits with big empty bosoms sticking out, and a few gay two-pieces.

In front of the tents in aluminum lawn chairs sat overweight middle-aged women in sleeveless tops and shorts, their arms and legs rippling with fat, the men in undershirts fixing fishing reels or holding a beer can or throwing a ball for a dog to chase. The McPhersons had moved up a little in life, to a middle-class neighborhood during the work/school year, but when it came time for vacation, they vacationed back into Mother and Daddy's past.

The radios provided a supermarket of music, from rock 'n' roll to hillbilly to Lawrence Welk as they drove by. Most of the kids presumably were at the beach, because it was a perfect hot July day and even Moira felt good and couldn't wait to dive into one of those great big Lake Superior waves.

Daddy got their lot assignment for the tent and they drove over to take a look. Their lot had two pine trees and a big green oak tree. You could see a little bit of the deep blue water of the lake. They were between a tent with a mauve bathing suit on its line and one with several children's colorful bathing suits and pajamas.

Two tents over, Moira saw the bare back of a teenage boy, muscular and tanned the color of cinnamon, as he climbed onto a motor scooter. A girl in a halter top and a chiffon scarf over her bouffant hair got on behind him.

"Can we go swimming now?" Taryn said impatiently as Daddy began to pitch the tent and mother unpacked dishes and food.

"The beach is beyond those two rows of tents," Moira said hopefully. "Not far at all."

"No, I need your help pitching this tent," he said.

The girls had to help pull the corners out, then hold the stakes while he pounded them into the ground. The yellow convertible they'd seen out on the road went by again with the radio playing Connie Francis. Daddy stopped pounding, hammer in air, and glared at the car. "Goddamn punks," he said, then raised his hammer and with one mighty blow drove the stake into the sandy soil.

Moira wondered for just a split second if Daddy was like Mother —jealous of teenagers because he'd married and become a parent so young. Forever prevented from being a teenage boy and forever jealous of them.

It was three o'clock by the time Daddy said they could go to the beach.

"Be back in an hour," he said. "Eleanor, why don't you go with them. Hell, maybe I'll take a dip, too. I could use some exercise."

"I thought you got plenty of exercise lifting beer cases from the car into the kitchen."

Daddy smiled but it wasn't a real smile. "Come to think of it, you get enough exercise, too, yakkety-yakking and bitching and moaning all the time. Or at least your mouth does."

Taryn, trying to be the peacemaker, jumped in with, "Come on, Mother."

"No, thanks," Mother said. "I'll get the sheets and blankets out, then I'm going to do some reading. You go ahead and swim."

It almost seemed as if Daddy would like to have gone swimming with them all. Taryn said, "How about you, Daddy?"

"Nah, to hell with it. I'm going to see about renting a fishing boat for tomorrow and getting some bait. You girls be back in an hour," Daddy said. Mother never told them when to come back. It was almost as if Mother hoped they'd get lost.

"Thank goodness he didn't want to come with us," Taryn said on their way to the bathhouse to change into their suits.

"Yeah," Moira said, happy for this rare time of sisterly comradeship because Taryn's friends, whom Mother called the "gaggle of gigglers," weren't around. "Who needs him?"

But then Taryn turned on her. "You shouldn't be so negative. Half the problems in this family are your fault anyway."

"Come on, Taryn, let's try to be cheerful," Moira said. The air smelled of Coppertone and the sun was still bright and someone's transistor was playing "Teenager in Love." Moira was high on the potential for fun, love, whatever.

They went to the bathhouse to put on their bathing suits. Moira had a black-and-white knit that Mother had broken down and bought her for the vacation. And when she came out of the changing room, Moira felt as if she had *really* changed—because three boys looked up at her immediately with a sort of double-take Moira had begun to understand, and one said, "Wow." And she felt power now, real power. She was important, even if it was to these guys who were (a) too young, and (b) obviously from a small town way north. One whistled. Something went through Moira. A feeling that she really was okay, that other people would appreciate her one day.

As they crossed the sand, still hot, still bright gold and welcoming even though it was almost three-thirty, the yellow convertible went by again and it was playing "Itsy-Bitsy-Teeny-Weeny-Yellow-Polka-Dot Bikini." The air now smelled of the cold, clear lake. Taryn jumped up and down when she saw dozens of people still in the roped-off area swimming and grabbed Moira's hand and pulled her, running, down toward the water. A couple of boys looked up at Moira, and they weren't laughing at her and none of the girls were snickering because no one knew her here and Moira felt free and new and pretty. She was brand new. She was Eve.

Swimming side by side with Taryn, Moira felt a hand on her ankle. She squealed and turned around. A boy with wet spiky hair down on his forehead and a brown tan that made his teeth look impossibly white was grinning at her.

He pulled her under and then ran over and helped her out. She laughed and he lifted her up onto his shoulders and gave her a ride. Another boy did that to Taryn and pretty soon there were other girls on shoulders and they were all laughing and splashing. Time stopped, it was so much fun. Moira was actually having *fun*.

Moira wasn't used to fun, and suddenly she felt guilty. What if Daddy came down to the beach and saw them? But he was busy getting fishing stuff and beer, most likely.

As the group swam out to a dock, she caught some names—Doug, Bobby, Carla, Ted, Audrey, Walter. New names, new people. Fun. Moira was having fun.

They dove in and boys chased girls and dunked them and the girls squealed together. Every now and then, Moira would glance up to make sure Daddy wasn't thundering down the beach toward them.

They all decided to go buy Cokes and french fries. The group gathered on Audrey's blanket and listened to her transistor radio. Doug, the boy with the white teeth, asked Moira where she was from. It turned out he was from Mitchell, not far from Sioux Falls.

He was a sophomore and was here with his parents. He was an only child and hated vacations with his parents.

Moira and Taryn sat together and it *felt* like they were sisters. They both teased and laughed with Doug and the others. Doug rubbed Coppertone on Moira's back, even though it was almost five o'clock and the sun had retreated.

It was time for a walk down the road. That's what they did, the ones who couldn't drive yet. Took endless walks down the pine-forested roads, laughing, joking, snapping towels, acting like normal teenagers, and Moira was one of them.

They stood up and wrapped towels around their waists. Moira wrapped the little towel Mother had gotten out of a Breeze detergent box. It still had detergent on it and left white powder on her back and it was itchy. But who cared? And just then, the yellow convertible went by. One of the boys looked at Moira and whistled.

Moira felt that power again. Who could ever sit around being depressed about their screwed-up family when they had this kind of power?

"Let's go for a walk," Doug said. Moira had long ago hidden her glasses in her beach bag and didn't have a watch and couldn't see the clock at the refreshment stand. But she was having too much fun to care about five o'clock and having to meet Daddy's deadline. Let him kill her. She was going to have her last request—a real, honest-to-God fun time with kids who liked her.

"We can't," Taryn said. "Our dad would kill us."

"So would everyone's," Audrey said. "But we do it anyway."

"But she really means it," Moira said, perfectly serious. "Our dad really would kill us."

The others laughed. "I know what you mean," Audrey said.

Taryn, whose vision was perfect, just like the rest of her, looked up at the refreshment-stand clock and grabbed Moira's arm and pulled. "It's ten after," she said. "Let's run."

Taryn hurried her to the tent, and they arrived twenty minutes later than Daddy had said. Moira didn't care if he kicked her all the way across the lake. She had had fun enough to last a lifetime. And she had gotten some confidence. Some kids had liked her. Some boys had admired her.

The yellow convertible floated by and Moira looked again. The boy in the back seat had a girl with a ponytail flying behind her. He waved at Moira. Moira smiled.

"You shouldn't smile at boys going by in cars you don't know," Taryn said. "I should tell Mother."

Moira noticed she didn't say "I should tell Daddy." Taryn might be near perfect, but she wasn't totally sadistic.

As soon as they got back to the tent, Moira knew it was going to be hell. Daddy's face was already a brilliant red, and not from the sun, was Moira's guess, and he was fussing over something to put on the Coleman stove. Mother was sitting with her arms crossed and her eyebrows in perfect arches.

Moira was all prepared with an excuse when he asked why they were late. But he didn't even seem to notice, and that almost made it worse—sometimes he got mad when they were late, sometimes he was mad about too many other things to get mad at her.

Moira saw that it was his special kind of hamburgers he was making, where he mixed horseradish and onions into the meat. They all hated those stinky kind of hamburgers. He made them when he was really pissed off at Mother.

"Can I have mine plain?" Moira said, and Taryn, forever the peacemaker, kicked her ankle.

Daddy was patting one of the hamburgers between hands that were the same shade of red as the meat. "You can have yours the same goddamn way everyone else has theirs."

Mother pursed her lips, then said, "Don't make me one. I won't eat it."

He looked up slowly. Things were already flaring up, and here Mother just tossed a hand grenade into the fire.

He let his head nod a little bit as he digested this act of defiance. "Go to hell, Eleanor." Then he took the hamburger and threw it into the sand over by the pine tree. "There's your hamburger, Moira. Is that the way you like it?"

This was it—Daddy had thrown down the gauntlet. Everyone froze, and then Mother's face changed expression just slightly. Moira now saw the open pint of whiskey sitting on one of the folding lawn chairs, two chairs down from Mother. The familiar terror of family living returned. Now, it was time to stop fooling around and to step cautiously, as if on eggshells, around the situation.

But Mother wasn't in the kind of mood to walk on eggshells. "If you don't stop drinking, I'm going into town and staying in a motel," Mother said.

"I've heard about enough," Daddy growled. "You've been bitching at me all afternoon about the hamburgers, Eleanor, and now you start in because I want to have a cocktail before dinner like every other man around here."

"Oh God, why did I come on this trip?" Mother said.

Daddy looked at Moira's sunburned legs. "What the hell are you doing without any pants on?"

Taryn jumped up and pulled her shorts over the bathing suit, sunburn and sand notwithstanding.

Moira got up a little more slowly. Her emotions during this fight were changing. Instead of being so godawful scared, she was now getting mad. So mad she could push him into that fire.

She looked around the campsite for her shorts. They weren't out there, so she went into the tent. She took off her bathing suit and it felt as if she'd gotten a little sunburn and she was reminded of the fun she'd had. She felt a little bit of strength against Daddy. After all, she wasn't going to have to live with him forever. She rummaged through the suitcase for her clothes. Clean ones. Her skin was very sensitive, and she couldn't stand sand on it under her clothes. She found a pair of shorts and a top and some underpants and her bra. As she stood up to put them on, Daddy pulled the tent door open and said, "Eleanor, where's my sweater?" and when he saw Moira he said, "Jesus Christ, what the hell are you doing? What's wrong with you?" He'd forgotten that he'd told her to get dressed. He jammed his eyes shut as if a hurricane were blowing sand in them, and backed out of the tent.

Moira pulled her clothes on fast. Sure, she'd get away from them in a few years. She was going to a really good college, like her biology teacher, Mr. Bailey, said she should, and she was going to be something important, a doctor or a scientist. And she was going to do good works for the world, just to show the world that it couldn't get her down. She was going to show her parents that they couldn't ruin her, no matter how hard they tried.

But the reality now was that she was stuck here and she had a sick feeling in her stomach. She hoped she wouldn't throw up. That would just piss Daddy off more.

She came out of the tent. Daddy lurched past her and went in and you could hear his heavy breathing and see his shoulders and head bumping the top of the tent as he put on a sweater.

He came back out and put the hamburgers—three of them—in a frying pan on the Coleman stove. Then, slowly and painstakingly, he opened a can of pork and beans, swearing about the inefficient camping can opener. He finally got the can half-opened, and through the jagged half he'd gotten through, poured the beans into the old camping pan and put them on the stove. "You can have beans for dinner, Moira," he said. "If you don't like the god-damned food I make, then you can eat beans. I'm sick and tired of your complaints, sick and tired of you thinking you're something special around here."

"I didn't say I wouldn't eat it," Moira said quietly. "I just said I don't like my hamburgers that way."

"Well, I'm not eating that crap," Mother said.

Daddy glowered at her, then went over and raised his hand and brought it down on Moira's thigh. It made a loud smack into the night, at odds with the laughter coming from other camps. "You'll eat what I say."

Moira glared at Daddy.

The onion smell filled the air. As the burgers cooked, lanterns came on and the sun faded and the air filled with a rather sudden darkness.

"Why don't you get off your butt and set the table, Eleanor," he said.

"Don't talk to me like that."

"Okay, let me put it another way. Why don't you get up off your lazy ass and make yourself useful."

"You put that bottle of booze away."

"Oh, is that what's bothering you?"

"Yeah, that's what's bothering me. Surprise."

"Oh really?" Daddy said in a polite, sugary tone. Then Daddy took the whiskey bottle, screwed the top on it, and put his arm way back. Then he hurled the whiskey bottle at the oak tree. It shattered and sent whiskey—admittedly not very much left—raining onto the ferns below.

Mother pushed up out of the aluminum chair, took Taryn's arm, and pulled her into the tent.

None of the other campers seemed to notice. Laughing and playing cards and drinking sodas and listening to radios, they were having too much fun to observe that the McPhersons weren't.

"Okay, Moira, you get a clean hamburger by default." He got a beer out of the cooler and opened it and then directed her to sit down at the aluminum table. He put hamburgers on their paper plates, and piles of beans. Moira had to eat the sickening hamburgers with Daddy alone. In the middle of the dinner, Daddy stood up and in a too-loud voice said, "Eleanor, are you eating?"

"No," she said from the tent. "In fact, I'm packing up. I'm going back to Sioux Falls."

"That's what you think," Daddy muttered. He took the last bite of his hamburger, got up and fumbled around noisily in the dark for his car keys, and went and got in the car. In a frenzy of sand and gravel he spun off into the dark.

As they were laying out the air mattresses and shaking the sand out of blankets, they heard Daddy pull up in the station wagon. The door closed and he came into the tent. He had a paper bag with a large bottle in it.

They lay down on the mattresses. But Daddy didn't want to sleep. He stumbled around in the dark, narrowly missing stepping on Moira, and lit the Coleman lantern. His air mattress and blankets were over by the door, as far away from Mother as she'd been able to get them.

He unscrewed the bottle and took a sip. Some of it had already been drunk.

"What are you going to do now, Eleanor?" Daddy said.

"I'm going to stay in this tent and sleep, then I'm getting up in the morning and calling a lawyer. You can drink the whole quart for all I care."

Daddy burst into laughter. "That's how much you know—it's not a goddamn quart, it's a fifth."

"Drink a whole gallon, for all I care," Mother said. "Drink a lakeful of it."

Daddy sat up drinking for another hour or so. They all lay still in the tent, not moving a muscle. You could hear faint laughter from the tents of other campers. Moira heard a car go by—it must have been the convertible—and the radio softly playing Elvis. Her arms and legs began to ache from not moving. There was sand grinding into her sunburn. But she would survive the night if she lay very still. She was a cowboy with Indians surrounding the tent, she was a wild deer with wolves sniffing her out in the woods.

Daddy got up, lurched drunkenly against the sides of the tent, then went outside. Moira heard him pissing against a tree. Then he came back in and tripped over the stove. It went out. He didn't bother with his sleeping bag and lay down next to Moira on the tent floor and pulled a blanket over himself. His snorty breathing ruffled her hair. Soon the smell of whiskey and onions took over her entire air space. Moira lay trying not to breathe herself so he wouldn't wake up. She accidentally twitched and bumped him.

But he didn't move. Probably Daddy had passed out. No fireworks display this time.

Moira took her blanket and silently sneaked out of the tent. With the quiet of a wood-savvy animal, she opened the door to the station wagon and got in. Now the night opened up to her. Crickets beat the air with their optimistic noise, the occasional owl hooted from the woods.

Moira listened to nature, remembered Paul Whitefeather, wondered where he was tonight. Would he ever come back into her life? Her soulmate, her renegade friend?

Somehow she knew that it wouldn't be for a long time. Maybe she would marry Paul Whitefeather. Until then, she'd have to make do.

Music, as if from a million miles away, came through the heavy night air. There was life, even happiness and love, a million miles away. Maybe it would come to her.

But it wasn't a million miles away now. It was just down the road. She sat up, hugging her kerosene-smelling army blanket around her, and saw car lights bounding over the road. The car caught her in its lights, came over, and stopped. It was the yellow convertible.

"Wanna go for a ride?" the boy inside said.

She got out of the station wagon, left the door open, and went around the glare of lights to see who was in the car. It was the boy who before had been in the back seat. He wasn't laughing or leering or anything, just looking at her as if she was a normal girl. Maybe he liked her.

She tiptoed on her bare feet back to the station wagon, took great pains to close the door without making a sound, and tiptoed back over to the convertible. Without a word, she got in.

They drove along the cold, black lake, the wind in their hair. Elvis sang on the radio again. The boy pulled over to a small parking area facing the lake. With the lap-lap sounds in the background, the boy kissed her neck, ran his chin along the edge of her ear.

With a long kiss her stomach dipped and he put his hand on top of one breast. She wanted him to touch it. His hand went down slowly, asking if it was okay. It was okay and she wanted more. He rubbed her nipple lightly in his big, calloused, boy hand, then opened his shirt and rubbed her breast against his chest.

There was a wet pulsing between her legs. Was that an orgasm?

She forgot all about Daddy and Mother and Taryn. This would help her survive. Sex would help her survive this horrible family. Oh, kissing, touching, that handsome face so nice and kind to her. Oh, it felt so good. He ran his fingers ever so lightly along the insides of her thighs. The rest of her body was forgotten by this one area of her body. There was no reason to be sad and depressed and miserable and alone. There was something she could do that would make her feel good. And make her feel wanted or at least desired.

They climbed into the back seat and he helped her take off her shorts and pants. He took off his pants, and then they did it.

It hurt. Then she went numb.

Moira had found an escape from her life. And as she lay there thinking about what fun she'd just had, she felt a little less ashamed.

And everyone else in Moira's family could spend all their time trying to figure out the secret of being normal. But not Moira. Not anymore. She didn't care about being normal and average. She knew she could never aspire that high. She was going to have to make the leap from oddball to—well, she wasn't sure to what.

Because Moira knew that no way was she ever going to fit in the way Mother wanted them to. Mother and Daddy were raising a couple of kids in an oddball household and then telling them to go out and become normal people. Not just normal, but average. Super average. Right smack in the middle—home economics teachers. That may have been okay for Taryn, who was always trying to please Mother and Daddy, but not for Moira. Her brain worked differently from other people's, from nice happy average people's.

And if Moira had to be an oddball, which seemed inevitable, then she was going to be her own kind of oddball. And Taryn and the rest of them could go on pretending that with a thin coat of normal paint on the outside they could pass, but Moira knew that wasn't true.

The unknown boy drove her back to their campsite. He kissed her goodnight. Without a sound, she got back into the family station wagon. She wrapped her sweater around her and prayed to God to forgive her. When she felt that forgiveness from Him that she'd never get from anyone else, she fell asleep.

She woke up to the sound of birds and crickets. The sun was throwing orange wiggling light onto the lake and then coming up itself, big and red.

She inhaled the piney air and felt optimism surge through her veins. She wasn't ugly. She was maybe even pretty. And she had a beautiful body that boys loved. And she had her wits. And she had something else—she had a sense of wanting to do something good for the world. That would be her life. And all of those things—sex, God, school, and goodness—were going to get her through life.

Her family life might be hell, but there was a whole big world bursting with a million more sunrises in her life, and if she just bided her time and kept her sanity—she'd be okay. The wind rusting the riotously light-dappled leaves of pines whispered *Everything will be okay, Moira, everything is going to be okay if you just listen to me and not to your family.*

The next morning, the McPhersons packed up and returned to Sioux Falls.

Thirteen

Moira's penny loafers silently headed down the empty hallway toward biology lab.

She loved the school early in the morning before anyone else was there. It was the best time to work on her biology project.

But before she could do anything, she had to fix her face and change her clothes.

Moira had begun to study the beautiful women on TV. How they applied their makeup. The kinds of dresses they wore.

Into the empty girls' room. In the air were dusty old heating pipes, girls' illegal smoking from yesterday, and her own loneliness. And that naked face in the rust-spotted mirror.

Somewhere in her oversized purse was a bottle of Cover Girl Ivory makeup. She shook it, took off the cap, poured a good amount into the palm of her hand. She rubbed it all over her face, enjoying the slightly antiseptic Noxzema smell that meant she was cleaning the old, lonely Moira McPherson off her face.

She found her powder and dusted it on. Her face looked a little orangy but smooth.

Then contour powder. Under the cheekbones, around the forehead to make it more oval—the perfect shape, according to all the magazines. White undereye cream to get rid of premature bags. Then green eyeshadow on lids, iridescent yellow highlighter above that. As a contrast, shiny black liquid eyeliner, a thick, smooth line next to upper eyelashes. Now black eyebrow pencil in a thick line underneath her lower lashes. Next, green eyeliner inside the lower rims of her eyes. They glowed like a cat's in the dark. Two coats of mascara and finally, pinky-white iridescent lipstick.

There. Now she looked like someone new.

Out of her purse came clothes. She took off her A-line skirt and white blouse and put on a slinky iridescent green dress slit high up the back. Next, into a stall to stand on the toilet and look at her figure. She was beginning to lose her baby fat. Her waist was beginning to turn in above her hips. She turned around three-quarters to see how her rear looked. Like a four-leaf clover.

And now for the pièce de resistance—her hair. She ratted and teased and sprayed, let it dry, then ratted some more, let it dry, then when it felt like barbedwire, she backcombed it again and smoothed the top over slightly, then sprayed until it felt as if it had been glued in place.

She was going to dye it maybe. Dye it black. Then she'd have someone else's hair, too.

Kicking off the clunky loafers, she dug pointy-toed flats out of her purse and put them on. She smiled at her pretty new someone else's face in the mirror, and went out down the empty hall to the biology lab.

Fourteen

It was an autumn day out of a dream. The leaves were dry and smoky; good-smelling stuff crackled out when you walked on them. The sun seemed to be doing a dance with antique veils, shifting the light in different curtains of yellow and white. The air on her bare arms felt like a beautiful sweet tune in her ears, like sugar dissolved on a hungry tongue.

Moira could feel every nerve in her body. She was so alive, so happy to be a part of this earth. People were scary, but nature, science—they were friendly. Her saviors.

Everything is going to be okay, the gentle, silk-gloved wind whispered to Moira just as it had long ago when she came out with Paul Whitefeather to the woods and to the prairie. *Everything is going to be all right if you listen to me, if you pay attention to me.*

What was it? Where did all this happiness come from? The beauty of the world? Nature? It just wasn't fair to the rest of the world—Moira didn't deserve to have all the happiness the trees and good-smelling, soothing earth had to offer. Yes, in the long run, the breeze told her, everything was going to be okay.

Today things were going to be more than okay with just nature. Today things were going to be okay with real people. In fact they were going to be downright exciting, because she was meeting Gary Racer to collect leaves for a biology assignment.

Moira saw a chestnut tree and jumped up to grab a branch. She held it, inhaling the good smell of autumn. Gently, so as not to disturb the rest of the branch, she twisted off a couple of leaves. She loved biology, all aspects of it—field work like this, as well as the lab and the reading and the problems. Earlier that day Mr. Bailey had said she was destined to become a scientist of some sort. "You're creative enough to be in research science," he'd said in his cultured, tenor voice. The boys at school said he was homosexual.

They always made loud expressions of alarm at the thought of his approaching them to help with their projects. No one had ever reported being bothered for real by Mr. Bailey, but they all made fun of him anyway.

They made fun of Moira, too, for her braininess. Mr. Bailey said her brain would take her a long way in life.

Mother and Daddy always told her to be realistic. "My parents want me to be a home ec teacher," Moira told Mr. Bailey.

Mr. Bailey had stroked his tiny beard and stared at her. "I recommend teaching, as well. I happen to think it's a noble calling. One good teacher in a student's lifetime can make a difference. But is that really what you want to do?"

"That's just it, I don't know," Moira had said. "I start giggling when I have to get up in front of classes and give book reports. And I'm not sure I have patience with people who don't understand what I understand. And I can't see myself teaching home ec—I'm not neat and dainty enough."

He bent over and helped her adjust her microscope. "Then do what you want, Moira. You can be anything you want. Even a doctor." He'd stood up and patted her on the shoulder of her lab coat. "You'd make a good doctor, come to think of it. You're bright, and you have a heart."

Moira had blushed. Having her soul bared and examined was almost more embarrassing than having the body laid bare and examined with sideways glances in gym class showers.

"Maybe one day you'll come up with a cure for cancer," he said. "Fight evil with good works."

Fight evil with good. And Moira had seen so much evil that she was going to be good at fighting it. But all that aside, what an incredible thought—doing something wonderful for the world so that maybe the world would start loving you! And if the world loved Moira, would her family love her then too?

She rather doubted that, but again the idea of helping sick people gave her a feeling of calm and strength the way it had in the biology room, as she paused at the edge of the woods by the river to look for Gary Racer. Maybe while they looked for the silver maples and the white birches and the red oaks she could talk to Gary about it, see if he felt the same way, that life had to be dedicated to something to be meaningful.

A tickle ran through her when she thought of Gary and how good-looking he was. The only way she had caught him, she had to admit, was because he had his leg in that cast from his motorcycle accident.

She found a locust tree and looked for a specimen for herself and one for Gary. The thrill ran through her like a cold slippery gel as she remembered how he'd stopped suddenly while they were coming out of biology class. Gary had settled onto the one crutch and reached out with his free hand and touched her shoulder. "You got notes I can borrow?" he had said. "My old man says if I flunk biology again he's gonna kick me out of the house."

Her hands had shook as she pulled out her carefully written, thorough notes. She was almost unable to speak, she was so shy with him. Silently, she held them out to him. He took them and looked them over as if he were counting long overdue money she owed him and was now paying back.

He tucked her notes under his arm. He looked her up and down and said, "I got an idea. You gonna go collect them leafs we gotta do?"

She had said yes, that she was going that afternoon, in fact.

"Wanna go together? I don't know all that shit. Man, I can't tell a—what was that crap he was saying today?—a coniferous tree from a Christmas tree."

Moira had had the impulse to laugh so he'd know she got the joke, but then she wasn't absolutely positive he knew it was a joke. She didn't want to do anything wrong around Gary; he was unanimously agreed to be the best-looking of all the greaser guys in school but was always seen around with his girlfriend, Doris Bronwin. Doris had been riding on the back of his motorcycle when he had the accident, and was at home recovering from an arm injury.

"Doris is pissed at me and gave my ring back," he had said, showing her the class ring on his finger. Moira had thought of how that big ring would look bouncing on a chain between her own breasts. She had wondered if Gary was thinking the same thing.

*   *   *

As she looked up the orange-and-yellow-dappled path for Gary, Moira's heart pounded so hard in her ears that now she couldn't hear the wind or feel the beauty of the day. If he stood her up, she'd feel like a complete fool.

As Moira waited she tried not to compare herself with Doris. Last year, Doris had been voted the girl with the prettiest eyes in school. Those eyes were light green with eyelashes the color of daddy-longleg spiders, and they reached all the way to her eyebrows. Moira would never forget how she'd seen those eyes up close once. It was when Doris was a gym captain picking her team. Moira had been, as usual, the last one standing. Darlene had rolled her prettiest-in-the-school eyes and gone up to Moira's face close and said, "Okay, out of all the possibilities, I pick Moira." That had gotten a laugh from the other girls as well as from the gym teacher.

What if he was standing her up? Telling people how he had agreed to meet in the woods, then left her standing? Moira could see the boys, Darlene, the gym teacher, everyone in school, laughing.

But no, here came Gary Racer along the edge of the river, swinging back and forth on his crutches, a transistor radio with the earpiece in his ear, a blanket, and no leaf identification book.

Fortunately, Moira had brought hers.

He half-smiled when he saw her and stared straight at her breasts. Suddenly she was uneasy; did she really like him all that much? He was bigger than the other sophomores, so big, too big. And now that he was standing in front of her, chewing his gum and nodding his head to his own private music and spotlighted by nature's light, she could see his pimples and how at odds they were with his strangely soft and jowly fifteen-year-old face.

But she didn't want to be confused, it was too beautiful an autumn day, so she reminded herself that he *was* tall, and he *did* have a cleft chin, and he *did* wear his hair all swooped up in a perfect D.A. with a fancy flip in front that made it look like he was wearing a great big rose at the top of his face. And, she also reminded herself, the girl with the most beautiful eyes in school used to love him.

"Let's go, baby," he said, nodding toward the path. He didn't take the radio earphone out. They began walking slowly. She couldn't think of anything to say, and he didn't seem interested in talking much. They went in silence along the path, he on his crutches with the transistor radio dangling out of his pocket and humming to the music, Moira with her leaf identification guide and a bag to put the leaves in.

She saw a group of sugar maples and pointed it out.

He didn't look.

"Should we get some leaf specimens?"

"Huh?" he said, taking the earpiece out.

"Sugar maples."

"Forget it. We'll get leaves later. I need to rest," he said in a loud voice, still listening to the radio.

So they sat down on a little clearing on a hill. Autumn leaves rustled and shook some sparkles of sunlight on them. There were patches of sunlight on the leaf-covered ground, and the air above those spots seemed to have rising little particles of light emanating from them, as if they were part of some holy shrine, like something important happened in this spot once, an animal was born or died, an Indian sat and found God, a pioneer ate his first meal in a week, or maybe just a little wildflower germinated and grew and blossomed and died there.

"I got you a honey locust specimen," she said, and took it out of her bag and gave it to him.

He twisted it around absently and chewed his gum.

"Do you live nearby?" Moira asked, desperate to keep a conversation going for fear he'd get up on his crutches and walk away without saying goodbye.

"Huh?" he shouted, and took off the radio earpiece.

She asked again.

"Naw," he said, putting the honey locust branch on the ground with a bunch of other broken branches and leaves. He took out a cigarette and then shook the pack in her general direction until a couple of cigarettes stuck out. She took one, even though Daddy had told her he'd shove her teeth down her throat if he ever saw nicotine stains on them. He lit his, then hers.

"Where, uh, do you live?" Anything to make conversation.

"North Prairie Street."

"I live on Boxelder Court East."

"No shit." He looked down at Moira, not smiling.

She tried to look confident and alert and told herself that he was being attentive in his own way. "It's a nice street."

"Yeah? That's cool," he said, stretching and looking around behind him.

She fumbled for another topic. The teen magazines said to ask boys questions about themselves. She asked Gary what he wanted to do when he was out of school. He said he might want to be a motorcycle mechanic. Moira said that sounded interesting because aptitude tests showed that she also had mechanical ability.

"Yeah, man, maybe you'll be a mechanic, too, huh?" he said, almost smiling. "The world's first chick mechanic. Man, I'd like to see you bending over my engine in a pair of short shorts."

She imagined Mr. Bailey knowing she'd collected leaves with Gary Racer. She felt as if she were betraying Mr. Bailey by having agreed to work with Gary.

Moira said that Mr. Bailey thought she could be a doctor. "Can you imagine finding a cure for cancer?" For a moment, Gary looked at her as if she'd said something almost interesting, but then he tore off a long piece of grass and put it in his mouth to suck on and looked around again, bored.

"How do you like Mr. Bailey?"

"Bitch Bailey? Old Worm Lips? Hey, I hear he sucks off them worms before we gotta dissect 'em."

Moira could feel her face blaze red as Gary laughed. "I think he's nice," she said. Mr. Bailey gave Moira projects that would help her win the city and statewide contests, got her a job as lab assistant so she could start saving money for college in case she decided to go to a better one than the one her parents wanted to send her to. She liked Mr. Bailey a lot, even though she knew the general opinion of the student body more closely matched Gary's than her own.

So she tried to make herself look down on Mr. Bailey. To feel contempt for him. But the only person she could feel contempt for was herself.

Gary put his arm around her, but she was out of the mood for romance. If she had had fantasies of kissing Gary, dancing with him at a sock hop, having that class ring that Darlene had always worn, even in gym class, those fantasies had gotten lost somewhere between the cold brick school and the delicate chatter of the wind overhead in the autumn leaves.

But it did seem she was at some point of no return. If she didn't let him kiss her, it would mean she had been duped into this whole expedition. She would seem stupid, like someone who didn't know the rules, didn't know what the cool kids did.

His fingers did a little dance on her hair, then he put a finger in her ear, barely touching the tiny hairs in it. She felt a tickle, a chill. He bent his face down and gave her his famous smile. He *was* sexy. Now his mouth was on the side of her neck, taking little pretend bites out of it, and then in the part just above her collarbone. It felt good. Maybe she did like him after all. Maybe she even loved him. And he was acting as if he loved her. He wasn't very articulate. Maybe he was just shy, that was why he didn't talk to her much.

He caressed the inside of her arm, lightly, almost as if he were a gentle breeze. "I like you a lot, Moira. I've been noticin' ya for a long time. You're real cute without them glasses on. You're really stacked, you know? You've got a real shape, a real set there."

Handsome Gary Racer whom girls were dying to go out with was saying these things to her. He kissed ever so lightly along the side of her neck again and her nipples went painfully erect and she moaned and fell to the ground like a rabbit whose jugular is in the mouth of a fox.

Now she wanted to make out with Gary Racer more than anything. It felt so good, so awfully good. It was so obvious now why Mother and Daddy had been so worried about this. It could be addictive.

Now his fingers were running along her neck and it felt so awfully good some more. It made everyone—Mother and Daddy and the kids laughing at school—insignificant. And if kisses with Gary —someone she didn't even like very much—were this good, what were they like with someone you *did* like?

Oh, if kisses were this good with him, she had to know the rest.

Still kissing her, he reached and fumbled with his transistor radio, yanking out the earphone. The Paris Sisters cooed out a song from two years ago when Moira had been so lonely watching the prom party across the street. "I Love How You Love Me."

Maybe she was going to be like the other kids, other kids who were starting to go steady. Maybe this was how it started. Maybe Gary loved her.

If Gary loved her, maybe she was wrong about not liking him. Maybe she loved him too. Maybe Gary loved her, wanted her, thought she was important, important enough to come out to the woods with, attractive enough to want to make out with. She felt more important than she ever had topping the honor roll. Now Gary was kissing her mouth with loose, wet lips. She was so weak she knew what dying was like. And then he was on top of her, rubbing his pants against her, and then his hand was on the edge of her breast.

She cried out because the feeling was so good it shocked her. He pulled her sweater up to expose her bra, then pushed up her bra above her breasts. The radio played "Hey Paula." Moira saw the couples on "American Bandstand," kids holding each other, gazing into one another's eyes. She saw the girls' long swish of skirts, their thick legs over bobby socks, the boys' swept-up hair and hungry expressions.

And then she remembered that her bra had brown underarm stains like rust because she'd been wearing it for a whole year now. But he didn't seem to notice the stains, and when he saw her breasts pushing up and part of them spilling over the sides onto her ribs, he whispered, "Jesus fucking Christ, willya lookit this," and for the first time in her life she was glad they were growing so big. So she just lay there feeling his eyes on her nipples, feeling embarrassed and feeling pleasure at the same time. And he kissed her nipples and she had that same feeling at the quick point between her legs, the way she'd had when she was fucking the air, and the same way she felt when Daddy slapped the inside of her thigh.

She became aroused again, aware of the wetness in her pants, and she cried, cried because girls aren't supposed to come, not until they're married, and she cried because she was ugly and she cried because Daddy and Mother didn't love her enough. Then she cried as he blew on her nipples. It felt like he was blowing fire on them, and she cried some more because she liked it so much and when he licked and kissed them she cried and cried and cried because girls weren't supposed to like this and she liked it.

And then Gary was rubbing against her and breathing hard and she felt happiness, she felt in control, and she put her hand on his hair and ran her fingers through it, and her hand came out smelling like the leftover french fry grease Mother kept in the refrigerator to use over and over again. He rubbed and rubbed and reminded her of a locomotive going up a hill, and he rubbed crazily and yelled and bit into one of her breasts and it hurt and she screamed.

Then he was fumbling with her slacks, her one pair of pegged black pants she'd hoped he thought she looked cool in, and he got the side zipper down, then tugged at them, Moira lifting her hips to help them slide down.

Jerkily, he put his hand inside her pants and stuck his fingers inside her. He pushed and pulled out and it didn't feel good but she was afraid to say anything. Saying anything would make her a fool somehow.

And then he put her hand on his crotch and rubbed against her hand. He rubbed harder and harder and harder and harder. The zipper scraped her wrist. Anger tried to seep into her throbbing blood, but she wouldn't admit it because then maybe what she was doing would be wrong.

Twitching like someone with palsy in his excitement, Gary undid the snap of his pants and unzipped them and reached down and she felt his thing probing, then swiftly, rather expertly, he stuck it in her.

It was so big. Was it supposed to be this big? How old was Gary? It repulsed her and it also felt good, exciting, dirty, wrong, exquisite. He pushed a couple of times and then rammed her deep and yelled out and then collapsed onto her, sweating and breathing deep into his too-big, too-old-for-his-age chest.

He lay there panting, his face looking away from her, for a few minutes. Moira lay very, very still. She had done it again. Had it been worth it? Those few moments of pleasure? But then that wasn't the point. There almost was no choice anymore. If she wanted to escape the horror—yes, the horror—of her home, this was the escape. She didn't know of any others. Algebra wasn't enough anymore.

There was a sticky mess on her stomach, just above her pubic hair. She had done it. Again. Gone all the way with Gary Racer. It was a little like murder. No going back. And so what if this was the second time? They could only hang you once, right?

But maybe she was exaggerating the importance of all this. Maybe she was feeling guilty for nothing. In fact, maybe this was a major step in her relationship with Gary. Did this change everything for him? Did he love her? Would he ask her to go steady? If so, why did she have this feeling in her stomach like she'd swallowed a million gallons of just-cried tears?

He grunted and pushed himself up to a sitting position. With difficulty, because of his leg, he pulled his pants back up. All of a sudden it was cold. Moira turned away from him and pulled her bra and sweater down and her pants up.

Gary looked off in the distance, chewing his gum again, then looked at his crutches. "I better go," he said, still not meeting her eyes. "I gotta catch a bus."

Moira helped him with his crutches. Her teeth were chattering and she didn't know if it was because of what had just happened or if it was because the sun had gone down and there was a mean chill in the air now. The gluey cold in her pants was unbearable if she thought about it. She couldn't stand to think about it, so she'd pretend nothing had happened.

As they walked back to the bus stop, she smiled and raised her eyebrows in a confident way. She kept trying to say things, light things, nothing-happened things, but her throat was froggy. She kept clearing it and finally as they got to the street she was able to say, "Do you know when you'll be done with my biology notes? I need them for the test."

He looked at her as if she were asking about something that had happened ten years ago, then said, "I dunno. I can't even remember where I put them."

Something was wrong. Something was very wrong.

But maybe it was just her. Oh, she wished she had someone to ask about this. She tried again, something gay and light. "What's your favorite song?"

"Huh? I don't know, honey," he said, looking down the tracks. "I gotta go now."

She waited for a moment. "You're going home?"

He kept looking down the street for the bus. "Nah. Over to Doris's."

A panic grabbed her throat. She inhaled in short little breaths. "I thought you broke up, that you weren't steadies anymore."

He shrugged. "We got back together. I just called her before I came over here."

She swallowed. "Are we . . . are we going out again?"

He turned and looked down at her as if he'd forgotten she was there. His face was jowly, square. The rose shape at the front of his hair was lopsided now. "Wanna meet me here next week? I didn't bring no protection this week. I can bring a rubber next time."

She looked down at her empty leaf sack. She didn't know what she should do, what she should say. "Maybe." Having a guy like you this way was better than no one liking you, wasn't it? Wasn't it?

She laughed and waved and walked off, trying to look dignified, like she knew what she was doing, like she had meant to do this, like it was no big deal.

And she kept from crying all the way home. She actually kept from crying, you had to hand that to her.

That night, when Taryn went out to a friend's house and Mother went to bed in her room to stare at the white walls, Moira thought about what she had done.

It had been exciting. The physical thrill had been intense, almost unbelievably pleasurable.

The aftermath, the hangover, was something else.

Yes, something had gone wrong.

Moira lay in bed praying that God wouldn't make her like sex and that he'd make her beautiful and normal like everyone else, with a thin little figure and straight blond hair and a burning desire to become a home-economics teacher and not a doctor or a scientist.

Sometime late at night she opened her eyes and Daddy was standing in her bedroom doorway, his arms up on the frame, his legs out for balance. His half-opened eyes and sweating red face told her he was drunk.

Did he know somehow about Gary Racer? Is that why he'd gotten drunk tonight? Was this all her fault?

He filled the frame of the doorway like a big X, his posture like one of those characters in the superhero comic books. She could hear his loud breathing. She lay almost not breathing, careful not to move, like a rabbit playing dead.

If she didn't move, he'd go away.

At times in the past when he'd done this, she had rolled over, scratched her nose, moved her feet, and he'd come in the room closer and stood over her bed breathing loudly, smelling of beer or whiskey, his movements jerky, unpredictable. He'd stand there, looking out her window for a long time—she had no idea if it was hours or minutes—the belt of his pants sticking out in front where he hadn't looped it back in. He'd look out her window, breathing loudly, snorting as he stood there with his strong arms that used to hit hockey pucks and catch passes from the quarterback and that now lugged the weight of the sporting goods sample trunk around. Then, finally, he'd leave the room, and she'd break out into a cool, thin sweat of relief.

Was he going to leave this time? Through the slits of her eyes, she saw him staring at her. His breathing was raspy and strong and the sweet-sour whiskey smell took over the room. She felt like screaming out. The heavy breathing was almost the worst thing. She kept her eyes open just a bit, careful not to close them all the way or the movement might let him know they'd been open and she was awake.

He could have been the devil from hell, the way the hallway back-lit him in an orangy yellow.

Finally he took the doorknob and drew the door shut, and she heard his heavy, staggering, drunken footsteps down the hallway.

What had she done to make him so mad at her? Did he somehow know about what she had done with that boy at the beach? With Gary Racer? Did he know what she was like?

She dreamed that night that she and Daddy were friends again. That she was a little more grownup, and he had taken her to one of those cocktail bars.

Her legs were crossed. She wore black fishnet hose and high heels with ankle straps that accented the slimness of her ankles, the length of her legs.

Daddy asked if she would like a martini. She smiled flirtatiously, and in her dream she was beautiful, with a regulation beauty magazine oval face and big eyes and perfect Revlon lips. Daddy smiled at her with his black-fringed eyes and said, "It's time we stopped playing around. It's time we got down to it, stopped pretending something's not there when it is."

"Yes, Daddy, whatever you say, Daddy." And her body began to melt and her legs opened up for him to see.

She woke up with a throbbing between her legs.

No. To hell with it, she thought. She'd find more boys to go out and have fun with. Otherwise, living in this household, she'd go insane.

Fifteen

DORIS MUST HAVE found out about what Moira and Gary did in the woods, because Doris's daddy-longleg eyes followed her in wonder, as if to demand how Moira could do something like this to someone like her, someone with such pretty eyes.

The word, in fact, must have been all over the school, because now instead of ignoring Moira for no good reason, people were whispering around her. Their gazes, in fact, carried a bit of awe, as if Moira were a dog that had gone mad and attacked a human and could do so again at any moment. They'd look at her with wonder, then they would turn away again, condemning the mad dog to the pound and its gas chamber.

Although admittedly not *everyone* turned away immediately. Some people smiled at each other first. With some people she was a joke. Maybe being a joke was better than being invisible.

But even though she had goals in life, wanted to be respected, sometimes she thought maybe she preferred the mad-dog image, at least for now. It certainly seemed to draw attention from the boys. Now the boys talked to her, talked to her a lot. They talked to her in packs, though, never alone, calling out to her from groups, sniffing around her, inviting her to walk with them, talk with them, joke with them.

She was a sophomore now and boys liked her a lot. The hangover from Gary Racer was still in her head, but so was the pleasure. Pleasure sometimes has a louder voice than pain, and she was ready for fun and love and excitement again. Sex could be a wonderful distraction from unhappy circumstances. She must be wild. Sexy. Irresistible. Was it possible that Mother was wrong, that Moira was indeed attractive?

It was very confusing.

* * *

Artie Ballenger, a junior who told her he liked younger women, offered Moira a ride home one afternoon in his father's new four-on-the-floor Pontiac. The way he was looking at her made her feel beautiful. She was important. People wanted her. Actually wanted her, admired her, wanted to do something to please her.

Artie drag-raced around Jerry's Drive-In with her, then headed down to a field by the river. They made out in the Pontiac, the vinyl seats creaking noisily under them until they were both panting. He reached under her blouse and Moira fell helpless back against the gearshift. He sucked her breasts, first one, then the other, then back to the first one, then he did it to her, jamming into her and rocking her back and forth against the car door as she pretended vaguely to be fighting him off and then losing. Moira pretended that she'd been forced, that she was like a dying rabbit and limply giving in to her fate. But she was really enjoying it.

Sex was so much fun. How did other people resist it?

But afterwards he drove her home in silence and didn't look at her anymore. She went to her room and lay in bed trying not to feel anything, staring up at the light on the ceiling.

And then Vern Horister offered to walk her home, carried her books, and even bought her a milkshake. At least she had some value. She was worth a milkshake.

They went down to the river and he put his hands on her bottom and pulled her up close to him and rubbed his hard bump against her. After a few minutes, she pulled away and they kissed and he stuck his fingers under her pants before she wriggled away and she ran home, not knowing why she'd come there with him in the first place, and not knowing why she was running away.

Maybe it was because she wanted to reform. Was that it? To become a nice, normal girl?

If that was the reason, it didn't last long. The next day, she let him walk her home again. This time, they went all the way. Out by Hinkley's farm in a grove of trees with ants crawling on them and biting and with Moira on the bottom, the cold hard earth under her.

Boys hung around her in packs. With girls it was the opposite—cliques of girls would have nothing to do with her, but individually one might chat with her, especially if she needed to borrow class notes, or if she wanted an explanation of something she'd missed in class because she was part of the clique in the back of the room that was too busy passing notes and whispering to hear the teacher.

Like the other nice girls at school, Taryn now steered a path around Moira, too. At home, Taryn seldom spoke to Moira, and Moira often noticed the exchange of eyebrows between Taryn and Mother when Moira came into a room.

It would be more fun to be one of those girls like Judy Riley, who wore a different expensive outfit every day and had golden skin and golden hair and was head cheerleader and class secretary and who lived in a big sprawling ranch house that the school bus stopped right in front of instead of on the corner, as if her parents had paid off the bus driver just to show off.

It would have been really nice to be like Judy, but she wasn't. She hadn't gotten the same cards in life.

But if Moira had to be the class slut, it was better than being the class weirdo-egghead-Coke-bottle-glasses loser.

And all she could say was, two years ago nobody in the entire world would have given you two cents for Moira, and now she was one of the most noticeable students at North Prairie High School.

Sixteen

Mr. Smealz was the most respected teacher at North Prairie High. Not the most liked, because he was so strict, but the most respected, by students and parents alike.

All the worse for Moira, who sat in his office on the second day of her junior year, her back hunched in shame, her face down in confusion because she wasn't exactly sure what she had done wrong, what he was driving at.

"Young lady, sometimes I think you're asking for trouble. Do you know what your reputation is around this school?"

Moira didn't say anything, just continued to look at her lap. If she just pretended she was walking through a beautiful meadow, she could forget she was here.

"Yes, you have a reputation as a very loose young lady." He let that sink in, then said, "Can you tell me again why you're wearing that blouse?" he said. His voice had gone razor-sharp. She was so nervous she felt like laughing anyway to release the tension, and now that he'd called her sweater a blouse, she couldn't help it—she burst into frantically nervous snickering.

"Oh, it's funny is it?"

She looked back down, covering her mouth with the back of her hand. He wouldn't understand why she wore the sweater. Or be sympathetic. Any more than he would be sympathetic about why she sometimes ended up at school wearing two different shoes. The reasons were different—the sweater was tight and sexy and bright red to fool people into thinking she was attractive, the shoes sometimes didn't match because she had terrible eyesight without her glasses and she was always thinking about something more interesting when she was getting dressed on cold, dark school mornings.

"And look at me, young lady, when I'm speaking to you."

She looked up. He was so very thin that his cheekbones came to points under his eyes. When he smiled or looked like he was trying to figure something out, the flesh over the cheekbones rose like a cat's. He had those thick lashes like Daddy's, and when she looked into his eyes she got confused.

But she couldn't look for long and hung her head again. "I don't know."

Couldn't she just die and get it over with? Couldn't God just reach down with his big hand and scoop her up? But no, that wasn't going to happen, God put you through all this for a reason, to see how much you could take. Like the Sioux Indians with their sun rituals, cutting holes in their skin and tying themselves to a pole with a leather throng and standing in the sun in pain. Well, people took a lot in this world, and if it wasn't self-inflicted it was nature or other-human-inflicted, and if you thought what people put each other through in civilized society and then thought about what they did in the past or today in other countries, like killing female babies and cutting the fingers off thieves, you saw that things were the same, only in civilized places the misery was likely to be mental rather than physical. And once you were a grownup, you had a chance to defend yourself. She was going to college, and she was going to have to bide her time, this year, then one more school year, then she wouldn't have to come back to this awful place, this horrible school, ever.

"Don't know, huh?"

His voice had changed a little bit, and she could tell he was ready to shift gears.

She shook her head. Please God, just get me out of this room. I'll never sew up the sides of my clothes again to look like the ladies on TV. I'll never try to be beautiful, I'll never try to be loved. I'll be ugly and horrible and accept being ugly and horrible.

"You're cute, you know that?"

Moira stopped squeezing her arms. She looked up. There was a slight twitching under one of those cheekbones. Had she heard right? Did he call her cute? Only yesterday Mother had told Moira, again, that her eyes were too small and her nose too flat and she'd never get a man with those wide feet of hers.

"And you know it. A very pretty little girl, too pretty for her own good, who's going to get herself into trouble someday."

Moira's face went hot. Why was he saying this? She wasn't pretty. Boys just wanted her for her big breasts, because she was easy, because she was a sex maniac.

But Mr. Smealz was the best teacher in the school. Whatever he said was true, wasn't it?

"Do you know what wearing those provocative clothes does to boys?"

Moira shook her head.

"To men?"

His voice had shifted gears again. She dared to look up. He was looking at her hard, but there was a softening, too, a softening she knew in the eyes of males. A softening that said they were saying one thing and thinking another. A softening that said she was special, that she had something special, and that maybe the rules changed when she was around.

"It puts them under your control."

Moira felt lightheaded.

"Stand up and let me look at that blouse again," he said, and that involuntary smile at his calling it a blouse came to her again and she could just picture herself telling Mother about him calling a sweater a blouse and Mother laughing at how dumb men were and saying something like, "Well, if I can't sew up the sides of my blouse, then is it okay if I just do it to a sweater?" Mother would laugh hilariously about it, then go off into her depressed fog, then later tell her it really was wrong of her to sew up her clothes to make them tight. Especially if you had bosoms the size of Moira's.

She stood up and stretched the involuntary smile into a look of meekness. He was looking at her breasts. A thrill stabbed her like a sword grittily coated with sweet, hardened sugar. She began to cry.

Mr. Smealz picked up the yardstick next to his desk. The yardstick was sort of Mr. Smealz's trademark. He used it to point to kids when he called on them in class and to tap on his desk when he was watching someone pass notes. He was forever breaking yardsticks over his desk suddenly, out of the blue. He'd be discussing the Crimean War, pointing at the map with the yardstick, then, wham, turn around in mid-sentence and whack, over the desk, and a good foot and a half of it would go flying and if you were in the first five rows or so, you'd better duck. He always told the class his favorite use for it was to whack boys in front of the class.

Was he going to whack her? She'd die. She'd feel like a boy.

He began to tap his hand with it as he swiveled back and forth in his chair. "Come here, Moira."

Moira walked over to him. She stopped crying. Now she was going to pay for being bad, so she wouldn't have to cry anymore. She stood next to Mr. Smealz. With the rule, he pointed at her left breast. "Much too tight, young lady. Much too tight."

Moira felt a stream of pleasure stabbing her abdomen. She looked at him, into his eyes. She had a grownup man's attention like no one would believe. He was bothered by her. He was enraged by her. His whole grownup, sanctified teacher's world was upset by her. When she stopped to think about it, she could be pretty important sometimes. Important enough to make a grownup, important, respected man like Mr. Smealz—a schoolteacher, the most revered person in the world to Mother and Daddy—angry. Spitting, red-faced angry. Angry so that his cheekbones sucked in underneath and made the points look like little pyramids.

The yardstick accidentally touched her breast, then her nipple. Her face felt hot, her nipple went erect. She sneaked a look at Mr. Smealz, hoping he hadn't noticed what had happened.

His tongue was flicking on his lower lip. He tapped her nipple with the yardstick again, and this time she could almost believe he did it on purpose. She felt heat all through her body. She felt that involuntary smile again. He tapped harder on her nipple. Then he tapped the other with his yardstick. Her hands reached up to cover her hard nipples.

She looked toward the door. He had locked it, but only to keep people out. She could run and scream if he tried to stop her. Someone would hear. But she was afraid to. All that anger of Daddy's, all that criticism of Mother's had made Moira want people to *like* her, not to get mad at her.

And Mr. Smealz seemed to like her. He reached his yardstick out and rubbed her nipple with it. It felt horrible and underneath it all it felt good, too. And then he groaned and began to sort of whimper. He was out of his swirling swivel chair and his hands were pulling up the "blouse" in question. Moira felt wet between her legs. His mouth was in her cleavage, his thumbs were rubbing her nipples. His crotch was rubbing her leg just below the knee.

He laid her back on his desk, and pulled her skirt up and kissed her thighs up near the elastic part of her pants. She felt humiliated, but the sensation was so strong she couldn't stop him. She heard jingling and rustling as he undid his belt and loosened the brown suit pants he wore almost every day. He fumbled with his shorts, and then he was on top of her.

Now she was frightened. She felt his thing, rubber with springs in it, and it bounced against the upper inside of her thigh, which was somehow more disgusting and maybe more pleasurable than if it was inside her.

"No, no," she said.

"It's okay," he said. "It's okay."

"No, don't. I don't want this."

"Just a minute. Hold still."

"Please, no."

"It'll be okay. It'll be over in a minute."

"No, you can't do this." She meant it and then again she didn't but then again she did. She really did. And he was the voice of authority, wasn't he? She wasn't supposed to argue with authority, was she? Oh God, she didn't know. She probably deserved this. She just didn't know. She could scream, call for help, but she didn't want to make a fuss. Everyone in school knew she was a slut anyway, so they'd find a way to blame her for this, and by the time she gave this horrible mess some thought, she'd probably think they were right.

She tried to wriggle away, but his hands grabbed her hips and he backed up a little to look at her.

"You little cockteaser," he said, then kissed her hard, his teeth grinding against hers. His pointed cheekbones were on her pudgy cheekbones, and they hurt. "You little slut. Do you know how long I wanted you, sitting in my class? Bitch, cunt."

And then he was putting his thing into her. She cried and he stuffed his handkerchief in her mouth and pushed and pushed and oh it felt so good, she couldn't help it, it felt good even though the whole thing could make her puke. Streams of warm tears washed down her cheeks, trying to wash the awfulness of this away.

And in the middle of it he stopped and grabbed his yardstick, and slapped her on the thighs, slapped her until she was crying and moaning, and then he went inside her again and again it felt so good. The tickly little hairs of his legs feathered over the part of her that had been slapped. And he banged and banged, and came out and turned her over and spanked her on the bottom with his yardstick, and turned her over and did it some more and then he chugged and chugged again like Gary Racer and that boy at the beach and all the others. Then he had a spasm and backed up and pushed it against her leg and then he howled and wet sticky white stuff came out and smeared all over his yardstick.

She couldn't believe it later. She felt the way someone must feel when he's killed another person in the heat of passion.

That night she tried to make her brain work the way a good girl's brain is supposed to work. Marriage. Maybe Mr. Smealz would marry her. Maybe he wanted to. Maybe he loved her. Wasn't that really what sex was all about? Love?

The next day, Mr. Smealz didn't look at her, just walked by her in the hallway. The day after that, she wore the "blouse" that he had been so interested in, but he still didn't look at her.

Seventeen

SHE LIKED IT BEST when Jack started out by slapping the insides of her thighs. He could work her into a frenzy by this slapping, then fucking her for a little bit, then turning her over and putting his finger in her ass and fucking her while she rubbed her legs together.

He'd turn her over and hold her hands up with one hand and her throat with the other. "Call me Daddy," he would say, and kiss her. "Say, 'Please slap me some more, Daddy.'"

She'd groan, "Slap me some more."

"Say 'Daddy.'"

"Daddy."

"Say the whole thing."

"Slap me some more, Daddy."

"Say 'Please.'"

"Please."

"Please what?"

"Please slap me some more, Daddy."

He'd slap, gently at first, hard, fast, mean slaps later, then when her skin was red, he'd take little tiny bites in the flushed skin. It would usually be enough to make her come without his ever having to touch her between the legs, as long as he pulled on her nipples at the same time and called her a whore and a slut.

She had won the statewide high school sophomore science competition and was invited to an awards ceremony over at Augustana College. There she met another science genius, Jack Locksmey, a classic nerd in every sense, and one who hated women. Just what Moira felt she deserved.

He was a nerd in every sense, except that he played basketball on the intramural teams and was tall. Everywhere.

Moira would let Jack know when Daddy was going to be out of town. He would call from his off-campus roominghouse, talk about his math homework, arguing theories with her, sometimes helping her when she was stuck on a problem. "Maybe you need a little help," he'd say. "I'll be at the corner of Thomas Street and Third Avenue. We'll go over to my place and discuss what kind of help you need."

Jack was the most intelligent person she had ever known, the first man who could challenge her intellectually.

But he had a funny-looking, give-a-shit haircut and wore Sans-a-belt pants from Sears, and he walked in doors ahead of her and slammed them in her face, and he brought the cheapest beer and never took her out to dinner.

He talked all the time about a girl he was in love with back home. The preacher's daughter. "She's gorgeous, smooth blond hair down to here, green eyes. Face like an angel's. Pretty. She's going to be my walking, talking baby machine. Nice girl, too. A nice girl. Unlike you, you little whore, she won't let me fuck her. A virgin."

Moira would yawn when he talked about her, but she wasn't really jealous. Jack Locksmey was good for three things: fucking, help with a tough physics class, and forgetting that she'd even been born and lived the first sixteen years of her life.

Eighteen

AND THEN THAT WINTER, Moira developed an itchy red rash on her face, arms, breasts.

Mother said, "It's just hormones. It'll clear up."

"I look horrible," Moira said. "Can I stay home from school until it clears up?"

Mother's eyebrows hit the ceiling. "Moira, I really don't know what makes you think you're special. That you can loll around the house while other kids with acne—and that's all it is—go to school. You're much too vain. This'll do you good, maybe take that vain streak out of you."

But it wasn't acne. She looked up medical books with pictures of people with skin diseases just to make sure. No, it wasn't acne. Poison ivy? In January? Well then, maybe it was psoriasis, or ringworm.

She showed Mother the pictures in the books. "Maybe I ought to go to a doctor," Moira said.

"I'm not raising a pair of spoiled brats that I run to the doctor every time they get a little rash."

But it wasn't a little rash, it was a big one. It covered her cheeks and the sides of her neck and her wrists. Mother insisted that it was barely noticeable and temporary. "Don't worry, it'll go away."

But it didn't go away. And it itched. It got worse. Spread so that her face, breasts were big, red, scratched-up wounds. Oozing pus here and crusting over there.

Daddy noticed it and said, "Moira, what the hell's wrong with your face? Eleanor, what's wrong with that girl?"

"Adolescence," Mother said.

Daddy gave Moira a suspicious look. Moira shrank. *Adolescence* was a synonym for *sex*. Then it hit her—what if she'd gotten this because of the bad stuff she'd been doing? What if this was the first sign of syphilis? She looked up venereal diseases. No, it wasn't venereal disease. It was God's punishment.

Moira's face and the insides of her arms were covered with the rash. It bled when she scratched, but she couldn't leave it alone, it itched so much.

Someone in Latin class tapped her on the shoulder to borrow a pencil. Moira turned around, and the girl said, "Is that stuff on your face and arms contagious?"

"I don't know," Moira said.

The girl made a face. "Never mind the pencil."

No one would touch Moira. Mr. Bailey took her aside and told her it looked like eczema. "You'd better tell your parents to take you to a doctor."

"My parents won't take me to a doctor."

"Don't tell me they're Christian Scientists?"

Moira wished they were. Then her parents would make sense to someone else. "No, they just think it spoils kids to take them to the doctor whenever anything goes wrong."

It went on for another week, and finally Mother let her stay home from school. Her face was red and so painful she couldn't wash or even get in the shower because the water felt like flames on the rash. Her nipples oozed, crusted, cracked, oozed some more, and stuck to her bra. She screamed each night when she took off her bra—her nipples would be stuck to it, and she had to pull the crusted skin off. Her nipples would be freshly exposed, a thin layer of skin bleeding. The crusts of eczema would stay in her bra at night. Her one bra, the annual one-size larger single bra that Mother reluctantly bought her.

Even in bed it was misery. The wool blanket stuck painful little tendrils into the eczema, and even the smooth sheets were painful on her nipples, so she had to sleep bare, and it was cold because Daddy stubbornly refused to turn the heat on because officially it was spring, even if it did go down into the forties at night.

The school nurse finally called Moira in, took one look at her, and wrote a note to Mother. The note sat on the kitchen counter for a few days, then the nurse called. Mother spent some time arguing with her on the phone, then when she hung up, told Moira that she had decided to take her to a doctor. "Here goes twenty bucks up in smoke because you're allergic to chocolate or some damn thing you won't stop eating."

The doctor gave them a prescription for some pills and cream. He told her she was probably allergic to something like wool, or wheat, or orange juice. "Or boys," he joked to Mother. Mother didn't laugh.

The next day, the rash turned brown and crusted over. In a few more days, the crusts began to peel off. Soft, pink, new skin shone forth underneath.

The doctor had told her to watch her diet carefully and to see if she could figure out what it was that caused her excema.

No matter what she cut out of her diet, though, the eczema kept coming back, and Moira had to keep using the cream and pills for months.

Her reputation around school by junior year was widespread. In the lunchroom cafeteria, boys began whistling in unison when she came by with her tray. "Hey, d'ja get any last night from Wendy Whattapair, Mike?" Or Bill or Tom or Jim or Fred, they'd ask each other even though none of them had gone out with her.

One cold winter afternoon, she accepted a ride home from school with a boy in one of her classes. He drove out to a cornfield and parked and grabbed her and pushed her down.

She was afraid to fight. In a fight, she might lose. If she didn't fight him off, then it would be her choice, wouldn't it? In a way? Wouldn't it?

So she lay still as he pulled her pants partially down, unzipped his fly, and went into her.

But as he began to move back and forth, she suddenly became enraged.

She yelled so loud he pulled out, stunned. She reached her arm back and knocked him on the side of his head. Then she held him away with her foot and pushed in the cigarette lighter and popped it out and held it toward him. "I'll put this on it, see how you like that."

He opened the car door and pushed her out. The cigarette lighter fell out of her hand. The boy reached out and took it and pressed it on her leg. It was still hot and she screamed out.

She lay in the corn row as his wheels spun on the slick corn stalks, then screeched off.

Afraid to hitchhike, she'd walked home. It was dark by the time she got to the house and Daddy saw the burn on her leg. "Cigarettes," he shouted. "What'll be next out of you?"

She was cursed. She was a slut.

She grabbed the scissors out of her desk drawer and locked herself in the bathroom and cut off all her hair, all Mother had left her, cut it way down short and let it scatter all over the clean bathroom floor she was always scrubbing, cut it short and uneven, a convict's haircut. She put her arms up on the mirror and burst into tears because she was such a whore and because she wasn't pretty. "I hate you," she'd screamed into the mirror, and she slapped the mirror, slapped her reflection, and then slapped her own face, slapping loud and screaming and crying out and hitting until it became swollen and red, and then she scratched and drew blood.

She looked down at her body. There was nothing she could do to ruin it. She couldn't even try to get fat—she ate as much as she wanted, and the food around there was so starchy, if it didn't put weight on her, nothing would.

She held the scissors over her right nipple. How much would it hurt? Could it possibly hurt more than it hurt to have it? She pressed the scissors against her flesh. The aureola flattened and the nipple jumped out and the edge of her breast pinched as the scissor blade nicked the flesh of her breast. How much would it hurt?

She squeezed the scissors together, making a tiny cut at the base of her nipple. She would be in a car with a boy, he would beg her to take off her bra, and would see this. She would laugh then. He would think she was crazy, jump out of the car. She'd run after him, holding up her breast, laughing.

It began to hurt wildly, just this little cut, and she put the scissors down and went to bed and even enjoyed the pain.

She went out the next day with her swollen face, with a jagged scratch next to one eye, smaller fingernail crescent marks elsewhere on her face, and with the money she had saved bought the ugliest clothes she could find—colors that had always made her look awful, purples and aquas and off-whites—in three sizes too large. She bought old ladies' housedresses, nylon prints with puff sleeves, and a pair of oxford shoes and men's socks with clocks on them.

Evenings, she would pull aside her curtains and look out at endless snow or lifeless tan prairie, and remember the feeling she used to get as a child playing with Paul Whitefeather, the only person who had ever understood and accepted her.

Maybe it really was boys that she was allergic to.

She was going to change. Be a good girl.

Moira gave up on any ideas she had had about going off to a private college in the East, despite the continued urgings of Mr. Bailey and a couple of her other teachers. Mother and Daddy were right—who on earth did Moira McPherson think she was, anyway, wanting to go off to some place where there were rich snobs and people who were really smart and privileged and went to private schools instead of ordinary public school like Moira? They would turn around and know that it was Moira's fault that she went to public school and not some snazzy boarding school in the East.

Moira resigned herself to Dakota State Normal College, though from the title *Normal* she had an inkling that she wasn't going to fit in.

But she was going to try. She was going to be so good and obedient—to her parents, to the other students, to God—that no one was ever going to think she was a dirty girl again.

By the end of her junior year, she began to almost see herself as a home economics teacher. Unmarried, as Mother wanted, because Mother wouldn't want Moira to carry on the slut gene.

Nineteen

THE SUNDAY SCHOOL bus tore down the street, rushing them to church as fast as possible so that not a minute could be lost before salvation.

Rosemary had invited Moira to attend one of her church's Wednesday evening youth-fellowship hours. Moira had decided to switch from the easygoing McPherson Methodist church to Rosemary's God's Witness Fellowship, as someone with an exceptionally dirty house might switch from watered-down Mr. Clean to full-strength ammonia cleanser.

Though Rosemary never said anything about it, Moira worried that Rosemary had heard not only about Gary Racer, but about the other boys; or worse, she thought with a terror that made her break out in sweat, about Mr. Smealz last year.

Sometimes when she looked at Daddy she got that sick feeling of revulsion and panic that she got when Mr. Smealz was around. Mother wasn't any comfort; in fact, Mother just stared at her with raised eyebrows and gave Taryn those looks that said they both thought Moira was tainted merchandise and they'd all be glad when she finally got out of there and went off to Normal and they could all be a nice, happy family.

Moira shifted in her seat and sat straight and took a deep breath. But now, as far as she was concerned, none of the things she'd done with any boys had happened, because she was turning over a new leaf. She was going to try to find a new Moira at church. Church was the only thing she could come up with, because the only two people who accepted and maybe forgave Moira her sins were Rosemary and God. And when it came right down to it, Moira wasn't always so sure about Rosemary.

It seemed that nothing had happened as far as Mr. Smealz was concerned, because he refused to acknowledge her anymore. In class, where he used to call on her all the time, especially when she was daydreaming, he didn't look at her, never spoke her name anymore. Why was he acting like that? Was she so disgusting? He couldn't even stand to look at her, she was so repulsive—his eyes would sail over her when he appraised the class, tapping that awful yardstick against the desk, walking around the room, the sucked-in cheeks under the pointy cheekbones shiny and sallow in the harsh fluorescent light of the classroom. The tiny, sharp eyes that used to look at her in anger and disgust didn't even know she existed anymore.

Maybe it hadn't really happened. Sometimes she wondered herself. If she'd ever had to tell anyone about this thing that had happened, she wouldn't be sure whether she remembered it right at all.

Or maybe *something* had happened but it hadn't really happened the way she thought. She'd been so frightened and turned on at the same time and disbelieving that maybe she was all mixed up. And she couldn't remember how it felt, because the whole thing was a blur now. And besides, grownup men weren't supposed to do it with teenage girls. So it probably hadn't happened. She'd probably mentally made up half of it. She was probably becoming crazy like everyone else in the McPherson family. After all, Mother and Daddy always thought the rest of the world was right, not them. And Mr. Smealz was the rest of the world.

But most of the time she knew what he had done. And she lay in bed sometimes at night, thinking of him tapping her breasts with the yardstick, of him grunting against her.

She thought about it now as Rosemary opened her Bible. She had a Bible bookmarker that told you which verses to turn to for various reasons—when you felt lonely, when you felt temptation, when you were afraid of death, when you were sick, when you were angry.

They didn't have one for when you felt like the slut of Sioux Falls. She wished she had the nerve to ask the preacher if such a passage existed—it probably did, since Jesus befriended adulteresses and such—but she was afraid even a preacher would react the same way other men did to her.

Moira put her hand over her face and wondered if she was too far gone even for God.

But that Mr. Smealz business was all over. She took a deep breath as they neared the church. It was in a neighborhood of small new ranch houses with lawns full of ceramic deer and rabbits and spinning pinwheels to scare away moles. Another deep breath. She had told Jack she wouldn't see him anymore. He still called but she hung up on him. She could get rid of most of them, but she couldn't get rid of the image of Mr. Smealz and his yardstick. Well, she had to deal with it. Here was an idea—she could just brush it off, the way people brushed off things and went on with their lives as if it was no big deal. *If* the Smealz thing had really happened, it was just one of those things. Right? People did worse things, right? You read about it in the newspaper. They shot other people, they beat their kids to death with belts, pulled wings off baby birds, poured scalding water on cats, sold drugs to kids. Robbed banks, tortured prisoners, killed people with machine guns, lots of people. She was just going to forget about it and go on with her life, that was all. You could just put those things behind you, couldn't you?

She looked around the bus. It was full of a lot of weirdos. But what else would you expect—this wasn't the Presbyterian church or the Lutheran church or the Catholic church, it was a weirdo offbeat church for people who didn't fit into normal churches. It was a bus full of outcasts, misfits. And Moira fit right in.

No one had cool clothes or cool haircuts. But that was only for starters. For instance, there was Kimberly Haggensworth, who had never been known to speak to any other kids ever, and she had a mustache and sideburns and thick dark blond hair on the backs of her hands, fingers, and even her toes (Moira had seen them in gym class). And there was Hal Wiscott, who was a nice guy, extremely polite, but whose father made him wear a bow tie and carry a briefcase. Then Hector Ainsworthy, who was the size of a ten-year-old kid and acted like one, and Olivia Bartsend, who had to wear not only regular braces on her teeth but also a big one on the outside that went around to the back of her head and made her spit all over you when she talked. There was Sally Dardenel, who always wore a Band-Aid over one of the zits she'd been picking, and she was so skinny you could see the bones of her spine when she wore a thin sweater. She tried to play on her skinniness by dressing like a Vogue model in clothes she made herself. She came to school in such weird homemade outfits the other kids called her Spaceship Sally. Moira should talk—she looked down at her own clothes. She had on one of Mother's specials, a straight skirt that was too long and too tight in the rear and a jersey top that was too tight in the neck so Moira had to leave it unzipped with the result that it sagged in front—and ended up looking sexy, in spite of Mother's attempt to desex her.

Yes, and here you had the odd couple—Rosemary Jenks with her hair fastened back so tight that the scalp in places was pulled, and Moira McPherson, with turquoise Cleopatra eye makeup to hide her face that she thought was ugly and ratted hair and size 36D boobs fighting for attention.

The bus bounced into the parking lot of the little church, a pale brick building on a sea of concrete, a church that looked like it was scrubbed completely clean of the world's filth. Moira was doubly glad that she had come. Maybe this was all destiny. Maybe her sins would be forgiven.

Hers and those of this bus full of weirdos—fat Mike Brostman taking up an entire seat and sitting there eating a Mars Bar, goody-goody Shirley Heathley and her bouncing sausage curls talking to her friend Evie Wendell, who didn't have parents and lived in some kind of a home and had bad teeth; Lars Muller, who had a buzz haircut so short his almond-shaped head showed through the top and who also had a severe speech impediment because it was rumored he had once put his tongue on an ice-cube tray; poor Nancy LaModde, who had a raging red birthmark like a pinto horse all over her face and arms, and the list went on through every single seat on the God's Fellowship after-school youth-fellowship bus until finally you got to Moira McPherson, queen of the misfits.

But wait, who was that slumped in the back of the bus? Not Les Bowen.

Les Bowen was sort of normal. He was on every sports team there was, or at least he seemed to be. A tall, pink-complexioned redhead with blurry orange freckles, he was no genius but he was quite well-liked around the school. You'd always see him taking big strides down the hall, feigning football passes at all the people that called out "hi" to him.

When Les tried aiming a pass at the girls as they were getting off the bus at the church door, Rosemary acted more indignant than usual. "Oh, I hate him," she hissed, but then on the sidewalk she circled back in front of him again and he made another football pass and she gave him a look out of the side of her eye and if Moira wasn't mistaken, she was looking to see if he was still looking.

Rosemary sat staring at Les during get-acquainted time. Whenever he looked at her and Moira, Rosemary would turn and look at Moira with a fake smile, as if they'd been discussing something and were oblivious to Les.

This went on until dinnertime. Someone said a very long grace and then they lined up. Dinner was undercooked hot dogs, lukewarm ketchupy beans, metallic-tasting green Kool Aid, and not-bad chocolate cake. Les sat down next to Moira. Rosemary glared at him and talked nervously about nothing to Moira and made more chattery conversation in those ten minutes than Moira had heard her deliver in a month.

After dinner a glassy-eyed, smiling youth leader asked everyone to get out their Bible and turn to First Thessalonians.

" 'That they all might be damned who believed not the truth, but had pleasure in unrighteousness,' " he read.

Wooden mallets inside Moira's head pounded the words "pleasure in unrighteousness" into her brain. Moira stared down at her Bible so that no one could read her frightened face.

He went on, " 'Comfort your hearts, and stablish you in every good word and work.' "

She looked up. Good works. Yes, she wanted to do good works.

During the reading, Les sat with his Bible upside down on his lap, making little ball-throwing motions. "He looks as if he'd rather be somewhere else," Moira said to Rosemary.

Rosemary sent him a smoldering dirty look.

After a prayer, the youth leader sat the students down for a discussion: "How cool is it for a Christian to be cool?"

"For example," he said, "what if someone should say, 'Hey, excuse me, fellow, but would you like a smoke?' What would you say?" And then he turned his glassy look onto Les. "Les, what would you say?"

"I'd say only if you've got my brand."

Rosemary and some of the other kids gasped, but Moira couldn't help it, she turned around to get a look at him and laughed before she knew what she was doing. Les winked at Moira, and Moira turned around.

The leader stopped staring at Les and started staring at Moira. "Judgment Day will be no joke."

Moira thought of Mother and her sarcastic jokes. Would Mother try to joke her way out of hell or into heaven in the afterlife?

"Moira," she heard the youth leader say. "You seem to be reflecting on something. Would you like to share your thoughts?"

Even at school, Moira normally got away with as little class participation as she could. It was hell having to say things out loud and have all the people who hated you staring. "No, I guess not," she said quietly.

"What would you say to someone who makes a joke of God's Word?"

Moira thought of Mother again. "Maybe for some people jokes are the only truth."

"Can you explain that a little better?"

Moira thought, then said shyly, "The rest of the time they're lying, trying to act the way people expect them to act."

"Very interesting," the youth leader said. "So for some people a joke is their only means of communication. Even with God."

"I guess that's what I mean."

He chuckled. "Do you think God jokes back?"

Moira thought for a moment. "Maybe God deals with people on an individual basis. Those with a sense of humor get one from God, those with none get none from God."

The youth leader laughed. Pretty soon some of the other kids were laughing. Not Rosemary, of course, but Olivia and Lars and Les Bowen.

Rosemary turned and snapped at her, "Don't your parents teach you not to laugh at serious topics?"

Poor Rosemary. She was so dead-serious about Moira's salvation.

"*Au contraire,*" Moira said to herself. And she thought that Mother probably could do it, get God laughing so hard he'd forget about anything she'd done wrong on earth. Or if Mother was in another kind of mood, she could get God so goddamned mad he'd end up kicking clouds around and getting drunk and hurling lightning bolts all over the heavens and forget all about her so she could sneak in the door while he was throwing his fit. Or, more in Mother's style, she'd make God think Moira was the bad one, and while God was busy yelling at Moira, Mother would sneak into heaven through the back door.

In her own case, Moira wondered vaguely if God was indeed male, and if so, was he like other males and willing to overlook a lot of things he didn't like about you because you were sexy? Or was he more like Daddy, capable of great jealousy and rage because you were sexy. Surely he couldn't be like Mr. Smealz, could he? Respected by everyone because he was so strict? And she began to worry, because Mr. Smealz was God at North Prairie High School and he thought Moira was so awful he wouldn't even look at her. Her heart raced and she felt short of breath, but she tried to concentrate because she wanted so very badly to be good. These were the kinds of questions she would like to have asked, but something told her not to ask them.

Les Bowen stood up and pretended now that he was a baseball player. He threw a pitch and then batted at it. A lot of kids laughed. "He's a troublemaker, and you shouldn't encourage him," Rosemary said.

"Don't you think he's sort of funny?" Moira said.

Rosemary looked at him and wrinkled her face. "He's a shit bastard."

Moira looked at Rosemary in disbelief.

Rosemary turned a brilliant red and yet looked almost proud of herself at the same time.

Later they saw a film about the mission in Africa that had been founded by Rosemary's parents. They were in part of it, smiling their odd smiles as they handed out Bibles to a group of grinning if slightly perplexed-looking Africans. The camera panned the crowd. Some of the Africans looked so happy and so much more at peace than any Christians Moira had ever seen. They were so at peace that they didn't even bother to brush the flies off their eyes or mouths. She wondered why Rosemary's family came back, because surely Africa in its naturalness must be as close to paradise as anyone would ever see on earth. And for people so bound on seeing paradise, Rosemary's parents would be the first to recognize it, you'd think.

But then the Jenkses wouldn't be selfish enough to look for paradise on earth for themselves. They had work to do, souls to save. They might yet save Moira's. No, that wasn't true. It was up to Moira to save her own soul. They had introduced the idea, now it was her turn.

Rosemary's expression was hard to read as she watched her parents. But Moira wasn't so sure that Rosemary was going to turn out like her parents. Why would she be friends with someone like Moira, the class slut? Moira suspected Rosemary wanted a little bit of Moira's wantonness to rub off on her, just as Moira welcomed any of Rosemary's wholesomeness that might rub off on her.

As she watched, Moira envied Rosemary her family. Her parents looked so sweet, serene, innocent, that Moira felt proud to know them. And she looked around the room in the dark, and she almost felt proud to be part of this group. After all, it *was* a group, and it was a group that accepted her. How could she dislike these people, weirdos or not, how could she even be ashamed of them if they accepted her, took her in, taught her hope?

After the movie, they had a prayer and then it was time to get on the bus. Les came over and pretended to be dribbling a basketball to Moira. Moira assumed Les was in on all the gossip about her, and she didn't want to do that stuff any more, even if at nights she would lie awake masturbating until her fingers or something else fell off. Rosemary could have him.

Moira reached for Rosemary's arm and said, "She's the basketball player, not me."

Les sized up Rosemary. "Now she's a baseball catcher." Les wound up and pitched one toward Rosemary. Rosemary shrieked in an exaggeratedly feminine way and covered her face with her arms.

Les laughed loudly. "That's a curveball." He pretended to spit on his hand. "This is illegal." Rosemary pretended to be disgusted. He wound up again. "You sure you want to learn how to throw a sinking fastball?"

Rosemary nodded. Moira walked off and got her jacket and left them to flirt with each other and climbed on the bus ahead of them with all the weirdos. Rosemary really was about the most boy-crazy person in the entire school, but who knew it?

On the way home, Moira felt happy about playing matchmaker for Rosemary. Moira McPherson had done something unselfish. Something nice for someone else.

No one in her family had ever, that she could recall, done anything unselfish. The concept didn't exist.

Maybe that was why her family never felt normal. Because they lacked the kindness and generosity of other people. Maybe that was why they'd never really be normal. Normal people were nice people. The people in that church bus were more normal than her family would ever be, because whatever their outward defects, inside they were still nice people.

But then even if Moira was nice, Moira could never be a real normal person. But that was okay. She could be a weirdo who was a nice weirdo and happy with being weird. And now, thanks to Rosemary, Moira was now an official member of the outcasts club. She had just joined voluntarily. And while it wasn't the greatest thing in the world, it was better than being a reject of the outcasts, and it was better than being like the people in her family, trying to pretend they were part of the normal in-crowd and knowing they weren't and letting it eat away at them all the time.

And suddenly she didn't feel like one of those African masks on Rosemary's wall anymore. She felt like part of something.

Maybe that church business had saved her after all.

Twenty

ROSEMARY AND LES BOWEN became an item in the school cafeteria, and Moira had to go back to eating lunch alone. But after a few weeks of trying to hold a conversation with him about anything other than sports, Rosemary decided Les wasn't her type.

One Monday after a big sports weekend, Moira saw Rosemary waiting in her usual place by the crates of milk cartons as Moira slinked into the lunchroom trying to be both unnoticeable and noticed at the same time.

As they ate their lunch, feeling comfortable and happy again, Rosemary told Moira, "I was so crazy about him. And it was so depressing when that feeling went away. I'm going to find someone else. What do you think about Freddie Hansen?"

Her brief romance had certainly made an impression on Rosemary. Now she had her eye on the coolest guy in the school. "He's cute. And maybe he'll like you, too. But you sure are setting your sights high, Rosemary," Moira said.

"Yeah, I guess I'm getting cocky. Having one guy like you makes you see that you aren't a hopeless loser. So why not reach for the stars?"

"Good luck," Moira said.

Rosemary made a few attempts at attracting Freddie Hansen the same way she had gotten Les Bowen's attention. Freddie finally got annoyed and said to her one day, "Hey, Sister Rosemary. Thou shalt not stare at thy neighbor. Fuck off."

Rosemary was depressed for a few days, but it was obvious that she had started changing. And so had her family.

Her mother seemed to be waking up to the fact that they were no longer in Africa but in America where the name of the game was spending money on the latest stuff. She was becoming aware of how people lived in America.

Mrs. Jenks stopped wearing thick-heeled Red Cross pumps and got herself a pair of pointy-toed heels. Her hemlines crept up to where they almost brushed her knees as she bustled about her Sunday school work. You didn't hear the loud organ music from their house anymore. They bought a TV set. Rosemary was allowed to wear shorts. Then lipstick. Then she was allowed to learn the cha-cha along with everyone else in gym class instead of having to stay on the sidelines doing situps and knee bends. Rosemary's mother even suggested Rosemary might someday meet a boy whom she could go to the prom with, now that she was a senior. Because next year she'd be off to college in Ohio, and even if it was a conservative Christian college, students without any worldly experience could get into trouble their first time away from home.

Moira was afraid that they were going to become normal, and then they'd see through normal eyes what Moira and her family were really like, and that would be the end of her friendship with Rosemary and then Moira would be completely, utterly alone in the world.

Rosemary's mother took Moira shopping with them one day. Rosemary got a yellow mohair sweater that made her blond hair look even blonder and her skin look creamy.

"God made her pretty," Mrs. Jenks said. "That's a gift." Then she turned to Moira. "And he made you very pretty, too. Lovely figure, pretty face."

Moira took off her glasses, now that she'd been reminded that she could be pretty, too.

"Even with your glasses, you're cute," Rosemary said.

"So intelligent," Mrs. Jenks said. "Rosemary is always telling me how you amaze teachers and students at school." She looked at Moira's clothes, which were the best Moira could buy with what money she made from the extra work Mr. Bailey got her in the science lab. "Do you suppose your parents would mind if I bought you a gift?"

Moira pictured a new Bible or a wooden cross to hang on her wall.

"I guess not."

"Then you go pick out a sweater, too."

Moira was so touched that someone would buy her a gift that she almost started crying.

On the way home with the sweater she had finally chosen, Moira continued to worry that Rosemary would become so cool that she'd leave her behind. The Jenkses, after all, were missionaries, going from one sinful person to another.

What would she have done without Rosemary? she asked herself as they headed toward Moira's subdivision. Would she have curled up and died by now? A friend is so important. Anyone who accepts you is something. And she began to feel nostalgic for the old Rosemary, the odd one who forgot not to smile with her gums showing and put her hands over her ears every time someone played a Rolling Stones or Beatles record on a passing radio. Because she'd felt comfortable with the old Rosemary. With a new, cool, updated Rosemary, Moira was going to have realize that it was possible to change yourself, you didn't have to become a hopeless victim of weirdness, even of a family like Moira's.

And Moira realized that even though Rosemary had been a missionary to her and saved her from despair, any kind of nice friend would do the same. And between Paul Whitefeather and Rosemary and someone like Mr. Bailey, she had been really quite lucky, because those friends had accepted her the way she was and hadn't asked her to be normal.

It was Rosemary who came up with the idea of going to a dance the next fall, senior year, at Saint Francis Catholic School for Boys. At Catholic school no one knew them. With savings from her after-school job in the lab, Moira had gone out and bought herself the requisite collegiate outfit—cranberry V-neck sweater and A-line skirt, pink button-down-collar Oxford shirt, madras headband, cranberry knee socks. If she felt odd when she looked at herself in the mirror in this get-up, she told herself that since it was close to Halloween, she was going in disguise to the Catholic school as a nice, wholesome girl.

Rosemary's parents had never been crazy about the idea of her getting mixed up with Catholics, and yet it seemed to Moira that they were catching on to the fact that Rosemary was regarded as a bit of a weirdo, and they were actually concerned about it, Catholic menace or no Catholic menace. Rosemary's mother actually took Rosemary out shopping for a new outfit, and allowed her to wear nylons instead of anklets.

As the girls entered the Catholic school gym and wandered among the lavender haze, the boys began to look them over. Rosemary licked her lips and managed to smile starry-eyed at nothing the way fashion models did, and Moira smoothed her hair and tried to remember that no one here knew anything about Mr. Smealz or Jack or Gary or Daddy. They didn't know about Mother, either, she added, then wondered why she had thought that.

A pair of boys appraised their figures, then their faces. The girls waited to see if the boys would make their move. They didn't, but there was always hope. Hope winged its way through the airwaves and was inhaled and pumped into arteries; Avon perfume, English Leather cologne, Arrid deodorant, AquaNet, Wildroot Cream Oil, and hope surged through the thick atmosphere, mixing with the Supremes and Sam Cooke and the Four Seasons. And Moira felt light, ready to dance, as if she'd shed her reputation like a heavy suit of armor.

She and Rosemary looked at each other, Rosemary pretty in pink lipstick and with a maybe-God-will-forgive-me-for-stepping-out-of-my-oddball-role glisten in her eyes. Yes, Moira told herself, this was the beginning of the rest of her life, as Daddy liked to say on the morning after a big drinking binge.

Thank you, God, for giving me another chance, Moira whispered, thank you for creating Catholic schools. Now I know why you made them, now I know why Catholics are always naming things Sacred this and Our Lady of Hope that.

But by the time the evening was half over, they had sat out every dance from the Animals to the Zombies. They didn't say it out loud, but Rosemary and Moira were wondering why. And here they'd done all the things you were supposed to do to get boys to find you attractive, from the egg-white facials that afternoon to the English Leather behind their knees just before they entered the gym. Maybe Mother was right when she always reminded Moira that it wasn't a fair world. Maybe you could do every goddamn thing on earth that Seventeen and Glamour told you to do, and you still wouldn't be loved. Maybe there were people who were unlovable.

They continued with their brightest smiles and talked to each other and acted oblivious to the dancers around them, trying to give the impression that they had come to the dance just to listen to the music and chat with each other. Every now and then, Rosemary would turn and look at the dancers on the floor, a tiny flicker of her eye giving away the fact that she was lonely and scared.

And boys continued to wander through the crowd, looking at each girl's face up close, appraising, deciding whether they were going to bid or wait and see what other girl's floating love they were going to try to capture for the evening. Most of the girls here were in fact like Moira and Rosemary, unknowns from other schools, girls with no histories, like brides sent from back east to the cowboys out west, no questions asked.

Rosemary looked at her new watch with the cool plaid watchband. "It's nine-thirty."

And no one had asked either of them to dance. Rosemary's face had lost its confidence and had taken on a look of desperation and resignation. Moira's cranberry knee socks were starting to droop.

"It's still early," Moira said.

"I think I'm tired," Rosemary said.

And just then someone tapped Moira's shoulder.

The guy was stiff and danced like Frankenstein, and he didn't say a word the whole time, but as far as Moira was concerned, the evening was already a success. Someone who didn't immediately expect to get laid wanted to dance with her. Just because. Just for the hell of it. As she danced, she looked around to see if Rosemary had gotten asked, but she didn't see her, and when the song was over she found Rosemary standing alone and looking like her old hunched-over self and with her gums showing in a fake smile.

She twisted her fingers together. "You almost ready?"

"No, not yet," Moira said. "I want to stay just a little longer. Please, Rosemary. You'll get asked. You're prettier than I am. Boys are afraid of the really beautiful girls, you know. That's your problem. I read it in a magazine."

"Thanks, but it's not true, Moira. Besides, you've got what really matters—a nice figure. Come on, we have to share the cab."

They played "Eve of Destruction," and Rosemary said, "That does it, I hate that hippie song. Let's go home. I'll call us a cab."

But Moira wouldn't admit defeat. "I'm staying."

"I don't want to have to pay for a whole cab by myself. I can't afford that."

"I'll give you the half I would have paid if we'd shared."

"Sometimes I wonder how much of a friend you really are," Rosemary said.

"Maybe I'll meet someone. Maybe you'll meet someone if you stay."

"You probably just want someone to go out in the woods with."

Moira got that old familiar feeling of self-loathing.

"Why don't you want to go home, huh? Is your dad drunk?" Rosemary went on, her lip up like a snarling dog.

"Stop it, Rosemary."

Rosemary lapsed back into the old Rosemary. "Moira, you should try to be a better person and go home and pray for your salvation."

Moira's face burned with conscious, renewed self-hatred.

Rosemary went in for the kill. "Everyone knows all about you."

Moira felt her body turn to steel. She waited to hear her mention Mr. Smealz, but the words didn't come and she mumbled a prayer of thanks to Rosemary's God.

Moira briefly considered calling Rosemary a holyroller, but she still couldn't hurt someone's feelings, even if her own had been hurt. "Oh, never mind, Rosemary. Please stay here with me."

"You're just trying to get us into trouble. Maybe people are right, I shouldn't hang around with you."

As Rosemary stalked off in big angry giant-steps, Moira wondered who else Rosemary was going to hang around with now that she was cool.

Rosemary had been her last friend on earth. Now she had no one. And if that was the case, she had absolutely nothing left in the world now to lose.

It was terrible standing there alone, and she began to regret what she had done, burning her bridges with Rosemary. She thought of the warmth and comfort of Rosemary's neat little bedroom as they gossiped and did homework with the snow packed three feet deep outside, and of her smiling mother coming in as the new Mrs. Jenks the other day with two cups of hot chocolate with melted marshmallows. She thought of Rosemary's generosity with her possessions, her family, and her religion—and whatever you thought of the style of all of them, they were better than most of the alternatives. Now Moira was stuck here and would go home depressed because she wasn't pretty enough for anyone but Frankenstein to want to dance with, and she'd have to give up on the fantasy of being the belle of the Catholic school dance and go back to being the slut of North Prairie High School and not even have a best friend. She went into the girls' room and sat on the couch and tried to figure out what to do, what to think.

The loudspeaker blared with "Leader of the Pack," the song that glorified rebel outcasts. Hope began to return, the kind of hope a gambler has. The thrill of a boy noticing you must be like a gambler throwing out the dice. The boy asking you to dance was like winning. So what if it ended badly, if you lost your bankroll? There was always the chance you were going to win tomorrow, hit the jackpot.

She got up and looked in the mirror. She put on some lipstick and hiked up her cranberry skirt a couple of inches, and took the stiff, scratchy Oxford shirt off and folded it into her purse and tucked her sweater into her skirt. To hell with being cool. To hell with being collegiate. She drew on some eyeliner. She looked like a greaser again. She began to cry, crying off the black greaser eyeliner. She looked better. To hell with being a greaser, too. If Rosemary had done nothing more, she'd helped Moira see that being a greaser wasn't all it was cracked up to be.

Oh God, how she missed Rosemary. She considered finding a pay phone and calling her, but she wouldn't even be home by now.

She chewed her fingernails that she had taken such pains over during a manicure with Rosemary that afternoon following directions in Seventeen magazine. Now that she was completely alone in the world, she had nothing to lose. She felt strong suddenly. She pushed open the door to the girls' room to face the gym full of boys all by herself, hoping even Frankenstein would lurch back over to dance with her.

As the Beach Boys began to croon she smelled English Leather before she felt the tap on her shoulder, that magical tap that she could live and die for. Ready, get set, turn: A guy with hair combed so that it wasn't sure if it quite wanted to make the transition from Elvis to Beatles mumbled, "Wanna dance?"

She danced with three different boys. She enjoyed the feel of the solid shoulders, the anonymous bodies. She could create her own two- or three-minute fantasy with each of them, that they loved her, wanted to go steady with her, thought she was okay. Those anonymous bodies were reassuring in a way—there would always be more. For a few moments, she actually loved her body—breasts, hips, legs, and what was between them.

And then she met Corey.

Corey was tall, with floppy blond hair and an appraising look in his alert, intense eyes. He didn't squeeze her too tightly, and he talked a lot, asking lots of questions like where she went to school.

"North Prairie High," she said, hoping to God he didn't know anyone there.

"Hey hey, North Prairie Dogs, we played them last Friday night and they killed us."

Moira didn't understand.

"The game. Didn't you see the game?"

Moira shook her head. Was he going to walk away in the middle of "Hey Paula"? Daddy had been home last Friday night and he wouldn't let her go to football games because there might be boys there.

"Yeah, hey, I'm on the team."

"Which position?" Moira asked, assuming this would be her last question ever, that he'd probably walk away and not even answer it.

"Linebacker."

"Oh, great," she said, having not a clue as to what that meant.

He didn't walk away. Instead, he asked what clubs she was in.

"Just Science Club," she said, embarrassed, wishing it were Majorettes or Boosters or French Club or something classy and feminine.

"Hey, that's cool," he said. "I like smart girls."

"Well, yes, I *am* smart," she said matter-of-factly, and she was surprised to see him burst into laughter.

"Modest too, huh?"

He said he liked smart girls, especially when they were pretty, and Moira didn't know if he meant she was smart and pretty or he liked other smart girls who were pretty, unlike Moira.

But so what? Moira would never be the same again. For two minutes and however many seconds the song went—she didn't hear what they were playing—she was dancing with someone who liked smart girls and who was nice and normal and even cute.

They told each other which classes they were taking—he was struggling through chemistry for the second time. Somewhat embarrassed, even though he said he admired brainy girls, she said she had advanced calculus, physics, and fourth-year Latin.

"Wow, don't you ever have any fun? Any class that's not for geniuses?"

She thought for a moment, then mentioned her Abnormal Psychology class. He laughed.

They danced to "Twilight Time," then she hurried away so that she could reject him before he rejected her and got her coat from the checkroom and went to call a cab. She thought about how she, an egghead and a greaser, had attracted someone as neat and fratty as this Corey. Her whole life could be different.

As she waited for her cab, Corey pushed through the crowd and asked for her phone number. She pictured Daddy answering the phone and almost laughed.

"I can't give it to you, but maybe I'll come back again," she said, and seeing her cab, hurried down the steps feeling like Cinderella of the Greasers.

Twenty-one

"WOOEE, THERE GOES Wendy Whattapair," a boy yelled as Moira walked down the hall.

Moira passed them stone-faced. And then, like an apparition, Rosemary appeared.

"I told my Mom about our fight, and she said I was wrong," Rosemary said with an apologetic face.

Rosemary asked if she could borrow Moira's physics notes, and they were friends again. They walked down the hall together, Rosemary almost cool and Moira almost not a greaser anymore, but still they received cold looks from other girls and grins from boys.

"Let's go to the Catholic dance again on Saturday," Rosemary said, taking out her new blusher compact and checking the swoop of liquid eyeliner she'd put on that morning.

Moira pictured herself in the size 44½ car coat Mother had recently bought her.

"Okay, and can I wear your chesterfield coat to walk in in."

Rosemary agreed, if Moira gave it back for her to walk out in.

They continued down the hall, past a group of boys horsing around swatting each other with their jackets. A boy yelled, "Hey, I hear Moira's not really stacked. I hear she has foam rubber titties."

Rosemary gave Moira a shamefaced look. "I have to confess something. I was mad at you and I told someone about your Mom's falsies. I guess the story got garbled."

"Oooh, I'm allergic to foam rubber," another boy said loudly. "Achoo."

A chorus of sneezing followed them down the hall.

"Hey, Chuck Lester knows whether they're real or not," someone said. "Let's ask him."

"So does Denny Thrushton," someone else said.

"So do half the guys in the school."

"Achoo, achoo."

"Don't pay any attention to them," Rosemary said.

"Yeah," Moira said. She tried to tell herself that it was a relief, in a way, to have them think her breasts weren't real.

At the Catholic school, Rosemary met a boy she liked and danced with him all evening. And Moira ran into Corey Donogan again.

He asked her to dance to the nice normal Beach Boys—not the bad boy Rolling Stones or the Animals.

They danced all evening. "Science," he repeated as they stood together and heard the last dance announced. He had an appraising look, and I'm-looking-at-you-and-trying-to-figure-you-out look that didn't go with his pretty-boy face, the kind of face that usually said you're-looking-at-me.

It was as jarring a combination as Moira's sexiness was with her egghead brain and her timid personality.

Football team. Imagine that—a jock.

He asked her to dance to "Twilight Time." She concentrated hard to make it last in her mind. Because of course the whole thing was impossible—someone like him with someone like her. Not to mention Daddy.

But if someone nice like Corey didn't see anything wrong with Moira, maybe there wasn't anything wrong with her. Or at least nothing wrong to the naked eye that she couldn't do something about.

Mother came into Moira's room the next day.

"I see you've been getting money from somewhere and spending it all foolishly, when you should be saving for college, for Dakota State Normal."

"How have I been spending it foolishly?" Moira asked.

"On clothes."

"I need clothes. Anyway, it's my money. Mr. Bailey pays me to be a lab assistant."

"Is that all he pays you for?"

Moira looked at Mother in disbelief. Mother wasn't kidding. Moira felt like pushing Mother through the bedroom wall. But then Moira reminded herself that she was, after all, the slut of Sioux

Falls, two evenings of dancing with Corey Donogan notwithstanding, and Mother's opinion of her was no different from anyone else's. And it was true.

"Yes, Mother, that's all."

"You've developed quite a little reputation for yourself, young lady, from what Taryn tells me. Although Taryn thinks you'll eventually grow out of this," Mother said, taking a strand of Moira's hair and rubbing it between her fingers.

"Oh, Taryn does, does she?" Moira said, jerking her head back. She pictured Taryn's tiny face looking at Moira with that expression that said okay, now what the hell is my older sister going to do next?

"I don't care what Taryn thinks."

Mother reached for another tuft of hair, and Moira drew back. "Leave me alone, Mother."

"I do believe you're jealous of Taryn," Mother said quietly.

"No," Moira said, "I feel sorry for Taryn. She's sensitive, and she's afraid to do anything on her own."

"What a rotten thing to say about your little sister. You *are* jealous. I can see that."

Moira felt like crying but then she realized that crying was what Mother wanted.

It came to Moira that Mother went so far in her mistreatment of her, so awful, so beyond belief, in order to get a reaction. Like Daddy's behavior, Mother's was so disturbed that you realized the behavior had nothing to do with you, and then it stopped hurting so much. It left a numb spot where it was supposed to hurt, and you realized that the person hurting you was hurting more herself.

"Anyway, that's only natural for sisters," Mother said, and her face brightened and she put her arm around Moira. "Guess who called today?"

"Who?" Moira said, not really interested.

"Ralph Smealz. Your teacher."

Sweat sprang out along Moira's armpits. Something started drumming inside her head. She waited, like a boxer expecting to have his face pummeled, for Mother to spew out a venom-filled accusation of her, then talk about how this was proof that her daughter was a filthy slut.

"He's a very nice man."

Moira's breath came in little spurts. Even if Mother slapped her, she wouldn't feel it. She was numb.

"Good-looking, too, I must say, in a cold way," Mother said. She smiled. "He thinks I have acting talent."

The drums stopped.

"It all started when he saw me one day at the drugstore having an ice cream soda. God, I feel like Lana Turner. I was reading my *Adventures in Drama* book as usual. *Macbeth.* I was so caught up in it I was saying the lines out loud. He asked if I was an actress."

Did Mother know? Was she playing some sort of game?

"You know something funny? He reminds me a little bit of your father. Those eyes. And that tough-guy way about him. Your father is horribly jealous of him. You know how much he looks up to schoolteachers." Mother laughed again.

When Mother left the room, Moira sat against the wall and thought about all the things she'd been confused about. Suddenly she just didn't give a shit about Mother, Mr. Smealz, Daddy, or anyone. She just didn't give a shit.

And something else. If Mr. Smealz was going after Mother now, if he went after all the women, maybe Moira wasn't so bad. Maybe she wasn't such a slut. At least not such a bad one. Maybe the real slut was Mr. Smealz. And then she thought that idea over. They were all sluts—Mr. Smealz, Mother, Daddy, all of them sluts, for their dirty minds. The world was made up of sluts.

Moira got up and walked around the room for a little bit. Then, slowly, she twirled around, around again, feeling light on her feet, like she was floating in relief.

It hurt a little bit less. Everything hurt a little bit less. This, Moira said to herself, was Mother's way of *being* Moira. Keep Moira from being herself, a teenage girl with sex appeal, maybe too much of it. Keep Moira under control, convince her father that she was bad, and then Mother could be Moira.

Well, she wasn't going to keep Moira under control the way she kept Taryn under control.

What a disaster her life had been so far! She would graduate next spring, and what was she going to do? Go to Normal. Learn how to be a nice home-ec teacher, although she doubted she had the talent for it with her clumsiness. Learn how to be not too intellectual and not too sexy.

She reached for last year's North Prairie High yearbook. She found her picture with all the naked white space next to it where other people had clubs listed. Her hair was ratted so high that the photograph had had to be reduced and her head ended up being smaller than the others on the page. Looking at that picture, she realized why she'd teased her hair so high and worn those sexpot clothes—she didn't want a big head full of brains. Teasing her hair made her head seem smaller in proportion, but in true Moira Mc-Pherson style, she'd carried it to the extreme so that she was still an oddball. She'd escaped looking like the brainiest, but she'd ended up being the shrunken head in the yearbook.

She looked down at her new clothes. It was amazing how much energy she had to devote to just keeping up with what other girls took for granted. How she had to study what they wore, things they did, boys they went out with. Moira understood what it must be like to be a refugee coming from another country, trying to fit in. She was indeed a refugee from another country, from another planet—this household, which orbited its own sun a million light-years from everybody else's.

And now her parents wanted to send her to a college where all the other girls had been coached in being perfect little middle-class specimens, and they hadn't coached Moira at all. She pictured herself in a college dorm with the same girls who snubbed her, she pictured herself becoming an actual teacher for these nice, normal, well-adjusted girls. No, normal school was not the place for her. Miss Abnormal Psychology. But what could she do?

Moira looked out her window the next evening at the setting sun. It seemed that somewhere out across that long, flat prairie there was a place for her. Out west. On a secret dare to herself, she did what Mr. Bailey had been urging her to do all along and applied for admission to Stanford and Berkeley. She even got nervy and sent applications to a couple of Ivy League schools. And to New York University and Barnard College, because they were in New York and New York seemed like a place as mixed up as Moira. The day she mailed off the applications, she looked up at the crisp blue northern sky and said to God that she wouldn't do anything to get kicked out if he got her into one of those schools, she wouldn't go out on dates, she'd spend all her time studying.

While she was waiting for responses, the recurring eczema miraculously stopped coming back, seemingly for good. Moira put the pills and cream away.

And then Mother one day asked if she'd gotten her application ready to send to Normal. Moira went to her room and got the copies of the applications to the other schools. "I don't think I want to go to Normal," she said.

Mother looked at the application forms briefly, looked up and pursed her lips and gave Taryn one of her famous knowing looks, and changed the subject.

Moira began to doubt herself. Maybe this was silly, maybe she really didn't belong in places like Stanford or Berkeley or Barnard. She went to her room. As she lay on her bed thinking, Mother came in.

Her Mother's face was covered with cold cream, slick, each rise and fall of her face highlighted and shadowed. She sat down on the bed and leafed through Moira's trigonometry book.

"Those colleges you applied to," Mother said, composing her face into something that was supposed to look motherly, "are for rich people. People with nice clothes and nice manners. People who don't have to face reality."

Moira sat up and pulled the blanket around her shoulders.

"Frankly, I can't picture you there." Mother let that remark set in, then raised her eyebrows. "You should also watch the way you present yourself. Whether you're in Timbuctoo or Harvard. Your father thinks you're much too provocative for your own good. And that's going to get you into trouble someday, mark my words, young lady."

Moira felt a slight ringing in her ears.

Corey looked up her phone number and called and asked Moira for a date.

Moira approached Mother that evening after Daddy left for his business trip to Duluth. Mother sat sipping coffee and reading *Adventures in Drama.*

"Mother, a boy I met at one of the Catholic school dances, Corey Donogan, asked me for a date," Moira said, her voice shaking.

Mother snapped *Adventures in Drama* shut. "Do you know what Catholic boys want from Protestant girls?"

Moira shook her head.

"I'll tell you what they want. They want the same thing Protestant boys want, only more so because they think Protestant girls are wild."

Moira hung her head. Mother was probably right.

As Moira started to walk away, Mother called out, "And then they have it in their religion that they can do anything they want as long as they have a dozen brats running around the house and have one of those rosary-things dangling out of their pocket and go to confession every week and tell some priest about it."

This wasn't making much sense, but then, that was nothing new.

"Do you want your name coming up at some confession every week?"

"Never mind. I'll tell him I can't go."

Mother leafed through her book, recited a few lines from *Macbeth,* made a sigh of exasperation, and said, "What's his name?"

Moira looked out the window and swallowed hard and took a deep breath, remembering his intense eyes that had shown a little light when she'd said her best subject was calculus, and heard his soft voice in her ear saying, "So cute, and in Science Club." She repeated, "His name is Corey Donogan."

"Dona-who? Irish. That's all you need. You can bet he drinks like a fish. Can't you find a nice Norwegian boy? Or at least someone who's not a Catholic?"

"He's on the football team," Moira said.

Mother looked at Moira's hair and reached for her scissors. She wiggled her finger for Moira to come over. "Football team? That means he can't have a dirty mind, like they all do?"

Mother clipped some hair at her temples. "Where does he want to take you? To some lover's lane, I suppose."

Moira swallowed hard again. "No, to a movie."

Mother snorted softly. "Which movie? Something dirty, like a Sophia Loren movie, I suppose."

Moira felt anger rise to her head like the red mercury in a thermometer. She pulled away from Mother. Mother had the scissors up in the air like a weapon. She looked at Moira in surprise, then put the scissors down.

"Well, what movie?"

"A musical. With Julie Andrews."

Mother rolled her eyes. "Jesus," she said, as if she were spitting out something that was oily. "That disgusting broad? She has the biggest jaw on any woman I've ever seen. And that sickeningly sweet way of hers makes me want to puke."

"Never mind," Moira said irritably, gathering up her books and heading for her room.

Mother put the scissors away in the drawer and said in her sweetest voice, "Well, since your father's out of town . . . I guess it's all right."

Moira felt like squeezing her Mother's squarish body in gratitude, but she remembered that the last time she tried to hug Mother she'd recoiled.

"I don't know what to wear," Moira said, hopeful that Mother would give her the money to buy an outfit. Besides her cranberry outfit, which Corey had already seen, the only other clothes she had were her sewed-up greaser outfits.

"Want to wear my new 'nothing' blouse and the herringbone A-line skirt?"

"I don't know if they'll fit."

Moira meant the skirt might be too big in the waist, but Mother said, "You're so big in the bust"—the word "bust" came out of Mother's mouth like an assault—"I hope you don't stretch it out." Then she threw in, "You're not wearing padding, are you, Moira?"

Moira turned to look to see if she was joking. Her face felt hot and embarrassed and she was glad she hadn't hugged Mother. "No."

"Come here, let me feel."

Moira stood and let Mother feel her breasts.

Then she hurried into Mother's room to look for the outfit.

* * *

Mother's outfit was okay if she wore a belt around the waist to keep the skirt from falling down. The blouse was perfect, a "nothing" blouse, sweet and demure, that buttoned up the back, the latest style.

Corey had combed his thick yellow hair down into a modified Beatles haircut. He wore a madras shirt and a navy blue V-neck and white jeans. All the experience Moira had—Gary, Mr. Smealz, and all the others—was erased, and she was a virgin trying all over again to learn how to do these things right. She felt so nervous seeing him coming up the driveway just as he'd promised he would, actually showing up, that she started giggling uncontrollably, unsure if she was laughing or starting to cry.

Mother came out of the kitchen, and for a split second she wore a motherly, concerned face. "Come to the kitchen, hon, I'll get the door."

Mother was dressed up in a red knit sheath and red-and-black high heels. She even had red button earrings on. She looked as pretty as Moira remembered her ever looking.

Where would she be going? She never got this dressed up when she went to the movies. There was no PTA meeting tonight, and Daddy was out of town so they weren't going to a company thing, and it wasn't her birthday so they weren't going out to dinner.

"You must be Corey," Mother said, trying to sound flirty-tough in the nineteen-forties way that she always had with that librarian over at the North Side branch and the way she did lately with that grocery store manager. And probably—most lately—with Mr. Smealz. Moira wondered if Mother's Puritan act really was just an act, an act to convince Daddy and the girls but, more to the point, to convince herself.

"Yes, ma'am. Nice to meet you."

"Oh my God, don't call me ma'am. I'm not a hundred years old, even if I look it."

Corey's appraising eyes looked the way you would look if a stranger on the street said that to you, but then he laughed. "No, I mean . . ."

"Oh, I know, you're from the South. I can hear a trace in your accent."

"No, just Illinois, near Springfield, ma'am. I mean, Mrs. Uh—"

"Eleanor."

"Mrs. Eleanor."

Mother laughed.

"Well, the old fogey is going to leave you two young ones alone," she said, then called, "Moira."

"No, you look young enough to be her sister. Like on that Ivory Soap commercial."

"Well, let's not carry this too far," Mother said with a little chuckle in a deeper voice than she usually used.

Moira went to the bathroom to check her makeup and calm down. It almost seemed as if Mother, not she, were going on this date. Mother was asking if he wanted a drink, "A highball? A beer before you go?" Corey sounding surprised, then saying he wasn't allowed to drink during football season, Mother ignoring that and asking if he liked her new earrings.

Moira came into the room and Mother even seemed to give Corey the Look, the Look she gave Taryn, the Look that zeroed in on someone and said, *I know it, you know it, everyone else knows it. This girl is fucked up and we don't like her, but remember that I have to be her mother.*

Mother turned the radio on and slipped into her sarcastic mode. When "Sukiyaki" came on, Mother said, "Too bad they couldn't find any American records to play. Singing about sukiyaki! I'm going to record a song about macaroni and cheese and send it over to Japan."

Corey chuckled. Moira came to the living room, wishing Mother would stop or at least change the radio station. When the Angels sang "My Boyfriend's Back," Mother raised her plucked-out and penciled-in eyebrows and said, "Poor girl, she's so popular that her boyfriend has to beat them off with a club. You should have such problems, huh, Moira?"

Corey gave Mother the appraising look again, and then he laughed out loud. Moira doubted he'd had much experience with sarcasm in his life.

"You look nice," he said, giving Mother's outfit on Moira's body a quick look. "Well, come on, Miss Straight A's." He held the door for her, Moira not knowing what to do and motioning for him to go first, then too late realizing that must be one of those polite things you were supposed to do on dates, let the guy hold the door while you walked through ahead.

"When will you be home?" Mother asked.

"We're seeing *The Sound of Music*. It's kind of long, so we may not be back until almost midnight," Corey said.

Mother muttered, "Julie Andrews—the jaw on that woman could be used as a nutcracker. *The Sound of Music,* oh Jesus," then she added under her breath, "Julie Andrews, yech." Then she called out cheerfully, "Okay, before midnight. Otherwise she'll turn into a pumpkin."

They all laughed and Moira felt buoyed with relief that Mother was maybe approving of something for once.

Corey's car was not a souped-up Chevy or hot-rod Ford but a respectable little navy blue Volkswagen.

The VW shook to a start and they were wheezing off, the sound of respectability bouncing through the subdivision street, to see Julie Andrews.

Twenty-two

ALOYSIUS PULLED ONTO the highway. He wasn't expected home for three more days, so he'd tried to call Eleanor to say he'd be home early, but there'd been no answer. Probably out shopping.

He pictured Eleanor walking out of the house, tall and elegant, her hair so short that just above the nape of the neck it was bristly and made him think of the old expression about not getting your dander up. Eleanor had her dander up all the time. Ah, but hell, she was an impressive woman. Intelligent, attractive, respectable. A saint, that woman, and he still loved her every bit as much as the day he met her.

It would be late and they'd be finished with dinner, he supposed, but he wasn't hungry. Just needed a drink. Should he start off with a nice strong shot or two? He closed his eyes for moment, imagining the impact of the whiskey on his brain. That made it all worth it, didn't it?

But no, a cold beer, *m–m–m–m*, so cold you couldn't taste it at first, would be better, because it would be late and whiskey kept you awake before it put you to sleep. Hell, he didn't have to have whiskey every single night. Nope, a beer and maybe a plate of snacks. Piece of some of that boiled ham Eleanor kept around for sandwiches, some black olives, some green onions with lots of salt. He wondered if by some miracle there were green onions in the house. A cocktail, some snacks, some quiet. Not some goddamn motel but his own house, for a change.

Every time he thought of that house, he was reminded of the ten-thousand-dollar mortgage he had on it. The whole thing scared him, because having a mortgage implied stability, steadiness. He hadn't grown up around people who lived like that. Ma and Dad had only finally settled down when Ma came into that little bit of money.

Aloysius always felt kind of bad when he thought about that law-suit. It happened way back when Wish was just starting high school. Ma had been over at that old lady neighbor's house bor-rowing something. That nice old lady who always gave Wish a piece of licorice. Ma had tripped on the stairs on her way out. Skinned her ankle a little bit or something. So what does Ma do? She goes out and hires herself a slick lawyer who gives her the name of some slick doc who says she'd injured her back through the old lady's "willful neglect." The old lady doesn't have any insurance—in those days, in that neighborhood up in International Falls who has insurance?—but the old lady is from the old country and does things the old country way and Ma knows about the cashbox under the bed. Turns out there's pretty near eight thousand dollars under the old lady's bed. Ma gets the bulk of it what with the old woman not hiring a lawyer herself, being so confused. So with that nice cash settlement Ma buys herself a Model A and a liquor store to run.

Sometimes Wish felt bad about that, but then he'd remember that that was how the world was. *They're all out to get you. So you gets them first.*

No, until he got away from home and went to college Wish hadn't been around people who believed in steadiness and hard work. He'd been brought up with the attitude that you had to keep your eye open for the weak, the suckers of the world, and if some-one was nice to you they wanted something, or if they really trusted you, well, that was their problem.

Maybe that was why he was such a good salesman. He hadn't entirely shaken that attitude. And yet the good part of him some-times felt bad when he gypped someone, like the store up in Black Falls that he sold those inferior fishing rods to. Some kid would get one for his birthday and it would snap off the first time he got a bite. Sometimes it bothered Wish, the way the world worked. Some-times Wish thought he was the only goddamned person in the entire world with any morals.

Yes, a cold beer was going to taste good. Jesus Christ, he could hardly wait. A couple of cold ones. Just two or three tonight. He could almost feel the moment of truth when the alcohol hit his brain—like a big boxing glove on the brain, knocking hard enough yet soft enough that the kicks and bites of the day would begin to recede into the background and you could laugh about them.

What was on tonight? "The Rifleman"? "The Rebel"? "Gunsmoke"? Hell, he couldn't keep them straight. All good shows, though, all teaching good, honest American values.

Maybe he should stop off and have a few to get him by until he got home. Hell, he deserved his little reward. It was a tough world for him. Hell, a tough life. A tough life made up of tough days. And it had been one hell of a day.

First, he'd woken up pissed off again about that time he saw Eleanor sitting there on the side of the road talking to that librarian, her face looking so relaxed and friendly. Their cars side by side the way cops do it so they can talk, front end to ass end to front end to ass end. Like the cars are getting ready to mate or something. Surprised the hell out of him. There he was driving down the goddamn county road and he sees his own station wagon and just about faints. Looks and it's a woman with that dander-up haircut like Eleanor's. Stops the car and he'll be goddamned if it isn't Eleanor. Looking at Aloysius like she can't even remember who the hell he is, then remembering, oh yeah, her husband, and looks defensive. Gives him some story how she was asking that librarian for directions to Dell Rapids. Since when did she need directions to Dell Rapids? The two of them looking like the cat that swallowed the canary.

But what the hell could he say? He'd been almost as embarrassed as he was confused and almost as confused as he was mad.

Drove off, watched in the rearview mirror as Eleanor drove off too. But it ate away at him. Happened a month ago and Wish still couldn't get it off his mind. Someone trying to make a pass at his wife. His good wife.

Then what? He lost a piece of the sales territory to some young punk, that kid everyone was so impressed with. Connersen had called Wish in and broken the news to him, and Wish had frozen for a moment. Could not believe his ears when he heard they were taking Northern Iowa from him and giving it to that punk. That punk had started to really burn Wish's ass last spring when he won the company award and he got a free trip to Mexico, son of a bitch

came in wearing that sombrero to show off. Then that company
bonus . . .

Wish had gone out and had a few at lunch. That had helped for a
few hours.

How the hell was Wish going to pay his bills next month? It was
so goddamned expensive to live these days. What if he couldn't do
it? What if he never sold another Louisville Slugger again in his life?
What would they all do? Go live in a teepee?

Wish wondered about his sales ability. Was he as good as he
thought? He knew he was smooth, he knew you just had to out-
smart people, just be a little bit smarter and if you get pissed off
don't show, just be smooth as ice. Glide right over that ice with
your stick ready, then slam that puck right past the sons of bitches
into the goal.

There was a bar, but it looked like the kind of place where a guy
in a suit would be asking for trouble. Sometimes it would be nice
not to be the guy in the suit. But then he never had fit in with the
lumbermen up north. Wish McPherson had been too intelligent.
School had been easy for him. Okay, so he didn't get all A's like he
bragged to Eleanor and the girls, but he'd had passing grades, better
than passing grades, and that was a lot more than anyone had ever
expected from him.

Not that anyone had expected anything from his report card—he
didn't recall Ma ever looking at it once, Dad either. And not that
anyone had expected much of anything from him; the best lesson
Wish McPherson had learned as a kid was to run the other way
when he heard his name called.

Ah hell, but he'd had fun anyway when he was a kid. He could
still picture the new black hockey skates he'd won from Mr. Du-
bois, the owner of the hardware store. Winning those hockey skates
had been the best thing in his life. Nine years old. Nothing like that
had happened since.

Oh, that wasn't true. A hero. Wishbone McPherson, and all the
broads loved him. Eileen what was her name? A lady, not a broad.
Church every Sunday.

Unlike Mom and Dad, who never went to church. Funny how the
church catches up with you, though. They find someone to tote you
along to Sunday school. Did him good, too. Otherwise he'd proba-

bly have ended up in jail, like Johnny Hartlee or Virg Cummins and some of those other punks back home.

Instead, he was a respectable family man. With a respectable wife. When they first knew each other, Eleanor had been just about floored when he told her he was still a virgin, that he didn't believe in sex before marriage. She was a virgin too, of course, but didn't know a fellow could be that way.

Wish jammed the accelerator to the floor. He knew he was a good salesman—hell, last year he led the company in ammunition sales. Oh, he knew he pushed too hard sometimes and that he let the edges of his temper ooze out too much sometimes in front of a prospect. On the annual personnel review, Jack Connersen told him that. As soon as Connersen started criticizing him, Wish had felt that goddamn thing where his eyes started to water, and had had to blow into his handkerchief. "Allergies," he always said when that happened. Connersen suggested Wish excuse himself for a minute whenever he felt hostility building toward the client, go into the crapper and take a few deep breaths, wash his hands and face.

What pissed Wish off the most was when people were inconsiderate. When they didn't observe common courtesies and show ordinary consideration. Like this: you walks in hauling your samples trunk, say it's full of baseballs or footballs or dart boards or hunting rifles. So you opens the goddamn thing up and starts demonstrating. Say you brings out your best deer rifle; you tells about the special you've got this month, you goes on talking, and looking over at the prospect, you sees that he's all ears listening to you tell about your line, and then, after he's let you waste a frigging half hour on him, he shakes his head and says he isn't interested. Just like that!

Jesus, that's inconsiderate. You feels like taking aim at the son of a bitch.

But as Connersen said, clients were going to do things like that, "browse," dick you around and waste your time, then buy their line from the next guy who came in. Connersen reminded him that you had to be cool even if some son of a bitch was going to waste your time, knowing he's not interested.

Still, sometimes he wondered where people's sense of decency was, anyway.

Wish saw a liquor store and stopped and went in for a pint.

He came out of the liquor store, unscrewed the cap, and felt that familiar satisfaction as the seal broke on the pint. He looked around and took a nip. Jesus, that was good. Firewater. Ha-ha. He took another long one, then one more, then one more and screwed the top on and put it in the trunk where the spare tire was supposed to be. As a gesture to Eleanor, he kept his pint in the trunk rather than in the glove compartment.

Spare tire being repaired now because of the general lack of concern of people in this world for others.

He got into the car and turned on the ignition. Losing half his territory, then getting a flat tire by running over a nail some asshole left right in the middle of the road. Now what in the hell kind of person would do that, anyway? Did no one have any respect for other people? Any concern? He wouldn't do anything like that. In fact, Wish was the kind of fellow who would stop his car and out of consideration for others pull over to the side of the road and go and pick the nail up, so that no one else would run over it. And what thanks did he get? Someone leaves a nail in the road for *him* to run over. Wish's blood surged angrily and he remembered Connersen's words about taking a deep breath and calming himself: *Oh well,* Wish said up to the heavens, *that's how the world works. That's human nature.*

He felt just a little bit better now, now that the fingertips of the alcohol were starting to massage his brain. So then what had happened? Oh yeah. While he's trying to swerve out of the way of the nail, some other son of a bitch comes barreling through the intersection, misses Wish's Ford by a hair, then goes on his merry way. So Wish screeches the brakes loud, extra loud, so the asshole can hear what he's done to Wish.

Wish felt tears start to come to his eyes remembering it. Dammit. This was so embarrassing. It happened in front of people and he always had to turn around and pretend something had blown in his eye if he couldn't pass it off as allergies. When he got mad, felt like the world was turning on him, his goddamn eyes watered. Couldn't he just get rashes or ulcers or heart attacks or some goddamn thing other fellows got?

And then what the hell had happened? Yeah, I'll tell you what

happened, Wish said to himself out loud. I takes the goddamn tire
to the goddamn gas station to get the hole patched, and the sons of
bitches just sit there smoking their cigarettes while I stands there.
The sons of bitches. So I stands there looking at them, just looking
at the bastards, waiting for them to acknowledge me, and the more
I stands and looks impatient, the more slowly they puffs on their
goddamn cigarettes and shoots the breeze. So I finally picks up my
tire and walks the hell out. One of them is calling out as I hurl it
into the trunk, "Sir, can I help you," and I acts like he doesn't exist,
just like he did with me, and I goes screeching my brakes out of
there and goes to the gas station over on the other side of the street.

It had been the right thing to do. A person had to have standards.

Wish spotted a bar with a cocktail-glass neon sign: The Starlight
Club—Cocktails, dancing. He pulled into the parking lot. To hell
with the dancing, but he was going to have a cocktail, by God. And
why not, why shouldn't he? That's what cocktails were for, the end
of a tough day. Jesus, it wasn't illegal or anything, although you'd
think it was a capital offense the way Eleanor carried on.

Jesus but Eleanor griped his ass sometimes. That librarian ought
to have his teeth knocked in.

It was fairly crowded with what looked to be salesmen and secre-
taries. He sat at the padded bar and got the bartender's attention.
He enjoyed the feeling of being part of a crowd without having to
talk to anyone. Here was the thing about drinking: you likes to get
drunk because then your head is handed over to another power.
Your brain is on hold. Vacation time. Vacation from responsibility
you can't really handle. Well, it's time to hand over the old brain
and take a rest.

He finished his drink in three quick gulps and ordered another.
He was going to have two. After he'd downed the second, he figured one more wouldn't hurt, and as he drank that, a woman in a
low-cut dress sat next to him. Her hair was gray but she looked
fairly young. No, he guessed it was that platinum blond all puffed
up the way the gals fixed their hair nowadays. Purple stuff smeared
all over her eyes. He ordered another shot.

She held a cigarette in front of his face. He reached for matches
on the bar and fumbled until he lit one. Having been an athlete,
he'd never even been tempted to smoke. She leaned down to his

match and gave him a too friendly smile. She was a tough-looking broad. The thought of going to that motel up the road came to him, but then he'd have to get another pint somewhere if there were going to be two of them. He wondered vaguely if there was a liquor store on the way to the motel, tried to remember but he would have noticed. He wondered vaguely whether the bartender would sell him a pint for the road.

A lot of the fellows boasted about the women they picked up, but the funniest thing was Wish had never done it. It just didn't seem like the right thing to do.

It was also inconvenient. He couldn't imagine going with some strange woman without a bottle, and when he really thought about it, he couldn't imagine spending more than two minutes with some cheap, brainless tramp. That was the thing about Eleanor. She was an intelligent, refined woman. Wish was proud to be married to her.

Something inside Wish felt hollow. He counted out change for the bartender's tip, exactly ten percent to the penny, and walked out without saying goodbye to the blond or whatever the hell she was. There were times when Wish thought he was something of a loner.

He felt nervous now and wanted a beer. Just a beer or two. What awaited him at home? A beer. But then Eleanor giving him a hard time about it. Taryn going to her room, Moira watching from behind those glasses that made her look so wide-eyed and pinched at the same time.

A mystery, that Moira. Probably in her room with her nose in a book right now. An odd duck. Who had said that about someone before? His mother's unevenly dyed hair came into his mind again, and he remembered people saying that about her, that and worse, laughing but their laughs fading as they got to know her, got to know that she wasn't a woman to fool around with, her and that cold, calculating look in her pale eyes, her and her law books, threatening to sue people, outsmarting the cops. Moira must have gotten her brains from Ma. Smart as a whip. He clenched his fist and closed his eyes and the picture was gone, only to be replaced by his father walking around the house looking for defiance among his sons. All the time in his long underwear, smoking those stinking cigars, his teeth out, five days' growth of beard when he gave up on

working and just sat around the house dreaming up ways to sue the
government or cheat someone. When Wish and his brothers pissed
him off, him going out in back and staying out in the shed working
on some whittling project and ignoring Wish, not speaking to them
for hours, for days. Doing that to his mother, too, sitting there and
not speaking to anyone. Hell, that could go on for weeks or sometimes months. One time his old man went from summer to Thanksgiving without speaking to anyone in the house. Broke his silence as
he was carving the turkey. Cut out the tail and handed it to Wish,
telling him he'd like this piece because it had extra flavor inside.
Broke into hilarious laughter. They'd all laughed. That had done it
—and the silence was over for a while, all the way through Christmas, as Wish now remembered.

Wish laughed nervously now. His laughter ran out of steam as he
remembered the time Ma, too, went for two months not speaking
to Wish. Ma not speaking to Wish and the old man all the time
with a snootful. Jesus, he'd thought for a while he'd go crazy. How
old had he been? Nine, ten? But he took it, took it like a little man,
not some crybaby sissy.

Wish felt his face turn red and his eyes water.

Lying in bed sucking his thumb—sucked his thumb until he
started drinking whiskey—and feeling as if the walls were getting
higher and higher and yet moving toward him so that soon he'd be
crushed to death.

Wish had had a dream about his father recently, a dream he
didn't like to remember. He was asking his father a question, and
he got one of those silences, as if Aloysius didn't exist. So he dared
to stand up to the old man, shouting at him, letting loose, pounding
the old man with his fists. Suddenly the old man got up, stubbed
out his cigar, and went and got his hunting knife. He chased Aloysius around the house with that knife, upstairs and back down and
then into the basement. Somehow he got out of the house and ran
into the street in the dream, yelling, screaming, asking people for
help, but they just looked at him like he was crazy or a siss-ass
fruit. He'd awakened shaking and covered with sweat and feeling
so damned alone in the world.

No, he wasn't alone. Not as long as he had Eleanor. A fine
woman. A respectable woman.

Wasn't she?

Hell, he wouldn't care what the hell she was as long as she cared for him. Maybe that was what gnawed away at Wish. Eleanor never had cared for him, if he really wanted to face the truth.

The kids liked him. Or used to. Something had gotten into that Moira. When he thought of that little greasy-haired punk in the backyard with her, he could almost taste the metal fillings in his teeth. He was angry at Moira that she would get involved with a boy like that. That she would let any boy kiss her. Moira didn't love her father anymore. Wanted to leave him.

The thought of that was unbearable.

Aloysius had the nagging feeling that Eleanor meant it sometimes when she said she hated him. When it came right down to it, the first person who had ever returned love to Aloysius Wesley McPherson had been Moira, that little girl with curly hair who liked to feed birds and read books. As if to make up for twenty-odd years of loving without ever being loved in return, this little girl worshiped him and he responded with love that would fill the Grand Canyon.

Little bastard punk kissing his curly-haired girl. Wish knew what he wanted. It was the same thing Wish wanted from girls when he was that age. The same thing he almost got from that tramp Lenore-what-was-her-last-name before he came to his senses and stopped himself. Only one he didn't stop himself with was Eleanor. First time and bingo, she was in trouble. Eleanor just a kid in school, Wish still in college himself, having to drop out and move into his aunt's house and work in that hardware store. Although those were the days.

Well, some little shitbird wasn't going to touch his daughter. No punk was going to knock up his daughter. They were going to change some traditions in this generation. Neither Wish nor Eleanor could remember a woman in the family who hadn't had to get married. Neither of them could recall a real family wedding. Neither had wedding pictures in their family albums. No white dresses and veils and church altars. Just a lot of big bellies.

Eleanor said that Moira was starting to think she was better than the rest of them because that science teacher who probably sat down to pee made her think she was something. Hell, it was true, she was smart, all right. Too smart for a girl. Too attractive, too, or maybe he was prejudiced. The worst thing was the way she walked around in those short skirts. Eleanor said it was best not to say anything, that she'd grow out of it. As far as he was concerned, that wasn't his little girl anymore. He didn't know how to feel about Moira. Didn't understand the whole goddamn thing.

Eleanor also told Wish to keep his eyes off Moira's bosoms. Wish felt his face go red. What was he, a sex maniac? If it weren't for Eleanor, he wouldn't know what the hell was wrong and right in this world. He wouldn't have anyone to tell him he was a naughty boy.

And he was a naughty boy. A naughty, naughty boy that Eleanor straightened out.

Sometimes he could feel that he hated Moira as much as he used to love her for not becoming what he wanted—a modest, nice schoolteacher lady he could be proud of. Instead, they had this. You just didn't know what got inside that girl's head, why she acted the goddamned way she did. Hell, he didn't tell her to go around with her ass sticking out, Eleanor didn't tell her to spend all her time in that bedroom with her books. Everything Moira did she did to excess, goddammit. Why the hell couldn't she be like anyone else? *What the hell was wrong with that girl?*

And yet somewhere deep inside, Aloysius knew that Moira had integrity. Real integrity. And the whole family was jealous of her for that one thing, her integrity.

But he didn't like to look below the surface of things. Best to judge things as they appear, he always said. Be up front yourself and judge others up front, too.

Well, there was always Taryn. She was turning out decent. The thing was, Moira was the one with spirit. The interesting one. And, yes, the one, in spite of the makeup and the boys, with integrity. Wish slumped a bit. Integrity was such a precious commodity in this world. Lord knew he didn't have much of it himself. But that didn't mean he couldn't admire it.

By the time he got onto their street and saw the familiar pattern of lights in his own house's windows, he was remembering the way Moira's eyes crinkled when she was a little girl, the way her little-girl voice laughed when he gave her a horsie ride, and he wondered why God had to be so cruel as to take away your little girl.

No lights on in the house. Surely Eleanor was home by now. Probably in the bedroom. She'd goddamn better be. If Wish wanted to be honest, he'd say he wondered what the hell she did when she went out to the movies. Somewhere, he knew she wasn't at the movies.

Somewhere he didn't want to know that he knew it either. He seemed to be able to not know it most of the time, especially when he was drunk.

And Moira, goddammit, was just as sneaky as her mother.

But let's try to stay in a good mood.

It was just about dark as he pulled into the driveway. But he could see well enough to see that someone had left the lawn mower in the driveway. He swerved wide and slammed the brakes loud, so that whoever left it there—Moira probably, she was so absent-minded—would hear and see how he'd almost hit it, then almost ran over the shrub trying to avoid it. That would have taught her a lesson, dammit, if he'd run over the shrub. Would have taught her a damn good lesson. He'd have made her go out and buy a new one with her own goddamn money, if she had any, and get out there and plant the damn thing.

But disaster had been averted. Or was the correct word avoided? Hell, he didn't know—he wasn't some goddamn intellectual. Let's the girls be the intellectuals, the schoolteachers. Damn, he had wanted to be a schoolteacher so bad. A coach. Kids looking up to him. Order in the classroom. But he had a family to raise and couldn't go back to school.

He pulled into the garage, but the station wagon was gone. He pressed the garage door closed and now the day and the world were behind him. No disaster, Aloysius, so relax. He laughed out loud, feeling good now that he was a little relaxed, and shook his head.

The shrub was safe. And Taryn was so cute, so damn sweet. What a kid. And he pictured her when they brought her out after she was born. Tiny, premature. Almost died. Eleanor said she'd never lose that preemie look. Cute as a button, though—dark hair, like Wish's, blue eyes, too. "She looks just like you, Mr. McPherson," the nurse said. Nice nurse. Nice girl. Nice job for a girl, nursing. That nurse was a truly wonderful person. All nurses were probably wonderful people. Not like doctors, just after the money and the glory.

Schoolteacher's better than a nurse, though, more job security, prestige. Teachers are wonderful people, like nuns.

Where the hell was the station wagon? Eleanor must be out at the grocery store. A wonderful woman. Forget his stupid suspicions. A pain in the ass sometimes, but wasn't that their role in life, to keep men in line? To be the good ones while men went out and did bad things? To let you know when you were a naughty boy?

Hell, they were okay, women. Not level-headed like men, not rational and basing decisions on the facts, but okay. Eleanor was a fine, clean, good woman. Decent, no tramp, that girl he'd married. Despite the rough beginning, her being pregnant. Those things happened.

But he thought briefly of that lecher over at the library, the one always making eyes at Eleanor. Wish's blood gurgled. A feeling that was almost sexual ran through his gut as he felt jealous anger course through his body.

Moira's too nice to ever want to hurt you back. Eleanor, on the other hand . . .

He got out of the car and went to the trunk and got the pint and went back to sit in the car a minute. He took a few nips from the pint. Ah, hell with it all. He paused to think of all the wonderful people. Charlie Hargreaves at work. A wonderful person. Cooper Smith, a helluva wonderful guy. Just wonderful. Even Connersen. One helluva wonderful guy when he wasn't being your boss. Wish looked down at the cement floor and gave a little laugh. And his kids were so wonderful. They should never grow up. Where was Moira?

Wish felt a panic at thinking Moira might be out somewhere, defying him, getting into trouble, endangering her life, and his heart began to pound and his eyes began to water just a little bit. He got so scared that something would happen to one of his kids he almost couldn't stand to live sometimes, like you should kill yourself first so you don't have to face anything happening to them. If anything ever happened to those girls, some punk high-schooler driving the way they do, wrapping the car around a tree like that one he saw out on Route 115. The windshield shattered like a big spider web, dried blood on the steering wheel, on the car seat. Christ, he'd been eating a cinnamon Life Saver at the time when he saw that up-close at the gas station and just about puked. Couldn't ever eat a cinnamon Life Saver again in his life.

His thoughts of Moira rested on her bosoms. The thought of someone looking at them, wanting to . . . but this was disgusting. And he pictured them again growing out plump and juicy . . . but wait, this was his daughter . . . as far as he was concerned, there were no bosoms, none in the house.

And yet he was surrounded by them in that house. He felt an onslaught of shame, like something rotten rushing through him. It tasted like bile in his mouth. He almost felt like crying. He saw his father's long underwear, the fly, the bagging seat. He saw his mother giving men the eye like she did when they came into the liquor store, until the men came in with the law.

His mother was a tramp. He'd never been able to admit it. Oh, they'd said it was the drink or this and that, but she was a tramp. And the old man knew. Wish felt himself slump at this realization, then felt a panic in his bowels.

Another sip and it didn't matter so much about Ma. He put the pint back in the trunk and pulled out the sample trunk and the two-suiter.

He pushed inside the door with his two-suiter and his sample trunk—never liked to leave the trunk in the car, you never knew, what with crime rates these days. Empty house. Helluva greeting. Where were the girls at least? Out shopping with Eleanor, he supposed.

Or were they? His heart bumped around in his chest.

Letting go of the sample trunk by the door, he took his suitcase to the bedroom and tossed it in the corner. He changed clothes and went to the kitchen. Reached up into the cupboard and found his bottle and took a nip and put the bottle back and went to the living room to turn on the TV. He liked to have the TV singing to him from the other room while he was fiddling around in the kitchen.

He spotted flowers on the hi-fi next to the other phone. The kind the florist delivered. What the hell! Eleanor never bought flowers. Oh yeah, there was that one time. The blood in his veins jumped at the memory. He'd wondered for a moment that time, as he did now, if she'd really ordered them herself.

He went to the kitchen and opened the refrigerator and got out a cold bottle of Black Label. He jerked the drawer open to find an opener, frantically rustling through the kitchen paraphernalia until he found one, and popped the cap. He took a long, cold swig. Like seawater to a fish that someone caught, put in his creel, then decided to throw back in.

Just like seawater to a fish. Its oxygen. Without it, the fish couldn't live.

He wandered into the living room. Where the hell was Eleanor? Oh yeah, at the grocery store. He spun on his heel and went to the kitchen and put his empty in the cardboard case under the sink and got himself another beer. Oh, that first sip of your second beer at home. Just like a fish with his seawater. He opened the refrigerator. Black olives, yes, salami, yes, green onions, no. He took a couple of slices of Velveeta and got a box of saltines. Then why was the grocery list still on the refrigerator under the magnet? Out at the shopping center. Buying clothes. He checked his watch. Nine o'clock. Store'd close soon.

A little while later he heard footsteps on the little cement stoop and in came Taryn.

"Daddy," she said happily.

Nice kid. The only person ever happy to see him.

"Where's your mother?"

"I don't know."

"Moira?"

"I don't know. I went to Mary Lou's after school. I haven't been home all day."

Goddammit, where the hell were they?

Flowers on the hi-fi. What in the goddamn hell was going on here?

He got another drink and Taryn disappeared into her bedroom.

Wish had fallen asleep in his chair. When she came in, she was a little blurry but he could see that she was dressed up and that her lipstick was smeared and that she looked first angry then scared when she saw him sitting there.

"Where the hell have you been?" he said.

"Out at a movie."

"You sure get dressed up these days for the movies."

Eleanor didn't say anything.

"Where'd the flowers come from? You got a boyfriend?"

She made a barely inaudible snort. "Wouldn't you like to know! What are you doing home, anyway?"

An old annoyance, maybe an old rage, flirted with him for just a moment.

"The head office called me back. They want me to go to Fargo tomorrow. Where's Moira?" Taryn and Eleanor exchanged looks— they had this look that bound them together. Sometimes when he saw them doing it he felt like knocking their heads together. But right now it wasn't that important. After smiling at Eleanor, Taryn gave him that half-smile, a copy of Eleanor's cynical ain't-life-shitty smile from the stool in the kitchen, but didn't miss a beat picking up the phone. He didn't like it when she was on the phone.

"What the hell else goes on around here when I'm on the road?"

"Wild parties with a conga line down the block," Eleanor said in her Mae West voice. That was the thing about Eleanor. She was a funny woman. Life of the party. When they got invited to parties, about once every ten years. Which suited him fine.

"I said, Where's Moira?"

Eleanor seemed to hesitate just slightly. "She's over at Rosemary's. They have a science project."

Rosemary. Wasn't she that girl with the hangdog expression whose parents were some kind of Bible-thumping holy rollers? Oh well, to each his own, he always said. That was Aloysius's motto— he was as easy to get along with as the next guy.

"When is she coming home?"

"Oh, soon, I should think," Eleanor said, not looking up.

"Maybe you'd better give her a call."

"I'm busy."

"What's the number? I'll call. Get off the phone, Taryn."

"No, it's all right."

Eleanor had turned the TV to another station. He went and changed the channel again, to something less stupid. Some cheap floozie with her tits hanging out. She looked a little like the secretary over at Bub's Hardware, the gal who did the books, what was her name? He pictured the woman at Bub's wiggling her ass off to tend to some customer's complaint, and hit the dial so hard it hurt his hand.

Eleanor looked both scared and mad at him for hitting the dial. He didn't so much mind her looking mad, but when she looked scared, it pissed him off. Like he was some kind of a monster.

His hand was hurting like hell. He put it next to his mouth and rubbed it on his cheek. "Ouch," he said.

Eleanor's expression changed. She almost looked genuinely sympathetic. One thing Wish was always getting from people was sympathy. People seemed to feel sorry for him a lot. He guessed if he got it a lot he must deserve it. Although he never seemed to be able to muster up any sympathy for himself.

But now Eleanor looked nervous, if Aloysius wasn't mistaken, glancing at the picture window every now and then, at the aluminum screen door with the moths buzzing against it.

"Where's Moira?"

"Sometimes I think you worry too much about Moira," Eleanor said. "Anyone would think maybe your interest in her is a little excessive." And her voice raised a suggestion like the upswing of someone's very delicate handwriting. He looked and saw that she had that raised-eyebrow look. Wish felt like he was four and had just been smacked for doing something he didn't know was wrong.

He went to the bathroom to get a Band-Aid. He opened the medicine cabinet to look. Shit. None up there. This goddamned household. They were always out of everything. He looked under the sink. There they were. Wait a minute. What the hell was this. Oh yeah, Eleanor's diaphragm case. Did she usually keep it here? He closed the cupboard and put on the Band-Aid and went back to the living room. Eleanor was in the kitchen.

Just as he sat down, the phone rang. Eleanor could get it on the kitchen phone. But it rang again and again and again, and she didn't answer it. When a commercial came on, he went to the kitchen to get a shot. Just a small one. Hell, he deserved it, with all the aggravation you had to put up with in life. Maybe another shot because this had been a doubly aggravating day. And another because the day wasn't done yet and probably wasn't done yet being aggravating.

There was the goddamn phone again. Now why the hell did Eleanor look so nervous? What had she done now? She was just looking at the phone, not answering, drinking her milk. "You going to get that?" he shouted.

"Just a minute," she said, but she wasn't moving.

"I'll get it," he said, and marched over, but when he picked it up the caller hung up.

She returned to the living room. He followed her. His show was back on so he sat down. The sight of those flowers sitting on the desk next to the phone aggravated the hell out of him. Eleanor went to look out the front window. The sight of Eleanor aggravated him now. She had on that dress she wore the time he took her out for the steak dinner.

Then he put the flowers and the dress and the phone call together.

"Got your good dress on, I see," he said when the next commercial came on.

"It's not such a good dress." Eleanor was looking daggers at him, so he retreated a half-step.

"Any special reason?"

The look on her face was disgust. "Any special reason for what?"

He took a swig. "For the not-so-good dress."

"None that I can think of. Any special reason why you're wearing your chinos and T-shirt?"

"Yeah, because I wear them every night." He went to the kitchen for a shot. Jesus Christ Almighty, that tasted good. Another and he'd start feeling the way he liked to, where his brain was sort of coasting along in perfect happiness and contentment. Where not a goddamn thing could get to him. Another shot and the feeling would be even better. His arm accidentally knocked a glass off the counter and it shattered on the floor. He could see Eleanor tensing in the living room, and *that* pissed him off.

"Who the hell is leaving glasses all over the goddamn house? Eleanor, can't you do the dishes every few weeks, whether they need it or not, instead of plunking your ass in the movie theater every night. *If* that's where your ass was tonight."

"You know where the soap and dishcloth are."

He was getting more and more pissed off about the flowers and the dress and her going out to the movies alone tonight. But what could he do? Deep down inside, was he afraid of Eleanor?

The thought of that made him feel like a trapdoor had just opened up on him. The thought of that was . . . *unbearable.*

"Wish, you'd better stop drinking. Right now."

No, he wasn't afraid of her. And it really pissed him off when she started nagging about the drinking. Couldn't a man have a cocktail once in a while and have a little peace around the house? He'd show her.

"Eleanor, I think you'd better shut up right now," he said through the kitchen entranceway, listening to see if his program was on. He couldn't remember what he was watching. That was the thing about TV these days, it was so goddamn lousy you couldn't even remember what you were watching when a damn commercial came on.

"If you don't stop drinking, I'm going out somewhere for the night."

"Looks like you're already going out," he said. What he meant was "Looks like you're ready to go out" or "Looks like you're already ready to go out," or whatever. He took another beer out of the refrigerator and came into the living room. He was starting to feel happy now. But as usual Eleanor was trying to ruin it. Why did she always have to ruin his good moods?

He glanced at Eleanor over in her chair now, and didn't like the expression on her face. He just didn't like it.

"What the hell's the matter with you, anyway? Why are you always starting a fight? Can't you stand to have peace around the house? Huh? Is a little peace too much for you?"

"Not when you're drunk."

"And leave me alone about it. I am not drunk."

Wish took another look at the flowers on the table next to the telephone, and goddamn if it didn't occur to him for the first time that that skinny-assed skirtchaser at the library hadn't always had flowers on the desk every time Wish came in there to check up on him.

The phone rang again and this time he lunged for it. He just held it to his ear, and he heard a male voice, and possibly a male voice that was beyond teenage years, say, "Hon?"

Wish felt very cool, super-rational, as he ripped off the cord and threw the telephone into the hallway. Then he picked up the vase of flowers, and hurled it at the wall. Daisies or whatever the hell they were, roses, all over the floor, walls, chair. That cleared his head. It got the anger out of it as if he'd just shattered all the anger inside his head, too. Eleanor, who had her drama book opened, didn't even look up. Bitch. Wish went and sat back down and watched his show until a commercial came on. He went to the kitchen and tripped over someone's shoes. He lifted his foot back, and with a mighty heave the shoes went sailing into the living room. Eleanor ducked. One of the shoes made a nice thud on the wall. He could tell Eleanor was getting pissed now. Good. Let her know how he felt.

Had the caller said *Hon?* Or had it just been *Huh?* or *Hi, uh?* Or had it even been a complete "Hello"? Wish wondered if he'd made a mistake.

He wasn't going to think about that phone call just yet. He was going to concentrate on his years of anger at Eleanor, gnaw on that for a while and save that phone call for dessert.

Was it possible? He'd kill her. Easy. Himself, too.

Now where did he put the shot glass? Goddamn it, it was somewhere in this pile of dishes. Look at this mess. Why did he have to come home to a shitpile like this? With his arm, very, very slowly, he swept the dishes onto the floor. The crash was louder and lasted longer than you would expect. It was very, very satisfying.

The anger was shattered again. He sipped from the beer in his hand and looked around at the floor. Goddamn mess now. And whose fault was it? Eleanor's, for leaving the mess around just to get knocked on the floor. Goddamn Eleanor was a slob, and she was always provoking him, too.

As he started to walk out of the kitchen, trying to avoid stepping on broken glass, he fell back and bumped the back of his head on the edge of the cupboard door. "Son of a bitch, that hurts like a bastard," he yelled as he rubbed the back of his head. No blood.

He reached up and got his pint and unscrewed the top and drank from the bottle. A good long drink. Then he put it back in the cupboard.

He crunched over the broken glass on his way out of the kitchen, and sat back down in his chair and watched his show. Glass was stuck to his shoe. Son of a bitch, he cut his thumb and finger pulling it out. Blood trickled down his arm, onto his shirt. He couldn't stand the sight of blood.

"Look at this, I cut myself," he said to Eleanor. "Get something for it."

Eleanor hadn't moved. She was staring at him as if he were the one who had started all this. It was hard to figure out whether he should be jealous or not, it was hard, because Eleanor had this way of looking at you. Hell, maybe he had had a little too much to drink. Maybe Eleanor was a nice clean girl still. It was hard to know. But he had this goddamn feeling that wouldn't go away that something was wrong.

It was Moira who was the bad one. Wasn't it? He knew someone was bad and now he couldn't remember who.

Maybe that just had been a boy on the phone. Some punk who would get nowhere, once he encountered Aloysius McPherson. Or some girl's father, the Bible thumper. On the other hand, the voice had sounded oily, predatory, ready to make an obscene remark.

He went back to the bathroom to get another Band-Aid. He fumbled with the box, goddamn way they made these things. He accidentally knocked out the diaphragm case onto the floor, and it opened when it fell.

No diaphragm inside.

His head went hot with jolts of blood.

That librarian. She was carrying on with that librarian, he'd known it all along. He walked into the living room with the diaphragm case. He tossed the empty diaphragm case onto the floor, casually.

"Read any good books lately, Eleanor?" he said calmly, more sober than he'd ever been in his entire life.

"What are you talking about?"

He pointed to the diaphragm case.

Eleanor smiled. "You're on the wrong trail, Sherlock. It's not the librarian. It's a schoolteacher. How do you like them apples, huh, Aloysius?"

Aloysius tried to picture a teacher with Eleanor. Aloysius knew he'd never been good enough for her. Not intellectual enough. Or for Moira, but then who was for that girl? He tried to remember the girls' teachers, and the effort made him feel drunk again. Then he heard a wheezing in the driveway, the sound of a car, unmistakably a Volkswagen. He didn't recall the Bible thumpers having a Volkswagen. He stood there for a split second, or was it a million years? A few minutes later, there was some commotion at the door. He went to take a sneak look, standing on the balls of his feet, and there was Moira reaching up to kiss some boy.

His daughter, kissing some sexed-up punk. He knew what the punk wanted. His face got hot and his wrists began to shake. Tears came to his eyes.

He made his way over to his sample trunks and pulled out his High Standard Duck Rib Twelve. He went to the utility room, opened the cupboard where he kept the shells, boxes and boxes of them, found the right ones, and loaded the gun.

Twenty-three

THERE WAS A yellow glow behind the drawn sheer drapes inside the house. Cricket song vibrated in the cool black air. Corey and Moira sat parked in the Volkswagen down the street from her house, both reluctant to let the evening end. He gently pulled Moira by the shoulder toward him and leaned down and kissed her.

When Corey had first dared to put his arm around her in the movie, she'd felt a part of him and his sweet life. She'd felt herself melt into him. It was the way girls who weren't sex maniacs were supposed to feel.

Now if she could just figure out a way to sneak out with Corey all the time, if Daddy went out of town enough, she could have a real boyfriend, be seen as a normal person at this Catholic high school. *If* Corey would sneak out—he didn't seem like the sneaky type.

"You're so different," Corey had whispered in her ear, making it tingle. How did the vibrations travel? Hammer, anvil, stirrup, tympanum, wasn't that it? "You're cute," he'd said too. "And nice. And have a great figure."

Corey liked her figure, all right, but he said what he really admired was how smart she was.

"You don't look like what you are," he'd said.

"I always assumed that was good," Moira said.

"It is and it isn't. Why not wear your glasses all the time and broadcast it to the world? That you're beautiful *and* smart at the same time?"

Beautiful and smart. Moira repeated that silently. She'd had her glasses on during the movie and felt self-conscious, and took them off whenever he turned to look at her.

"You look so intelligent in your glasses," he said. "It really turns me on." She'd put them back on.

"Something else I like about you."

Moira was in shock at the adulation she was receiving, but she managed to say, "What's that?"

"You're so good. You're a good person. I can just tell."

"No, you are. You play football, you talk very nice . . ."

Corey was a football hero. Well, maybe not a big *hero,* but he was on the team and played a lot, or so he said. And here Moira was an outcast, and he was with her.

But then she had it over him in the fact that her father had attended college for a while, and no one in Corey's family had. His parents were saving so that he could be the first. Corey told Moira that his whole family admired educated people, people like Moira's father.

After the movie, they'd driven in his bouncing little Volkswagen to Smitty's Drive-In over on the other side of town, where nobody knew her, and they had Cokes and fries with some friends of his.

He tried to kiss her again but Moira pulled away. She was in love. Oh please, God, don't let what happened with Gary Racer happen here. Don't let me do like I did with Jack or the others. Or Mr. Smealz. And the thought of Mr. Smealz made her furious at Mother as well as at Mr. Smealz. She was still furious at herself, but not quite so much. With Mother flirting with him, maybe doing more than that, now that Moira thought about it, she felt a little less dirty herself.

"I can't believe I'm really out with a girl who got an A in physics and is sexy on top of that. You're neat, Moira. My mother will be crazy about you, too, even if you're not Catholic."

Moira savored that, then said, "My mother is already crazy about you."

"What about your father?" Corey said. "Will he like me?"

Worry washed through Moira, but then she forced a smile. "He doesn't trust boys with me."

"Who can blame him?" Corey said. "Hey, I'm very good at buttering up fathers. Old Silver Tongue here. You say he sells sporting goods—hey, maybe I'll buy a ball from him, and I bet I'll end up selling him tickets to our next game."

Moira looked down at her fingernails. "Maybe."

"Science is my worst subject. I'm so dumb in it I couldn't even

come up with a science project last year. How about you? I'll bet
you had one."

Moira brightened now that the subject had changed. "I was in
the citywide science fair last year."

"Did you win a prize?" His voice was so eager, wholesome, innocent. The sound of respectability, along with the wheeze of his respectable little bouncing Volkswagen.

"Second. For a Neanderthal skull I made out of plaster of Paris."

He was looking at her as if she had some secret to the universe.

"Neanderthals," he said. "Oh yeah, I remember them from history. How do you know so much about Neanderthals?"

"I live with them," she said suddenly, surprising herself, breaking
out in laughter.

He laughed too. "Hey, that's no way to talk about your family.
I'll bet they're real nice."

Moira looked out the window for a moment. Then she tried to
laugh casually, and said, "I was just kidding."

They talked some more about Neanderthals and evolution. Corey
said he didn't know whether to believe in evolution. Moira said she
didn't think evolution was incompatible with religion. "I think that
at some point in evolving from *homo erectus* to *homo sapiens,* an
Adam and an Eve were born. The first real humans."

"You've got an explanation for everything, don't you? Listen, I've
got a problem with this friend of mine." And he went on to tell her
about a guy he'd been close friends with and now the guy was
hanging out with another crowd and Corey wanted to know what
to do.

Sometimes people thought that if you were smart in science, you
were smart about everything in life.

She didn't want to tell him that she was the last person on earth
to be consulted about problems with friends, since she'd only really
had two close friends in her life. "Why don't you just come out and
ask him why he's running around with the wild crowd?" she ven-
tured.

"Yeah," he said, as if that were the most brilliant thing he'd ever
heard. He kissed her ear again and she felt the tympanum ringing
with pleasure. Then her neck, and she cried out, it was so painfully
pleasurable. But she moved away again because this was so scary,

and smoothed her skirt and hugged her breasts and said, "What are you going to do after high school?"

"I want to go to college, then be a policeman. I'm going to be in the detective bureau and investigate crimes. But you need science for that," he said. He nuzzled her neck. "I'll need you around to coach me, I guess."

He told her his father had been a cop and was killed in the line of duty.

Moira squeezed his hand and felt so awfully bad for him. She tried to imagine how she would feel if her father were killed. It was strange, but she couldn't project herself into the situation, couldn't empathetically feel what Corey must feel.

Corey's lips brushed against her eyebrow.

He turned the radio on. They were playing an oldie from five, six years back—"To Know Him Is to Love Him." Moira saw herself in a pink prom dress, like the dresses the girls wore to Phil Ettinger's prom party that she hadn't been allowed to go to a few years ago and had been so miserable about. She saw herself now dancing with Corey to that song. His hand touched the side of her breast. She wanted him to touch her hot nipples, her thighs as sensitive as if someone had been gently poking them with hundreds of tiny pins. But she pulled herself away, the way you're supposed to. She was going to be in control. Sex when *she* wanted it, not when someone talked her into it. "I have to go home now," she said.

He looked a little annoyed at first but then said okay.

He pouted a little bit that she wouldn't make out anymore, but by the time they got home he was bright and cheerful again and wanted to know if she'd come watch him at the next football game on Friday night. She ached with the wish that Daddy would go out of town next Friday. She even prayed silently, please God, make Daddy go out of town next Friday. Then she smiled confidently, as if she were the kind of girl who could go to any game at the high school, as if her father actually encouraged her to have dates with nice young men, and said, "I'll have to ask Daddy."

His car idled in the driveway. The car radio sent "Hey Paula"— also from her loneliest years, now long gone—out into the translucent black night as he walked her up the sidewalk to the door. When he leaned down and kissed her at the doorstep, a big curtain opened on her life. She could see a path leading to college, getting married, having a house, being in love with your husband forever.

She was okay. If Corey liked her, she was okay.

After the kiss, he said, "Guess I'd better go," and his eyes were genuine, lingering. "There's a party after the game at the captain's house."

"I'm sure Daddy will say okay. I just have to ask him first and . . ." She started to lie gaily, but before she could finish her answer, the light from inside the house dimmed and she heard something and felt heat, and she turned and there was Daddy at the door, his light blue eyes sparking inside all those black lashes, his shoulders up, and a shotgun in his hands.

Daddy kicked the screen door open and it hit them and rattled. Corey looked at him, then at the gun, then back at Daddy with his eyes almost blank with unbelieving. "Who's this?" Corey said to Moira.

Daddy came outside and stood on the porch. They stepped backwards onto the lawn.

"You rotten little son of a bitch, what are you doing with her?" Daddy yelled.

"What?"

"Where were you?" he said to Corey, pointing the gun at him, then swinging toward Moira with the gun, then back to Corey. "What were you doing?"

Moira's throat wouldn't make a noise for a moment, then she thought she heard herself say, "Movie." But it was only a whisper that came out, so she shouted it out. *"A movie."*

Daddy stopped and looked at the ground, as if he were trying to figure out what the word *movie* meant. Corey was backing quickly down the lawn and Moira was up against the house. Daddy headed toward Corey, staggering worse than she'd ever seen. Moira went after him. "No, please." Out in the middle of the lawn, Daddy almost fell, then recovered himself and put the gun up in firing position.

"No!" she screamed. He turned toward her, the gun's barrel aimed right at her forehead, and she was looking down the face of horror so absolute it became nothingness. She backed up toward the steps and he came toward her in big, faltering steps.

"Eleanor," he said, then seeming to realize his mistake, he halted and put the gun down lower and stared at Moira, as if trying to remember who was who and what all this was about. He looked so sad and defeated, his shoulders hunched over and his jowls hanging like a bulldog's.

"Daddy," she said. Everything could be okay now. They'd gone to the end of the line. "We went to a movie, that's all."

"A movie?" he repeated, managing to slur even that word.

And then he grabbed hold of her sweater and fell back to the ground, pulling it off. Moira lurched backward into the shrubs. He grunted and pushed himself up and came over and grabbed, trying to help her out of the brambles, sobbing and saying he was sorry, and this time he got her blouse—Mother's blouse—and as he pulled, the buttons in back snapped like popcorn and the blouse swung open. She got up and as she stood out on her lawn in her open blouse and Mother's herringbone A-line skirt in front of Corey, she thought of Mother trying to laugh at this incident the next day, and she found herself wondering if there was still time to save things and not lose Corey.

Moira covered herself as best she could with her arms. She looked for Corey. Corey was looking at Daddy. Suddenly he shouted, "No," and Moira turned to see that Daddy had lifted the gun and was squinting down through the scope that was aimed at her face.

But it was as if the gun and Moira were magnets, the repellent ends, and the gun wouldn't point directly at her.

She looked into his eyes. Tears streamed down his cheeks. Where was Mother? Why wasn't she stopping him?

He tried to steady his arms and aim. He pointed the barrel at her, squinted into the sight.

Moira waited for the end, for unconsciousness to come.

He lowered the gun and let it droop tiredly toward the ground. "No, Moira," he said. "It's not you."

He let the gun dangle, then picked it up and put his finger in the trigger and turned it so that it was pointing at himself. She heard Mother open the kitchen window. She turned around to look at Mother. Mother was staring at Daddy with absolutely no expression on her face.

"Is this what you want, Eleanor?" he yelled. "You always knew I'd do anything for you."

And then she heard a shot, so loud in her ears she was deaf for a few moments. Mother's face didn't change. But Taryn, peering from behind her, had covered her eyes and was screaming.

Moira turned around. It was so dark, hard to focus. The scene came to her in jolts of consciousness.

Daddy was on his back on the porch, his legs spreadeagled, his hands stuck together in the trigger of the gun, the barrel of the gun inside his chest. Blood pumped up in a six-foot-high arc from the bloody mess where his heart used to be.

Part II

Twenty-four

Who shall I marry?
Tom, Dick or Harry?
I won't marry Tom
'Cause his dick's too hairy.

WHEN TARYN THOUGHT of life at home with Moira, that chant always came to mind. It was a chant the girls had said one night at a slumber party. A few months after Daddy's death. Taryn had gone into the bathroom and thrown up because she couldn't stand the thought of sex.

And it was all because of Moira. Moira had been the bane of Taryn's existence and the bane of poor Daddy's existence. As far as Taryn was concerned, Moira had caused Daddy's death, and Taryn would never forgive her.

Now that Moira had finally gone off to college, maybe Taryn and Mother could hope to have some semblance of a normal life. Though it would never be really normal, not without Daddy.

Taryn wanted nothing more than to be normal. Average. And Moira had always screwed it up by screwing up the family. Been a troublemaker one way or the other—by being brainy and weird when she was little, with all those chemistry sets and aquariums full of bugs (Taryn still had nightmares about bugs getting out and crawling over her at night), and then the greaser bad-girl when she was a teenager. And consequently all of Mother and Daddy's attention went to figuring out what was wrong with Moira. Taryn sometimes felt that if she left home they wouldn't know she was gone. One time, in fact, they'd been at a restaurant and before they left Taryn had gone to the bathroom and when she came out they'd left her behind. Mother and Daddy had been so busy fighting about something having to do with Moira that they'd forgotten Taryn was with them and drove off. It had been nearly half an hour before they came back to get her.

I want to be normal. I want to be a good girl the way Mother wants me to be, the way Daddy would still want me to be if Moira hadn't killed him.

Which she had done, in a way, as far as Taryn was concerned.

Moira and her superiority complex. Moira thought that even though she was a slut she was better than the rest of them. Better than everyone in Sioux Falls. Wanted to be a scientist. At one time she even talked of being a doctor. A lady doctor. Well, la-dee-da— maybe Taryn would be President.

Realistically speaking, Taryn had once wanted to be something special, too. But that was when she was a child. Before she grew up and faced reality, like a normal person was supposed to.

Some teachers, long long ago, had said Taryn had musical talent. Dancing talent.

But there had never been much music around the McPherson house because music had always bothered Daddy's nerves. Because Moira made him nervous.

So Taryn had found her own music. Back in the old country house when she was little—Taryn now laughed to remember it—she taught herself to cha-cha to the thumping of the pump in the basement that came on when someone flushed the toilet. The toilet pump had the same beat as Perez Prado's "Patricia" she'd heard on other people's radios, and the steps were those she'd learned while watching "Ted Mack's Amateur Hour" and "Your Hit Parade."

"Da-da, beep-beep-beep, da-da-da-da-da-da-da-da-daa-dah-beep beep-beep-beep-beep-beep"—she sang out to the tune of "Patricia" as she did her routine, turning counterclockwise then clockwise twirls while tapping.

She could dance to anything. Even when Daddy came home for lunch in the old days and turned on the noon market report from the stockyards, Taryn would clack away as the man on the radio chanted in his auctioneer's voice: "Hogs—steady to strong with cattle steady to fifty higher; heifers fully steady to twenty-five cents higher; barrows and gilts active; sows and bulls steady, stockers and feeders active . . . tappety tap tap tap tap," wearing shoes she'd made of some old Mary Janes with bottle caps nailed to the bottom.

Self-taught Taryn got to be so good that she was chosen over girls who'd had lots of real dance lessons for the starring role in a school spring pageant.

The pageant featured highlights from *West Side Story*. When the class broke into singing, "The Jet Song," she and co-star Billy Johnson were to break away from the group and hold hands and stroll around on-stage and then sing a duet of "Tonight."

When the big moment arrived, however, Billy got stage fright and stood staring into the colored lights at the top of the stage. Taryn watched him out of the corner of her eye and kept on singing, and when people were done tittering about Billy, the auditorium got almost quiet—flashbulbs stopped popping, feet stopped shuffling, and then it felt as if the auditorium belonged to her.

Taryn sang "Tonight" as a solo, taking long strides across the stage the way Dinah Shore did on TV. "Tonight there will be no morning star." She made her teeth stick out buck like Dinah Shore's, and picked up her skirt and twirled and did a little tippity-tap dance. A few people laughed. At the end of the song, there was a thick silence.

Taryn wanted to own that silence, and the auditorium, and she broke into a little tap dance routine and then she sang "America," in a Puerto Rican accent like she'd heard on TV. Then she sang in a deep southern accent like she'd seen on TV, too, and the audience began to laugh so she did a little solo square dance, then she sang in a trilly voice like an opera singer she'd seen on TV.

The audience laughed and when she was done they clapped and called for more. She thought of Daddy down there in the audience watching and thinking she was talented and popular—much more talented than eggheady old Moira.

But then she saw Mother's eyebrows down in the audience, or at least she thought that was Mother and her penciled-in eyebrows up in thin arches, and the mouth pursed in an expression that said "You just wait, you're going to be sorry," and Taryn grabbed a tiny quick bow and ran backstage.

Miss Moesley got up from the piano smiling and came and got Taryn and said, "Our little star."

Taryn could have died happily now that Daddy had heard someone call her the star.

Afterwards, though, Daddy just patted her head and said "That was good, hon," in an absentminded way, and walked toward the Exit sign down at the end of the hall in a nervous way that meant he wanted to get home and have a beer and turn on the television.

This was a huge letdown. Could she never get his attention, even if she won an Academy Award?

Daddy may not have been moved by the performance, but Mother was. She didn't say a word until they got outside on the steps to wait for Daddy to bring the car from the parking lot. Then she whirled Taryn around and reached way back and sent a slap across her face that was so hard it took a while for the sting to set in. "I was never so embarrassed in my life. People knowing that was my daughter up there." And Mother slapped again but this slap landed on her head and knocked the crepe-paper flower clear off so that it dangled by one bobby pin. "Taryn, you can't do things like that. People will think you're strange, or a tramp like . . ." but she didn't finish because someone walked by and said, "Heck of a talented little girl you got there."

Taryn knew exactly which tramp Mother didn't want her to be like, and she knew exactly what Mother's problem with dancers was—Mother was enraged by show-offs.

Mother wanted nothing more than for her daughters to blend in with the crowd. And here Taryn had just made a fool of herself by being a show-off. Taryn watched all the nonshow-off kids walking by, the normal kids like Mother wanted her daughters to be, and suddenly felt so ashamed of herself that she wished she could take a knife and cut out that part of her that had made her do all that stuff. But before she could say that, a lady with hair the color of Turkish Taffy came rushing up to Taryn.

"Tell me, dear, where do you take lessons?"

Taryn checked Mother. Mother's lips were pursed so tight it looked like the area around her mouth could break out into blisters. Taryn looked back down at the ground and said, "I don't take anywhere. I just learned from TV."

"Oh my God, she's a natural. Wouldn't you like to take lessons, honey?"

Taryn shrugged. Daddy pulled up in the car and honked.

The woman looked up at Mother and out at Daddy, and cried out, "Oh, pardon me, my name is Marlena Bishop, and I teach ballet and tap."

She gave Mother a card and grinned at Taryn as she put on a chiffon head-scarf and disappeared into the night like a fairy god-mother.

Later that evening, Mother's mood had improved and she was laughing about Mrs. Bishop. "Did you see her fat legs? That's what happens to ballerinas. One day you're a show-off on the stage, the next thing you know you're a pair of walking tree trunks. And that hair! Bleached-blond Bishop."

Whenever Taryn said she wanted to be an actress, Mother and Daddy would laugh and say no, she was going to go to Dakota State Normal College to be a teacher, just as Moira would.

Taryn would try to imagine being one of the college girls they saw at Augustana College, their arms wrapped around books as if they were babies they loved. She worried that she wouldn't love books, or babies, or children that much.

Mother would pat her hand and say, "You don't have to like children to teach them how to read. You just have to love knowl-edge."

"But I don't love knowledge. I love dancing and acting," Taryn would persist.

"Oh, malarkey. All little girls want to be actresses, and it's time you realized you're no different from anyone else. And no better than anyone else, either, mind you."

Mrs. Bishop called Mother and offered to let Taryn take a free class to see if she liked it. Mother couldn't get out of this one, so she said okay, they'd try it.

The classes were in the basement of the teacher's house. It smelled of mildew and sewer water down there, and soggy lint from the wash was everywhere, clogging the floor drain so a puddle of rancid water sat on top.

But the basement was pure beauty when you looked at the girls and heard Mrs. Bishop playing an echoey piano and sweetly calling out commands in French.

There they stood on the linoleum placed in front of the wall-to-wall mirrors, girls in slumpy positions, wearing pink tights, leotards, crumply shoes with a little elastic band across, their hair in buns or slippery ponytails; when Mrs. Bishop said so, their arms went out in deliberate, I-want-to-be-pretty gestures, their legs in deliberate, I-want-to-do-this-exactly-right positions. Mrs. Bishop got up and in her big leotard with the little skirt demonstrated an arabesque and various ports de bras, and soon the little girls were swooping down and twisting around, then coming up and framing their head with an upturned arm, all the while checking themselves in the mirror.

Ballet class was everything Mother thought was vaguely immoral —vanity, bodies exposed with the outline of your bummy and worse showing, pink and white and black instead of the browns and beiges in which she dressed herself and her daughters; wasting your time trying to do something perfectly right was not only frivolity and egotism, it was an affront to other people because you were trying to be better than them.

No one could like you if you tried to be better than them. And the thing to do was to let the other person be better. Or prettier. And they'd like you for it.

Taryn turned to Mother and smiled. Surely Mother saw what she saw, that there was nothing wrong with this, that beautiful was okay. "What do you think?" she dared to ask.

Mother lifted her head so her nostrils showed. "To tell you the truth, I don't get where the art is in this. It's not like a painting or poetry, something that makes you think or that's hard to do. I could stand there, too, waving my arms around with a snotty look on my face, but I have better things to do and I don't crave attention to the extent that I'm going to make a fool of myself. But if you have to get this out of your system, better you do it now than later."

At the next class, Taryn appeared in an old leotard and tights that Mother bought from a neighbor for twenty-five cents because Mother said she didn't want to invest in new ones in the event

Taryn had no talent and gave it up. The tights had a Clorox spot on the rear part of the thigh that was about the size of a quarter and Taryn asked if that was why they cost twenty-five cents. Mother looked like she was going to slap Taryn, but then said no that wasn't why and added that no one would notice the bleach spot if Taryn twisted it to the inside. "Besides, Madame Bishop seems to have nothing against bleach—look at her hair."

The ballet slippers Mother found at a rummage sale were a little big so Mother had told Taryn to wear bobby sox under them. "I hope this is okay," Taryn said, worried.

"If this outfit isn't good enough for her, I'll tell her that her school isn't good enough for us."

All the little girls stared at Taryn's outfit. Mrs. Bishop smiled and said, "I have some extra ballet slippers. I'll bet we can find her size."

With that, Mother grabbed Taryn's arm. "Come on, we're getting out of this dump. If this ballet school weren't in someone's stinking basement, I might think about getting you new clothes. But why waste them?" And they made their exit up the basement steps, with all the other girls watching, the bleach spot in the back having stretched out to a fifty-cent piece and the shoes flapping sloppily off her feet.

As Mother drove home, she ranted about Mrs. Bishop's bleached hair and how she was wasting her life on showing off and teaching others to show off.

There were shrubs she could hide in to watch the classes from the basement windows of Mrs. Bishop's house. She stopped by after school and sneaked over on Saturday mornings and sat among the cobwebs listening to the piano and the shuffling of ballet slippers and smacky clicking of tap shoes. It was dark down there, but when the sun came in just right, it shone like a spotlight on the girls and she could see them taking their lessons.

She could watch until the sun started to go down, when it glinted off the window and blinded her view and left her in late afternoon nothingness. Then, she'd go home and practice in the bathroom with the door locked.

What was the problem? Was it that Mother was jealous of Taryn? But no. Taryn couldn't think that. If she believed that, she'd go crazy. Better to think that Taryn simply wasn't cut out for the stage, the way Mother was. She said prayers sometimes at night, asking God to make her quit wanting to be a show-off and a peeping Tom. But so far it hadn't worked, and she still wanted to be a dancer and a show-off. Maybe, she said to God, if he'd make Mother change her mind about the classes, Taryn could quit being a show-off after this one time. Maybe she'd get it all out of her system.

God never answered that prayer, but in November He took care of her problem, sending an eleven-inch snowfall and covering up the basement windows at Mrs. Bishop's so she couldn't see through the window anymore.

It was a cold winter and never without a thick cover of snow on the ground. And by spring, when the snow was melting, Taryn had convinced herself that Mother was right, and pretty soon, she too disliked Mrs. Bishop and all her show-off spoiled brats.

One day, when Mrs. Bishop came rushing up to Taryn on the street and asked how she was, whether she was dancing or doing anything on the stage, she was so cute and talented, Taryn shook her head without a word, then stuck her tongue out at Mrs. Bishop and walked away.

Taryn had decided then and there to quit wanting to be a show-off and to stand out from the crowd in any way. Then her parents would love her more than they loved Moira.

And she was going to be a nice girl, too, unlike Moira, so they'd really love her.

Taryn remembered the first time she realized her big sister was a bad girl. It was at Rollerama, the night Moira skated with Dennis Wildersen.

As they drove over, Mother was chewing and snapping her usual Wrigley's Doublemint Gum (Mother chewed gum only at home or in the car, not in public, and thought the sweeter flavors like Juicy Fruit were low class), and that, along with Daddy's sporting goods samples knocking around in the back of the station wagon, seemed to clack out that refrain: *Who shall I marry? Tom, Dick, or Harry?*

The only reason Taryn was here tonight was because she had

turned down an invitation to a slumber party. She had turned it down because of the dirty jokes like the Tom, Dick, and Harry one they'd started telling at the parties now that she was in sixth grade. Taryn was a nice girl. Wait a minute. And she remembered another little chant from the slumber party—"Nice girls go out on a date, go to bed, and come home. Good girls go out on a date, come home, and go to bed."

Taryn was a *good* girl. Her big sister Moira was the *nice* girl. Daddy's "nice" little bad girl, and Taryn was his good girl.

Oh my God, what was she thinking? What did Daddy have to do with girls going to bed? She put her hand over her mouth. She could just about die for thinking things like that.

But then her mind wandered back to the last slumber party. The girls had said the Tom, Dick, or Harry chant over and over at the last one, and that was why she'd decided not to go to the party tonight.

Taryn slapped the sides of her head with the heels of her hands and hummed until that chant left her mind.

No more slumber parties. But as they got closer and closer to Rollerama, a notorious hood hangout, she'd rather almost be at the slumber party. Moira had caught her in a weak moment and asked if she'd go. Otherwise, Moira would have had to go alone. Moira didn't have any friends other than that new girl who always wore that moth-eaten gray sweater, and the new girl's parents didn't let her go to places like Rollerama.

"Taryn," she said. "Be sure to ask if there's a lower admission price for kids under twelve."

Taryn, now wishing she hadn't let Moira talk her into going to Rollerama in the first place, said okay, she would ask.

"You too, Moira, lie about your age, say you're only eleven and a half." Mother waved her wrist to emphasize her point and her wrist crackled.

Moira gave Mother a look of alarm. "But I'm thirteen. And besides, it's not right to tell lies."

Taryn and Mother exchanged irritated looks. They knew that Moira was a fraud, she didn't care what was right and wrong any more than anyone else did, she just said it to be a spoilsport and weird and different. Moira knew that Daddy was right, that anyone who professed to want to do the right thing was using it as a coverup for doing the wrong thing. That, or they were a fool.

Mother looked at Moira and said, "Whose money do you want to save, the man who owns Rollerama, or your own father's?"

Moira's face got that super-reasoning look it took on for any kind of question, from "How are you today?" to "What's the square root of ten million three hundred and forty-seven billion?" When the super-reasoning look happened her eyes looked all glisteny.

Mother went on. "When it comes to money, as with social graces, there are little white lies. And this is one case where you should lie—lie like a rug." Mother laughed loudly. She often used teenage slang with them. It almost made it seem like Mother was another sister instead of your mother. "I mean it. We're broke. Flat busted." Mother laughed again. "All except for you, Moira."

The city was behind them and they were almost on the outskirts of town where Rollerama sat by the old two-lane highway against a long stretch of scrub land. The flat land stretched off, broken by an occasional tree or bush, to a cold, orange-sherbet sunset.

Mother started talking about how bitter Daddy was over the Minneapolis territory that Roy Janssen had taken away from him. Taryn felt just awfully sorry for Daddy. He tried so hard and the world was always against him.

Taryn felt so sorry for her father that it felt like all her insides were made of lead.

She thought of Daddy right now, out on the road, out there trying his damndest to get the quarterly sales up for Heartland Sporting Goods, Inc., or trying to excite the stores about a new line of hunting jackets or basketball hoops, and she wanted to go out there and stand next to him and threaten to punch the store buyers if they wouldn't take the new item. In her fantasy, she'd tell Daddy to just sit down and take it easy while she chewed out the clerks about falling sales and inventories piling up. Taryn had to take a deep breath so that she wouldn't cry for how much she pitied Daddy. And loved him, though if there was a difference between love and pity, Taryn didn't know what it was.

When Mother waved and drove off in that big lumbering station wagon with the football helmet samples knocking and the basketballs rolling around in back, Taryn felt as if she'd just been dropped off on top of Mount Everest.

Taryn bought an under-twelve ticket. Moira pursed her whitened mouth as she thought about it, then lied about her age. The woman inside the booth stood up and looked Moira up and down, then sat back down and with narrowed eyes asked for a birth certificate. Moira's face turned dark pink against the white lipstick. "Oh, I'm so sorry, I really am," Moira said, and she quickly counted out the nickels for the adult ticket. Taryn felt like slapping Moira.

Red, blue, and yellow lights rolled over the wooden floor and a scratchy sound system was playing "Everybody's Somebody's Fool" by Connie Francis. The girls pushed into the thick, warm crowd. The stale popcorn and sweat and dark dampness smell was the same as that in the creepy carnival funhouse last summer.

Again, Taryn felt the slight nausea that followed her around always looking for an opportunity to settle in. A place like this was all that nausea needed. Moira put her arm around Taryn and led her to the restroom. Girls were lined up in front of the mirror, writing on it with lipstick and laughing and shrieking, ratting and hairspraying huge clouds.

Moira didn't seem to notice them. "Wait here," she said to Taryn, and went into a stall. Taryn saw some commotion with clothes in the stall, then Moira emerged from the bathroom stall in a lavender Orlon sweater she'd sewn the sides of the waist of to make tight, and a short purple skating skirt. Taryn was startled at first by how large Moira's bosoms had become, how they were beginning to arc out like the shapes Moira was always drawing on her pre-geometry homework pages with that protractor. Moira got in front of the mirror and drew black rims around her eyes.

Thank God Mother was a decent person. Taryn thought of calling Mother and saying she was sick suddenly and wanted to come home. But Mother probably wouldn't be home for another half-hour, the way she drove.

"Hurry, Moira," she said. Taryn absolutely refused to believe that boys and men in real life had a dick, a long pink thing like in the slumber-party traveling-salesman jokes.

And thank God Daddy was a decent person. Certainly Daddy

didn't have a long pink hairy thing. If he did, knowing Daddy, he'd be so embarrassed he'd probably kill himself.

"How do I look?" Moira said, turning.

Her eyes glowed the way they always did, maybe because they were high-IQ eyes inside those rims of black eyeliner and mascara. Eyes like a nocturnal animal's at dusk—all set to go. The light lipstick made her lips look too big.

"Too much makeup, too much hair, too much lips," Taryn said.

Moira's face disassembled into disappointment, so Taryn added, "But you look sort of pretty, too."

Moira broke into a smile and her smile made Taryn think of a kaleidoscope, it was so frank and big and it used up all of her face —eyes, nose, forehead, cheeks, mouth. It was not the McPherson smile—a little twitch at the side of the mouth, raised eyebrows— that Moira had. Not the famous McPherson "ain't life shitty" smile. Taryn thought how painful life must be for both Mother and Daddy when they had to be out in public, how shy and afraid of people they must be; and Taryn wondered if she had inherited that smile, so she composed her face into public neutrality.

Moira looked back in the mirror. "But if I didn't have too much hair and too much makeup, I wouldn't be pretty. Is it better to be ugly with no makeup, or pretty with a lot?"

Taryn just stared at Moira. Sometimes there was no answer to what she asked you. At any rate, as they stood in line for their rental skates, Taryn felt somewhat reassured that she was in with the majority of girls, even if they were tough girls, wearing a blouse and slacks. Only a few of them out on the rink had short skirts like Moira—the girls who were really good skaters, and those who were really bad.

Some greaser boy had skated up to Moira and put his arm around her and led her out to the rink, and Taryn knew then and there that this was the last time she'd ever go anywhere with Moira.

When Moira's reputation started going all over the school, that was when Taryn wrote her off.

Marilyn Hofelt had turned to Taryn in study hall and put her hand over her mouth and whispered, "I hear your sister let Gary Racer feel her up."

"What?" Taryn burst out, trying to look surprised and innocent and even trying to change her facial features so she wouldn't look related to Moira.

Marilyn gave Taryn a conspiratorial smile, as if it weren't Taryn's sister she was gossiping about. "She went out in the woods with Gary Racer while poor Doris was home with her elbow in a cast."

Taryn heard crackling in her ears. This was what she'd always feared. Out-and-out, no-holds-barred public disgrace.

"I hear she does it with all the guys," Marilyn continued, then went in for the kill. "I hear she's a Friday-night girl."

Friday-night girls were the girls your steady boyfriend took out on Friday night to get his rocks off with. Saturday night was for girlfriends—the kind boys wanted to be seen with in public.

Taryn tried to look as if the whole matter meant nothing to her, but her hand shook while she did her English.

Taryn had seen this coming, of course. It had become fully apparent on Shorts Day that Taryn was not going to be able to go on pretending that her sister was not what she was.

And Shorts Day had started out so well. Taryn and her friends had gone shopping together with their babysitting money to buy an outfit to show they were a clique and that they wouldn't have anything to do with girls who weren't as pretty or as cool. They all bought the same outfit—navy blue sleeveless Banlon turtlenecks and red-and-navy plaid Bermudas. Shorts that hung like paper bags over their legs. Good-girl shorts. They had all agreed to wear the same brand and style of tennis shoes and they had all agreed on no socks.

Taryn and her friends had all met under the flagpole, the wind whipping it and making that clanging noise with the rope against the metal pole, almost as if it were announcing that here were the clean, upstanding all-American girls that flag up there stood for.

And what had Moira showed up in? A pair of short shorts (which, admittedly, Mother had made her wear) and a tight tube top that showed off her great big bouncing whatchamacallits to the world. Taryn had been standing at the top of the stairs with her girlfriends when Moira appeared at the bottom of the steps.

Everyone had stopped talking, then boys had started whistling and shouting "Ooooee, pussy."

Moira's hairspray glistened in the morning humidity, and with her glasses off (she'd stopped wearing her glasses most of the time and would walk right by without seeing you—either that or she was thinking about one of her stupid science projects) you could see that her eyes had so much black around them they glistened animal-like. Tough-looking but, Taryn admitted, sort of unknowing and star-struck.

Then some teachers, including Taryn's English teacher, Miss Juneson, had given each other a look. Miss Juneson gazed at Moira the way she would a stray cat, and Miss Juneson was not the type to take in a stray cat. As Moira passed within earshot, Miss Juneson said, "My, my, and what have we here?"

"Hey, it's Marilyn Monroe," another teacher said.

"No, Jayne Mansfield."

"Where have you been? The new one is Joey Heatherton."

Taryn sat in study hall remembering this, thinking this was the end—she would never have friends anymore because of Moira. They'd all leave her. They'd think she had Moira germs.

But then Taryn was in for a surprise, because when the bell rang for study hall to end, one of the popular girls came up to her and looped her arm under Taryn's and said, "Hey, I'm chairman of the Boosters Club this semester. Since you're my best friend, I want you to be secretary."

Taryn was so relieved she broke into laughter. People really didn't associate her with Moira.

No wonder Daddy got drunk all the time and Mother was depressed. Moira was obviously the problem. Taryn would just have to make up for it. Mother and Daddy were depending on her to be the good girl of the family.

The big love of Taryn's life had been Jay Schmidt.

Jay was like Taryn, small and slight. Where Taryn had no figure, no bosoms—thank God—Jay had narrow high shoulders and slender but very muscular arms. His yellow hair was in a perfect, sort of respectful-looking crewcut, and his pale blue eyes were almost but not quite crossed, giving him a dreamy look.

He kept beaming that dreamy look on her a lot, turning around to smile at her whenever she got an answer right.

Jay lived just a few blocks away, and began walking his cocker spaniel in front of the house and lingering with his starry-eyed gaze directed toward the big picture window whose curtains Taryn was wrapped up in, peeking out.

Remembering Daddy chasing away Dennis Wildersen, Taryn didn't want to take any chances with Daddy and Jay. She was afraid he might come home early again.

As always, Mother could read her mind. "Look," she said. "Lightning never strikes twice. Your father won't come home early anymore. In fact, I'll let you in on a little secret."

Taryn looked at Mother.

"He doesn't worry about you the way he does Moira. He knows you're a nice girl."

And then Mother said something else. "I have a plan anyway on how to handle your father on this matter. You see, he knows you're not a tramp like Moira. Let me take care of it."

One night when Jay was visiting, Daddy's car came tearing up the driveway unexpectedly.

Taryn whispered, "Oh my God."

Mother went to look, shouted, "It's him," and drew the drapes. She turned around with an excited look on her face and said to Taryn, "Don't worry. I have a plan."

"What's the matter?" Jay said.

"Nothing," Taryn said, looking nervously at Mother.

Jay's dreamy, slightly crossed eyes looked confused.

Daddy didn't say anything when he saw Jay.

"What are you doing home?" Mother said, and turned and gave Taryn the raised-eyebrow look, which Taryn returned. Fortunately, Daddy never noticed these signals between the two of them (though there were times when Taryn thought maybe he really did see them and that was half the reason he got drunk, so that he wouldn't have to confront Mother, because those raised-eyebrows and half-smiles were really powerful weapons).

"Front office called the dealership I went to this afternoon, said they want me back here this week."

Daddy passed through the living room in his chinos and one of the low-cut sleeveless T-shirts he'd taken to wearing.

When he was in the kitchen, Taryn heard the cap of a beer can pop and then do a little tap dance around the sink. She heard it scrape as he fished it out of the sink and plink as he threw it into the garbage can.

He came back to the living room, went to the TV set, and turned the channel.

During a commercial, Daddy turned and looked at Jay and gave him a good once-over. "Aren't you the kid who lives up the street?"

"Yes, Mr. McPherson," Jay said. "In fact, I'd better call and see when they expect me home."

While he was on the phone, Daddy turned to Mother. "What's that little punk doing here?"

Mother said, "The little Schmidt boy? He's awfully, uh, sweet, isn't he?"

Daddy looked at Mother as if he were waiting for her to say something else.

"Sweet?" he said.

"Well, you know what I mean."

"How the hell do I know what you mean?"

"Well, he's maybe a little too sweet."

"He's not a fruit, is he?"

Taryn froze. She could hear Jay still on the phone with his mother, so apparently he hadn't heard.

Taryn started to say no, he certainly was not a fruit, but Mother was giving her a look, so she didn't, and Mother said, "Well . . . I guess you *could* say he's one of those boys who doesn't like girls. Except as friends."

Daddy looked toward the kitchen, and just then Jay hung up the phone and gazed with his beautiful dreamy eyes at Daddy.

Daddy looked at him as if he were a cartoon character on TV or something, then gave his head a shake and made a little laugh. "That's what I always thought about that kid. Hell, maybe I'll get my wrestling mat out and make a man out of him."

The problem with that, Taryn thought, was that if Daddy "made a man" out of Jay and didn't think he was homosexual anymore, he wouldn't let him in the door. Daddy didn't want any other "real" men around. Just himself.

And then another thought occurred to her. Maybe Daddy just didn't care. Maybe he just didn't care as much about her as he did about Moira. And her hatred for her sister burned as strongly as her love for Jay and Daddy did.

Well, all that had been going fine—she and Jay were even secretly going steady—until that awful night when Moira sneaked out with that boy no one even knew and Daddy accidentally shot himself just trying to defend their lives when he thought that Moira and her date were burglars.

At least that was what Taryn told people. Sometimes she even believed it herself.

Moira had gone off to college the next fall. But Taryn had to stay in town. Jay's family, who had watched from their front lawn as the police swarmed to the McPherson house, wouldn't let Jay go out with Taryn anymore. That first night and the few days after it, all the neighbors were so wonderful and helpful and la-de-dah. But soon, Taryn could see that people avoided them. And Jay's parents weren't going to change their mind.

Mother sold the house and she and Taryn moved to another apartment on another side of town and Taryn finished at another high school. But there was still no getting away from people who knew about it.

Moira hadn't gone to Dakota State Normal College like she was supposed to—she had gone far away. Well, Taryn was going to Normal, and she couldn't wait. Moira was going to be her anti-role model.

She was going to show Mother and Daddy that she was a good girl and make Daddy love her more, even if he could only do it from the grave.

Part
III

Twenty-five

MOIRA MET ZEKE on a cold rainy day in the midst of an SDS demonstration in front of the Columbia University library. Just as she had almost squeezed her way up to the library doors, the crowd erupted into cheers and began jumping and dancing around.

Someone picked her up by the waist and twirled her around, umbrella and all. When he finally put her down, he put a flower, a daisy, in her hand and kissed her.

He was very dark, almost brown-skinned, with large, hooded eyes. Exotic, Mediterranean, molded and smoothed with warm fingers like a sculpted face in a museum.

"Mark Rudd's up next," he said. "I hope every capitalist, fascist pig in the world is watching."

"Pardon me, I'm just trying to get through to the library," Moira said. He looked confused, so she said, "I'm a Barnard student and I'm using your library today." She held up a book she was returning.

He turned and looked at the doors to the library as if he'd forgotten that this was a college and that the libraries also contained books.

"Oh wow, sorry. Here, let me help you." He put his arm around her and pushed through the crowd. "Make way, man, we've got a Barnard lady here who wants to use our library. Out of her way." After they'd gotten inside the library, she shook her umbrella and folded it, giving him a token smile of gratitude.

"I like chicks who are serious, serious about anything—if not politics, then school, anything other than their hairdo." His eyes followed her hair, which she had let grow so that it flowed down her back in thick chestnut-colored waves.

"It frizzes in the rain," she said defensively, and turned around.

"I think you have the most beautiful hair I've ever seen in my life," he said, and grabbed the flower out of her hand and, before she backed off, slipped it into a ringlet in front of her ear.

"Any chance I could get your phone number?" His olive-gold corduroy jacket made his complexion glow as if it were reflecting the sun off a beach.

An immediate self-preservation response ran through her and she remembered her anthropology project. She pulled the flower out of her hair and gave it back to him and clutched her heavy plaid coat to her throat, covering her breasts that still showed even though she'd worn her baggy Dakota State Normal College sweatshirt inside out (a remnant from the summer class she'd taken there just to get out of the house before coming to Barnard College). "No."

"C'mon, take the flower at least."

He opened the book she was carrying and slipped the daisy in and closed the book. "I have to go," Moira said, and walked away toward the marble stairs that led to safety away from people.

As the crowd started chanting "Hell no, we won't go," she heard him say "You are so . . ."

Had he said ". . . so lovely?" or had it been her imagination?

Upstairs, she gave the book to a librarian. He opened it and found the pressed daisy. "This yours?" There was no wastebasket, so she stuck it inside her organic chemistry book.

She went to the anthropology section to do some research while she waited out the demonstration so she wouldn't have to go through all that mess again. In the cool, echoey anonymity of the upper reaches of the library, she still saw his intense face. She stopped and said to herself, *Lovely?*

She took off her glasses and blinked in the winter light shining in from the window overlooking the rally going on down below.

Not *built* or *stacked* or *sexy*, but *lovely*, with *beautiful hair*.

But no matter. She put her glasses back on and got herself interested in the carbon-14 studies of some Australopithecine tooth and skull fragments. These Australopithecines were her closest friends, and she wanted nothing to do with this dark-haired radical or any other man who'd been born within the last two million years.

Arriving at her part-time waitress job at Nick's Coffee Shop a little early, she went to the coffee station and poured herself the first of the two free cups allowed per shift, then got into a booth to review for an anthro quiz. The radiator in the coffee shop steamed and spat as a backdrop to the students' chatter and occasional shrieks of laughter and the clatter of dishes. It was a sublime place, this grimy coffee shop, as white January sunlight pushed through the droplets of rain on the storefront window and hovered in the smoke and steam over the people in the room, average Columbia-Barnard students, Moira one of them, part of them. For the first time in her life, almost belonging.

Moira enjoyed her job for several reasons: one, it called on her intelligence in a surprising way, having to keep track of all those orders, a fugue of demands to run through her head as she scuffled around the cafe and for once was too busy and too broke to be self-conscious or depressed about her past; two, it gave immediate gratification, all those tips jingling around in her pocket, the copper and silver rubbing against the white apron so that by the end of her shift the pocket was smudged dark with the color of money, going home and counting the tips into long neat rows, going to the bank and getting the little coin wrappers, taking them to the bank after a few weeks and getting bills; and three, she could move around the coffee shop and feel important, useful, needed, part of something.

As she now felt a part of Barnard College. Her scholarship, her schoolwork, her job, and her friendship with her roommate were all she had in the world right now.

Ironically, even though Daddy was gone and it was now possible to have a real, live boyfriend, Moira doubted she would ever have another boyfriend, or ever marry.

It would always be with her of course, every night when she lay down and closed her eyes. Blood had splattered through the open door onto the carpeting, onto a lamp, even onto Daddy's sample trunks, onto their lives.

Corey and his mother had stood at the end of the driveway while the police questioned the witnesses. When the detective finally said Corey could go, Corey said something Moira couldn't hear. She'd gone temporarily deaf. Maybe from the shot, maybe from fright. Corey led his mother to her station wagon and Corey hurried to his car and got in without looking back at Moira. Moira, standing wrapped in a blanket, realized she was still in her blood-stained blouse and skirt. Moira turned away as Corey drove off, and then she heard again and for the last time the sound of respectability disappearing down the street and dissipating into the cold November air.

A few neighbors hung around, staring, offering help. The Ettingers and the Mankowskis offered to put them up for the night, but Mother had declined. It was then that Moira noticed Mother's expression—composed, almost smiling.

Moira was confused for a while, and looked again. Mother's mouth wavered between a smile and a smirk and an expression of slight disapproval, the kind of face she would make if someone had spilled red punch and it was going to be hard to get out of the Formica.

And then Moira understood. Mother was trying to look as if it was no big deal, as if nothing really bad had happened, because she'd had a lot of practice. To Mother, this was just another embarrassing McPherson mess and she was trying to look just as unconcerned as usual, to trudge on. Moira even expected Mother to break out the ain't-life-shitty smile, to dismiss this as just another day in her life.

After the ambulance had taken away Daddy's body, Moira fell into an altered state of consciousness, as an almost super-calm, super-reasonableness fell over her. As the neighbors and the newspaper reporter walked off down the street, now brightly lit with porch lights, Mother looked at the spot on the porch and the grass next to it where blood glistened reddish black on Daddy's perfect lawn, the only thing he'd ever really gotten right. Mother had then looked at Moira. Moira had expected a cynical face and a punchline from Mother, but what she said was, "I don't know what to do about this." She'd looked up at Taryn and Moira, now with a pale ghost's face, and repeated, "I don't know what to do."

They went inside the house. Moira turned on every light in the house, even those in the basement. They'd stood in the cruel light of the living room lamps, looking around, glancing at one another's face. It was so horrible that it wasn't happening, really. Moira had stepped outside her body and was watching herself, Mother, Taryn.

It was Taryn who made it real again. "This is too horrible," she screamed, and began to cry. "You guys can stay, but I'm going over to Mary Lou's house for the night."

"No," Mother said. "We'll go to a motel." And once again she looked as if nothing much had happened, in fact she looked almost in control, as she had the night they all drove off in the snowstorm to a motel to get away from Daddy's drinking.

They drove in silence. Mother was confused and they drove all over town, getting lost, traveling to neighborhoods she should have known didn't have motels, ending up in the deserted middle of downtown at three in the morning. Finally, she found a Holiday Inn by the interstate. The clean, predictable, nondescript room gave a feeling that they were not really experiencing any of this. Maybe they would stay in this vacuumed plastic unreal world and wake up tomorrow and laugh with nervous relief at how this had been such a terrible nightmare. Maybe if they didn't touch one another or talk, the evening really wouldn't be real. The bland, plastic world of Holiday Inn went on forever—why couldn't that of the McPhersons?

But as they lay on the scratchy beds watching TV and inhaling the dusty, dry motel air, the evening gradually became real again. No one would mention what had happened. They watched television in achingly tense silence. If one of them got up to get a drink or to go to the bathroom, she was careful not to bump the others or even to accidentally graze another's flesh. If there ever had been any intimacy or trust among them, physical or mental, Moira felt that it was now gone forever.

They watched a Sophia Loren movie. Not that Moira could follow the story, but Sophia Loren's brassiness was riveting.

Moira couldn't close her eyes. She feared Daddy wasn't really dead, that he was going to burst through that motel door any minute with the gun in his hand and finish what he had started.

Mother was silent. After Sophia Loren an old black-and-white horror movie came on, and they sat for a few minutes in tense, embarrassed silence, no one daring to change the channel and thereby acknowledge the real horror that had just happened to them.

They had forgotten pajamas, and Taryn fell asleep on the bed in her clothes.

Moira climbed under the covers and Mother sat in the chair with the lamp over her casting shadows beneath her blank eyes and her lips with one corner turned up. When Moira woke up a few hours later, Mother was sitting in the chair, staring at her.

Mother's eyes were puffy and watery and her hair was sticking out all over the place and her face was serious, without the cynical set to her mouth. "He was the only person who ever cared for me," she said, looking at Moira and Taryn in surprise. "The more he cared for me, the more I hated him."

Taryn began to cry. "I hate Moira. It's all her fault." And Taryn cried in the bed. "It's so awful. I miss him so much already. There's nothing left of our lives. What will my friends say?"

Mother looked at Taryn with all the humor gone out of her face, still without her ain't-life-shitty grin. Her face was so dead-serious it frightened Moira. It was the first time in her life that Mother didn't have a sarcastic quip. This was almost as scary as Daddy killing himself.

It was as if, in shooting himself, Daddy had killed all the jokes in Mother.

She felt him before she even saw him.

"Hey, man, imagine us meeting again in a greasy-spoon coffee shop. It's as if our bodies had been born on opposite sides of the earth and some kind of magnetic force is bringing them together, isn't it?" He laughed to show he knew he was being corny and slapped down a pile of leaflets that said something about "The Resistance" supporting Dr. Spock. As he slid into the booth, Moira took off her glasses and looked up at him. He had on that same olive-gold corduroy coat and his hair, like hers, was frizzed from the wet snow that was skittering about outside.

He put out his hand. "Hi, Zeke Beaustein. Remember me? Are you alone?"

She didn't answer and she didn't put out her own hand.

He looked around the coffee shop, then looked back at her and then twisted his head to read the title of her book. He smiled and his mouth was like those Botticelli paintings in the museum, curving red and full. "I've seen you around a lot. You have a quality about you . . . dreamy. Did you know that? It's very appealing."

Moira looked back down at her book.

"Hey, how about a cappuccino and a pastry?"

The jukebox started playing:

> *I saw her sitting in the rain.*
> *Raindrops falling on her.*
> *She didn't seem to care*
> *She sat there*
> *And smiled at me.*

And Zeke started singing along:

> *And I knew—I knew, I knew, I knew, I knew*
> *She would make me happy, happy, happy . . .*
> *I love the flower girl . . .*

And he hummed along raggedly and then said, "Do you still have the flower I gave you, Flower Girl? Hmmm?"

"I don't know," she lied. She'd been studying organic chemistry the other night and came across it. She'd left it in the book.

"Never mind, there'll be more where those came from," he said in his maddeningly cheerful way.

Before Moira could respond, he called out to the waitress on duty, "Miss, two cappuccinos—do you like cappuccino, Flower Girl? 'I knew, I knew, I knew, she would make me happy, happy, happy . . .' Never mind, you're going to, the way I put the cinnamon in, a little dash of salt—my own special recipe—and those pastries with the poppy seeds, hey, Miss, are they fresh? Bring two of those." He flipped open the metal cream pitcher, looked in, snapped it shut and put it down. "We need a refill on the cream, too, when you get a chance."

He turned his black-brown eyes that were deep with interest onto Moira. " 'I love the flower girl, oh I don't know just why, she simply caught my eye,' " he sang along. She wondered if she had enough money to cover the coffee and pastry. She was used enough to boys paying on dates, but this wasn't a date, and besides, she saw that his wrinkled black turtleneck had a tear in the seam and he could use a shave. He was probably just as broke as she was.

"No, really, I can't eat anything," she said.

"Don't tell me you're on a diet," he said. "I don't want to hear about it. You're perfect the way you are, not too fat, not too thin like some of these New York chicks. Man, they all want to be Twiggy." He waved his hand in a twirly way, and his face showed exaggerated, kindly concern. "Come on, do me a favor, you should eat."

He was so excessive it was kind of funny. Well, the pastry did look awfully good, and why make a scene? She could pay for it later, out of her tips.

Though Daddy had left life insurance, Mother had refused to give Moira a penny when she decided to attend Barnard instead of Normal. Moira had a decent financial aid package, and her part-time job helped, but New York prices even here around the Columbia/Barnard campus were hardly designed for scholarship students from South Dakota. Last term, before she'd gotten the fringe benefits of a free dinner on the nights she worked, she used to buy the institutional-size cans of pork and beans, chili, and Spanish rice at a Puerto Rican market on Amsterdam Avenue. The cans had to last her four dinners each. And she would never admit it to anyone, but she had accepted a few dinner dates last semester just for the free dinner, she had been that desperate—but after a few of those kinds of dates, she decided she would rather starve to death. Which at times did not seem an entirely remote possibility.

For snacks while she studied at night, she allowed herself a pack of gum a week (saving the chewed pieces in a secret spot she hoped her roommate wouldn't find), a large bag of potato chips, and two Cokes. And in some perverse way, it was all rather satisfying and not a bad life, compared to the one in the past.

"Eh?" he said. His face made her think once again of something that belonged in a museum, with its five o'clock shadow and high forehead. "I saw you through the window. With that dreamy look."

"I wasn't dreaming, I was studying. I have an important test tomorrow."

"When you look up, when you tear yourself away from your book, then you're dreamy-eyed. When you walk around, you're dreamy-eyed. You have that look now." His voice softened. "You do remember me, don't you, from the rally the other day?"

Moira let her fingers touch the page of the book she'd been studying, her security blanket, then closed it. "Yes, I remember you."

"Hey, man, you're just like me," he said, looking around. "You like to study in weird places. At home I have to have the radio on, noise of some sort."

"No, I work here. I'm about to go on duty."

He looked at her oddly, it seemed, for a split second, then returned to his jovial mood and asked if she could get a discount on the food, and when she began to explain that they got only one free meal at dinnertime, he playfully took her hand that was clutching the pencil and shook the hand wildly and laughed loudly and said he was just kidding.

Now the jukebox was playing " San Francisco," the song about wearing flowers in your hair. It made Moira feel part of something, though she wasn't sure exactly what.

He ate his pastry in big chunks, bursting with energy and enthusiasm, animated, waving his hands, gesturing—telling her how he got into SDS, how it started with his being a political science major who didn't like the system he was studying.

"There's a sit-in in two days, you know?"

Moira said she didn't know, and nervously opened her book again.

"It's about the gym the fascists are trying to put in a black neighborhood, just to drive them further into the Bronx. I did tutoring with those kids . . ." He shook his head sadly. "Unbelievable the way some people have to live in a racist society, unbelievable . . . Hey, why don't you come along? I'll take you."

She looked down at the Formica table that she'd have to rub with vinegar water at two in the morning after they closed and before she could go home with her apronful of tips. She could almost smell the vinegar, feel the good ache on the soles of her feet, feel the wonderful weight of tips in her apron pocket. "I don't have time to protest against the world. I'm too busy trying to join it."

He threw his head back until he was staring up at the glaring fluorescent lights and gave a big belly laugh. When he'd recovered, he reached for her hand and leaned over the table and put his face close to hers. "I swear to God you're the most entertaining chick I've ever met." Then he checked his watch and reached back for his coat. "I gotta run. Hey, I mean it, come join us."

She folded her arms across her breasts with the words *South Dakota* pressed against them in her turned-inside-out sweatshirt. "I can't attend, I have to study, but . . ." Something made her add, "I do admire what you're doing." She was afraid to elaborate on the dumb thing she'd just said, so she couldn't tell him that she didn't have time for protests and marches, that she was in a hurry to grow up, to be an adult in the real world, to wear nice clothes and drive a nice car and have her paycheck and her own apartment and never to have to go to Mother for a single thing. She just wanted to have a job, to live a calm, orderly, decent life, the kind of life the hippies were trying to knock down. Not that they weren't right that it was an unfair, racist, materialistic society, but she wasn't sure what that had to do with her and her problems.

"We're making political history out there. It's going to be a new society. A fair one."

"Oh, I see."

"You're humoring me."

"No, actually I have a feeling I understand black people's problems better than a lot of white people do."

He struggled with his corduroy coat, catching his fingers on the torn lining in one of the armholes. He finally got it on and stood up. A button on his coat dangled on a few threads; he would look like a ragamuffin except that the coat had a dull, expensive sheen to it and he had a stiff-necked way of holding himself that suggested, to Moira's admittedly inexperienced eye, the kind of ease with the world that a comfortable childhood gave one.

"You probably don't even know any blacks personally," he said.

She could have asked him if knowing an Indian would do, and she saw a blurry image of Paul Whitefeather and of trees next to the Sioux River big as the arches that held up the George Washington Bridge. She saw Paul's calm eyes and his gleaming skin. She could have told him that skin color was nothing to her. But Paul Whitefeather was none of his business, and neither was Moira McPherson.

"I have to get to work." She got up, wrapped the apron around her waist, and felt him looking at her legs for just a second, and she felt the old enemy sex trying to come back into her life; she snatched up the coffee cups and hurried over to the counter where the dirty-dish bin was kept. She pulled the checks out of her apron and began to fill in at the bottom, "Thank You—Your waitress, Moira," to save time when things got busy later.

He came over and sat on a table. "Come and join us."

And he looked so damned innocent. Like he wasn't even thinking about going to bed with her, and he was so very intelligent with all that theoretical political stuff he'd just been laying on her, so she said, "Oh, I'll think about it."

"I'll pick you up at four sharp right out there on the corner."

As the door closed behind him, she went to take an order from a party of five stoned-looking hippies who had collapsed into a booth, the males with headbands and feathers and beads, the females with long braids and peace-symbol necklaces. Moira already missed Zeke, and almost wished she'd admitted that she too wanted to someday devote her life to helping people who were less fortunate. And she saw in vivid colors the African masks on Rosemary's wall. She shouldn't get involved—even if he wasn't after her body, this Zeke could be another missionary, someone who'd spent a different kind of life so he wouldn't know at first what a weirdo Moira was, wouldn't know that awful things ran in her blood, that the blood was both inside and outside of her.

All that blood. Yes, for the first time in her life, Mother didn't have a joke to pull out of her pocket and wipe away the hurt or the happiness from a situation. No jokes with which to mop up the blood.

A few months after Daddy's death, she'd been rummaging through a drawer—the same drawer in which Mother had hidden *Peyton Place* long ago—and she came across the death certificate. Cold letters typed onto a piece of paper now summarized the evening.

The death certificate said the death was the result of a self-inflicted wound.

But the wounds weren't really self-inflicted. Moira put her face in her hands and wept for her father. Say what you would about Daddy, the wounds were, well, life-inflicted.

Mother walked around pale, confused, and she'd glance up at you and just say, "Well . . ."

That *well*, Moira came to realize, meant *I feel bad*, and it was the first time Moira could ever recall Mother seeming to feel bad about something, not covering it up with sarcasm.

And then she stopped the *well* and became bitter and angry. Her eyes were cold now. "I never cared for him," she said one day. "That was the sad thing. That was the really sad goddamned thing."

"Do you know what, Moira? He was faithful to me. The poor sap was faithful to me."

Moira had gone back to North Prairie High, endured the staring and whispering, just as she had endured staring and whispering all her life.

Daddy had died because Moira had disobeyed him. So what if it was an idiotic rule of his that she had disobeyed? She was still responsible.

But maybe that hadn't been the point.

The real point had been that he felt insanely jealous over Moira.

Daddy knew that Mother didn't really love him. So he'd loved Moira—desperately.

Mother knew that. Taryn knew that. Moira, deep down, knew it.

And when she was old enough for boys, it was too much—he couldn't stand to lose her.

But he had Taryn. He tried to make that enough. Poor Taryn, he tried to hate Moira enough to love Taryn. And he'd just about succeeded.

Take one very unstable and jealous man, put him with one very unstable and jealous and very, very unhappy woman. Throw in a third female, and to make it even more interesting, another—and you've just come up with the formula for gunpowder.

Of course it took her a while, and it took talks with Mr. Bailey and with Mrs. Jenks and letting a distance grow between herself and her mother and sister to come up with that.

*   *   *

Zeke had a toylike red sports car—she had no idea what kind—with a grumbly engine when it idled.

"Hey," he called from the car, "where were you the other day?"

He clambered out of the car and stood in front of her.

"I never said I would go," she said.

"Come with me now. Let me give you a ride, Flower Girl."

"No, thank you. I can walk."

"I know you can walk. But you don't have to."

Her feet were in fact awfully sore from work last night. Her arches ached with every step. And what harm would a ride do? He wouldn't have to know anything more about her than he did now if he just gave her a ride home.

"You'd think I could take a hint. But there's something about you I can't resist. You're so damned—what is it?—serious about everything you do—from reading your class notes to giving the busboys in that joint their share of the tips. I watched you through the window as I passed by the other day—by the way, the other waitresses cheat that skinny Puerto Rican kid."

She looked up, feeling the ugliness of the world, wondering how you could combat it. "Oh no," she said. Raul was her friend. On late nights he walked her home, sharing a joint, warding off potential muggers.

"Tell him to watch things more carefully. After he knows what's going on, believe me, he won't let it happen anymore."

Oh, all right, Moira said, maybe she would take a ride. After all, her feet *were* killing her.

He ran to the passenger side and opened the door in an exaggerated doorman's gesture.

As soon as she sat down inside the little car, she knew she had crossed some threshold. She put her hand on the leather dashboard. This was what nice things felt like. Looking at his handsome profile, seeing the look of confidence and of knowing his way around town, around the world, around life—she felt slightly corrupted.

"How about if we go down to the Village for a coffee? I know of a poetry reading this afternoon, in fact."

"I really can't. I have to study."

"Okay, okay. Where to?"

"My dorm," she said, pointing the way.

"Hmm-hmmm," he hummed. " 'Oh I don't know just why, she simply caught my eye . . . I love da-dum-de-dah.' "

Moira looked out the window and tried to suppress a smile.

"I apologize for the lousy weather," he said as the car skidded in the snow that was wafting onto Broadway. The car slid to a stop at 116th Street for a red light.

"Oh, this is nothing. This is spring where I come from," Moira said.

Zeke laughed and she realized she must have said something funny so she laughed too.

"Where are you from—the North Pole?" he said.

When she told him South Dakota, he gave her that look that people around here did when she told them, then made a loud noise and pounded the palm of his hand against the steering wheel. "I don't believe this. I'm driving down Broadway with a beautiful long-haired, long-legged girl from South Dakota." They scooted around a corner. Was she wrong, were people looking at them? Admiring them in this embarrassingly, outrageously comfortable car?

"I'll bet it was all very wholesome."

"Wholesome?"

"South Dakota."

Was he making fun of her? Was this a sick joke? Did he know about Daddy? Had he checked up on her, read the *Argus Leader*'s small news story on page nineteen about that awful night?

"Yeah, Ozzie and Harrietland, Father Knows Best, Princess and Kitten and Bud, all that."

She looked at his face and saw that he really meant that, and it struck her now how naive in a way this guy was. Then, the thought of telling Zeke about Daddy flashed through her mind, then the thought of him knowing anything about her past, and suddenly it felt as if there were a ten-ton anchor attached to the rear bumper that was about to jerk them to a halt.

But he turned on the radio and as it played "Incense and Peppermint," Moira felt as if a small opening had come about for her, and as Zeke talked on and the car went further, she thought, after all, this *is* 1967, and this *is* New York City, where millions of people over the past four hundred years started new lives, and who knows?

* * *

Sometimes she thought it had been some sort of terrible freak accident. Daddy wouldn't kill himself. It wasn't like him.

Now she was weighed down with the sadness of his poor life. She began to dream about him. She dreamed about him still. He would appear in the dream, younger, in his thirties.

"I thought you were dead," Moira would say.

He would look at her calmly and say, "No, I'm okay, Moira."

He wouldn't ever be crazy or drunk in this dream. He would be *normal*. Normal like other people's fathers. Death had made him okay. Blowing his heart out had cured him of his terrible jealousy. The jealousy over Moira, fueled by Mother's jealousy of Moira but which was really, Moira now knew, jealousy over Mother.

Daddy hadn't been the only cruel one in that household. Moira guiltily recalled how badly they'd all treated each other. She'd joined in the chorus of silence when Daddy came in from work. There had been opportunities to show she cared, but she had not taken them. He was a tyrant, but he'd been made one, she sometimes thought. It was a cruelty she had learned from Mother—that when someone loves you and leaves himself vulnerable, you stick the knife in. Right in the spot where he loves you. And then you twist it. Because that's the part of him that loves you and you despise it because you despise yourself—you're not worthy of love. If someone does love you, there's something wrong with him. Kill his love, and you kill yourself.

You could talk to him in this dream if you wanted to. Instead of sizing you up warily and sadly, he regarded you calmly and steadily the way one imagined a father should. He was a real father in these dreams, and he loved her the way he had always wanted to love her —without the sexual side of it that had come creeping in and that he'd been unable to control. So he'd had to kill himself. A very moral man.

When Zeke went around corners she had to hold onto the handle on the door; he hardly seemed to be looking where he was going, he was so busy talking, talking about blacks and civil rights and Vietnam and black power and students' power as the insubstantial little car skated down Amsterdam Avenue.

"So here you are in the big city with a nice Jewish boy."

"Jewish?" she said. What did that mean to her? All she could think of was Jews in the Bible. Moses, Abraham, David.

"Surely you've figured that out by now?"

"No, I . . ." she began. "I didn't."

"Uh-oh. Is something wrong?" His face was so worried that she had the urge to touch it, to smooth it back to the noble-statue face.

"Oh no," she said quickly. "It's just that I've never . . ." she started to say "dated," but wasn't sure this was a date and the coffee definitely hadn't been a date ". . . had coffee with anyone who was Jewish before."

He laughed loudly. "Oh my God, I hope that coffee was kosher." He looked at her again, his eyes big and round and dark as brown can get. Eyes that were as intelligent as any she'd ever seen, and yet there was something soft and right about him and she just wanted to put her head on his chest and wrap that worn corduroy coat around the two of them.

"What did you think I was? Ezekiel Rosengarten Beaustein. A great old Irish name, huh?" He reached his arm out and hugged her and said, "Or what the hell do they have out there in South Dakota? Swedes? Huh? Eskimos? Yeah, that's me, a Jewish Eskimo."

There was something very sexy about all this, about how different they were and about how much it seemed to delight him. "I didn't think anything. I don't think about that—about what someone is."

He pulled up at a stoplight, looked at her, lightly touched the bridge of her nose. "No, my little South Dakota *shiksa,* I don't suppose you do."

She wanted to know what a *shiksa* was, whether it was an insult or a compliment, but his voice seemed to tell her it was both.

"My mother would die if she saw you," he said.

Moira laughed and said, "Well, I think we're even."

"Your parents don't like Jews?"

"Oh, I don't know about that. I don't think they think about it, either." Why not say *they?* Why tell him about Daddy right now and spoil a perfectly beautiful evening? "I just mean the car, your politics."

"And my parents worry about some *shiksa* getting hold of their nice little Jewish boy."

"Oh," Moira said playfully. "Am I getting hold of you?"

"I'm yours, baby." As they took off from the stoplight, heads turned to watch them.

"Thank God they retired to Florida and can't see me realizing their biggest nightmare. Or make that plural—getting hung up on a *shiksa* and trying to let the blacks into their neighborhood."

"Your neighborhood?"

"Riverside Drive near Eighty-second Street," he said. "Penthouse Ten-A. Now what do you think of me? Surprised? Angry? Disappointed? Thrilled?"

"I don't know the area," she said. "I haven't been off-campus much yet, other than the bus ride into New York, a cab ride to the dorm from there."

He reached over and squeezed her. "I feel like a little kid and you're a roomful of brand-new toys." He looked in the rearview mirror and stomped on the accelerator and yelled happily out the window as they belted their way down Broadway.

Twenty-six

"Okay, you're going to think this is crazy, but I sometimes wonder if democracy isn't bad for the human soul," Zeke said one night as they scooted around the corner onto Central Park West on their way from a concert to dinner. "I mean, it assumes human selfishness as a guiding rule. What do you think about that, Flower Girl?"

"I don't know," Moira said, grabbing the little strap as he accelerated toward a corner. She no longer closed her eyes around corners but was enjoying herself, no longer feeling self-conscious but as if she belonged in this car with this man with big, dark eyes and a turned-under nose and generous scarlet Botticelli lips. "You don't think we're innately selfish?"

"I don't think we have to be. Maybe there's a whole mess of altruism in all of us, just waiting for the right system."

Outside of church, Moira had never met anyone who talked like this. In her experience, people expressed love for humanity at church, then went out and looked down on poor people and hated anyone who tried to change the conditions of the poor if it meant taking something away from everyone else.

"The problem with democracy is that you're supposed to vote for what you need, for your own selfish ends. If you care about the other guy, vote for his best interest as well as your own, for everybody's, it fucks up the system. It's like our system preys upon man's basest instincts, encourages selfishness. It's a drag."

Moira liked Zeke's way of looking at things, and even if she didn't always agree there seemed to be a certain logic to it all, and she couldn't quite decide if that logic was zany or terribly profound. "But maybe that's the way nature wants it. Selfishness, competition are built into our genes, into all animals' genes. All plants' genes, too," Moira said. "People, rats, plants. Not that I like to believe it myself, but it seems to me that selfishness is the law of the jungle."

"But this isn't the jungle," he said in an alarmed voice which she had come to know was not so much alarm as an exclamation point. "This is Eighty-seventh Street."

And he put his arm roughly around her neck and pulled her to him and kissed her, scratching her face with his perpetual five o'clock shadow that was impossible to shave away. As they headed into Central Park, he took her largish hand with its ragged nails and burns from a chemistry lab experiment and squeezed it in his gentle, thin, brown hand with its smooth, even nails.

"I can't stay out too late tonight," Moira said. "I have an eight o'clock class in the morning."

"That's all right," he said. "I'm having a hellish time with that statistics class. I have to write a paper, too."

"I'll be happy to help you with it," Moira said.

"Would you, Flower Girl? That'd be great."

"You can show me your term paper after you write it, and I'll check it over for you, if you'd like."

"I'd like, Flower Girl. Thanks."

Central Park unfolded in front of them. Snow whirled down, some resting on the brown, searching branches, while the rest fluffed to the ground. Yellow cabs and black limousines raced them through the park. People walked by in bright winter reds and yellows and greens. A cardinal flew by. Someone had just adjusted the color knob on the world. Real happiness, Moira realized, came in full, living color.

Zeke pulled aside the collar of her big plaid coat from high school to see what she was wearing. Zeke had a way of looking her over in a way she didn't really mind—not the way boys before had, but the way Zeke also looked over menus, shelves of books in antique book stores, sets at the opera when the curtain had just come up. "Nice dress. Is it new?"

"Sort of," she said. She'd run out of clothes to wear on these dress-up dates. This one was a chartreuse bouclé minidress that used to be a calf-length dress she wore on high school dress-up occasions. She'd altered it that afternoon with a pair of lab scissors and needle and thread from the dorm sewing kit.

"And new shoes?"

As she had headed out with the dress and her old worn-out flats, her roommate Roberta, an overweight chemistry major from Maine who liked to mother Moira, had raised her head from her book and said, "Wait a minute."

She'd then gotten up and in her methodical way went to her own closet, fished around at the bottom, and pulled out a pair of never-worn black high heels. "Mom sent me these. Take them, I'm not the high-heel type."

Moira had never held expensive dressy shoes in her hand before. The pleasure almost frightened her as she put them on. They were a little wide, but they were without the nicks and toe-shaped bulges and slick worn-down areas at the heels that marked Moira's shoes. In fact, they were so good-looking that Moira felt the rest of her now appeared doubly shabby by contrast.

Moira had been amazingly lucky to get a roommate like Roberta, she always reminded herself, when she looked around the residence hall and saw all the women in cashmere and silk-lined suit jackets going out on dates with men who wore vests and smoked pipes— what a disaster a roommate like that would have been for both Moira and the roommate! Not that Moira wouldn't like to have been one of those people—but she knew how they felt about schol-arship students from South Dakota.

"I'd like to buy you a dress," Zeke said. "I'd like to buy you clothes. I'll take you shopping to Bergdorf's one day."

It had become increasingly apparent that she was falling in love with someone who had a lot of money. She wondered if accepting a dress from Bergdorf's would make her a prostitute, or if that's what one did when one had a rich boyfriend. She'd never considered the question before because she'd never known anyone before with a rich boyfriend.

If only Mother could see her now. What would she think?

Mother would be appalled by her relationship with Zeke. And Moira was beginning to like that idea.

The restaurant was crowded and had that modulated-voiced New York energy Moira had come to like. She had also come to like New York's roomfuls of people who wouldn't care what Mother or even Taryn thought. Moira suddenly felt glad that she was smart enough to have gotten herself to New York and pretty enough to have gotten herself to this New York restaurant full of svelte, soft-voiced people who looked up and admired Moira's figure as Zeke took her coat. Yes, Moira liked New York.

The walls were dark wood, interrupted by big plate glass mirrors. Lace curtains fluttered behind the dark leather booth that groaned as they scooted into it.

Zeke ordered wine. The waiter returned, all bows and flourishes, with the gleaming bottle and two glasses. She loved the ritual with the cork, the whiff, the sip, the nod to the waiter.

As they sipped their wine, he talked of the SDS's plans to boycott the building of the new gym that would displace blacks in the university area. "Do I sound like some sort of moral snob? I worry that I've developed a superiority complex."

"I think you are very moral, that's why I . . ." She wanted to say *love,* but that hadn't yet come up between them, not in earnest, so she said, "That's why I like you. Sometimes I think that's what saves us, those of us who have had difficult lives.

"I guess the reason I want to go to medical school and help people in misery is that I had a difficult childhood. I think goodness is the only thing that really saves people."

"In the long run, it's the only constant, the only sure thing," he said, looking at her with glowing black eyes.

"The only thing that can get you through hell on earth."

Zeke squeezed her hand. "I understand, believe me, I understand."

"You couldn't," she said. "Your life must have been a lot different."

"Yes, I was a spoiled if neglected brat. I had every toy invented by man to keep a kid and his nanny busy and out of Mother and Dad's hair. I went to school with rich, neglected kids. That's part of why I like you so much. I'm tired of spoiled brats."

He still thought she was Rebecca of Sunnybrook Farm. What if Zeke knew what she'd been back home? She could never take him home, not really. But before she could dwell on that depressing thought, Zeke was off into politics again. "Most people aren't like you. Man, the gall of racist, fascist war-mongering white people never ceases to amaze me."

Moira sipped the wine. They both were aware of the irony of the situation—dinner at a French restaurant while they discussed poverty and revolution; they were little more than radical chic innocents but it was okay because eventually they would help make the world more fair. And she would have loved Zeke as much had he been either poor or (even more difficult to imagine) a Republican.

She was a limousine liberal tonight but she really felt almost like a black person—one of "his" black people—passing for white, black inside, white on the outside, the opposite of an Oreo. She would like to tell him that she had all the sympathy in the world for minorities. That she had once been an African mask on a South Dakota missionary's wall.

He took small, quick spoonfuls of the soup. "I sound almost corny, I'll bet, but I can't help it, I feel so responsible, so guilty"— he looked up and laughed—"as if I'm carrying the burden for the whole white race."

Here he was: the Jew come to save her soul. As he spoke on, she felt as if a wedge had just been dug into her, that something was trickling in to fill that little wedge. On and on he went, this time about a protest march, how he envisioned the world after the revolution, and she felt almost a relief. A relief that said the only way she could find happiness was to follow that instinct inside of her that wanted to help others, and to do it in her own way, not the way other people thought she should. And she would stop feeling guilty about doing what she wanted to do—it was her own life, after all, not Mother's, not Taryn's, not her poor dead father's— and she would find a way to go to medical school, if she had to take out loans she'd be paying off until she was ninety years old.

She'd build an armor of virtue around herself to keep out the evil spirits. An unassailable armor of goodness to protect herself from the terrible things that went on in this life.

Barnard had had new students coming in from thirty-eight states but no others from South Dakota, she found out later, and she wondered now if that was why they had accepted her, as their token hick.

And yet odd as it might seem, she was a girl from the Plains who had dropped down in the middle of New York in 1966 and felt that she almost fit in, that she came closer to belonging here than she ever had at home. And whatever happened to her in New York, she knew one thing for sure; she was never going back home to live.

She had taken a Greyhound Bus all the way from Sioux Falls to New York. She was astounded by New York City. Looking up, she was so overwhelmed she imagined the tall buildings must feel overwhelmed and dizzy themselves, and she almost felt as if her presence was going to make them all topple onto the streets, cave in, as if she'd been wrong about New York, that it wouldn't tolerate her either, that New York had been waiting for someone like her to come to town and that would be the final straw, they'd had a lot of oddballs blow into town over the years, but this one took the cake and the whole city would collapse to the ground.

And when she got off the city bus at Broadway and 116th Street, her mother's words rang in her ears: "Ivy League, Seven Sisters, for God's sake. Just who do you think you are, anyway?"

She had gotten away from home, but it was not without loneliness that she lived her quiet life as a biology major on a scholarship. Her first semester, Moira would see girls going out on Saturday night and would throw herself onto her bed and begin to study furiously, angrily, hungrily, like a religious fanatic going to her knees and praying for help from God. Only her God was the God of blessed science and study, the God who had brought her to a college that would take the likes of Moira in and give her a chance to make something of herself other than a home-economics teacher, a profession for which she was now absolutely convinced she had no talent.

There were times when Moira would still have liked to be the kind of person who fit into a niche, and there were some nights when she lay in bed in her room, her eyes blurred and red from studying, and out of habit worried that she was crazy, that she was immoral, that she was a slut, that she was a bad soul headed for hell. She didn't know, she just didn't know. Thank God for science, she would say, whispering real prayers to the God of science, also to the God of lonely people who had been to church only a few times a year. "Thank you, God, for giving me science and getting me out of my hometown."

God had done his part, gotten her out of town. The rest, she guessed, was up to her.

Zeke's apartment had an endless series of dark rooms in which faded antique furniture sat stiffly reminiscing about the glory days. There were paintings on the walls with individual hooded lights on the frames that you could turn on by pulling a little chain. Most were old landscapes, but there were a few modern pieces—a de Kooning scrambling all over one huge wall, a Frank Stella and a Warhol shoulder to shoulder on another, a Picasso giving her a curious three-quarter stare from down the hall.

There were both a large formal dining room and a small room with a glass dining table and six chairs, and the walls covered floor-to-ceiling with wine racks.

"Dad is a wine importer, among other things. This is our wine cellar, which they also use for smaller, intimate dinner parties." Moira looked around at all the bottles, which caught the chandelier light like green and red and yellow gems. "Some night I'll have Mabel serve us dinner in here."

She was becoming more and more surprised at the extent of Zeke's wealth, but for some reason she wasn't intimidated. Maybe because he took it all so much for granted. Maybe because the apartment was, in fact, a little worn in parts, past its prime. Maybe because Zeke in a way felt guilty about it all. Maybe because Zeke made her feel like she belonged there.

Zeke picked out a small bottle of dessert wine. He uncorked it and poured them each a glass of the heavy golden nectar. Then he put Bob Dylan's *Blonde on Blonde* album on the stereo, and lit a joint. A white cat appeared from a dark hallway, joined them, making figure-eights around their legs, then leaped onto a chair. Zeke and Moira went to the center of the floor and danced silly, exaggerated steps and laughed and sang out in hoarse voices with Dylan's "Rainy Day Woman" about getting stoned.

They settled onto a thick white rug on the floor and took turns with the joint as they watched the lights of the boats travel like bejeweled water bugs down the Hudson River. A deep blue melancholy hovered in the room, Moira thought, because the residents were Jewish and the Jewish people had always had so much trouble. She loved him for that, for his vulnerability, for his being Jewish and still trusting, still wanting someone like her.

He took her to a Christmas party at the French Consulate. Zeke knew so many people that he was off socializing—in French—most of the night. Moira stood in a corner with her champagne.

Back in his apartment, they kissed as soon as he opened the door, then they crumpled into a loveseat near the door and he held her and let his hand run over her bare arm.

She loved him so much she was frightened and so she said no.

"Moira, my love, this is nineteen sixty-eight. It's okay, everything's cool. Let's make it."

"I can't. I don't take birth-control pills."

"Why not?"

"I don't want to. I don't plan on needing them."

"Time to change your plans. Get with it, my love."

She got up and went to one of the paintings—a landscape—and pulled the little light on. The little brass nameplate underneath it said *Frederic Edwin Church*. She turned it off and went to the next. It was a woman in an old-fashioned evening gown and dark, blossoming lips like Zeke's.

Moira looked around the room, at the wavery glass in the windows, the high old wood bookshelves, the chandelier that tinkled every time a big truck went by on the street below. She looked up at Zeke's grandmother, great-aunt, whatever she was, and thought all of a sudden, "What am I doing here?"

He'd dump her if she went to bed with him, and he'd dump her if she didn't. Ultimately he wanted someone from Riverside Drive. One of those girls with pierced ears and designer peasant skirts.

She moved into the hallway to view the Picasso. The face resembled an African mask like the ones on Rosemary's wall. A fuzzy, marijuana-induced fear came tiptoeing into the room, settled over her head. Another missionary who would never really understand her. She was exactly like one of Zeke's "blacks." A charity case. Some little poor girl to assuage his conscience, an avenue for rebellion against his parents.

Wasn't this what people warned against? Was she going to be used, fucked, and discarded as usual, just in a classier setting? She

could see her father bursting down the door, taking her by the hair
—hair that was long now that Mother couldn't get to it with her
scissors and which fell away from her face like a mass of tumble-
weed—and hurling her against the wall, threatening Zeke with a
fist.

She pulled the chain to turn off the light under Zeke's rich family
and panic came flapping in. Why hadn't he told her he was rich?
She didn't need a lot of money. She'd never wanted a rich husband.
She'd never even wanted a husband. And now she was involved and
she had made Zeke her everything, her family, her boyfriend, her
God.

The marijuana made the room spin. A thousand needles were
sticking into her arms, face, eyes, nose, navel. Big, white, muscular
boy-hands fumbled inside her blouse, pulling at her nipples,
scratching the sides of her breasts, pushing under her skirt to feel
her crotch. She was sixteen again, and boys sucked on her tits in the
backseats of cars and didn't even say hello to her at school the next
day. She was seventeen and Jack Locksmey was forcing himself into
her mouth and talking about his prettier, more moral, more desir-
able girl back home.

"I have to go," she said.

"Sshh," Zeke said. "Come back. I need some company. So do
you."

"I'm frightened," she said.

"Me too," he said.

With that, she became calmer and sat back down next to him.
His eyes were closed as he held her hand and listened to Dylan sing
"Desolation Row."

"Why are you frightened?" she said.

"Because I've always been alone. Because my father wants me to
go into his business and I don't want to. So I'm not a real man.

"And because I want to stop the war. And not just because I'm
some noble motherfucker, either. I have selfish reasons, too—I
don't want to die young."

She reached up to touch the black curls spilling onto the neck of
his shirt. She was doubly frightened now, not so much of seeing
him weak, vulnerable, but because he seemed to be reaching to her
for something she didn't know how to give him. She could give him

her body, her romantic love, but she couldn't give him what he seemed to need.

He put his face on her chest, just above her breasts. "Oh, God, Moira, I don't want to shoot people, I want to help them," and it felt like he was crying. "And I'm afraid of getting hurt."

The next weekend, he took her to hear the New York Philharmonic and then they went to his apartment. He put a Brahms piano trio on the stereo and poured them some pale perfumey dessert wine and lit a candle and a joint.

They smoked, listening to the melancholy music, looking out at the black night and the lights twinkling across the Hudson, and here, on the white rug, he unbuttoned her blouse, and his mouth traveled down her chest to her breasts.

She was too numb, too much in love, too frightened of never seeing him again, to enjoy it. "I'm afraid of sex," she said.

"Let me teach you. We'll make love all night."

She moved away. "No, I can't, I won't."

He stopped for a moment. "Don't tell me you're a virgin. Impossible. The species is extinct. Hey, come whisper square roots in my ear. You're so intelligent, so sexy, so pretty. Mmmm. I love the Flower Girl." Then looking her in the eyes, "And you're so *good*. That's why I love you, Moira McPherson, the girl with the mysterious past, the girl with no past. I love you I love you I love you. Because you're so good."

They made love the next night. Then they lay on his bed and she told him about her father's suicide. "Sometimes I tell myself that there was something almost normal about what he did. Yes, it just seemed like such a normal thing to do. I mean, suicide is something you can understand, something with a name. So far, he's the only one of us who ended up making sense."

Zeke didn't really understand, but how could he? And he didn't want to understand. He wanted to be in love with an uncomplicated midwestern girl, not the mess that she really was.

But she went on. "All my life I felt as if no one understood me and my family's problems. They don't sympathize with craziness or alcoholism, but they do feel sorry for someone who kills himself.

Yes, the only thing that saves me is that my father finally did something that made sense."

Zeke said. "All that's behind you. Come join the sixties. Come join life, Flower Girl."

Zeke fished around on the floor for a pack of cigarettes. He lit one, and with his delicate fingers tossed the match into the ashtray. Daddy would have thought Zeke was a "fruit" the way he smoked the cigarette. Maybe that was one of the reasons why Moira loved Zeke. Because he wasn't what Daddy would call a "real man."

They went to a party and came home sick from the apple wine and the strobe light. He put *Sergeant Pepper* on the stereo and poured Cokes.

They smoked cigarettes, looking out at the black night and the lights twinkling across the Hudson, and there on the white rug he unbuttoned her blouse again.

He kissed her throat, and she kissed his face, his neck. They began to make love.

They rolled around on the floor, fucking, rolling more and working their way, it seemed, down the hall and into the kitchen.

Just as Moira was beginning to enjoy the fucking, being awakened from a two-year freeze, Zeke said, "Let's do it the way they do in India, make love for a while, stop before we come, then take a break, then go back," Zeke said. "That way, we can do it all night."

"All night, yes," Moira said, and they wrestled and laughed and kissed and he went into her again and they rolled around on the cold kitchen floor, onto the cat's dishes of kibble and water. Icy water dribbled onto Moira's back and hair and cat food went flying over the floor and they rolled back to the refrigerator.

They made love some more, gently, then roughly, violently. Moira broke her promise and came, Zeke pulled out before he came. They lay breathing and feeling each other's wet bodies. Moira felt the inevitable letdown. What in God's name were women supposed to do? There were no answers. Guilty and wrong no matter what they did. Come on, get with it, Moira, it's 1968 now, she said to herself. But she couldn't get the image of Daddy charging down the hill out of her mind, of Mother's disapproving, penciled-in eyebrows, of the boys calling her a slut, of girls avoiding her, of Mr. Smealz, of Daddy sliding into her sleeping bag.

Goddammit. Goddammit all.

They fucked some more. She let go as fully as she could. All the guilt, the shame of her body. After a while, out of breath, they paused and looked around.

"I don't know about you, but I'm starving," he said.

"I've never been so hungry in my life," Moira said.

Zeke stood up and opened the refrigerator and got out a bottle of already-opened Beaujolais and pulled out the cork and took a swig and handed it to her. She stood up. His penis, still hard, bobbed, his pupils were huge with exhaustion and sex. He took a swig of the wine, then another. It tasted foreign and musty and raw and appropriate for the evening. He got out a hunk of cheese and gave it to her, holding it while she nibbled. He took a bite. He got out a salami and they ate bites out of it and she played with him and they drank the Beaujolais from the bottle. Then they went to bed and made love Indian-style.

It was amazing how much love she had ready to give. With Zeke, it came pouring forth, knocking her off course. She felt she had finally been released from her past.

Twenty-seven

AND THEN DADDY'S ghost returned to haunt Moira. It crept in during the McCarthy presidential campaign.

They were on a bus heading for New Hampshire to go door-to-door canvassing.

Zeke was struggling with a reading assignment for his statistics class and Moira was reading *Manchild in the Promised Land* for an English class when one of the organizers came back and took an aisle seat across from Zeke. Her hair was black and parted down the middle, her eyes were lined in black and her mouth was plump with white lipstick. Moira's old look had come into style.

Handing them packets of materials, the organizer said, "Remember, with these blue-collar types, we don't stress the ethics of the campaign, we stress how much tax money the war is costing them." And she gave Zeke a tiny smile that said they were of the superior class, despite their genuine proletariat work shirts and gnarled sandals and frayed bellbottoms.

Zeke smiled back but, Moira was happy to see, didn't acknowledge the message. The organizer went on about the canvass and her flirty tone made Moira angry. So did the tone that was creeping into Zeke's voice—it was the same circling tone that he had used when he was first pursuing Moira.

And then she wondered why she was so insecure.

When the woman went on to another seat, Moira, trying to make herself sound funny, said, "Just what do you see in me anyway, Zeke Beaustein? Is it my family's millions you're after?"

"I certainly hope not. From what you tell me, I'd be sorely disappointed."

"Well, what is it, then?"

"Okay, Moira, I'll take the bait. It's your body I'm after," he said. "Are you happy now?"

Moira felt heat rise to her face. She decided to take him literally. She seemed to be itching for a fight. Why, she didn't know, but she snapped, "Well, I knew that, I'm just wondering what else of my many assets you find attractive."

"What else have you got?"

"Well, you've got me there. I have nothing else to offer, I guess. Just a body."

Zeke sat in silence for a moment, reading through the pamphlets, then said, "Moira, you have a nice body, but I've seen better. Is that what you want to hear? What do you want?"

"Where have you seen better bodies? On her?" Moira realized how stupid she was being and yet she couldn't stop herself.

He laid his head back and closed his eyes. Moira looked down and saw that her hands were shaking. She clasped them and sat feeling self-conscious, then got out her book again.

After napping for half an hour, he stretched and hugged her and said, "Do you know what I really like about you? You act any way that you want to."

She looked out the window at the mountains. She wasn't sure she wanted to act any way she wanted. "Maybe because I don't know how I'm supposed to act."

Eyes still closed, he laughed the way he often laughed at things she said in earnest that he seemed to think were meant to be witty.

"My little iconoclast," he said and took her arm in his.

The neighborhood Moira canvassed reminded her of the small South Dakota town her family left for Sioux Falls. The possessions of the people looked so pitiful under the endlessly melancholy sky. Big cars with mud flaps and rusting junk in backseats sat in driveways of unfriendly-looking shingled houses. How had she ever been born into a family like that?

That was a good question, but a better one was: How had she gotten out?

But her parents hadn't really been like the families she had met working here. Not intellectually, anyway. Her parents had proved that people could realize the American dream by moving up in the world with their brains and talent. But they hadn't gone as far as they wanted because the American dream didn't take into account the emotional toll on those who made it.

And Moira got the uncomfortable feeling that maybe that was happening to her, too. Maybe her own emotions were going to stand in the way of her own sixties brand of the American dream.

After a party thrown by one of the big supporters, they returned to their motel. She and Zeke stayed up most of the night drinking Grand Marnier and smoking Tiparillos, talking—she about what it must have been like to have been early *homo erectus,* he saying he loved it when she talked dirty and then talking dirtier about Sartre and Allen Ginsberg and then Descartes—and making love Indian-style, pausing every now and then to watch the black-and-white Kirk Douglas-Lauren Bacall movie flashing light and trumpet music into the room.

Zeke was speaking to a group, urging them to join a boycott of classes at Columbia to protest the draft. As Moira watched him speak, she wondered if the others listening felt a pang at the sincerity in his voice which pleaded with them in that beautiful New York accent. "Listen to your conscience," he said, and there was silence for a few moments. They loved him too. Did they also love his thin figure with those perfect wide shoulders and that worn-out coat he didn't believe in replacing. Did they, too, think of him as something almost religious, someone come to teach them ideas they might not ever encounter again, not in this world? Was he teaching them a new way to pray?

Zeke was on the nightly news, quoted in the newspapers, reading from student publications. He was preoccupied and almost irritable and overwhelmed, at times anyway—the SDS was protesting the building of the gym, and Columbia University was a media event for the world.

Still, when he was done with the blacks and the communists and the celebrities and the poor people, Zeke would pick up Moira at her dorm and whisk her off to eat in a variety of restaurants to match the variety of his personas, one night at a brown-rice and broccoli place, another night at some decadent restaurant with tinkling china and crystal and Bearnaise sauce.

They were becoming comfortable with each other, and at the same time the illusions were starting to fade. She saw that he could be arrogant, and he saw that she really *was* from the homogenized heartland.

"Did they even *have* spaghetti in Sioux Falls?" he said one night at a brassy little overly lit place in Little Italy.

She laughed, fork twined with pasta in midair. "Yeah—haven't you heard of Franco-American?"

Zeke's eyebrows expressed his irritation. "Please don't say 'Yeah,' Moira. And by the way, maybe you should try not to drop your 'i-n-gs,' too."

They ate in silence. Was he kidding? Yes. No.

After dinner, they took advantage of the warm early spring weather and walked through the streets. Men ogled Moira, Zeke noticed and took her hand in both of his and said, "You're going to have men admiring you for a long time, Moira. You'll have lots and lots of boyfriends."

She turned to him, anger pouring out uncontrolled. "I don't want any other boyfriends."

He looked at her, detached, maybe annoyed, she thought. "I don't want you to, either. At least not while I'm still in the picture," he said, kissing her forehead.

Moira tried to let that remark fly into the warm air, but then a girl in an orange mini and hot pink tights walked by and she smiled at Zeke and he smiled back. He gave Moira a sheepish look and she erupted into tears. She couldn't stop crying at the thought of him ever leaving her, so she ran off to a subway station and rode home by herself.

This time he didn't call to ask her what was wrong, what he had done.

She couldn't eat and she couldn't study. She called him and they patched things up. But then the next afternoon, a girl standing on Broadway in a dress that let her belly button peek out ran over and handed him a flower and brushed her lips against his cheek. He bent down and kissed her forehead. "Peace," they called to each other, and held up their fingers in the peace sign.

Moira felt the rage build, actually boil within her. It came up in waves up through her arms to her hands to her fingers, up from her chest to her throat to her head.

"What was all that kissing about?" she said too loudly.

Why was he looking at her like that? Surprised. Like he'd just noticed she had green skin or three eyes.

His expression went back to normal. "Peace, love," he said, then started singing " 'I love the flower girl, she seemed so sweet and kind, she swept into my mind. Da-da-de-dum-dum-dum.' "

The jealous feeling came back over her again and now it was as if she were standing off in the distance watching this scene. "You are always flirting and humiliating me."

Zeke started to walk away but she went after him and grabbed his shirt. "You bastard, don't walk away from me." And all of a sudden she stepped out of herself and was standing and watching herself. Or was it her father she was watching? She put her hands up on her cheeks, which were hot and wet with sudden crying. "You fucking bastard, what do you want to do with her? You want to lay her, too? Well, go ahead. I never want to see you again. You whore."

With all the bottled-up anger of a lifetime propelling her, she ran down the street and back to her room.

Maybe she'd had to do that, maybe that scene had been necessary.

Now she felt good, actually, glad to be rid of him. She'd said what she felt, and that was what you were supposed to do. No one was going to take her for a fool. No one was going to fuck her and leave her again, not that easily.

Moira got out her calculus. The little stack of fresh, white, impersonal paper with its little flaws here and there gave her a lift. Paper was so safe and neutral. She worked hard, emanating an aura around herself to scare off unhappiness and memories. After an hour and a half she put down her calculus book for a break, and a scared feeling came back to nag at her. She felt more alone than she'd ever felt in her life. And the truth was, she *was* more alone than ever.

By evening she was beginning to regret what she had done. She found the dried daisy he'd given her that day in the rain. If she had kept a memory book of her love life, this would be all she would have to show for it.

She considered calling him. No, he'd call her. Of course he would. He loved her, didn't he?

But he loved everyone, remember? He called everyone his flower girl. This was a new age of free love. The world was confused, Moira was confused. It was time to get out of this relationship. Time to get out before it was too late.

But then, as she lay in bed crying because she really didn't want to get out of this relationship, she wondered if she was only imagining all her problems with him.

A few days later he called and asked her to lunch. She looked up at the sky to where God was smiling down at her, and said yes, she'd love to.

But as she was heading off to meet him, full of apologies to him, she became angry. Lunch, and not dinner? Why not dinner? Who was going to one of those goddamn French restaurants with him tonight? Was he phasing her out? Who had he been with these past few days?

She couldn't do it. She couldn't be rejected by him. She turned and went home and waited for him to phone and ask why she didn't show up. The telephone didn't ring.

Martin Luther King was shot in April, and Moira imagined Zeke's reaction. Sorrow, of course, but also anger.

She cried for Martin Luther King, the man who spoke for minorities, like herself. And she cried because she'd lost Zeke, and he had been another teacher of hers, showing her that her basic instincts—the good ones—were the right ones.

A few weeks later, one of those soft afternoons when spring gently begins to descend and no real work is possible, she was out for a walk and saw him strolling in earnest conversation with a tall blonde. She followed them to his car, Zeke in his corduroy pants with the worn-out seat, the girl in hip-huggers that showed off her skinny little-girl body to perfection. Moira watched the back of the girl's bare tanned midriff as she climbed into the little car and thought of hurling something out of a trash can at that back, something that would cut her, make her cry. Something rusty that would give her lockjaw. The girl looked in the rearview mirror, Moira's rearview mirror, her tiny hips in the seat where Moira's fleshy thighs were supposed to be.

She stood with her mouth covered to keep from shouting, her eyes hurting to keep from releasing tears. When he closed the passenger door and walked around to his side, he saw Moira, or at least she thought so, but he didn't acknowledge her.

She soaked a cloth in chloroform, took a female white rat out of the cage, and held the cloth over its mouth until it stopped twisting its body and swimming with its legs. Moira revered the laboratory animals in that they lived a life with purpose and personal sacrifice. They were dedicating their life to the betterment of the world, to science, as Moira wanted to, but Moira wondered if she'd ever prove as useful as these animals. Both Zeke and the lab rats had that over her—lives dedicated to the betterment of the human race. She almost smiled at how Zeke would laugh if she told him his soul was as noble as a rat's.

She laid the rat in her tray and prepared to dissect it. Her hands were trembling.

She put her instruments down and took a deep breath and picked them up again. More students came in and got to work on their projects. There was a quiet tinkly sound in the lab, odors rising and falling. What if she didn't have the science lab? It was like a big cathedral, with the high windows and light lazily filtering in. She'd have been crazy a long time ago.

There was the liver. Now the lab was quiet, despite the students, and it felt so safe, she felt so right. Carefully, painstakingly, she cut a thin specimen from the liver and put it on the slide.

She twisted the dials on the microscope, enjoying the heavy, old-fashioned feel of it. It was reassuring in this era that humankind still put so much effort and expense into making such instruments.

Taking off her glasses, she put her eye to the lens with the same excitement she had when she fanned out a freshly dealt hand in one of her late-night poker games with Roberta where the stakes were who would answer the phone and how many times they had to lie —Moira had to say Roberta wasn't in when her mother called, and

Roberta had to do the same for Moira when any of the slide-rule jockeys from the Columbia physics club called.

They just wanted to go to bed with her. Not like Zeke. She looked up and tears squeezed involuntarily from her eyes as they had been doing lately. Moira knew something was happening to her. That she was sinking into quicksand.

She put her eye back to the microscope. The cells appeared as they were supposed to under the magnification. Alcohol had destroyed this animal's liver, just as it had probably destroyed Daddy's. She clenched her fists, wishing she could get drunk like him. She now understood why he did it. To keep from going crazy.

But maybe Zeke would call. Maybe he would understand that she was just extremely jealous, that she could try harder not to be. Couldn't he see that she loved him, that she had never loved anyone before, that she would do anything for him, go to Vietnam for him —she swore she would, or at least go with him, like in the Peter, Paul and Mary song, "Cruel War."

She brought the slide in closer, twisted dials. The incredible predictability of it all, of seeing what you are told intellectually is there and yet cannot see until you go to all the trouble of finding a microscope and killing a poor little animal, it never ceased to amaze her.

Jealousy. She couldn't concentrate. Jealousy was going to destroy her, as it had the rest of her family. She'd come from a family of people trying to possess and control each other, seething with jealousy of and over one another. A rabid, raging jealousy that came from sexual repression gone berserk.

She had the urge to throw the microscope to the floor. To swipe it hard and make it crash against the wall, destroying the cabinet full of slides, to hear glass shatter and shatter and shatter.

But then she heard some noise outside, down on the street.

And suddenly there was an uproar in the hallway. Moira's head jerked up, her eyes adjusting to the unmagnified world of non-science. Something big was going on, she knew it in her bones. Something told her it was more than the usual kind of demonstration that was going on all the time across the street these days. She put her cirrhotic rat liver in the refrigerator and cleaned up and grabbed her sweater.

Hurrying over to the Columbia campus, she felt as she had when

Paul Whitefeather took her to an Indian neighborhood—excited, curious, welcome, scared, wrong, right. Hundreds of students were gathered outside the library. "Out of our way, fascists," the students were shouting. There was pushing, chanting, "Hell no, we won't go."

Something took hold of Moira. This was it. This was the real thing. This was the revolution Zeke had talked about. She pushed through the crowd, looking for Zeke. She heard Mark Rudd and some of the other SDS leaders arguing way at the front of the crowd. She was shoved back and forth; police sirens cut the air.

And then she saw Zeke. The black turtleneck, the leather vest, the corduroy pants with the worn-out knees. His hair longer now and his face shaded by that dark beard he could never shave away. She loved him so much that a sweet taste came into her mouth. She pushed her way over to him, and when he saw her, he frowned and turned away.

He knows I'm nuts. He knows I'm going out of my mind. I got in over my head and I'm going crazy. And then she was angry. He had played with her. Made her love him. She went after him, people pushing on either side, yelling and chanting, "Racist pigs. Racist pigs. Fascist pigs. Fascist pigs."

She tapped him on the back. He turned and now he was impatient. "Hey, baby, how you doing?"

"I'm okay. I hadn't heard from you."

"I've been organizing a march, speaking about this grad student deferment thing. I've been really busy."

"Busy?" She took hold of his shirt. Just the way Daddy had taken hold of her blouse. But she couldn't stop herself. "Don't tell me you're busy. You can't tell me to fuck off. You fucking bastard. How dare you talk to me that way? Nobody talks that way to me, not ever again."

Now he had stopped. Now he was tuning in. "Moira, what is wrong with you? Have you lost your mind?"

And then she was her father, running down that hill with the hedge clippers after Moira and Dennis Wildersen, aiming a twelve-gauge shotgun at Corey on the porch steps. She was Daddy slapping her breast, listening to Mother say that Moira was a little tramp and she'd better stay home. Oh, maybe Mother had been right. She didn't belong here. See what happened? She'd had her heart broken. She felt her mouth open, her eyes shut as she screamed out, "Go away, then. Go away. You little bastard. Leave me alone. Don't you ever come back or I'll kill you. I mean it, I'll kill you."

She went to her knees, sobbing, and the crowd pushed him on. Moira got up and frantically searched, calling for him through the chanting and pushing and shoving crowd that was now trying to get to the gym so they could tear down the fence around it.

And when they were at the gym, Moira had almost caught up to Zeke. Now she wanted to kill him, yes, she was going to kill him. A couple of students climbed the fence, and then some of them were tearing it down, and she had a knife in her hand, no, a pair of scissors, no, the dissecting knife from the lab, and she was stabbing Zeke in the heart with one of the sharp points, and he was screaming for her to stop, he was screaming that he had never loved her, that no one could ever love her, and her Mother was saying she was ugly, and then she was screaming at the top of her lungs, screaming and crying and squeezing her eyes shut, and she knew that now that Daddy was no longer around, she had to do his work for him.

And when she opened her eyes, the crowd was still there. There was no blood on her, no knife in her hand, and Zeke was gone.

She had chased him away. Someone who could really love her. Now that he wasn't around to do it himself, she had done her father's job for him.

Moira never remembered walking home, never knew what happened to her books, her lab kit, her purse. She went straight to bed and fell into a numbing sleep.

Only a ringing telephone could break into her stupor. Every time it rang, Moira would wake up and find the crackled daisy in her fist and she'd pray please God oh please. But the calls were invariably her roommate's mother. After a few days of this, Roberta called the student health service. Roberta and Melvin—a friend of Moira's from the Columbia biology club, a scholarship student from Ohio who had a crush on Moira, the kind of guy she should content herself with—helped her out of bed and walked her over to the service.

Two days in bed with intravenous feedings. Melvin found a friend with an old beat-up car and brought her back to the dorm. Roberta, who had never had a boyfriend, was sympathetic but lacking in wisdom that would apply to the situation. She just moved slowly around the apartment with an uncomprehending but concerned look, offering various tidbits of the goodies her mother sent in her care packages.

Moira felt as if she had the flu and was a hundred years old. She couldn't breathe. She would lie in bed and concentrate on breathing; if she didn't, her lungs would forget to do it for her. The sight of her only two friends—Roberta's 220–pound frame and Melvin's 120–pound frame—was both comforting and depressing.

Roberta and Melvin brought her homework from classes. She sat up now. She felt as if she were wearing one of those lead aprons they put on you at the dentist's office for X-rays.

Roberta turned on the radio to hear the news about the student take-over of the university president's office. Zeke was probably there. Maybe when the strike was over she could make it all up to him. Roberta changed the station, and the words "I Love the Flower Girl" came out. Her pulse speeded up, as if she had been shot with adrenaline.

One evening as she sat on her bed leafing through the copy of Ho Chi Minh's *Prison Diary* that Zeke had given her, her mother called.

"You're still alive?" she said. "I called because I was worried about those riots."

"Don't worry, Mother. I'm not part of that."

"Is something wrong, Moira? You sound tired."

"I've been sick, but I'm okay now."

"Sick with what?"

If only she could tell her. "Oh, just the flu."

"Drink lots of orange juice. Keep warm."

Moira closed her eyes and rubbed them.

"You're probably studying too hard."

"Yes, maybe."

"You can come back home if you want. If you're fed up with that place." There was a pause. Faint electric buzzing sizzled on the phone wire. "Maybe you *should* come home. It's not healthy there."

"I'm okay." And she burst out, "Oh, Mother, I just chased off my boyfriend. I don't know what's wrong with me."

Another long pause. "Moira, why don't you come home for a while."

The student strike closed Columbia, and enough Barnard students were with them that chaos ruled and Moira felt that she could get away almost unnoticed for a few days.

I'm so lonely, Moira whispered, so lonely I can't stand another minute of it. If I had let myself fit in back home, I wouldn't be so alone.

Mother's hair had gone mostly white, and with her grayish skin and pale hazel eyes she was so washed out that she stood out in the crowd at the airport gate like a specter in a row of real people.

Awkwardly, she put her arm around Moira in a halfhearted gesture. It reminded Moira of a little boy being forced to exhibit good manners to an aunt, and doing so reluctantly.

And yet, as they walked out of the airport, Moira noticed that despite the monochromatic coloring, Mother's face didn't look any older. She was like a character in a play you saw aging from scene to scene, her hair exaggeratedly white and her skin powdered to look old, but the face underneath the makeup was still the unlined face of a young woman.

Mother and Taryn's new apartment was in one of those efficient complexes with speed-bumps. Mother took them at exactly three miles per hour. She parked under a carport with her apartment number on it.

When Mother got out of the car, standing and waiting for Moira, Moira felt the rush of a new thought. That Mother was a child. Oh, Mother, she thought, can't you be like the other mothers of the girls I'm in school with now, vain and overdressed and obnoxious and ambitious for their daughters? A mother who wants to show her daughters the ropes in life. Why do you have to oppose me?

But she remembered that her mother *had* been ambitious for her.

After all, she'd wanted her to become a home-ec teacher. And as for
the ropes, her poor Mother didn't know them. Mother had used the
only weapons she'd had in her role—contempt and righteousness
and control and sex and then fear of sex. And now Moira wanted
to take Mother's plump arm and tell her everything was going to be
okay, that the South Dakota wind had once said that to her, and
she still believed it was true, despite the misery she felt.

But later she wondered if it was simply that Mother didn't want
Taryn and Moira to know those ropes, either, because they might
leave. As Moira had indeed done, at least for a while. Mother had
been so vicious with her daughters, Moira now realized, because
she wanted to make them incapable of having other friends. Like
always, she wanted her daughters for herself.

Mother had kept a few pieces of the old furniture—the colonial
buffet, the matching drop-leaf table with the old familiar nicks from
the vacuum cleaner, and Daddy's easy chair and ottoman. On the
bookshelf were four eight-by-tens of Taryn as a sober, deliberating
nine-month-old; as a pixie-coiffed seven-year-old with jagged teeth
growing in; as a twelve-year-old surrounded by her group of girlfriends clapping as she blew out birthday candles; as a member of
the Future Teachers of America club. Back in the corner was a
black-and-white snapshot of Moira in a winter coat and hat.

Moira was to sleep on the cot in Taryn's room. Taryn was still at
school—at a Future Homemakers of America meeting.

Mother looked at the clock to see how long it would be until
Taryn came home. Then she turned to Moira and said, "Well . . ."

And Moira felt a sickening in her stomach, that Mother was no
longer to be feared. Was she to be helped now? How could Moira
help her? How much did Moira owe Mother? Now that Moira had
survived, was she now responsible for Mother?

And as she unpacked, she wanted nothing more than to go back
to New York and pick up her classes. From here, the struggle back
in New York seemed so much more manageable, the struggle here
had always seemed so pointless.

What was she working for? She'd always wanted to escape all
this. And she did. Now did she have to come back here because

she'd left people behind? Was it up to her to help the people who had tried to drag her down because they didn't know any better?

As they sipped coffee and waited for Taryn to come home, Mother absently asked how school was going.

"It's harder than any school I've been in before, of course," Moira said, sitting on the cot and kicking off her shoes. "I'm not getting all A's this semester, that's for sure."

"See, maybe you're not so smart after all, Moira. Maybe this is the best thing that could have happened to you. Finding out now."

Moira looked up at Mother. The ain't-life-shitty look was back in full force. The look that went out in public with a smirk, a glance at a total stranger that asked for sympathy, that asked that total stranger to respond in some way to share her misery and anger.

And then the smile disappeared and now she had a pale imitation of the old expression of superiority and disapproval, the only way she knew how to be a mother. Mrs. Superior Morality. Oh, poor Mother, you can't do it to me anymore.

Taryn was still tiny, almost shrunken, in fact. It looked like Mother was still cutting her hair. She looked like a doll in a striped chemise minidress that emphasized her fashionably boyish figure. Her face was even prettier than ever in its preemie way with the wide, up-turned eyes, a flat nose, and little pursed, cynical mouth. "You're still just as cute as ever," Moira said.

"Oh," Taryn said, giving Mother the old knowing Look that the other person was meant to see, that was meant to be cutting and excluding. Moira would always feel bad about that look, but not as bad as when she realized where the Look really came from—loneliness, feeling apart from the world, and fear of abandonment.

Moira turned away from the Look.

In her tiny-girl voice, Taryn asked about New York City, how people could really live there, then gave Mother the Look again. Mother returned it, her mouth pursed and eyebrows arched. That was somewhat reassuring, that with Taryn, at least, Mother could be her old self, or at least an approximation.

"I actually like New York," Moira said.

The Look again, then Taryn said, "Oh."

Moira tried to sound jovial and said, "It's nothing like anywhere else. It's an abnormal place, and I feel normal there. I feel comfortable there." They all had an uncomfortable laugh together.

As Taryn walked out of the room, Moira noticed that Taryn had Mother's old walk now—hunched shoulders and back, shuffly feet; a don't-notice-me walk. Moira's insides sank. What could she do to help Taryn? Obviously she wasn't very happy in her righteous indignation. And Moira still loved her sister. As much as ever.

Mother turned to Moira, and there was that new, vague look, but something else in the look, too. Was it fear? Admiration? Amazement? Bewilderment? Anger? All of the above?

Mother moistened her parched lips and smiled at Moira.

As she lay in bed that night, she thought of Zeke's long, lean arm, how he'd keep it around her all night when they slept together, how she wouldn't want to fall asleep so as to roll over and disturb it.

She opened her eyes and looked across the room at Taryn, who was sleeping in the fetal position, her short cropped hair glowing in the moonlight. Poor kid. I'll always be around to help if you need it.

But of course, no one wants help from a sister.

And what did Moira want from her sister? Acceptance. Maybe a little love. But she wasn't going to get it. And now Moira knew why. Because it had always been she, Moira, who had been the loved one, and not Taryn.

And what about her parents? Well, she hadn't gotten the love she would have asked for from her parents. What she had gotten was a kind of love.

She rolled over. Maybe that was the best they could do.

And in the middle of the night there was another thought. Maybe, just maybe she had been in on the game of jealousy with them all. Maybe there had been a little thrill in making Daddy jealous.

Daddy thought she was a slut. Was jealous over his little slut. Who acted that way in part to provoke him.

But then again, she was tired of women being held down by such name-calling.

Besides, sex had been her escape from the misery of her childhood, and her parents and then the world called her a slut for it. Well, fuck them all.

She wasn't a slut. And, after all, it had been Daddy and Mother who thought about sex sex sex all the time. If anyone had been a slut, it had been them and a whole fucked-up repressed society.

Anyway, by comparison with all those dirty minds, Zeke seemed so fresh, innocent, wholesome. He who had always joked about her wholesome whitebread background being the real clean one. He, not she, was the wholesome one.

Well, she thought rather happily, rolling over again and punching her pillow, she could go back to Barnard and finish undergraduate school, then, if she still wanted to, apply to medical school.

And try to get Zeke back, too. Why not?

Twenty-eight

*B*LEND IN WITH *the crowd,* Taryn said to herself. *Just blend in and you'll be okay.*

Taryn now got panicky whenever she entered a roomful of strangers by herself. Not just the wet-palms panic that a lot of people have, but a searing pain in her chest, nausea wrapping around her stomach, her knees so weak she feared her legs would bend backwards like a bird's.

Afraid of being noticed, afraid of being ignored.

She was lucky, her husband Brock kept telling her, to have any job at all, but especially this job teaching home economics in this nice, clean suburb of Cincinnati during a time of teacher surplus.

And Taryn knew it was necessary for her to work, to supplement Brock's income, which depended largely on commissions he made as a pharmaceutical company's rep. Not that Brock didn't make enough for the basics, even for some small savings, but Taryn's salary provided the extras, the things that pushed them squarely into the middle class. And that was a nice feeling, being squarely middle class.

"I know I'm lucky," she would say to Brock, for the security and the extras her job gave them. "I'd feel even luckier if I enjoyed my work," she'd continue but then add that she supposed most everyone disliked his or her job.

"Work would have another name if it was any fun," Brock kept reminding her.

The parents' faces showed they were sizing up the home-ec teacher. If you don't keep a hold on yourself, they seemed to say, we'll see through you; we know about you, we know where you came from, we know about your family.

As she was about to speak, the urge hit her to say something funny, the way Mother would, like, *Hi, I'm here to teach your kids how to fly a microwave,* and she shook her head slightly and made herself promise just to be straight. It's okay, Taryn, you look like anyone else, you act like anyone else. You're a respectable person, Taryn, a teacher, a home-economics teacher. You hold down a job, have a nice husband and two perfect children, you live in a super-clean house, you belong to the Unitarian Church and the Meadow Grove Tennis Club and you are food-committee chairperson of the PTA.

She looked up and made a small smile, nothing too big and silly that might make people wonder about her, and began. "Hi, I'm Mrs. Hardison, and I want to tell you what your children will be doing in home economics this year."

And when she was done, she knew she had done well, that no one realized she had grown up in a weird family, knew that she was accepted, that she was a normal average person in town and that there was nothing to be afraid of.

When she first met Brock at a disco, soon after she arrived in Cincinnati on her first teaching job, she had fallen in love with his normalness, his averageness.

A group of teachers had talked her into going to a singles disco one Friday night. She'd been instantly turned off by the lounge singer and her ringing microphone and the way the leisure-suited, mustached men looked her up and down, from her shag haircut to her platform shoes.

And then Brock had pulled up a chair. He was so big, strong-looking. She had felt secure with him immediately. And when they got up to dance, she felt that the feathered hair and low-slung pants were as wrong on him as the clunky shoes and Olive Oyl dress were on her. There was something endearing, almost pathetic about that big muscular body in the slinky shirt that made his torso look too long and the tight polyester pants that made his legs look like they were attached to his hips at the wrong angle. It was as if he were trying to fit into the cool and the new and the modern, when he'd really never be anything but a nice average all-American boy. There was something vulnerable and pathetic about his ridiculous disco getup, and she'd instantly both loved him and pitied him.

She had decided that he was the one for her when he told her he'd been in Vietnam. And he was proud of it.

Daddy would have approved. At the wedding, she had thought constantly of Daddy. He would have admired Brock. And seeing that Brock loved her, maybe Daddy would have loved her, too.

It was almost eleven by the time she got home. Brock was on the couch in front of the TV, three beer cans lined up beside him on the end table. She hung up her coat, called out hello. Brock grunted a reply.

She went up to the bedroom to check on the children, Jason, aged four, and Jennifer, three. She didn't get to see much of them on days like this. Usually she was the one who picked up the children from day care. She'd take them with her to the grocery store and get things for dinner and run any other household errands that had to be done, and then it was dinner and time for a little play, and then bed. She kissed Jason, then Jenny, trying not to feel guilty.

She went down to the kitchen. Brock and the kids had eaten all of the Stouffer's lasagna and the Green Giant frozen pasta salad she'd put out for them to eat while she was at the PTA meeting. She felt a small satisfaction—she had fed them even though she had had to work from eight-fifteen until eleven.

People thought it was funny that the home-ec teacher never made any clothes on her sewing machine at home and rarely cooked dinners. She thought it was funny too. But who wore homemade clothes anymore? And Brock and the kids actually preferred the taste of microwave stuff to home cooking anyway.

Here was the funny thing; she rather enjoyed the creative part of cooking—planning the nutritional content of menus, contrasting textures, flavors, finding complementary colors—when they did it at school. She'd even dabbled in French and Italian and vegetarian cooking as a student at Normal. But people considered you a weirdo if you cooked French, Italian, or vegetarian food in real life, so she pretended she couldn't taste the differences in foods, too, and she bought frozen meals and canned sodas and packaged desserts so that the children could feel that they fit into the neighborhood, that they were like everyone else.

The dishes stood like the Leaning Tower of Pisa on the counter. She went to the hall and called out, "Thanks a lot for the Italian scenery in the kitchen, Brock." She said it in a joking way so he wouldn't get mad.

"Wait'll you see the laundry room," Brock said. "I spilled some beer and used the towels to clean up. They're hanging from the line. You'd better remember to buy paper towels tomorrow."

She got a Diet Coke and sat down at the table. A few minutes later, she called out, "I guess my hint to get some help in the kitchen is not being heard."

The cold Coke felt good. The lights in the home-economics room were so harsh and hot.

When she thought of the room and the parents a tiny panic began to flutter in her, and she pushed it away with the countdown she often went through: she had a nice husband, two lovely children, a good job in a decent school system when some people had to teach in the inner city, a couple of good friends and several other friends. She was doing very well.

Washing the dishes, she thought of the women she knew lucky enough not to have to work, like Paulette Frenner next door.

Brock said Paulette was lazy, that her husband should have kept her working after she had the baby. Taryn didn't say so, but she envied Paulette.

Brock came in for another beer and helped wipe one dish, then went back out to the living room.

She put the dishes away except for the drinking glass that said *Cote d'Azur,* which Moira had sent her from a trip to France. Taryn kept it out on the counter accidentally on purpose so that when people visited they would think that Taryn had been to exotic places or would at least know that Taryn knew people who went to exotic places. Not—though they were both in their thirties now— that Taryn was proud of having Moira for a sister in any other imaginable way. It had really grated on Taryn's nerves the last time she saw her, when Moira came down from Chicago to see her in the hospital after Jenny was born, that Moira had looked rather pretty. Quite stunning, actually. Her face seemed to be lit, she glowed. What caused that? Was Moira actually happy?

But then Mother had always said Moira was not pretty, so it had probably just been the light.

When the dishes were done, Taryn realized she hadn't even eaten dinner. She found the last granola bar left in the box, took a bite of it, and couldn't eat any more. She had this odd thing—she was way underweight at ninety-two pounds and she both wanted and didn't want to lose weight. She tried to eat more but immediately felt guilty when she did and got sick to her stomach. Men, she knew, found her excessively thin, almost frighteningly thin according to Coach Creighton—Mr. Tell-it-like-it-is. But then she'd look at that potbelly of his and say to herself what did he know? But a lot of women admired her and were envious that she shopped for jeans in the boys' section of department stores. She gagged and threw the granola bar into the garbage and went and sat down next to Brock on the living room couch and watched the news. She wondered why Brock was so interested in the news. It never had anything to do with anything. Certainly not their lives.

"Meeting go all right, little lady?" he said, patting her hand.

"Too long."

"Parents all happy?"

"I guess. I guess they're just as happy that it's me who is going to teach their kids to boil an egg as anyone else."

"Hey, don't put yourself down. You do an important job." Her hand disappeared into his big square one as he squeezed it. "For a runt."

Taryn herself was happy she was naturally skinny, but she would have liked to be taller. Brock liked her little-girl body, though sometimes he joked that she should get one of those boob operations so that she'd look older than twelve. Yet she noticed that the times he'd seen Moira, he seemed uncomfortable. She'd told him she was lucky she found a guy who was uncomfortable with big boobs. He'd said big boobs were one thing, but on Moira they were like a pair of boxing gloves she wore under a sweater that would take a swing at you if you stared too hard.

A commercial came on and Taryn felt more relaxed. "I had this one parent tonight who was as clumsy as her daughter. You wouldn't believe it, Brock," Taryn said.

"Oh yeah?"

"Like this." And Taryn got up and imitated the walk. "Like this, oof-oof," and she made the sour kind of face both mother and daughter had. Brock laughed. Taryn sat back down. It was fun, the reaction she got from people when she did things like that, but she had to be careful about doing it too much. With some people she couldn't do it at all, like Nannette MacGovern, the prissy English teacher who gave her looks when she did it in the teachers' lounge.

It was true that some people actually thought she was making fun of the kids when she imitated them. But that wasn't it at all. She just felt this compulsion to get into them, to see what it was like to be them. "It's my way of understanding them, I guess," she said to Brock.

But how else could you cope? You had to find the humor in the tedium of the day or you'd kill yourself. And she stopped, as she always did when she thought of killing herself, and allowed thoughts of Daddy to come to her.

Sometimes she couldn't face the idea that he had really killed himself. There were times when she wondered if Moira had done it. She lay awake sometimes thinking about that. Moira could have easily done it. In all the confusion, maybe Taryn had seen wrong. Maybe Mother had seen wrong or was covering up for Moira. Maybe Moira told Daddy to shoot himself, or pushed him so that the gun went off accidentally.

And thinking these things, Taryn would get so angry her fists would tighten up around her pillow. The only person out there in the yard with her that night had been that boy from the Catholic school. And he would have stood up for her, wouldn't he?

But it wasn't worth pursuing that idea, because when she thought of going to the police and asking if they were really sure it was a suicide (Could you really hold a shotgun up to yourself? Then pull the trigger yourself? Exactly how long was a shotgun?), when she thought of going to the police and asking to see the pictures (she hadn't seen Daddy after he was dead. Couldn't stand to. Had stayed in the house until the police covered him up), she would have to ask if they had considered the possibility of murder. But then she'd realized that she just couldn't open all that up again. That it would be too disturbing for her. Better to just forget the whole thing.

Although even if she didn't convict Moira of pulling the trigger on Daddy, she convicted her of being an accomplice. And she would never forgive her for that, for taking their father away from her. Mother had even said so, told Taryn that Daddy had always preferred Moira, and just when Taryn was getting Daddy to prefer her, Moira killed him with her wild behavior.

She began to imitate Shawn Orsley for Brock, and then Lisa Dettwiler, and Brock downed a beer and laughed so hard he made her feel relieved.

Someone recently had told Taryn that she should have been an actress because she'd been imitating someone in a movie.

"Frustrated actress, are you?" they had said.

It hurt like a red-hot burn from the stove to hear that. What if she really could have done something she enjoyed in life? What if she'd missed her calling in life by going to Normal?

She wondered if the other teachers came home and imitated their students to their husband or wife and kids when no one else was looking. If they were bored out of their minds, irritated by the way teachers were treated these days. Not exactly the revered Protestant ladies Daddy and Mother had had in mind.

But she didn't want the other teachers to think she wasn't just like them, and she told herself she wasn't going to make jokes about people anymore.

"Brock, I've been thinking. Teaching is so hard for me. I don't think I'm naturally good at it."

"Sure you are. Look, hon, everyone we know is a schoolteacher. The women, I mean."

"Yes, but I've been thinking of doing some other kind of work one of these days."

"Yeah?" He took the last drop out of the beer he had, crumpled it in his hand and then went to the kitchen and returned with a fresh beer. He poured some into a small juice glass and gave it to Taryn. "Like what?"

Taryn sometimes felt sorry for Brock. He didn't get a lot out of life. He didn't even get a lot of worry out of life like she did. He just sort of went through his day, no major cosmic problems, no major cosmic thrills. But then, let's face it, when was the last time *she* had had a major cosmic thrill?

"I don't know. Maybe a job downtown. A *job* job. A business-woman job. I don't know, maybe I could go back to school and get a master's degree or something. Or I could go into interior design, I don't know. Or get one of those franchises that sells hosiery, go into business for myself."

"You know you don't have a head for business. Let me worry about how the numbers add up, hon. You just keep bringing me that little paycheck you earn so we can have a decent life for the kids."

"That makes me feel like the packhorse following the leader up the mountain. Or mule. Donkey. Ass."

Brock turned and looked at her as he swallowed his beer. "Taryn, sometimes I just don't get you." She tried not to think about the comment Mother made about Brock, that he had a perpetual expression of trying to figure things out.

"I just don't like my job, Brock. I'd really rather be home than teach. I wouldn't mind being home. I'd like to be with the kids while they're little."

"What are you talking about? Job—hell, it isn't even a job you've got. It's a goddamn paid vacation. Job. Look, teaching is perfect for a woman—you get home when the kids do, summers and Christmas and Easter off. How would you see the kids at all if you were on some out-of-town business trip?"

He had a point there, but then *he* didn't see them when he was on out-of-town business trips.

"Hell, honey, I wish I had your hours. Do you think I like things the way they are? Unfortunately, pharmaceutical salesmen can't work nine to two-forty-five with three months off each year."

"I wouldn't call today such terribly wonderful hours."

"Today was an exception, hon."

Brock was getting puffy eyes as the people on his mother's side did when they aged, and his hair wasn't as thick and shiny as when she first met him that night at that disco, but he still filled up a doorway when he entered a room. Mother made fun of him all the time, but other women told her how lucky she was.

"Those nights I have parent conferences, teacher workshops, the time I spend grading papers and doing lesson plans?"

"Oh, I know, I know. But the time you have to be there, punched in, that's what I mean."

"It's just that I'm—"

"You're what, sweetheart?" He massaged her back ever so gently.

"Tired. Sometimes I wonder if I'm cut out for this. I'm not sure I understand or appreciate kids."

"You don't appreciate Jenny and Jason?"

"Of course I *love* them—they're *my* kids. I adore them. But I don't adore kids in general." It sounded so wrong to say that. So unfeminine.

He stopped massaging and slapped her on the back affectionately. "That's a hell of a way to talk."

"I don't mean it the way it sounds." Or maybe she did.

"Look, Taryn, I work hard too, you know. Do you think I like going in there day after day to sell a new kind of pill to those thick-headed pharmacists? Hell, they're all foreigners nowadays, half of them don't even speak English. I can't even say hello to them, let alone sell them a line of products, and then I go into the head office and get my ass reamed because I didn't make quota." He moved back. His voice was getting loud and gruff. "I'd like to quit working and I'd do something glamorous, too. I think I'll be a rock singer. Or a baseball star."

Brock took a long drink of beer. "I'll be assistant head of the department in a couple of years and then I can stop pushing pills all day long."

"Good. I hope it happens. But, Brock, my job isn't really taking me anyplace."

"Oh yeah? Honey, where do you want it to take you?" Before she could think of an answer, he took her hand and patted it and said, "Hey, hon, don't complain. You've got a nice soft job and the hours are short. Talk about security. Hey, half the world envies you."

She fingered the magazines she found boring and pretentious but which she left out on the table for when a neighbor dropped over— Smithsonian, House Beautiful, and Golf Digest to give the impression that they had upper-middle-class interests and tastes, and Skyliner to show they had gone on a vacation that had required a plane trip (instead of a cheapo car trip or, worse, a camper or trailer)—and got up to get ready for bed. Brock was right, she really shouldn't complain, she should feel very lucky. She'd been doing it for thirteen years now, even through her pregnancies, when the kids were babies. The job got easier every year, especially if she used last year's lesson plans.

It was just that she got so tired, and sometimes she got so bored, but when she thought of really trying to go against Brock, who had insisted on her going back to work right after she had the babies, her stomach got sick.

She had boys in home ec now, as well as girls.

When she'd told Mother that last Christmas, Mother had rolled her eyes. It had almost scared Taryn a little bit, as if she hadn't been able to predict this—Mother, who was supposed to know everything, who knew how Taryn should take care of herself.

"It's because women work nowadays. Men have to help out around the house."

Although she had yet to hear of one who did.

She'd shown Mother how the boys acted when they were doing flower arranging. "Pgggggge-e-ew," she shouted, making a bomb sound. "Like they were blowing the whole thing up once they've finished the arrangement."

Mother didn't appreciate her making fun of things quite so much these days. Of course, Mother had been different ever since Daddy died. That had been a long time now, twenty years, but it could have been yesterday as far as Taryn was concerned.

She still dreamed of Daddy at least once a week. He came to her in her dreams and he looked normal, just like he'd looked when she was a little girl. She'd say, *Daddy, I thought you were dead. I thought your heart was bloody, shot up.* And Daddy would say, *Heavens, no, where did you ever get an idea like that?* And Daddy would put his arm around her and they'd go for a walk in a huge meadow together. *I'm proud of you, Taryn,* he would say, smiling at her with his blue eyes under the soft sunlight.

Taryn thought the only possible good that could have come out of Daddy's death was to show her that she had to try really hard to be normal and to fit into the world, the way he'd wanted his daughters to, and to be a nice, wholesome, clean-cut, all-American girl.

That was probably one of the reasons why she stayed working as a home-ec teacher. That, and the fact that she sort of believed what

Brock said, that the more you hated the job, the more normal you
were.

Actually, she rather liked the young boys as students. They either
horsed around in home ec and took the whole thing as a joke, as an
easy grade, watching the toaster as if it were about to shoot off a
rocket ship, or they took it all so literally, as when hand-stirring a
cake batter, (a method she taught, because what if they were ever
left without a mixer and the stores were closed one night? Or on a
desert island, she always joked) counting to exactly 300 and not
overcounting just to be sure, as the girls did.

The girls were another story entirely. There was nothing funny
about girls. Girls were no joking matter.

What she liked about teaching home ec was this: she could usually find a core group of girls that she could relate to. They were the
middle-of-the-roaders, the average-to-good students, the average-to-
nice-looking ones, always the middle-class girls and not the upper-
upper-middles nor the handful of girls from Queen City Estates, the
trailer park that had been gerrymandered into their school district.

The girls in the middle paid attention in class, and when they
were watching her demonstrations of flower arranging or bathing a
baby, Taryn felt almost as if she were back in high school, her hap-
piest time, going out with Jay, her one true love.

Taryn had never been sure that Daddy really believed that Jay
Schmidt was gay.

And she was never quite sure that Jay didn't know that they all
pretended in the McPherson household that he was gay.

He had always wanted to go to college and study engineering.
Daddy had actually liked that about him. If home-ec teacher was
the perfect job for a girl, electrical engineering—no nonsense, good-
paying, always in demand—was the perfect job for a man.

But then Jay had dropped her. Just like a hot potato. The night
Moira ruined their lives. Well, what difference did it make now? Jay
could have gotten a college deferment, but he'd wanted to join the
Marines. And then he was killed in Vietnam within two months.

Moira had killed Jay, too, in her way, because he would never
have run away and joined the Marines if he had still been dating

Taryn. She would have wanted him to take a college deferment, and if he insisted on joining the Army, to wait until he got out of college. (And by then, the war would have been over.) He wouldn't have done anything dishonorable, like evade the draft, but he'd be alive, and maybe she could have gotten him back eventually.

And now Taryn felt like those little monkeys she saw in her high-school science textbook. Those pitiful monkeys clinging to wire-mesh surrogate mothers in the laboratory. Only Brock was a surrogate father. And now that she had her father back, or at least a wire-mesh version of him, she wanted Jay.

But no, she quickly told herself at such times. She was perfectly happy. She had an enviable life. She was normal.

Yes, there were times when she felt secure and happy and useful and deserving of her paycheck.

The problem kids, the girls around the edge, were enough to send her into the teachers' lounge with a weak stomach. "You look 'bout to lose your lunch," Coach Creighton had said in that Kentucky drawl of his once when he peeked into the room while they were preparing a picnic lunch. "You better stop eatin' what these boys is makin' in here."

Yes, joke about the boys, but the girls must be taken seriously.

One such girl to be taken seriously was Venus Shannon, a big-hipped, long-legged junior.

Venus had started out the semester by confiding to Taryn, just as the class was about to serve a luncheon to the principal, that someone had spit in the eggplant casserole. When Taryn asked who spit, Venus had made a smug little smile and said she'd sworn not to tell who it was.

"Then why did you tell me, Venus?" Taryn said.

"I just wanted to let you know."

Taryn wasn't going to give Venus the satisfaction of forcing the meal to be changed or canceled, so Taryn went ahead and served it. While the principal and his staff dug into the eggplant, Taryn found herself unable to eat, just pushing the eggplant around on her own plate, but then everyone knew that wasn't unusual for Taryn because of her weak stomach. But as she pushed the food around on her plate, she was thinking about the spitting, and she knew exactly who had done it—Venus Shannon herself.

Venus had that spiked kind of hair that was bleached on the ends and black at the roots, and wore black Spandex all the time when she wasn't wearing purple or chartreuse or hot pink. Her boots were black, with spurs, so pointed at the toes that they curled up, and they reminded Taryn of the ones Moira wore a million years ago back in the sixties.

The first time Taryn saw her, she thought she'd been in an accident. But it had just turned out to be purply-pink bruise-colored eyeshadow and blusher and dried-blood-colored lipstick.

Taryn had to admit that Venus might be pretty if she ever washed all the makeup off her face along with that smirk, but since that was as remote a possibility as her wearing normal pants and skirts and sweaters like the respectable girls, Taryn didn't really think about what she would look like without the makeup or the smirk.

In fact, Taryn avoided looking at her, didn't look at her, wouldn't look at her, refused to look at her. The poor thing was just desperate for attention, showing up late all the time, wearing those black Spandex outfits like some sleaze, sullying Taryn's nice clean kitchen, but Taryn wasn't going to let Venus get to her.

Don't let it bother you, Taryn, you're better than that. There are always a few in every class, she told herself as she stood demonstrating how to make granola cookies.

Taryn looked up at the class, holding her head high with the perfect posture they practiced for the fashion show when they modeled the jumpers and aprons they made in class for the assembly. She smiled and said, "Granola is very good for you. It has natural fiber. Fiber keeps your system regular."

Someone made noises in the back of the room that were, Taryn supposed, to sound like someone going to the bathroom. She looked up but couldn't tell who had made the noises.

"Now, we pour out two cups of rolled oats," she went on, showing how to measure exactly by putting the cup on the counter and then bending over to see if it came up to the line.

Those noises again. She ignored them and held the cup up for the class to see.

"Mrs. Hardison," she heard. She knew the voice—Venus, probably about to tell her someone had spit in the granola.

She pretended she didn't hear, and went on, "Now, you pour it into the bowl and . . ."

"Mrs. Hardison," she heard again, and again she ignored it.

"And add one egg."

"Mrs. Hardison," Venus yelled.

She stopped as she was about to crack the egg and looked at Venus, and after she had visually made her point, said in a cheery voice, "Yes, what is it, Venus?"

"I've heard that granola makes you high."

"High?" Taryn said, putting the egg down.

"Yeah, like stoned."

Taryn stared into Venus's eyes, lined in turquoise today, and made her own register polite surprise. "Wherever did you hear that, Venus?"

"I can't exactly remember, but I know I heard it somewheres."

"Well, that's absurd, Venus. It's just not true." She picked up the egg and cracked it against the side of the bowl and put it into a cup the way she'd taught the girls, so you can first see if it's a bad egg or not, then let it fall into the bowl.

The next class, Venus came in with a book. With a big, nasty smile, she opened it up and showed a passage she had underlined that said there was a theory believed by some scientists that granola has some sort of ingredient that causes a mild state of euphoria, and that it could be addictive.

"Well, I guess you're right and I'm wrong," Taryn said, snapping the book shut. "We'll certainly have to set the record straight on that one. Class," she called out in a calm voice, though she was barely controlling her wrath, "class, Venus has something to read to you, to correct an error I made in class last week. Venus, go ahead."

" 'It has been suggested,' " Venus read in a voice that tried to be as bored as usual but which showed a certain excitement, " 'that granola can induce a mildly euphoric state.' " And she read on.

When Venus had finished reading the passage, a group of girls giggled. But they were Venus's followers, more girls in Spandex who wore the look less shockingly and therefore, it was to be assumed, less successfully.

Taryn felt anger rise in her and she felt as if Moira had just walked through the room and someone said, "Is that your sister?"

"You seem to be quite the authority on getting high. Tell me, Venus," Taryn said, "where does all this interest in getting high come from?"

Venus's face froze for a moment. Taryn stared into the eyes that were lined today with green, a green that was an entirely different shade from the green of her eyes. Then her face went back to its old perpetual smirk with the sides of her upper lip drawn up, and she said, "My uncle lived with us and he used to get stoned every night."

Taryn tapped her foot and stared into Venus's eyes, which seemed to be challenging her.

"What a nice uncle you have," Taryn said, immediately regretting it. Rise above these kinds of people, Taryn Hardison.

"Had."

"Had?"

"Yeah, he's dead now."

"Well, you can see what happens." She might as well drive the point home. "I hope you don't follow his example. Or do you?"

"I hope not, too. He had cancer. That's what the dope was for. So he didn't feel like throwin' up all the time. You get that from chemotherapy."

The class went silent and Venus seemed to have gained sympathy, or could it possibly be respect? Taryn snatched the book out of her hand and said, "I'll hold this until after class. From now on, you should be paying attention to this class, not reading."

And afterwards, Taryn hated herself. Why had she let a girl like that bother her, one who deserved pity and needed help more than anyone? Why couldn't she stand it when the spotlight was on the little chit, especially for something like that? Why did these trashy girls get all the attention in life? Were people so stupid as to be unable to see that they didn't deserve it?

Taryn couldn't believe it when she heard that Venus had gotten the lead in the class play, *Oklahoma*. She had been just sure that Ginny

Quinn, who was president of the Future Homemakers of America Club and Taryn's pet, would get it.

But that wasn't her problem, it was the problem of the teacher directing the play. "Congratulations, Venus," she said anyway at the next class. "I hear you're in the class play."

Venus shrugged and went on stirring her roux.

Taryn stole into rehearsal the next week. There was Venus, in her tight little miniskirt and a see-through blouse with a black bra underneath, clomping across the stage in those boots with spurs.

Hugh Ellings, the history teacher, came in and stood next to her and made a low whistle.

"Yes," Taryn forced herself to say, so that it wouldn't be mistaken by anyone that she was jealous, "she certainly is an attractive girl." And Taryn suddenly saw herself the morning of Shorts Day, Moira coming up the steps in her short shorts.

Taryn could hear the teachers: "Why do her parents let her do that?" And for the first time, Taryn wondered, why did Mother and Daddy let Moira do that? And her anger with Moira jumped to her parents for a moment, then to herself for having grown up in a family like hers. Daddy's suicide had almost numbed Taryn to where she didn't think about her childhood, but it intruded into her consciousness every now and then like a big roaring monster waiting around a corner that jumped out at you when you least expected it.

Hugh turned to her with a thoughtful look. "Venus is doing okay, too, for the kind of home troubles she's had."

"You know something is up if they let her dress like that . . ." Taryn began, and she saw Moira coming up the steps and herself standing there listening to the teachers talking about Moira, and Taryn thinking what a bunch of jealous old biddies.

"Yes, she's a lovely girl," Taryn said quickly. "I hadn't heard about her family."

"That mother of hers is something else," Hugh said.

Venus's mother never came to conferences, so Taryn had never met her.

"They live over in Queen City Estates," he said. "Something like half a dozen kids in a goddamn house trailer. Can you believe that?"

*   *   *

That night she told Brock about Venus.

"She looks like this," Taryn said, then made her upper lip smirk like Venus's. "And walks like this," and she got up and walked a stomping kind of walk while wiggling her butt fast at the same time and saying out the corner of her mouth, "Mrs. Hardison, your class sucks."

Venus cut class. A week later, she did it again.

Taryn took her aside. Venus chewed her gum and nodded her head sideways and gave Taryn a look like she knew what was coming.

"Where have you been? You've missed two classes."

"Rehearsing for the play."

"There's no rehearsal during school hours."

"I was looking something up in the school library about it."

"You don't even know where the school library is."

"Neither do you, probably."

Taryn's knuckles and wrist twitched in an urge to slap.

"Honest, I was in the library. Then I was practicing—I had to have some lines memorized and I didn't have time the night before because my mom needed help. She's got a bad back and I have to drive her to the doctor."

"You can drive? You're only a sophomore."

"Yeah, but I'm sixteen, almost seventeen. I flunked a year."

"Look, I won't have you skipping my class, even if you are sixteen and even if you are in the play."

"It's not like my whole life is gonna be different because I don't know how to put a potato in a microwave oven. Or like I can't learn it myself."

Taryn looked into Venus's eyes and saw Moira looking at Mother a long time ago so clearly that she had to close her own for a moment.

"Please don't cut my class again, or I'll have to give you an Unsatisfactory attitude rating."

"You better not," Venus shouted out.

Taryn was taken aback by Venus's strong reaction—girls like that usually didn't care what kind of attitude rating they got. But then

Taryn remembered that if someone got an Unsatisfactory on their report card, they couldn't participate in school activities. That would include participating in the class play.

"I'll do what the rules say I'm supposed to do, Venus."

Taryn thought she heard Venus mutter "Bitch" when she walked by her the next week while they were making tapas.

"Did you say something, Venus?" she said, turning around.

Venus just looked down at the jalapeno peppers she was chopping and didn't look up. Taryn kept going to see what the other table was doing. She heard a chorus of low tittering behind her.

She thought, a little horrified, of how sometimes she'd like to take Moira and just slap that face of hers. Slap her hard, make her cry, make her repent. Taryn's hand would come away from that slap covered with gobs of that makeup—black and green and orange and God knows what else. Slap her hard for ruining their family's life, for killing Daddy.

And for all the talk about Moira, Taryn knew that Moira had been loved while they'd all pretended to hate her. Loved more than Taryn, when they'd all pretended to love her.

She brought her coffee into the teachers' lounge and sat down. Hugh was there, along with Elmer Creighton and Ruthanne Barkerson, the girls' phys-ed teacher.

"Nice suit," Janet Chadwick said. "You always look as if you spent the night at the dry cleaner's."

"Thank you," Taryn said, laughing, smoothing the skirt, then cupping her impeccably neat, short hair. She got her hair cut every four weeks. She couldn't stand it when one little strand was growing out of place, when it was at all uneven, off balance. "You should see the condition of the house I really walk out of, with two kids."

But it was true that she dressed up a little more than the teachers did nowadays, like teachers had when she was a little girl. Nubby wool skirts, soft blouses with ties at the neck, jackets with braid trim. She liked red, navy, gold, crisp colors that gave her a little height and breadth, because she was so small. Size two. People thought she starved herself for it, and it was just a nervous stomach. She probably spent too much on clothes. But she was the home-ec teacher, and people expected her to look neat and stylish, and besides, she wanted to look that way.

"You're one of the last of a breed," said Coach Creighton. "Ladylike, proper, well-bred. Yep, that comes with breedin'. And you can't fake that, breedin'."

"Want to bet?" Taryn said with a little smile, which made Coach laugh. Taryn was relieved once again that she was passing for proper and well-bred, even if it was only Coach who noticed. Did other people? Taryn composed her face so that she wouldn't look jealous or unduly angry and said, "Has Venus been cutting anyone else's class lately?"

The other teachers shook their heads. "I wish she would," Janet Chadwick said. "Awful, isn't she?"

Taryn didn't say anything. She sipped her coffee as the teachers gossiped about students, wondering why she always felt as if the rest of the world were sitting in a big happy circle with a glowing light over it, and she were over here in the dark spot in her red Butte knit suit with the gold trim around the collar, watching, just barely fooling everyone.

Taryn wondered what Moira looked like these days. Taryn didn't talk much about Moira to people. It was too hard to explain what she was doing, that she was married to some filthy-rich man, and lived in Chicago and was a doctor and traveled to places like Africa. People didn't usually believe Taryn anyway when she told them about the kind of life her sister lived, or else they thought she had the story mixed up.

And it was better that people didn't believe Moira, because she was pretty unbelievable. When Moira came to visit that one time, her neighbors had been shocked by long corkscrew curls on a thirty-five-year-old woman and a broad-shouldered, flapping mink coat that reached almost to the cowboy boots she wore with jeans. They'd thought only movie stars wore mink coats. And they weren't even sure they still wore them, that they hadn't gone out with black-and-white movies. That ridiculous noisy little car that made all the neighbors come to their window, a row of people looking out their picture window at Sandalwood Heights as she made off to get something for dinner, coming back with that extravagant meal she bought in the gourmet section just to show off.

Thirty-five years old, living in a crazy place like Chicago, working as a doctor, for godsakes. And that husband, so dark-skinned and sinister-looking. All those oddball ideas that they had about changing society. That was all so childish, so unrealistic, so weird. Oh, it was still so embarrassing to have a sister like Moira.

"I saw that girl you hate so much today at the drugstore, that Venus," her friend Linda said one night as they were cutting up a pizza that had just arrived. They had ordered it for the kids to eat while they watched videos and the adults played cribbage.

Taryn was feeling particularly happy because the Tylenol 3s she had sneaked from Brock's samples for her cramps were just at the point where they made that fuzzy little buzz in the front of your brain and made you realize that the world wasn't so bad after all. In fact it was not only not so bad, it was pretty wonderful.

"Good heavens, Linda."

"Mommy, you don't have to talk so loud," Jenny said.

Taryn tried to keep her voice lower. "My God, Linda, where did you get the idea that I hate the poor child?" And she really didn't. She actually felt sorry for her. It was just that something overcame her when that Venus was around, and she literally wasn't herself anymore, she was this thing that *reacted* to Venus.

"Well, you sure do put on a good act."

"I would like to set the record straight, my dear."

"Mommy, you're shouting."

"I do not hate my students," Taryn whispered. "I have some who are more difficult than others, and I'm only human if I don't completely adore them. As I do you," and she leaned over and kissed her daughter's cheek.

"Sorry," Linda said, handing the pizza slices around to the children. "Anyway, Venus was in the drugstore with some big fat woman. The woman was crazy or drunk, something, and wearing bedroom slippers. I guess it was her mother. It was all kind of sad. And Venus going around in those tight skirts." Linda started to giggle. "When she bent over, you could see her underpants, and the elastic was torn and hanging."

"Which drugstore is this?" Brock said as he ducked the doorway to come into the kitchen. "I just remembered, we're outta tooth-paste." He opened the refrigerator and got two beers.

"You men. All animals," Taryn said, playfully snapping the dishtowel at him, then taking Linda's arm to lead her to the living room. She smiled at Paul, Linda's husband who was always jok-ingly making passes at Taryn. Brock never worrying because he thought Taryn was not only above virtue but didn't much like sex because she was too much of a lady, too feminine.

Taryn liked it that Brock saw her as some sort of superhuman goddess that hardly even knew about evil—or sex—in the world. Taryn liked that role so much that sometimes she had to fake not having an orgasm when they had sex.

"Look at the jeans on that one," someone whispered.

"Poured into them."

"You can practically count the hairs," said Coach.

A group of the teachers had dropped in to watch the play re-hearsal. Taryn watched Venus, who was good, damn good, uninhib-ited and damn good, in her tight jeans strutting across the stage. Mother and Daddy had been right. That's the kind of girl who goes and makes a display of herself. Nice girls like sweet little Ginny Quinn eventually win, though.

Venus cut class again.

Taryn didn't have to open her grade book to check. Venus had three cuts already this term. She could easily give her an Unsatisfac-tory in conduct. She could send a failure warning to her house.

When Venus showed up for class the next time, Taryn said to her in front of everyone, "I'm going to give you a break, Venus. One more cut—one more—and you get an Unsatisfactory."

"I had to go home. There was a problem with my mom."

"Did you stop in the office and get an excuse?"

Venus looked daggers into Taryn's eyes. "I didn't have time."

"I can't accept your excuse, then. One more class, and that's it."

Venus cut the next class. Taryn filled out the sheet that notified her parents that she would receive the Unsatisfactory rating. As she was folding it, Venus came into the home-ec kitchen.

"Are you looking for me?" Taryn said from her desk.

Venus stopped chewing her gum for a moment. "Yeah."

"I was just filling out your Unsatisfactory notice."

Venus stopped chewing altogether, her Day-Glo purple eyes widening. "You can't do that. Then I can't be in the play."

"I warned you, Venus."

"But it means so much to me."

"You could have fooled me."

Venus came stomping over, her purse and book bag swaying and the jacket clutched in her fingers dragging on the floor. Taryn noticed that one sock was appreciably lower than the other. Come to think of it, Venus was always a little off, messy, runs in the hose, rips in the seams, as if the sexpot role wasn't even on purpose, just a byproduct of her slovenliness or lack of awareness. Like she'd always thought of Moira, only in Moira's case it was because she was the mad scientist, like Einstein with his unmatched socks.

She stopped in front of Taryn's desk.

"If it meant so much to you, you would have come to class."

"I couldn't, Mrs. Hardison." She started to cry, loudly, mucus in her voice, hair sticking out; she was almost pathetic in her messy attempts to get attention.

"Get control of yourself, Venus. Maybe you'll learn something from this."

"No," she said. She let her book bag thud to the floor. "No, Mrs. Hardison, I just have to be in that play. It makes me feel like somebody, makes me feel like I'm not a complete zero fuck-up. It's the only break I've had, the break I need."

"Why do you cut my class then?" But Taryn knew the answer. Because Venus didn't like her.

"I feel weird in this class. I feel like you're so squeaky-clean perfect, with your little dresses with jackets, and your shoes with the tassels. You're so pretty and dainty and perfect, and I feel like such a slob in here. I can't do none of that stuff, and I don't care about it."

Taryn watched her cry. The girl rubbed her eyes and the purple stuff on one was smeared all the way out to her hairline.

Well, she had to learn, didn't she? Rules were rules, weren't they? If the child ever needed to learn them, now was the time. And Taryn certainly didn't invent the rules.

"I'm sorry, Venus. Maybe this is a lesson you'll remember for a long time. Maybe you'll remember this when you're tempted to cut class again." And as she said it, a deep, sudden sadness overtook her, because that's what Daddy used to say: *Live by the rules, don't expect any favors in life.* And the image of Daddy came to her, and she slumped into her chair thinking how much she had loved Daddy. And she realized suddenly, with a thud, that *she* had never really been loved.

Venus stopped crying and looked at Taryn with all the hatred of the world. "Yeah, I'll remember it all my life. You goddamn bitch, I'll hate you all my life."

And for a moment Taryn was frightened as the girl's chubby fingers bumped all over with rings fanned out. But then she began slapping her own face, screaming and slapping and crying. Taryn jumped up and went to her and took hold of her hands. Leaning down into her line of vision, Taryn said, "Get a grip on yourself, Venus. Grow up. Do you want to be some kind of a slut, or do you want to be decent?"

And Venus began crying, weeping in a way that seemed to be asking for sympathy. But Taryn was fresh out of sympathy for people who didn't know how to behave, how to follow the rules.

Sally Westburn, who was directing the junior class play, came to her. "I see you gave Venus an Unsatisfactory. Did she really deserve it?"

"Five cuts."

Sally sighed. "She has an alcoholic mother. I heard their mobile home was just repossessed."

Taryn smoothed her skirt. "A lot of people have alcoholic mothers and fathers, and they don't cut five classes when they know what the consequences will be."

"So what do I do now with the class play?"

"Ginny Quinn told me that she tried out for the part. Did she read well?"

"Oh, she was all right, but she didn't have that . . ." Sally smiled. "That *je ne sais quoi* that Venus had."

"You can *je ne sais* that again," Taryn said.

Sally laughed. "Taryn, you should have been a comedian." Taryn must have stiffened, because Sally's expression changed back to official business. "Well, I'll have Ginny read for it again. I'll have to do something. You're sure you won't change your mind? She does have an awful lot of problems, that girl. Sometimes I think all she needs is someone to take an interest in her. A substitute mother. But she does make it so very hard, doesn't she?"

"Sally, I don't make the rules. If the school wants to change them, fine."

"I suppose you're right," Sally said. "Okay, Ginny can read for the part again. I'll have to ask a few of the other girls who read for it to come back, of course, to give them another chance, too."

As Taryn showed Ginny Quinn how to work the zigzag to make a buttonhole—just in case she was ever stranded on a desert island without a machine buttonholer—she said in a low voice, "Ginny, I understand that Mrs. Westburn is asking some girls to come back and read for the female lead in *Oklahoma.*"

Ginny took her foot off the pedal and stared straight ahead, her clear-skinned almost-pretty face alert with interest. "I thought Venus had that part."

"Not anymore. She got into trouble and had to give up the part."

Taryn and Ginny looked into each other's eyes and smiled.

"Look, Ginny, I watched the auditions, and I thought you were terrific. You should have the part. All you have to do is work on your Oklahoma accent. I'll help you with it."

Ginny said, "Well, I'll give it a try, but I don't know if I can ever be the equal of Venus." And they both smiled again.

And that was how Taryn liked it, Venus nothing more than a condescending smile on someone's face.

Taryn mouthed the words to the part as Ginny, up on the auditorium stage, read for the part. Ginny looked out every now and then at Taryn, and Taryn smiled. Elmer Creighton tapped her on the shoulder. "You're somethin' else," he said.

"What do you mean?"

"You know the whole goddamn play by heart."

Taryn felt embarrassed. It was embarrassing sometimes, this way she had of being able to remember song lyrics and dialog in plays.

See, she thought, watching Ginny on opening night, *see, I don't hate my students. Look how good Ginny is. It's not as if I'm someone who doesn't like people for no reason at all.*

Twenty-nine

TARYN WAS CLEANING up the home-ec kitchen when Sally Westburn stopped in, looking upset.

"Did you hear about what Venus did?"

Taryn rubbed a stubborn spot of marinara sauce with the Chore Boy. "No, I didn't. What did Venus do?"

"She tried to commit suicide."

Taryn stopped rubbing for a second, then continued.

"She swallowed a bottle of sleeping pills."

"Is she okay?"

"Apparently she'll pull through."

And now Taryn felt angrier than ever with Venus. She wondered if Sally thought it was somehow Taryn's fault. But Taryn hadn't even done anything—the board of education, after all, set the rules. But it wasn't even the board of ed's fault, it wasn't anyone's fault other than Venus's. Nobody skipped class for her. She did it herself.

Taryn rinsed out the Chore Boy and poured more soap on it and went back to attack the stain.

Brock came home and told her he was being transferred to Pittsburgh. "We'll have to move in April."

"The middle of the school year?"

He took off the light blue suit jacket that was his favorite and that Taryn didn't like because it emphasized his stockiness. He put his arm around her. "People don't turn down transfers any more unless they're planning to turn down promotions, too."

"But my job," she said, then added, not unhappily, "I'll have to quit." And now the thought of having time off was quite appealing.

"You can substitute again."

Taryn sat down. "But I hate subbing. I hate it more than regular teaching."

"You think I like working?" His voice was going loud and gruff and she was supposed to feel intimidated. And she did.

But she said, "Brock, maybe this is my chance to quit working for a while. Stay at home. Do some things with the children that I've always wanted to do."

"Yeah, maybe this is my chance to stay home too. We'll all stay home. The kids'll stay home from school, we'll all sit around in the poorhouse together."

"But, Brock, we're moving because of your career, not mine."

"You seem to think life is one big party, one big happy circus."

She threw down the rag that she was using to clean. "Yes, and I'm always following around the elephant act with a shovel."

"You try working as hard as I do."

"I wouldn't mind working if I were the elephant, too."

"Well, let me see now. You felt like a donkey before, as I recall, and now you're an elephant. Maybe you ought to go into politics," Brock said, getting a beer out of the refrigerator.

"No, I'll tell you what I am. I'm the girl who stands at the bottom while the acrobat is doing his fancy stuff, the girl who stands there with an adoring smile on her face and her arms pointing up in the air at the guy."

Brock flipped the top off a beer and stared at her. Just stared. Then he shook his head and ducked to miss the top of the doorway as he left the kitchen.

I want to be a good person, she said in church that Sunday during the silent prayer. I really want to be good. I love my children, I sort of love my husband. I want to be good. Please, God, make me good. Please, God, help me find some sort of peace.

Then she added, I'm sorry about what happened to Venus. I really am, God. She wanted to go on, But it wasn't my fault, but she didn't. She'd let God figure it out for himself.

The nausea went away for just a moment. But when she closed her eyes and saw Moira, she felt the same guilt and pity she had for Venus. Was God cursing her? The congregation began to read a prayer. Guilt and pity came back when she opened her eyes and looked around the sterile, modern church and felt, fleetingly, that nobody here, including herself, had the vaguest notion of what they were doing there, any more than they had the vaguest notion of why they really ever did anything.

She had never really believed in God. She assumed that everyone else at this church felt the same and just put up the pretense. Out of politeness.

And yet she still prayed sometimes to the God she didn't believe in. That was all she had in her life to *really* talk to, a God she didn't believe in.

Three weeks before they were to move to Pittsburgh, she heard that Venus was back in school. Not only that, she had gotten the lead in the spring production of *My Fair Lady*.

Venus as Liza Doolittle? "The *before* Liza Doolittle, maybe," Taryn said to Linda. "But can you see her as the *after?*"

"Oh, I don't know," Linda said. "I hear she's a pretty good actress."

Taryn fumed all day long.

The next day Venus passed her in the hallway. She didn't give Taryn the usual sullen look. Didn't acknowledge her at all.

In the teachers' lounge, Taryn said to Sally Westburn, "I can't believe you have Venus playing Liza Doolittle."

Sally took a bite of her sandwich and chewed thoughtfully. She swallowed and said in a musical voice, "I honestly don't know what you have against that poor girl, Taryn."

Sally was looking at her like she was crazy. Taryn's body flashed hot, a hundred and ninety degrees, and someone was sticking needles in her all over. Sally Westburn was so hateful that Taryn could shoot her. Right in the heart. But what a thought. Taryn hoped her face wasn't red and embarrassed and guilty at thinking such a thing. Taryn licked her lips and composed her face and went to her class and waited for the ninth graders to come in for sewing.

Her hands shook as she showed a student how to pin on the interfacing for a jacket. She grabbed for scissors, picked up the pinking shears by mistake, used them anyway, enjoying the sight of the teeth marks into the show-offy expensive wool that this girl had bought. Her hands shook so much that she cut way too far into the jacket's armhole.

"You ruined it and that was expensive material," the girl said. "My mother's going to kill me if I have to buy some more."

Taryn hurled the heavy pinking shears across the room. They hit the floor and skated around and twirled and spun before coming to a halt by the door. Every student in the room stopped, watched her.

"Maybe she *should* kill you," Taryn said, then turned to the rest of the class. "Get back to your sewing, goddammit, and leave me alone."

And then she ran out of the room and out of the school. She raced willy-nilly through the parking lot. It was drizzling rain and she was without a coat. She ran around the lot as if it were a maze, confused. Couldn't remember where the car was parked. Her shoes smacking against the rainy parking lot pavement was all that let her know she was still awake and not in a dream. By the time she found her car her hair was dripping in her face.

She climbed inside. Lightning and thunder rolled over the school and rain pounded her car. Taryn laid her head on the steering wheel and sobbed.

She reached one shaking hand into her purse and felt around for the tranquilizers Brock was pushing this week. She took three. That was better.

By the time the rain stopped, she had missed two classes. She went back inside and tried to teach the junior cooking class, but she was so sleepy she talked like a retarded person and put anchovies in a cookie batter and coconut in a Caesar salad. Finally she had to give it up and go home for the day.

She assumed that word had gotten around about her throwing the pinking shears and that everyone at this school thought she was crazy now. Maybe moving to Pittsburgh wasn't such a bad idea.

She wondered what it would have been like if Jay hadn't gone to Vietnam and been killed. Gentle, sweet Jay, whom her parents made fun of. Her parents hadn't loved her, but Jay had.

She shouldn't have married Brock.

But at least she wasn't like Moira, who for God's sake had been running around with all those communists and black people and nuts in New York and Chicago and Indians back in South Dakota.

The thought of Moira always made her angry, then she had to

compare herself to get rid of the anger, to show herself that she wasn't at all like Moira.

And then she got angry at Moira because she couldn't quit comparing herself to Moira. Every damn thing she did in her life was meant to illustrate the words, "Well, at least you wouldn't see Moira doing this."

And then she turned on herself for being such a goddamned bitch. Why did she hate her sister so much? She made herself think of the nice things Moira had done for her, especially when they were very little, like reading her stories about animals, always about animals or stars and never princesses or things she was interested in. But stories, anyway. She'd gotten her that *Little Golden Book of Insects,* which had grossed Taryn out, and bought her that disgusting book about what's inside you, with all the guts and everything, and had looked at Taryn with such sparkling eyes when she'd opened it. And Taryn had made a bored face and put it down. It felt good to be cruel to Moira. Moira set herself up for it. Made a career of it.

Taryn always felt a sweetish taste in her mouth when she thought of cruel things she'd done to Moira. Then the feeling would dissolve and an aftertaste would remain, and then she'd feel pity open up like a huge ocean.

Venus was leaning against the doorway to the home-ec room, her black-outlined eyes narrowed.

"May I help you, Venus?" Taryn said. She had the scissors in her hand, and she automatically began snapping them open and shut, a nervous habit she had, especially when she'd just taken one of those cold tablets for her allergies.

"I'm waitin' for someone."

"Who are you waiting for?"

"None of your business."

"I will not have students talking to me that way."

"I'll talk to you any way I want." The eyes were lazy. Resentful. Sluttish. She could poke the two prongs of the scissors into them and get rid of that look forever.

"No, you won't. You'll show some respect."

"How can I show something I don't got?"

Taryn walked over to Venus and stood inches from her. "Answer me. Why are you loitering here? Don't you know that loitering is against school policy? I could send you to the principal's office."

"I think you're nuts sometimes, Mrs. Hardison."

Taryn grabbed a fistful of Venus's blouse and pushed her. Venus jerked away and made a threatening motion with her hand. With the heel of the hand that held the scissors, Taryn slapped her across the face. Hard.

Venus recoiled, put her hand over her face and said, "You bitch. You goddamn *bitch.*"

Taryn's left arm, the one without the scissors, went back again and she took a full swing and got Venus on the side of the head. It made a hard noise and it felt good. She took the other hand and with the scissors still in it grabbed Venus's hair. She was screaming now as Taryn grabbed a handful of that disgusting hair and began to swipe at it with the scissors. She cut off a clump of that god-damned blond hair, then another, this time getting the fuck-you-on-purpose black roots. They were wrestling, moving toward the home-ec kitchen, and Taryn was powerful, all ninety-two pounds of her, and she was shoving big Venus and got her against the refriger-ator. Venus shoved and they hit the counter and silverware fell to the ground.

"Bitch," Venus yelled, grabbing at her hair where Taryn had cut it.

Taryn pushed her against the sink and Venus's head fell back and Taryn took the scissors to her again.

Venus knocked Taryn and the scissors went flying and Taryn knocked Venus against the faucet and the water shot on. Venus, her hair now wet where it was still long and sticking out where Taryn had cut it, screamed and pushed Taryn against the stove. Taryn slapped Venus and got her on the bare arm. It made a beautiful smack. Then she got her hair again and pounded Venus's head against the cement-brick wall.

Taryn wanted to knock her to the ground, but now Taryn herself was somehow on the floor, Venus standing over her. People were shouting, and then someone had Venus by the shoulders and was pulling her away.

Thirty

IT WAS A surprisingly pretty place, Pittsburgh, Taryn thought, looking around at the dips and hills as she drove over to the board of education office.

She wouldn't need to mention the incident in Cincinnati, of course, and no one there was going to bring it up, the principal had assured her. Why put any kind of blemish on the record of someone just because she'd gotten a rotten apple in one of her classes?

Anyway, she'd start with a clean slate here. No reason to think she'd go berserk like that again.

Besides, had she really gone berserk? Brock hadn't reacted much when she told him about it. Just shrugged and grunted and shifted his weight in his chair and asked when dinner would be ready.

No one at the school had ever once come out and blamed it on Taryn. They'd believed Taryn's story, not Venus's, and it was Venus who'd been expelled from school, permanently this time.

Coach Creighton, who usually had a comment for everything, hadn't had much to say to Taryn about it, though. In fact, after the Venus incident, it was kind of funny but students and teachers had stopped sitting with her at lunch or walking out to the parking lot with her after school.

Or was she just imagining that they were avoiding her? Maybe that was it. Maybe she'd been acting standoffish herself.

Anyway, her immediate problem was to find a job to pay some of the new bills that went with a new house. Since they were moving in the middle of the school year, there would be no chance of finding a full-time job, and as Brock wanted, she'd have to apply to substitute-teach.

She dreaded it—walking into someone else's classroom with the best of intentions to teach something. By second period, though, your only goal was to keep the classes quiet enough that you'd still get paid for the day and not get crossed off the substitute list. The thought of work, of facing a roomful of adolescents, gave her stomach a sick feeling, but she reminded herself that it was only six hours a day and with three months off in summer. Two weeks at Christmas, two weeks at Easter, other holidays and planning days. You had to look at it that way.

She wondered if other teachers secretly hated kids—except her own, of course—the way she did, if they were putting on an act, like people at church pretending they believed in God.

The man at the board of education said they were desperate for subs and she'd probably be called to work almost every day. She tried to look and act enthusiastic as she filled out the forms and chatted with him. She was barely able to get up the energy to walk out.

Sometimes she thought of doing what Daddy did. It would be so easy with what was in Brock's sample cases. But then she usually forgot about the idea after a while.

As she drove home, she became angry recalling her days of substituting when they first moved to Cincinnati before the children were born. Babysitting was what you were doing. Babysitting for thirty kids, and not getting paid as much as if thirty mothers paid you to babysit for their brats.

She felt a hypoglycemic attack and her hands began to shake. An idea came to her. She could say no on some days when they called. Tell Brock no one called. Pretend to be sick. Spend the day at home looking out at the trees in the backyard and maybe even reading a book. Take the kids out of day care and actually play with them. Or do something important to her. Paint, read a book. Try out for a play. Lie in the sun. Dream up a way to make her life *mean* something.

Jesus, she could do something really crazy like work for a theater. Be the damn cleaning lady but at least work around something she appreciated. Type newsletters for an orchestra. Be secretary to a director. A producer.

She should be in New York City, that's where she belonged. But then, that would be something Moira would do.

Oh Jesus God, I don't know what's right and wrong, what's me and what's someone else anymore.

She could see Brock's face, her mother's, Daddy's, if she dared to utter something like *Let's move to New York*. The thought almost made her laugh.

She imagined a scenario: she walking into her living room and announcing, "Okay, we're moving to New York."

She said it out loud: "We're moving to New York City. Brock, you can find another job. Oh, you don't want to move? You don't want to have to find another job you don't like as well? I'm sorry, but it's necessary for me to move to New York and follow my career for a change. You can get a job teaching accounting. They can always use a good accounting teacher at a lot of schools. Or substitute. The second half of our lives is going to be dedicated to my career. In the second half of our life together, you're going to be second banana."

She laughed out loud. Crazy. Was there a pill in Brock's sample case that you could take for crazy laughter? Brock probably had one. Women weren't supposed to laugh, they were supposed to be the stone-sober second bananas in life.

The feeling of power that idea brought soon dissolved, and she was back down into her nervous stomach feeling. Her wrists were so thin, so fragile-looking on the steering wheel. What the hell was wrong with her, anyway? Why was she so depressed? There was no reason for it. She had a life that ninety-nine percent of the world envied.

She passed another shopping center and thought of what her income was for—to help buy things to make their house nicer. A new bedroom set for Jennifer, new stainless to replace their mismatched everyday. They could get the sofa recovered, buy new speakers for the stereo.

She turned the car into the shopping mall. She would make herself want to work. She parked and went into Gimbels. The air-conditioning smell was like anesthetic. She went up the escalator to the home section and strolled around. She looked at guest towels, placemats, napkin rings. Almost-useless things, most of which weren't even pretty. They were just something to spend your money on. She stopped and looked at the different placemats with their nondescript patterns and tried to make herself want a new set.

Here were some dresser scarves, some candlesticks, candy dishes, picture frames, salt-and-pepper shakers of every imaginable description. We may never cure cancer, but by God we'll have invented every kind of salt-and-pepper shaker possible.

Now why on earth did she feel this way? She was supposed to want all this crap. Wasn't that the way it was supposed to be? Make yourself want this stuff, Taryn, or you'll be an oddball.

But she felt like an oddball anyway. She was a child now, listening to her parents' fights. She had a sister with a bad reputation. Her Mother was going around the grocery store making wisecracks and reciting poetry and people were looking at her as if she were strange. But, Mother wasn't strange. It was only Taryn's imagination.

Why did Daddy kill himself?

Because Moira was driving him nuts, right?

"Right, Taryn," she said sarcastically, out loud. And otherwise he was a perfectly normal person. She backed up against a wall in the department store and steadied herself because she felt faint. Otherwise Daddy was a perfectly normal person. Who was she kidding?

"Stop that," she said out loud again. A middle-aged woman who was sorting through tablecloths turned and looked at her.

She moved to another aisle. She saw some red-and-green floral mats with contrasting napkins. She tried to make herself want them. She pictured them in her new house. She closed her eyes and thought about the new placemats and napkins in her house, thought about the two-minute thrill it would give her to buy and own them. And through her incredible imagination, she succeeded in summoning up that two-minute thrill.

And then it went away and she felt the hangover of that high. When she opened her eyes, she felt nauseated and dizzy. She was out of Tylenol 3s. She was going to quit them anyway, except for cramps and when the headaches got really, really bad. Because the Tylenol 3s were killing her stomach. She took out the little bottle of Pepto-Bismol and with shaking hands poured some into the plastic cap and swallowed it. Oh thank you, God, for the chalky taste of Pepto-Bismol. The only other thing she allowed herself these days was cough syrup for her sinuses. She had to take it every night now, and sometimes she felt groggy the next day, but by afternoon she was okay and by evening she needed the cough syrup again.

Or, occasionally, Dramamine. Very occasionally Contac or Sudafed. But only very occasionally, no more than a few times a week. And okay, on days when work was particularly unappealing.

But this dizziness was getting bad. She hadn't eaten since—since when? She went to the furniture section and sat down on a chair. A salesman came over, put his foot up on the ottoman, and asked if he could help.

"No," she said, and she must have said it too loudly because he looked at her like she'd shouted or screamed. She grabbed her purse and got up and stumbled out of the home furnishings section and went down the escalator and passed cosmetics. She didn't look in mirrors anymore. Her face was too drawn and old-looking. She hurried to the parking lot and found the Chevrolet.

She drove out into the traffic and thought about subbing.

And then it hit her again, the thought that she didn't like to think because it was more depressing than anything. She wanted to be an artist, a dancer, an actress, even a painter, and nobody would let her. Nobody would let her, and she herself wouldn't let her. Tears stung her eyes like acid. She felt like a little girl. A helpless little girl. "Nobody will let me . . ."

But the real truth was this: it shouldn't matter to her if nobody would let her. She should figure out a way to do what she wanted to do. There was probably a way, and she was too much of a coward to find it. *That* was the most depressing thought on earth.

Despite the Pepto-Bismol, her stomach still felt nauseated and she cried out, "I don't want this. I don't *want* this."

She saw a grove of trees off the highway and inched over toward the right lane and drove into the little park. She pulled to the side of the road and put her hands to her face and cried. She wanted to be a little girl again. She wanted to think things that were stupid and ridiculous, the kind of things people didn't do in real life, like being an actress or a dancer or a painter. She cried loud and the sobbing felt good, as if it were massaging her stomach. People drove by and stared. A man stopped and rolled down his window and asked if she needed help. She shook her head and said she was okay.

What if she didn't take this awful job? What if she stayed home? What if she had another child and actually raised it herself, painted, took a dance class?

But that was for rich women.

What would it be like? What if she told Brock she wasn't going to work? That she was going to . . . to what?

What if she walked out of the house and got a cab to the airport and bought a plane ticket to New York?

What if she disappeared?

What kind of woman left her children? Her husband?

She thought of Venus. Living way beyond the rules of respectability. She thought of the overachievers, the popular kids, the oddballs. Better to be normal. Better not to stand out and have people think you were crazy. Taryn wasn't crazy. No, she was under control.

Under control. She dabbed at her tears and turned the key and waited for the engine to come back to reality with her. Then she slowly pulled out of the park and inched her way back into the stream of traffic.

Part
IV

Thirty-one

"ELEANOR LOUISE BERGSTREN."

It was her turn to read. Eleanor took her deep relaxing breath to keep her hand from shaking as she lifted the script. Without her bifocals she couldn't read it, so she held the script way out and began to read. " 'Why, Clyde, what are you doing here in the middle of my life? I mean, in the middle of my living room?' "

"Wait, wait, stop," the director said. "Read that last sentence again."

She read again and he told her to wait while he conferred with someone about something. She was nervous, of course, but part of her was also amazingly calm. Maybe because she had nothing to lose. Not even her pride or hope, because she'd never really had much of either. Does a poor person fear being robbed the way a rich person does?

She'd lost what pride she had when Aloysius did what he did.

As for hope, okay, she did have to admit that she had a little bit of hope in her life these days. She'd developed hope afterwards. Oh, not very much—just a bit. But she did have to admit that her first emotion at the sound of the gunshot had been relief, and relief had revealed itself as hope in disguise. Hope like a pinpoint of light in her black life.

The director down there was looking her over, appraising her. Wondering if a fifty-two-year-old woman who'd never acted before in her life was going to be the one he needed for this part.

Correction. A fifty-two-year-old woman who'd been acting all her life but who had never had a part in a play onstage before.

Boy oh boy, had Shakespeare been right when he said all the world's a stage. At least where Eleanor Bergstren McPherson was concerned. And she smiled at how funny she was. Always had been, except for those few years after what happened happened.

"Great," the director shouted. "I like that ironic look. Read again with that smile."

She kept that smile and began to read her lines. " 'Why, Clyde, I never thought I'd see you again.' "

The director crossed his arms. "Repeat that please, Eleanor, emphasizing the *never* and the *you*."

She read it again with the emphasis he wanted.

"Good. Continue."

Eleanor saw herself as this character—"an attractive, middle-aged woman of wit," "an upper-crust Boston woman." Well, she'd watched Katharine Hepburn enough on the screen and in the old movies on TV to know about what was upper crust, hadn't she? And she'd always been witty. And as for the attractive part, with enough makeup . . .

" 'But, Clyde, you've changed . . .' " Eleanor went on, her hands raised, her fingers arched just so.

By the time she was done, she was in command of the stage, the world. She almost didn't care if she got in the play; she had read well and she knew it.

Oh, but she did care. She fussed around the apartment that evening to keep from thinking about what she had dared to do—actually go out and audition for a play. She'd had the decorator do it all in peach. She had changed so very much from those old days where plainness was her only virtue. The days when Jergens Lotion was her fragrance.

The old days. Aloysius. Not a day went by when she didn't think of him. And when she did think of Wish, she felt like a blackboard someone was running their fingernails across.

The phone rang and the scratchy feeling disappeared when she heard that it was the director of the Sioux Falls Thespians.

"You got the part, Mrs. Bergstren." He laughed. "You were a convincing Boston snob, and your reading was just quirky enough. Exactly the right amount of irony. Now, are you prepared for a rather rigorous rehearsal schedule? We start Tuesday."

We start Tuesday. On Tuesday, after half a century, she was going to do something that she actually wanted to do. And that maybe she was good at.

She floated around the apartment.

Tea. She needed a cup of tea. She got her bifocals and went to the cupboard and fumbled with the glasses, she was so excited, and pushed things around in the cupboard without seeing what they were. Calm down, Eleanor. Now what kind of oriental herbal teas did she have in the box that Moira sent from, where was it, India, or from somewhere last Christmas? She bent her head back and held the tea packets out to look, and then she chose one and she didn't even know what it was she was so excited. Oh, they were all good. Moira was always introducing her to new things, and some of them Eleanor even liked.

Got the part. Her teakettle whistled its enthusiasm. She poured, spilling some water, her hand was shaking so much. It was only a little production by the Sioux Falls Thespians, but then it was something, wasn't it?

She sipped her tea. Peppermint? Wintergreen? She smiled at the darkening room, not bothering to turn on a light, just looking out the window of her third-floor apartment as the sun set over the low roofs of the apartment complex. *Got the part.* Weights had been unlocked from her wrists. From her ankles. Someone had just unlocked her face so that she could smile.

Who knew, maybe she'd be able to cry, too. There was a scene in the play where she was supposed to cry. She had cried for the director, that nice director. And she had almost lost control, because she was really crying when she cried. Crying for sadness, for nervousness, for happiness.

The room was getting darker. Calm fell gently over her shoulders like a beautiful warm shawl. It felt wonderful to sit here in the darkening room with her cup of tea and to think that she had gotten a part in life.

She felt like putting a new message on the machine. In her little-girl stage voice that she'd learned in acting class about talking from the back of your throat she left a message and then went down the street to McDonalds for dinner. By the time she got home she had recovered from the shock of being wanted for something like this and was ready to do cartwheels (she was so young for her age she almost didn't doubt that she could do one if there were room in this tiny box of an apartment).

The phone rang. "Hello?" she said in her new voice, her little-girl-sounding stage voice.

It was Taryn. The lift she felt about the play was suddenly reversed; now she was sinking.

"Hi, it's me."

Eleanor could just see the expression on Taryn's face. That smile where her mouth stretched up at one corner as if it were held by a rubber band that was about to snap it back into a resigned, pissed-off look.

"Hi," she said again in her lower, modulated stage voice.

"I was just wonderin'—"

Taryn dropped her *ings*. Eleanor should say something about that now that she herself was more aware as a result of all those speech classes. But she didn't want to be that kind of mother, too critical.

"—about Christmas. I wondered if we should come a couple days early. Brock has off on Friday. And I can tell 'em I don't wanna sub those days."

Eleanor winced. Either Taryn had become more low class in her speech, or she herself had become more careful. Well, she had had those acting classes at Augustana College. Eleanor was a college graduate now. Maybe Taryn had always talked this way and she had never noticed. Maybe she had talked that way.

She cleared her throat, and practiced her upper-class Boston accent. "Early, Taryn? What for?"

Taryn replied, "To help you with the shoppin'. Or to fix part of the dinner early."

Oh God, no, don't come two days early with those kids and that clod of a husband. With your nervous moroseness making even the suede on the arms of my new French provincial chair stand on end.

"Honey, I won't be back from Acapulco until the afternoon of Christmas Eve." And now Taryn would ask if they could come and stay in the apartment without her. And have those undisciplined kids tear the place apart and that overgrown hulk leave beer cans under the bed like he did last time. "And, Taryn, honey, I'm lending the apartment to a friend while I'm gone," she lied. "I just can't say no to her now—she's going through a messy divorce and needs a place to stay."

"Oh." Taryn's voice had that defeated, resigned tone complete with a vague whine.

"So tell me what's new," Eleanor said, now that she had control of the conversation.

Taryn went into a long story about the children's school and extracurricular activities. Then the song-and-dance about how much she hated her job as a substitute teacher.

"Taryn dear, I happen to know a lot of substitute teachers who enjoy their work very much. Who are grateful that they can say no on a day when they don't feel like going in to work."

"I don't feel like going in any day."

"If you don't like the job, Taryn, for God's sake, why don't you quit it?"

Taryn paused, and said, "I guess we can't afford it."

Here we go again, Eleanor thought. She didn't know what was wrong with that girl. What did she mean, *girl?* Thirty-one, thirty-whatever-she-was years old—Eleanor couldn't stand to add up the years—was not a girl.

"Well, what's wrong with that husband of yours?" Eleanor said. "Why can't he support you?"

"That doesn't work these days. Women have to work just to keep up."

"To keep up with what?"

"I don't know."

"You ought to know what you're working to keep up with."

"With everyone else, I guess. I don't know."

"Well, don't keep up with everyone else, Taryn. Be your own person, for God's sake."

"Yeah." Silence. That girl and her silences. Trying to make Eleanor feel guilty about something.

"What are you doing these days, Mother?"

Eleanor brightened. "Ooo, you'd never guess. I got a part in a play."

Now there was a real silence. What was wrong with Taryn? Wasn't she happy for her mother? Jealous, maybe. Was it possible for a daughter to be jealous of her own mother? That was kind of sick, wasn't it?

"You mean on the stage, that kind of play?"

"That's the kind."

"Mother, what on earth are you doing?"

Didn't even ask which play.

"I'm acting. Using a talent I'd buried all my life. What do you want me to do? Sit around knitting and baking pies? I don't even know how to bake a pie." And then Eleanor immediately felt guilty, or as guilty as Eleanor was capable of feeling regarding this wimpy daughter, because it had, after all, been Eleanor's plan that Taryn learn how to bake pies and knit because in the old days, the bad old days, Eleanor had actually believed that dancers and actresses were show-offs that deserved no attention whatsoever. But Moira going off and doing whatever the hell she wanted to do had affected Eleanor in a surprising way. She had seen that maybe you could do what you want. That you didn't have to fit the old Middle America image of housewife in clunky shoes and sensible haircut. And you didn't have to fit the new female image—getting some shit job to supplement your big cheese husband's job, then race home to cook his meals and take care of his kids.

Well, Taryn was going to have to just figure it all out for herself, if the girl was capable of figuring out anything for herself.

"You haven't heard the half of it, Taryn. I took a scriptwriting class and wrote a situation-comedy treatment and episode that the prof loved. He said I have writing talent, too."

It all came out so fast. She hadn't meant to tell anyone. But somehow it was safe to tell Taryn. Taryn was so . . . so innocuous she couldn't even jinx anything.

"This is so strange to hear, Mother."

"I went back and got my degree in drama, didn't I?"

"But you were going to teach."

"I don't *have* to work."

"I wish I didn't."

Here we go again. The whine and dance. "Well, it happens that I married someone who left me some money." And immediately she wished she hadn't said that. Sometimes she went too far. Sometimes there was something cruel about Eleanor Louise Bergstren (she had dropped the McPherson and gone back to her maiden name for professional purposes). Eleanor had a cruel streak, she knew that, as thick and slick and fast as a racetrack. Cruelty is the best medicine, along with laughter. A new Reader's Digest feature?

She'd make up for it by saying something catty about Moira, whom they referred to as their family doctor. "I don't suppose you heard anything from Dr. Kildare. Or is it Dr. Zorba?" She and Taryn still liked to make fun of Moira's wild hair that completed the picture of the mad doctor.

Taryn made a low laugh. "No."

"Me either."

They let the full impact of the nuances in their tones take effect.

"I don't supposed she'll be coming for Christmas." Taryn's voice was singsongy.

Neither of them ever referred directly to the fact that Moira had a Jewish husband. It wasn't so much that they disapproved as they just didn't get it.

"Though she said they still celebrate Christmas," Eleanor added in all fairness.

"No, I think she said *she* celebrates it. I don't know about him," Taryn said.

"That must be a lot of fun, sitting around on Christmas morning with a party of one."

They made some remarks about Moira's self-centered, childless life in the big city, and laughed together again. Eleanor didn't want to ruin their fun by letting Taryn know that Moira had written a letter saying she was thinking about having a baby—anyway, the thought revolted Eleanor, who couldn't stand Taryn's kids and would probably dislike any kids Moira had. She said she'd talk to Taryn tomorrow night when Taryn called as usual because her life was so goddamn dull she had nothing else to do, and said goodbye.

Eleanor needed another cup of that herb tea. And now there was that pinprick of hope again. Why, oh why, hadn't Eleanor known before all that she knew now? Why had she tried so hard to fit in in places where she had no business fitting in? Why had she wanted to be average when she had the special quality, a certain kind of craziness that a horrible childhood gives one? Look at Taryn. Look at what Eleanor had seen happen to poor Taryn. Trying so hard to gain this respectability that was never theirs to have. Not this family's. Too much history.

Taryn did live a rather dull life. So dull that sometimes it seemed that Taryn was on the verge of a nervous breakdown.

Well, that wasn't Eleanor's fault, was it? When she brought it on herself, marrying that pill-pushing lunk who guzzled beer night and day. Having those kids. Those pukey spoiled-brat kids of hers. God, Eleanor hated those kids. She really did.

Eleanor put on her mint cucumber facial masque and sat down in her new loveseat to relax. Oh, Taryn wasn't so bad. Thank God she still had Taryn when the thought of Moira came around. Moira had been a nightmare of a daughter. Just like Wish had been a nightmare of a husband.

She'd been practically comatose for a few years after Wish died. But then one day she got up and it didn't feel so oppressive around here anymore. After all, Jesus Christ, were you supposed to let yourself die? Kill yourself too? Climb on the funeral pyre? What was this, India?

She'd recovered from Wish. Spent two years as a zombie, those two months in the hospital, then that counselor. Thank God for that out-patient counseling. It was the best thing that had ever happened to her. Got her to get out and do what she'd been meant to do all her life. She'd marched over to Augustana College and enrolled in the theater program.

Of course, for a few years after *it* happened, Eleanor had been absolutely unable to believe the atrocious thing he'd done.

Why had he killed himself? Why?

Eleanor knew why. She knew why. Because he wanted to fuck his own daughter, that was why. He wanted to fuck his own daughter.

That thought sank in hard. But not as hard as maybe it should have. Theirs was a marriage that was never meant to be, anyway.

And he had been a moral enough man to know that it was very, very wrong. The only way of stopping himself had been with that gun. Maybe that was what had saved Moira.

But enough of this analysis. Goddammit, what an awful thing. Oh my God, but it had been unbelievable. Just simply unbelievable. Often she woke up dreaming of the blood. A couple of times she'd awakened screaming, "Oh my God, the blood everywhere."

Gil, now that he'd been able to come to her house, now that they didn't have to sneak around in the library stacks or wait until the library was closed to go into the office and do it on the couch, Gil told her she talked in her sleep about it. Screaming about blood on her yellow café curtains. Making motions of washing the blood out. Rubbing the sheets and pillows as if she were washing out the blood.

She didn't really love Gil. Never really had. She'd just always been impressed with his knowledge of books. She remembered Aloysius's jealousy of Gil. How he began hanging around in the library when Eleanor went. Finally Gil telling him he didn't allow loitering in the library. How Wish had grabbed Gil by the collar and said he was a taxpayer and he didn't like seeing him loitering on the job *he* was paying the salary for. How she'd had to laugh, in spite of herself. One point for Aloysius, one demerit for Gil.

She only saw Gil every now and then. No, she'd never really loved him. Hadn't really ever loved that skinny schoolteacher of Moira's either. Not really. It had just been sex.

Had she ever loved anyone?

She didn't want to answer that question.

The memory of Ralph Smealz came to her. How he had dumped her like a hot potato after seeing the article in the newspaper about Aloysius. That had hurt, Ralph dropping her like that. What an attractive man he'd been! He'd had those aristocratic cheekbones. That patrician aloofness, that way of looking superior and disapproving that was so attractive. Sometimes she wondered if she could have fallen in love with him. He was such a bastard. And she'd always been a sucker for that type.

Had she loved Aloysius?

She felt like the blackboard again. Yes, of course she had loved him at first. The crazy way his hair popped up all over his head in curls. Shiny black wild hair and shiny black curly eyelashes. He'd been so good-looking it had almost embarrassed her.

But had she loved him later? Were you even supposed to love someone after all that? The fights, the hatreds, the silences, the no-sex as soon as Moira turned thirteen and he got confused about who was who, his wife, his daughter, and then of course all the drinking, the problems with Moira, all that.

Well, did Aloysius love her though through all that? Poor Wish. Eleanor put her face in her hands. Oh Jesus God, there had been blood everywhere. You wouldn't know there'd be so much.

Splashed all over her yellow café curtains. Dumb little silly yellow café curtains with white pompoms she'd made—when was it? Nineteen sixty-something. Hot blood that dries dark, forming little spots that look like eyes looking at you.

The lawn had been soaked in his blood. His sample trunk had been soaked. Yes, there was something pitiful about that sample trunk soaked in blood.

Poor Wish, he'd worked hard. She put her face in her hands and this time felt something wet. Could it be tears for Wish? Yes, he had worked so damned hard, and where had it gotten him?

Blood all over the boxing gloves he'd used to teach Taryn's boyfriend how to box, the boy he thought was homosexual. Fat, orange boxing gloves stained with blood. Not an opponent's but his own. Big boxing gloves that would never come to life again with Wish's—what was it, left uppercut?

And God, those hockey skates—Wish loved hockey skates, actually liked trying to sell them to people, wanted them to get the same thrill he'd once gotten out of them—hockey skates soaked through with blood. Basketballs, baseballs, a box of arrows, the trunk itself.

Yes, where had that traveling salesman job with his sample trunk gotten him?

Well, it wasn't the job's fault. Not entirely. It wasn't even the booze. That had just been the tool. That and the gun.

The police had asked if she wanted the gun back. What were they, some kind of insane ghouls?

Yes, the whole goddamn sample trunk itself was ruined. Eleanor had had the crazy idea to bury the trunk with Wish, but that would seem too strange. And yet she hadn't been able to have those cleanup men take away the sample trunk.

Eleanor still had that sample trunk down in the basement storage area. And this was what sometimes made her think that there was a shred of decency in her. She went down to the basement every now and then to see the sample trunk. She couldn't see Wish, but she could still see his blood. She had that left of Wish—his blood on his sample trunk. She would lie awake at night and it was almost as if Wish were buried inside that trunk down in the basement.

Taryn loved the memory of him, still tried to please him, in a way. Moira had had sympathy, probably loved him. Poor dear Wish McPherson. His wife hadn't loved him. But the crazy thing was, she loved him now. Or was that love? Was it just pity and guilt?

Well, if it was only pity and guilt, it would still be an improvement.

Once Eleanor visited Moira and that husband she probably married just for his money—she knew Moira. And when she saw what she'd been missing out on in life, she actually went out and bought a living room set—French provincial chairs and tables and the whole bit. Got herself some paintings and sculptures, too, at that auction they held on Sundays at the Holiday Inn, and a chandelier at Sears, to replace that thing in her apartment that looked like the lamps the police use in detective movies to interrogate suspects. Moira didn't need to think she knew what was "correct" in decorating any more than her Mother did.

Chicago and that house in France to live in during the summer. A doctor. How embarrassing, really, to have a daughter who's a real honest-to-God doctor. People didn't believe her when she first told them. Didn't understand. Then they'd say, "Oh, you mean like a college teacher. A Ph.D. in elementary education or nutritional sciences, that sort of thing?" And Eleanor had to say no, a real doctor who spends five seconds making you say "Ahh," sticks a needle in your arm, and then sends you a bill for a hundred dollars. That kind.

She'd tried everything after Aloysius did the unspeakable thing that he did. She had even tried going to church regularly.

Every Sunday. Tried to pay attention to sermons about living God's word each day. But everything she heard in church sounded like a bumper sticker.

Oh to hell with it, anyway. Just show up and sit there and maybe something will happen. You'll become normal and your husband won't have shot his heart out on your front lawn and your eldest daughter won't have been the town whore and your youngest daughter won't be a washed-out wimp with a clod of a husband that she hates.

Of course, everyone at church knew the truth, but they were Christians so they were not supposed to hold something like that against you.

She even joined the Wednesday afternoon women's circle. After all, that was what Ann Landers always said to do when you're feeling blue. Quit thinking about yourself all the time and go out and do something for someone else. Get involved, toots!

First they were to make ashtrays to sell at the spring bazaar. "I'm going to make ashtrays to sell at the spring brassiere," she had joked to Taryn on her way out to the meeting. Taryn had laughed. Now she'd felt like herself again. Good old Eleanor. The family clown. Laughter is the best medicine. That page in the Reader's Digest would sometimes be the page hugging Wish's beer when he was half-trying to hide it. Oh, Aloysius, you poor crazy soul you.

Yes. Simple enough. Eleanor would become a part of the community. She would break away from that miserable depression tapping on her shoulder that whispered *Come with me. Come let me take you over.*

But when she walked into that room in the church basement and saw the card tables with their piles of buttons, sequins, tiles . . . smelled the glue, heard the relaxed voices of women who didn't question for one second whether they belonged, Eleanor had had the impulse to put her coat back on and run out the door.

But she'd smiled as best she could and sat down at one of the card tables. Seven well-meaning Christian faces smiled at her. The leader showed her a pattern of how to put the ashtrays together. It could have been a diagram of how to build a nuclear bomb, for all Eleanor could follow it, but no one was going to find that out.

"Oh, I think I can handle that," she sang out.

Simple enough—squeeze glue onto the tile, glue the tile onto the metal base. But she hated doing this. It was so damn boring. So awfully, terribly boring. She'd rather be at home reading. She hurried, trying to do it quickly and get it over with so she could just sit and drink coffee, but then she got her tiles put on unevenly. She did an entire row and the tiles were all wrong. And now they were stuck so she couldn't get any off without really messing up the others. But who cared? Oh, she hated this.

As a child, her brain had constantly been busy, busy running here and there to sew up tears in the fabric of her life, constantly working to keep up with the tears and rips and pulling-apart of the seams. Like trying to keep repairing a sail on a ship out in a hurricane at night.

That had been her life. She'd always wondered if that was normal.

And then she'd recovered her sense of humor to deal with life. Wish's cute little number out on the front porch had made her temporarily lose her sense of humor. And that sense of humor had been her essence.

She thought of her comfy bed back home. Of her *Adventures in Drama* book with its crinkled pages and the smell that she could hold to her face and rub against her lips the way she sometimes did and the way a child does a comfort toy.

They stared at her. And Eleanor knew what they were thinking. *Whore.*

Now that Moira wasn't around, Eleanor felt the way she had as a young girl, before Moira was born. Eleanor—the town bad-girl. The one who'd gotten in trouble and had had to go away for seven months when she was fourteen. Oh my God, that terrible abortion —ether, waking up with gut-wrenching pain and all that bleeding. Throwing up all over the stairs as her mother rushed her out, dragging her by the arm, looking around the corner before they went out on the street, hoping they didn't get caught. Seeing a cop and her heart stopping. Her heart starting up but the grinding pain in her belly returning as the cop walked off, ignorant of what had just taken place in that old merthiolate-colored five-story building.

Then Eleanor had turned around and done it again. Pregnant, this time with Moira, and married at age sixteen.

But no, these women didn't know about Eleanor's childhood. They just knew about Moira and Aloysius. Eleanor was clean—in reputation anyway. Unless they'd heard about the affairs. About Gil, about Ralph Smealz, some of the others. But no, how could they?

By three o'clock, everyone was sipping coffee and eating coffee cake as the ashtrays dried.

Eleanor could have just died. Her ashtray was over on that shelf slumped next to a half-dozen neat, perfect specimens. No one had said a word to her about it. But she'd felt—she'd been right, hadn't she? she really felt it—that they were more distant now, that their voices came almost from another room when they talked to her.

At four o'clock, when this interminable day finally broke up, the women went to the shelf to check their ashtrays. Eleanor picked hers up and it fell into four parts that clunked onto the table. One part disintegrated into bits.

Eleanor looked up at the other women. "I guess this would make a better gum holder than ashtray."

A couple of women made forced little laughs. They all put on their correct coats and their correct scarves and said goodbye until next week.

The following week, they were doing paint-by-number wastebaskets.

Eleanor couldn't paint within the lines, couldn't stand to wait until someone was done with green so she used red where she should have used green, yellow where black was supposed to be, and got it so mixed up you couldn't tell what it was—a lake scene with ducks flying over it.

As the women checked the wastebaskets at the end of the afternoon, Eleanor looked at her own, pursed her mouth up the way she did when she was about to say something funny, and said, "I guess mine's one of those modern abstract-art paintings."

They just stared at her with squared-off jaws. Thinking she was a whore. But Moira was the whore. Wasn't she?

Eleanor had gone home and written a nasty letter to Moira, telling her just what it had been like being the mother of such a girl.

But then just as she was about to drop it into the mailbox, something had hit Eleanor. She didn't mail it.

Why hadn't she mailed it? Because mailing it would give Moira the satisfaction of thinking that her mother was a nut. Only a nut would tell her daughter that she'd ruined her mother's life. Well, people didn't know, just didn't know, what a monster Moira had been. How could they? Other people didn't go around having kids like that. Most people went around having nice, normal, obedient, sweet kids. But not Eleanor McPherson, no, she had to give birth to the town whore.

But try explaining that to people. They'd look at you like you were nuts. No, you didn't explain, you didn't even explain it to the town whore herself in a letter. You just went on with your own life.

She didn't go to church anymore, either. It just wasn't for her. Maybe if the church had reached a hand out to her. A gentle hand to hold hers and say *It's okay, Eleanor. You can be yourself here.*

But no one did that. Maybe God would do it himself. Or maybe there was a church out there that accepted the likes of Eleanor Louise Bergstren McPherson, but if there was she hadn't yet found it.

Oh, don't get her wrong—Eleanor thought that people who believed in morality or religion or whatever were lucky. What a wonderful gift all that would have been, if she had only been able to believe in good and evil and then to care about them.

There was one thing that had occurred to her lately regarding morality and Moira. It seemed that Moira had provoked jealousy in all of them. And what had they all been jealous of? Her sexuality? Her intelligence? Her enthusiasm for life? No. Eleanor knew what they'd all been jealous of. They'd all been jealous of Moira's . . . integrity? A shocking thought, if true. And that had hit her from her blind side. A slip of the tongue, wasn't it, to talk about integrity and Moira in the same breath. What a thought—how could Moira and integrity be in anyone's mind at the same time?

But it was true, Eleanor admitted quietly to herself. It was true. Moira had some sort of integrity that the rest of them would never quite understand. And it enraged the rest of them. Made them hate her.

Because it went against the world's notions of female morality. Women only have to worry about one kind of morality—sexual. Let men worry about the big questions, the broader moral issues of war and killing and lying and hate and human decency to the less fortunate. Let them judge each other on those issues. Let women just worry about keeping their legs together. Because that's how they're judged.

Where did Eleanor fit into all that?

Let's not think about it. What the world didn't know about Eleanor Bergstren McPherson, they were better off not knowing. At least she had the decency to be a hypocrite about it.

She smiled. The old sarcasm was returning. Her old friend, sarcasm. Another thought: Do the people who moved in ever hear shotguns going off as they pass into the house at 47293 Boxelder Court East? Do they imagine, feel the warm blood spurting? Do the people living there now have nightmares as they take an afternoon nap on their couch near the front door, perhaps on the same spot that the McPhersons' couch used to be?

Right now Eleanor felt empty. The little mosquito of depression didn't buzz in her ear so much now. That vague uneasiness had gone away when she started her acting classes. But only to be replaced by Wish's whispering.

She could almost feel its—his—breath.

This presence was there all the time. Eleanor never told anyone, but it was Aloysius.

She often wondered if what the Catholics said was true, that people who commit suicide don't go to heaven. Eleanor wasn't Catholic, wasn't even sure she was a real Protestant anymore, wasn't even sure she believed in heaven, but she had to give the idea some thought.

Because it didn't seem that Aloysius was up in heaven. He was there all the time with Eleanor. He was a presence whose breath she could almost feel. Whose voice she heard at night, never sure that it was only a neighbor's radio or television. A presence whose image she saw when she woke up in the middle of the night and when the furniture in the apartment bent the moonlight just so.

Yes, people who died from illness or accidents could be buried and sent on their way to eternity. But that's not how it was with suicide. And you wondered, was there anything you could do to release this person to eternity? You thought there must be something, but you didn't know what it was.

And no matter what, Aloysius would follow her around for the rest of her life, whispering just behind her ear. *Eleanor,* he would whisper, sounding needier than he'd ever sounded in life. She could even feel his cool breath on her neck. *Eleanor.*

Maybe it would take her own death to release him.

That thought did occur to Eleanor sometimes. That the only way to stop that voice and the breath was to kill herself.

But she wouldn't do something like that. She would have to live with that whispering and the cool wind of his breath.

She picked up her playscript. Why, oh why, hadn't she gone ahead and done what she was meant to do in life instead of trying to conform to standards that were impossible for her? She might have left Aloysius and gone off and raised the girls on her own. The girls would have been happier. Aloysius would have been happier drinking alone, or maybe he would have quit drinking and they could possibly have worked it out together again.

She went to stand in front of the mirror, looked at her new blond-streaked hair and her new face that had an eagerness about it now. A show-off spoiled brat, she was. She blew a kiss at herself, then began to rehearse her lines.

Part V

Thirty-two

MOIRA DABBED ON makeup at her dressing table, which was all done up in white ruffles to match her canopy Civil War-era bed with ruffles, a silly bit of indulgence in fuss and frills; maybe to help make up for her no-frills childhood.

Outside the window next to her snow was beginning to fall, already slowing Chicago's Lake Shore Drive traffic. The scene—with the Italian Christmas lights and the horsecabs and the frothy black lake—was the kind of perfect prettiness that was a bit unsettling to Moira, and she looked away, as if trying to avert the evil eye, keep it from taking away any of her happiness. The snow invariably brought back her childhood, memories strung with flashbacks of brilliantly beautiful snow or wood scenes that knocked the breath out of her, then began to dissolve, to move indoors, where she felt anxiety gnawing like hunger, the empty belly of her soul aching, making that loud cat sound of hunger, yearning for the starvation to go so far that her belly swelled out and became weak and numb. She had been so terrified of her parents, she had spent so much time looking for logic in their actions that she had sometimes traded that fear for self-contempt so that her parents' contempt would make sense and this would no longer be a frightening, illogical world.

Her living room was a picture-perfect winter scene with the dancing snow outside and the dewy red roses huddling in bunches inside. The roses' perfume mingled with the odor of smoked turkey and salmon and chicken and tarragon from the spread laid out on the table for their guests. Her husband's family antiques against the high white walls with feathery cracks here and there made a statement, or at least his family's.

Moira's statement had not been made in this room, this apartment; so far only in that fluffy bedroom upstairs. Their friends thought it strange that they had separate bedrooms. They explained that they slept together every night, but they each had their retreats, he his dark room, she her virginal little-girl bedroom as a haven when all those memories tried to get her down.

Moira threaded her way between the caterers and went to the kitchen. Daisy, the cook, was complaining but didn't seem to need help. "You go relax, you," she said to Moira. When she was first married eight years ago Moira had made the mistake of trying to make friends with the help and they had never forgiven her. Now she stayed out of their way—anyway, she had her work at the hospital, and lots of friends, an active social life, crazy sometimes, so it wasn't so hard to let the cook and housekeeper run things.

Moira went to the bar and opened a bottle of the white burgundy and poured herself a glass. It was thick and yet light, dancing into her head like the Mozart piano concerto on the radio. She turned for a last quick look in the mirror.

She was really getting too old for long hair, but she'd had it cut once, and was shocked when she got home to see in the hall mirror her long fourteen-year-old face surrounded by what hair mother hadn't hacked off, and she heard once again the words of advice she'd once heard Mother giving Taryn: "Don't be like Moira. Be nice. A nice girl. A good girl." *Good*—not a greaser tramp.

Fifteen minutes to relax and then the guests would arrive. She went to sit on the loveseat next to the window. Now a Chopin nocturne was playing. It was unbearably beautiful. She switched to the oldies station and they were playing "I saw her sitting in the rain. Raindrops falling on her. She didn't seem to care, she sat there and smiled at me." She sipped her wine and listened and floated on the airwaves back twenty-some years.

When Moira went back to Barnard after her visit home in 1968, she tried to find Zeke, but he had disappeared.

He had become famous as one of the leaders of the student takeover of the Columbia campus. But then suddenly his name stopped appearing in the papers.

She heard he'd been arrested for burning his draft card. A month later she saw a leaflet announcing him as a speaker at a peace sit-in at Central Park. She went to the rally, but he didn't show up.

Then one day she ran into someone who had worked on the Mc-

Carthy campaign who said that he had gone to California to work for Bobby Kennedy. When Kennedy was shot, Zeke had gone to Berkeley. Then someone said he was back with the SDS, this time in Ann Arbor. The last she heard, he had gone to Canada.

She dreamed a lot those nights after Zeke had left the country. She would wake up in the morning thinking she'd been dreaming about Zeke, then realize that it had been Paul Whitefeather. Then she dreamed that Paul had died and that his soul had come back to her as Zeke. Then she would dream the next night of Jesus, waking up thinking she had dreamed of Zeke.

Slowly she resumed her fanatical studying pace, and her grades improved. Studying provided the relief it always had.

She tried to forget about Zeke. Still rooming with Roberta, she made new friends, activists, hippies, communists, civil rights workers. She even met Timothy Leary at a party, and danced with him. Some friends talked her into going to Woodstock in a van the next year. Moira wore bellbottoms and a beaded vest with no blouse underneath and a leather headband. She smoked dope and danced and slept outside and screwed. And all this was considered normal now. She had been validated by the sixties.

She wished Zeke could see what she had become. Maybe he would approve now. Because finally *she* approved.

She had several men after Zeke. Men whom she found attractive, men who took her to dinner and plays and all the other things never even dreamt of in her childhood. A couple of the men took her home to meet their families, nice families who welcomed her. But Moira didn't love these men, and though she longed for a family like theirs to attach herself to, to adopt her, she didn't marry them.

In medical school she fell in love with an intern, but she told him she didn't ever want to get married. She just wanted to be a doctor and to have her freedom. And, of course, that made him want her even more, and he pursued her all the way through medical school. It was sweet, having one of those busy white-coated figures running around the hospital in love with her, but no, she wasn't interested in marriage. She didn't even know what marriage was supposed to be.

She did know that no one was taking advantage of Moira Mc-

Pherson anymore, and she could have sex now when she wanted it, and without all that guilt. The world, after all, had now sanctioned Moira McPherson's own sexual revolution. No romance was ever to be the same, though. Some of the men were handsomer than Zeke, darker, more classic in their features. A few of the men were wealthier, one or two were smarter, and a few were even sexier. But no one was as idealistic as Zeke. He had spoiled her for anyone else.

After medical school, Moira decided to go to work with a poverty program on an Indian reservation back in South Dakota. It was probably because of a vague longing to see Paul Whitefeather again, to see her first friend, first of the disenfranchised. Out on the Pine Ridge Reservation near the badlands, she asked about him. One night at a party given by one of the legal-aid lawyers, as the party spilled out onto the prairie-grass lawn with pot-smoking, peyote-smoking Indians and some Peace Corps workers, Moira met someone who had known Paul.

They smoked and talked and watched the moon glide high up over the brown-gray plain, heard the wind smooshing in the background, and before this man even told her Paul was dead she knew it.

He'd never married. Had gone to law school. Had held some job as an adviser in the Indian Bureau in Washington. Gave it up because he missed South Dakota. Died in a blizzard out in the Black Hills. In 1967. The year she'd met Zeke.

For two years she worked on the reservation and only once went to Sioux Falls. She wanted to be close to home, yet she couldn't bring herself to actually go home and face Mother.

Mother was made of steel and Moira didn't worry about her. But Moira did worry about Taryn. Taryn, Moira felt, was still trying to please Mother and, in a way, Daddy too. She wrote to Taryn, offered to babysit while Taryn and her husband went on vacation, sent nice Christmas presents for the children, but all she ever got back was a Christmas card with the kind of Xeroxed notes people send to casual friends. She didn't hold Taryn's bitterness against her —she knew Taryn wasn't always happy with her life, and that

Taryn had made at least one suicide attempt. Moira wanted to help, but Taryn wanted nothing to do with her.

Taryn was angry, according to Mother, about Moira being a rich doctor and never sharing with them. That was all Moira ever heard from Mother about Taryn. And true, Moira was a doctor now, but she was renting a rundown old farmhouse and driving a broken-down Jeep. Not that she was complaining about her lack of status —this way, if she wanted, she could wear jeans and moccasins and a funky fringed jacket to work, and let her hair grow wild and long down to her waist or, when the mood struck, wear it in braids with beads wound through it.

After a few years, she began to miss New York.

It seemed, though, that Zeke's memory had become stronger, not weaker, and she couldn't bear to be in New York again without him.

Still, she needed a better-paying job—she was fifty thousand dollars in debt to college and medical school.

Chicago seemed like a good start back into the modern world. She found a residency at a Chicago hospital in—of all things— plastic surgery, and took it.

She decided on plastic surgery not because she wanted to give face lifts to society women but to help people with birth defects and deforming scars from accidents.

Her first patient there was a young black boy with ears that stuck out like funnels. She found some funding for his surgery, and then a scholarship to a private school so that he wouldn't have to go back to his old school and face the teasing. Her second patient was a beautiful young woman who had lost an eye in a car accident. She showed up at the office with what the surgeons had left her with— an eye socket completely covered over with smooth skin.

She wanted to work with these kinds of people, but she decided she wasn't going to be a reverse snob, either, by turning away people who wanted face lifts and other purely cosmetic surgery. She understood them, and they could help pay off her medical school loans.

Moira's style found a happy medium. She started shopping on North Michigan Avenue, and looking like a grownup.

She began to look like a normal, run-of-the-mill person now. Yes, Mother, normal.

One evening, after a long, rather depressing day, a male colleague asked her at the last minute to go to a party. She'd never been much interested in him, nor he in her (she suspected he asked her at the last minute because his real date had canceled out on him). But he was amusing and would be a welcome distraction after the kind of day she'd had.

"I'll have you know," he said importantly as they rang the doorbell at the brownstone, "that our host is *the* society plastic surgeon. His wife," he continued in all seriousness, "is *the* society veterinarian."

It was one of those Astor Street homes with butlers clicking their heels all over the marble floors. Moira was wearing a low-cut black satin cocktail dress, her long hair back in pearl-trimmed combs, and her expensive new Michigan Avenue coat (that had to go everywhere to earn its keep, from taking out the garbage to Buckingham Palace if she were ever invited).

"You're beautiful tonight," her date said.

"You're nice to say that," she said.

"No, I mean it."

She would never really feel beautiful, but she felt close tonight. "Okay," she said. "I'm beautiful."

"Don't let it go to your head," he said, tugging at a strand of her hair.

She knew Zeke was there at that party even before she saw him. Feeling his presence, she looked around the room, and there he was, over by a bookshelf, leafing through a heavy volume.

His hair was still dark (unlike hers, which was strewn with gray) and he seemed darker than ever. The expression was the same as it had been—intelligent, eager, kind, the way it had always been in those jeans and that torn turtleneck and ratty corduroy coat. Now he looked almost dangerous, foreign, and expensive, too, in his gray suit with the red tie that brought out the sensuousness of his full bow-shaped lips.

Moira's date went to get her a glass of wine, and Moira stood watching Zeke, not wanting to move for fear she was in a trance and he would disappear.

A woman in a pale gauzy dress, with pale hair swept into a perfect chignon, joined him. She smiled up at him and brushed something off his shoulder, and Zeke came to attention as men do when a beautiful woman is flirting with them. At seeing that, Moira was relieved—if Zeke were married to this woman, he wouldn't be so attentive. The woman tapped him with a folded-up cocktail napkin and he put a crooked finger to her cheek, but he wasn't flirting the way he had with Moira. She knew because she had memorized that scene over and over during the past ten years.

Or maybe she'd been deceiving herself. And now she was afraid, and decided to make an excuse to her date and leave the party before Zeke could see her and ruin the fantasy she'd been carrying around with her all these years by being less than enthusiastic at seeing her.

"I'm not feeling well," she muttered as he handed her a flute of champagne. But he wasn't listening. "There's the first violin for the symphony. He's an old friend. Best violinist in the country. Moira, come meet him. Fascinating fellow." And she must not have really wanted to leave, because she let him pull her arm to meet the man, who was standing next to a palm tree, the only thing that separated him from Zeke.

When Zeke saw her his eyebrows went up, unbelieving. Calling out no, yelling out to Moira, he excused himself from the woman and pushed his way over to Moira. He put his arms around her and buried his dark face in her long, wild hair.

Now he was a modern history professor at the University of Chicago. Taught two classes and spent most of his time writing and working on a project with underdeveloped countries. He was working on his third book, the working title of which was *How the Sixties Saved my Soul.*

He had lived in Canada, editing an underground newspaper until 1977, when Jimmy Carter pardoned the men who had gone to Canada to evade the draft. He came back to the United States and to school.

"And what on earth brings you to a party like this?" Moira said, gesturing toward the status-conscious crowd. "How do you know *the* society plastic surgeon? Or is it *the* society veterinarian that's your buddy?"

Zeke laughed. "I plead guilty to knowing the society plastic surgeon. And to liking him. I have to—he's my cousin."

"Oops," Moira said. "Sorry."

"That's okay. He's a pretentious bastard. But he knows a lot of people in the foreign service. Ambassadors, consuls, people who can help with my work. And I suppose deep down inside he's a decent guy."

"We've grown up, haven't we?" Moira said. "Politics . . . it has a new meaning."

Zeke nodded. He asked where she lived.

"In a politically correct Old Town apartment," Moira said.

He lived in a politically incorrect apartment a block from the party, on Lake Shore Drive.

"I've gotten old, haven't I?" he said. "I like to be comfortable. Hey, I happen to like lots of kinds of people. I like both socialites and socialists. I can't help it. I like poor people, I like rich people too. Hell, I guess I like everybody." He picked her up and swung her around. "And I love you, Flower Girl."

Someone sat down at the piano and started playing dance music. Zeke took Moira in his arms and danced her out onto an area by the piano.

"I go to lots of places that aren't so comfortable. I travel to Africa a lot. Asia, too. Want to go to India with me next winter? Don't answer, it's all set. You're going. Now tell me, Miss Sexy Brainy Flower Girl, what are you doing in life? Wait, don't tell me you're married to that fop over there." He snatched up her left hand and looked for a ring. "Thank God. Hey, everybody," he called out. "She's not married."

Five minutes to go now until their own party time. Zeke and Moira threw lots of parties. Zeke came rushing down the spiral staircase. He stopped in front of the full-length mirror and adjusted his tie in the mirror and asked how he looked.

"Irresistible," she said.

"I hope the ambassador thinks so. I'm going to hit him up for a favor tonight." He picked up the guest list. "Ha-ha, wait until the

Kenya crowd gets here. Trish Van Clyde is going to faint. What a mix of people we have coming! It's going to be a funky, far-out night."

His face screwed up in concentration as he poured himself a ginger ale and went into the library to look something up for the ambassador.

Moira had to laugh. She still enjoyed his earnestness, his concern. He'd always be that kid in the torn turtleneck. She'd never get tired of that image. And she'd never get used to seeing him dressed up the way he was tonight. And that was good, because it was a fresh surprise each time.

Marriage, however, had gotten her used to just about everything else. She'd gotten used to the look of perpetual distress on his dark face. But perpetual distress was only his form of energy.

Zeke reappeared. He kissed her on the cheek, failed to notice what she was wearing or to tell her she looked nice, and absent-mindedly took a rose out of a vase and stuck it in his lapel. It brought out the color in his lips and she hoped that no other woman at the party would notice.

After five years of marriage, they still loved each other. But, of course, it was that warm, floating, almost hands-off kind of love that survives in marriage.

Zeke would never have a crazy, sick adoration for her like her father had had for Mother and for Moira. Theirs was now a normal marriage—no more rolling around in the cat food.

They didn't even talk very much to each other anymore. But she guessed they didn't have to—they knew each other and were happy with what they knew. They found each other neither boring nor irritating, and there was a lot to be said for that. They worked toward similar goals—he had his writing, university politics, the projects in Washington and in Kenya. She had her own medical practice. They had lots of parties and a wide social circle and some close friends (she still saw Rosemary, who lived in Evanston and worked for a religious publisher—and was divorced).

And, Moira was happy. She was very, very happy, thank you very much.

And now she thought maybe soon she would have a baby. Zeke had suggested having a baby a few years ago, and when she'd said she didn't want a child, he'd let it drop. But now maybe it was time. Before time ran out.

It had always been hard to think of babies when you thought of yourself as a whore. She'd never yet run into anyone from South Dakota, anyone who remembered the slut of Sioux Falls. It frightened her a bit to think of someone walking into one of these parties someday who knew about Jack and Gary and Mr. Smealz and all the others, who knew about Daddy, who knew about Mother.

It frightened her a bit. But not all that much, she guessed, now that she thought about it.

Moira still believed in God—without God and the missionaries he sent, like Paul Whitefeather and Rosemary and, of course, Zeke, she'd never have survived. And the God she believed in said that adultery was a sin.

The caterers rushed by and Moira checked her face one last time in the mirror. Yes, maybe she was pretty. Maybe it took turning forty to realize how pretty she was.

Zeke hurried by looking busy and distressed, stopping to ask if she'd remembered the ambassador's favorite drink—she was the expert, not he—that special cognac or whatever it was. "Yes, my dear"—she had remembered the cognac.

And yes, she was the expert—Daddy had been the drunkard and she had been the sexpot. What other sexist words had been dreamed up to keep men from having to feel responsible for their own sexuality? Words that applied only to women, or gay men. Let's see—*promiscuous* was one, *slut* another.

Well, Moira wasn't going to call herself names anymore unless she could spread them around in all fairness. Daddy had been a slut —in his own mind, anyway. And so had all those boys and all those men. It had been a world teeming with sluts, male and female.

Except for Taryn, of course. Taryn had been the good one.

Moira McPherson, the slut of Sioux Falls. All the words applied: *whore, bimbo, tart, tramp, easy lay, round-heeled pushover, bad girl, fast girl, trollop, cunt, pussy, Wendy Whattapair, Miss Big Tits, Friday-night girl, trash, piece of ass, gang banger, fast fuck, good-time girl, woman of easy morals, woman of questionable virtue, woman of easy virtue, just plain loose, alley cat, pushover, cheap tramp, two-bit, jailbait, ass peddler, hot pants, hot mama, sex kitten, cockteaser, wanton hussy, the broad that's built like a brick shithouse, profligate little strumpet, fornicator, cheap crack, unchaste, wench, jade, baggage, bitch, Jezebel, scarlet woman, harlot, nymphomaniac, fallen woman, streetwalker, concubine*—well, there must be more words but she didn't have time to think of any more because the doorbell was ringing and their first guests were arriving.

My, my, my. What a bad girl she'd been.